ALASKA INFERNO

BLAZING HEARTS WILDFIRE SERIES BOOK TWO

LOLO PAIGE

Alaska Inferno
Blazing Hearts Wildfire Series Book Two
Copyright © 2021 by LoLo Paige
First published by Avoca Press 2021
ISBN: 978-1-7360951-0-2

Poem, "Phoenix Ascendant" by S. R. Cyres, used by permission of S. R. Cyres
"Lizzy's Song" by Craig Kuchler, used by permission of Craig Kuchler
Front Cover Design by Sylvia Frost at http://sfrostcovers.com/
Edited & Proofed by Karen Boston, The Word Slayers
Contact publisher and author at https://www.lolopaige.com/

DEAR READER,

LoLo's stories have brought me to tears, made me laugh, and made me cringe. Her characters are so very real to me. I know they're real, because I'm a retired firefighter with over 40 years of experience, most of it in the wildland fire world. I worked my way up from firefighter to Captain to Fire Chief and finally, as the Assistant Director of Fire Operations for the U.S. Forest Service. I can identify with LoLo's female firefighters, and I recognize the male characters as guys I've worked with, too. They're real to me. This may be fiction, but the danger and emotions we've experienced as wildland firefighters are very real.

Our nation's wildland firefighters tend to be young people looking for their future. They pride themselves on their fitness for duty and their commitment to each other, while facing dangers on the fireline. Along with that professionalism, are the emotions and drama of people working closely together in life and death scenarios.

I knew LoLo's stories would be good before I ever read a line. I knew, because while having lunch with her near a Forest Service heli-base in Arizona, watching firefighters responding to a fire in their helicopter, I recognized the person next to me was passionate about the work that firefighters perform; and she's a supportive advocate for those who risk their lives each day to save our nation's wildlands, towns, and homes.

—Bobbie Scopa
Former Wildland Firefighter & Fire Chief
U.S. Forest Service & U.S. Bureau of Land Management

PHOENIX ASCENDANT

Thought about giving up,
my life and friends up in smoke
in my dreams, now awake
I see with heart there is hope.

Who I was until now,
revealed to me in a flash,
lost my love gambling chance
against dreams, now burned to ash.

Not a swan song, my life
reborn from ashes, I pray
love returns, wise and strong,
herald of a perfect day.

S. R. Cyres, 2020
Anchorage, AK

CHAPTER 1

*E*lizabeth Harrington's heart jumped when the aerial tram swung in the wind as it hummed along its steady ascent up the steep mountain. The view grew more spectacular as the rectangular car climbed to the top of Mt. Alyeska, in the rugged Chugach Mountain Range.

Liz clutched the cool, metal pole, keenly aware the tram hung suspended from two skinny cables she'd scrutinized before boarding. She peered out the window at Turnagain Arm, the body of seawater that stretched along the Seward Highway south of Anchorage.

The car rocked even more when passing a lofty tower. She squeezed the pole tighter, chuckling at her intrinsic ability to twist herself around one wearing stilettos. This gave her a measure of stability on this quiet, breathtaking tram ride.

"It always does this when we pass a cable tower," assured the tram operator in his black vest, with the Alyeska logo. "We normally lift skiers, but ski season's over. Now tourists fill the cars."

"Right." As if that bit of trivia would soothe her nerves about the two skinny cables. Liz willed her heart to de-escalate to a simmer. *I'm a wildland firefighter for cripes sakes. Get a grip.*

The wedding invitation had boasted a spectacular ride,

1

with panoramic views of mountains, hanging glaciers, and fast-changing tidewaters.

Yep, the wow factor blew off the charts all right. A handful of tourists occupied the spacious tram, glued to the sizeable windows, taking photos of sea, mountain, and sky.

Liz caught the eye of a tall, smiling blond gripping the pole next to hers. He sported a charcoal-gray suit, with a turquoise carnation in the lapel, obviously heading to the same wedding.

"Are you in the firefighter wedding?" he asked.

"What gave me away?" Liz glanced down to make sure everything was good with the sleeveless turquoise dress that hugged her figure, ending above the knee.

"I'm a groomsman. Cohen Tremblay." He extended his palm.

She shook it. "Pleased to meet you. I'm Elizabeth Harrington. Friends call me Liz."

"The pleasure is absolutely mine." He flashed a bright mouthful of teeth.

The tram hummed low as it glided to a gentle stop, docking into a gray building with massive metal supports.

The tram operator pointed. "Welcome to Mt. Alyeska, folks. This here's the observation deck, where you get a 360-degree view that includes two mountain ranges. Above us is the Seven Glaciers Restaurant, named for the seven glaciers you'll view on the other side. And make sure you're wearing appropriate footwear for uneven surfaces."

The operator glanced at Liz's turquoise, peep-toed stilettos and flashed her a flirtatious grin.

The bride had dyed the heels to match the dress and sent them to Liz in Las Vegas. She would have worn her athletic shoes, but her flight had arrived late. She'd slipped into the heels as she scrambled for a rental car.

Liz had driven like a maniac to Girdwood after running late. Not a desirable choice, as an Alaska State Trooper cautioned her when he'd pulled her over at Beluga Point on the serpentine Seward Highway. After she shamelessly flirted and claimed tourist ignorance, he let her off with a warning.

The tram operator slid the door open. "Enjoy your time on the mountain, folks. Last tram leaves here at nine-thirty p.m. Plan accordingly."

"Duly noted." Liz nodded and stepped off the tram, holding her small daypack.

Cohen came up behind her. "This way to the observation deck. Be careful these metal grates don't chew up those sexy shoes."

"I'll be careful, thanks." *Dang these skinny spike heels.* She'd had nothing but trouble with them catching on every little thing since putting them on.

He held the door open, and she thanked him, then made her way out to a sizable observation deck that overlooked the world. Jagged snow patches etched the surrounding mountains.

"Hope to see you later, Elizabeth." His gaze lingered on her.

She blinked. "Good to meet you."

Cohen strolled to the end of the deck and down to the wedding guests gathered on the lush mountain slope. He was surprisingly good eye candy, for sure, but she was on the lookout for someone else.

"Liz Harrington!" a woman's voice called out.

Liz surveyed the tall, auburn-haired woman with the same turquoise dress coming toward her. "Tara Waters, how the heck are you?"

The two women rushed at each other and hugged.

Liz stepped back. "Hey girl, you clean up nice. Look at that, you have legs."

Tara laughed. "I know, right? We do have legs. Who knew?" She lifted the hem of her dress in a frivolous *check-this-out* motion. "Feels weird, seeing each other out of our stylish, Nomex ensemble."

A familiar voice with a Bronx accent piped up behind Liz. "Yeah, check out those legs."

She turned, impressed at a cleaned-up Nick Rego. "Look at you, rocking a suit."

3

"Gimme some sugar, Harrington." He opened his brawny arms to receive a hug. "I miss playing strip poker with you."

She hugged him. "Good to see you, Rego. How many from our crew are here?"

"About half. The ones who count are here." He winked.

One person interested her, but she didn't see him in the sea of guests. Instead, a massive guy with a man-bun in a long gray shirt with a black starburst on one side moved toward her.

"Tupa!"

He swallowed her in a bear hug. "Hot damn, woman, you're killing it."

Tupa had always reminded Liz of a Humvee. "Thanks, Tupa. Have you missed me?"

He let go and placed his hands on his heart. "I've pined for *all* the ladies of Aurora Crew. Mmm, you smell good."

"Hey man, no sniffing the female firefighters." Rego gave him a failed shove. Moving Tupa was like trying to budge a refrigerator. "Stop sucking up to our squad boss, Moose Breath." Rego pointed his thumb at Tupa. "Dress 'em up but can't take 'em anywhere."

Liz laughed, and it felt good. "God, I've missed you guys."

"Hey, Lady." Melbourne Faraday, Alaska Fire Service's renowned helicopter pilot, stood front and center in his dashing suit. He ferried crews and staff to and from fires, and he and Liz had become good friends.

"Mel, you look good." She hugged him, then tugged the bill of his ever-present baseball cap over his graying mullet. "Your ball cap matches your suit perfectly."

"I pride myself with my talent to accessorize." He tapped his lapel and rolled his toothpick to the other side of his mustache. "You're utterly stunning, Elizabeth."

She smiled sweetly. "Thank you, Melbourne."

"Come on, let's go help Angela." Tara grabbed Liz's hand and led her inside of the hexagon building called The Round-house. They strolled to a small room, where skiers changed during ski season.

"Angela Divina, you look fantabulous." Liz rushed to her

friend in a white floor-length dress that hugged her perfect form. Angela's breasts spilled over the top, like the cover of the Regency romance novel Liz read on the plane from Vegas to Anchorage.

Angela's risqué taste in dress style made Liz chuckle. She'd texted Liz photos of her strapless wedding dress. If anyone could pull it off, Angela sure could. And she made sure her bridesmaids exuded more flesh than fabric. Liz wasn't used to exposing all this skin in Alaska. In Vegas, yeah, it was her lifestyle. But up here? She mostly wore her yellow shirt and green pants.

"Oh, my stars, Liz. I'm so happy you made it. Tara and I worried when you told us you had trouble getting away from the dance club."

Liz clasped her hands together. "Lied to my boss. Told him fire training started early this year."

Tara spread her arms. "Group hug. The women of Aurora Crew."

The three women hugged as they had countless times during last fire season.

Angela stepped back. "I'm not on the crew this year. It seems one of Gunnar's condoms had a hole in it."

"You're—you're…?" Liz's jaw dropped.

The bride patted her still flat stomach. "Yep, there's a little Gunnar in here."

Liz chose a hopeful tone. "Is this a good thing?"

Angela nodded, smiling. "It is for me. Gunnar is still getting used to the idea."

"You came to Alaska to find a hot firefighter, get married, and have beautiful babies, as I recall." Tara smoothed out the folds in Angela's dress. "You hit your goal, Divina."

Angela beamed at her two friends. "I reckon I did. We'd better get out there." She inserted herself between her BFFs, linking their arms.

"Time for your last walk as a single woman," teased Liz, opening the door to step outside.

"Br-r-r, figured I'd freeze up here in this dress. I was determined to wear it even if a blizzard hit today."

Liz pulled out her fleece jacket from her day pack and arranged it around Angela's shoulders. "We can't have the bride freeze to death and shiver through your ceremony. Save your shivering for when you behold your naked husband on your wedding night." Liz elbowed her and shot her a cat-eyed look.

"Harrington, you're badass." Angela giggled. "Oh crickets, Mom is perturbed. See you after the big doings." She rustled off to the impatient woman standing with a flower bouquet the size of Denali.

Tara slipped an arm around Liz's waist. "Excited for another fire season?"

"Couldn't believe how much I missed Alaska. How's Ryan?" Liz gave Tara a light shoulder bump. "Did you guys spend the winter on the American Riviera—wherever that is?"

Tara brightened. "We had the best time. I flew with him to Pasadena to visit his dad, then he took me on his motorcycle up the Pacific Coast Highway—Hearst Castle, Big Sur, Monterey…" she trailed off and blushed.

Liz's lips twitched in amusement. "I take it you liked Monterey. Did you even leave your hotel room?"

"Bed and breakfast." Tara squeezed Liz's arm. "I'll fill you in later."

On the observation deck, Angela's mother gave silk bouquets of forget-me-nots and baby's breath to all five brides-maids. She organized the order of the bridal procession. Liz paired up with the tram hunk, Cohen, to march up to nature's wedding altar.

Angela's family had arranged rows of folding chairs, leaving a wide aisle of lush spring grass after snow had melted off the south-facing slope. The afternoon sun warmed Liz's shoulders, chasing away her goosebumps.

The surrounding mountains had dressed for the occasion in their green, blue, and white, with the gray-blue sea of Turnagain Arm, a royal carpet at their feet. A fitting backdrop for a wedding between two Alaskan firefighters.

She glanced around for her former crew boss, but he must not have attended the wedding. A twinge of disappointment poked her harder than she cared to admit. Since he no longer worked on the Aurora Crew, chances were she wouldn't see him anyway.

"Looking for someone?" Cohen followed her glances.

"Just taking in the view. How do you know Gunnar?"

"I fought fires with him a few seasons back. I'm from Salmon Arm."

"Alaska?"

"No, British Columbia in Canada. I'm a new hire on the Aurora Crew." He tossed her a toothy grin. "We'll be working together."

"Oh, welcome to the crew," she said mildly.

Hmm, there's a perk. Liz wondered if Tara would assign Cohen to Liz's six-person squad. The guy was incredibly buff and tempting, but as squad boss, Liz didn't get involved with her squad members. Not on the fireline.

Guitar music played, and a silver-haired man in a three-piece suit strode purposefully up the grassy center. He turned to address the group, ready to officiate the ceremony. Liz recognized Dave Doss, the incident commander from several fires she'd worked on last year. Gunnar and Angela had chosen well. Everyone on the crew had considerable respect for him.

Behind her, sounds of plucked strings on an acoustic guitar filled the spring air. She recognized the introduction to a song by Richard Marx, *Now and Forever.*

Gunnar Alexanderson proceeded up the center to stand next to Doss, rocking his usual blond, knockout self in his fabulous physique in that light-colored suit. No wonder Angela had fallen in love with him. In addition to his witty personality, he'd skied for Norway in the Olympics, and he kicked ass fighting fire as a smokejumper.

When the vocalist sang the opening notes, Liz sucked in so much air, Cohen asked if she was all right. Before she could glimpse the singer, he grabbed her elbow and nudged her to the front.

Liz craned her neck to sneak a peek at the back, but her spiked heels dug into the soft ground like two little backhoes. She lurched forward, out of her heels.

"Whoa, Elizabeth—" Cohen grabbed her waist to prevent her from swan diving into a face plant. He glanced at her bare feet, then back to her stilettos, which stuck to the ground like fire retardant.

"I'm fine. I've got it," grumbled Liz, smoothing her dress.

Amused snickers emanated from the firefighter guests at one of their own navigating stilettos on a soggy Alaskan mountain.

"Harrington, where're your fire boots?" sniggered Rego.

She shot him her resting witch face before bending to pry her stilettos loose. Heat crept up her neck as she clutched Cohen's forearm for balance, lifting one foot at a time to put her heels back on. Mortified, she hurried to the front on the balls of her feet, dragging Cohen.

"Hey, what's the rush?" he protested.

She gave him a polite smile. *I must check out the singer.*

Liz reached the front and parted from Cohen, taking her place with the other bridesmaids. Tara arrived and stood next to her as the maid of honor. Liz's radar swiveled to the singer, but Angela and her dad blocked her view as they stood on the ready to march down the aisle.

The vocalist began a new song, and Angela moved toward the Norwegian smokejumper, soon to be her husband. Liz was overjoyed for her friend, knowing that was the reason Angela came to Alaska to fight fire.

Tara elbowed Liz. "Check out who's singing."

"Oh. My. God." Liz did a double take at the tall, dark-haired man standing in the back, playing the guitar. Her eyeballs could have popped from their sockets and rolled off the mountain.

Jon. Freaking. Silva. In a suit, no less!

A thousand million moments of wanting him blasted her. When he'd been out of sight and out of mind the past nine months, she'd considered him an unattainable fantasy.

A lifetime ago. Someone she could never have.

Now here he was in the flesh. The burning desire she'd worked hard to extinguish and shoved to the basement of her heart rose like an untamed phoenix. The time she'd spent working with him last fire season flashed through her brain like a runaway wildfire.

"Now and forever…" Jon sang, his focus on the couple joined at the front. Without warning, his gaze shifted to Liz's and held it hostage. He faltered, flubbing the lyrics.

Liz beamed at him, praying she wouldn't spontaneously combust at the firestorm racing around inside her. Stripped of all reasonable thought, her mind wobbled off somewhere on vacation. Goosebumps blossomed like fireweed on her neck and arms.

He broke eye contact when he finished singing and took a seat in the last row of chairs.

The song may have ended, but Liz's goosebumps still danced their knobby selves on her skin. She became obsessed with *not* ogling him…like the day he'd announced he was the crew chief last year, on their ride to the Chinook Fire Station.

She sneaked secret glances at Jon and hated that he caught her doing it. He appeared spicier than when he'd busted the sizzling firefighter barometer last year. The Aurora Crew women had voted Ryan O'Connor, Gunnar Alexanderson, and Jon Silva as the three hottest Alaskan firefighters.

Jon had been her kryptonite from day one of working together on the fire crew. This bewildered her, especially after he'd revealed his three failed marriages. She'd sagely maintained her self-discipline, tossing out her lusty thoughts like an unwelcome relative.

As the ceremony progressed, Liz switched her focus to Angela and Gunnar, but her mind kept drifting back to Jon and how well they'd worked together last year. Clapping jolted her from her reverie as the ceremony ended. The bridal procession filed back to the photographer, who guided them up the stairs to the observation deck for the wedding photos.

Liz scanned for Jon, but he'd disappeared.

People stood tapping their phones and taking selfies with the spectacular scenery.

Cohen said something. She wasn't sure what—Jon's voice still reverberated in her ears. She'd not heard him sing or play guitar. He hadn't shared that aspect of himself. Then again, she hadn't shared her exotic dance world with him, and she figured that leveled the playing field.

While waiting for photos, Tara sidled over. "Did you have any idea Silva could sing? Why didn't he serenade us on fire last season?"

Liz stared numbly at her friend. "I haven't seen Jon since the crew party at Snowcastle last year. Except—once in January he called from his parents' place in Sonoma and wanted to drive up to visit me in Vegas."

"What happened?" prodded Tara.

"I panicked—told him no. Didn't want my fire world colliding with my dance world. Couldn't suffer the humiliation of our former crew boss seeing me dance half-naked in a dance club."

"I can understand that." Tara placed her palm on Liz's shoulder. "Now you're back in Alaska. Jon couldn't take his eyes off you during the ceremony. Remember, you helped save his life. That's not something any guy forgets."

Gunnar gazed adoringly at Angela, and a pain stabbed Liz's chest. "Silva and I are miles apart. We have nothing in common."

Tara smirked. "Right. That couldn't have been why you ate dirt on your trip down the aisle earlier. Pun intended."

Liz lifted a dirty heel and slapped at it. "Nothing like wearing swords of evil on your feet during spring thaw. Felt like they'd punched through to Antarctica."

"I know you too well. Silva distracted you with his golden pipes, and you became discombobulated. You guys had that spark between you last year, but the match didn't light. You should consider lighting it. I know he's into you."

"Yeah, for maybe two minutes. He lacks staying power and

changes women like underwear." Liz lifted her chin with resolve. "Besides, I can't get involved. I need to stay focused."

"On what?"

"I've invested in a new exotic dance club on the Las Vegas Strip. I'll be one of three owners. Running the business instead of dancing."

Tara's jaw dropped. "Liz, that sounds great."

Ryan O'Connor came up behind Tara and kissed her neck.

"I've always told you guys to get a room," snickered Liz, winking at the lovebirds.

Ryan spoke up. "Glad to see you back, Liz. Word on the street is, we're in for a busy fire season. It's drier than usual around south central Alaska this year."

"Like last year. Are all of you smokejumpers ready to go?" asked Liz.

"We're already on standby for fire call." He lifted his phone.

Liz nodded absently. This season's fire predictions weren't a top priority for her at the moment. The wedding singer had occupied her mind to distraction.

Gunnar made an ear-piercing finger whistle. "O'Connor, Waters, get over here so we can go party."

"See you later. I want to hear about your business plans." Tara moved off with Ryan for photos with the wedding couple.

Liz's thoughts drifted back to Tara and Ryan's whirlwind romance last season and how close they'd come to losing one another.

That's what happens when you fall in love. And it could vanish in a flash. I don't need the hassle, thank you very much.

But listening to Silva sing—cripes, she couldn't get him out of her head. The thought of getting hands across America with that badass firefighter's body buckled her knees. She'd fantasized a lighthearted fling during last year's fire season, then they went their separate ways. Over the busy winter, working in Vegas, he'd faded to gray.

She had no time for her own fantasies while she worked to sell them.

Now she was back in Alaska. Nothing holding either of them back. Maybe a one-night stand with Silva would get him out of her system.

Or not.

The 'or not' part was the wild card, but Liz was a gambler and reigned supreme on the blackjack tables back home. She'd not had an ounce of emotion for the patrons she'd danced for this past winter. No time for relationships. Too busy earning money.

An older man with white hair gave her a pleasant nod as he sauntered past. She thought of her dad, and her heart twisted with guilt. He hadn't recognized her on the last visit before she left for the airport in Vegas. He was the reason she'd taken the dance job at the gentleman's club. One night of dance tips alone paid for a day of nursing care.

By exotic dance standards, her employer considered her geriatric at the ripe old age of thirty-four. Business ownership was her ticket out of dancing and to finance her dream of owning a professional dance studio. She longed to teach ballet, jazz, and modern dance. Nothing would stand in the way of those plans.

Not even the one guy who'd ever mattered.

"Let's go, sports fans. Time to par-*tay*," hollered Rego. "Damn firefighters are like herding cats." He winked at Liz, rounding up the wedding party like a border collie.

As Liz posed for photos, she observed hang gliders launch from the edge of Mt. Alyeska to glide smoothly down to the grassy bottomlands sprinkled with Sitka spruce trees.

Where the heck did Silva go?

Unease nudged her—why hadn't he mingled with his former crewmates? Recalling last year's near-fatal situation on an uncontrolled fire, deep down she knew why. How vulnerable he must feel with these people right now. Disaster had taken only a moment or two—but the burden of it stretched for a lifetime.

And it tore her heart to shreds.

CHAPTER 2

*A*fter the bride and groom cut the cake, Liz stole time for herself and wandered over to the wall of windows. The seven cerulean glaciers presented a stunning view from the restaurant. She let the champagne bubbles tickle her throat as she took it all in.

His reflection in the window grew larger as he came up behind her.

"Impressive, aren't they?" The melodic sound of Jon's voice flickered up her spine.

"Thirteen-thousand-foot peaks, I hear." Her heart sped as she turned around, hating that she wanted to launch herself into his embrace. She told herself to be chill. "Hey, Silva."

"I'm supposed to return this to you." He dangled her fleece jacket from his forefinger. "Angela's orders."

She took it and draped it over her arm. "Thanks. Was a tad brisk up here today."

"It's Alaska." He stood a foot taller, and more swoon-worthy than he was nine months ago.

"Good to be back." She inhaled the familiar broad shoulders, narrow waist, and defined muscle, hard-earned mileage from fighting wildfires.

"I've been looking for you." He slanted her a scorching grin, with one hand in his pants pocket, rocking a white shirt with a royal blue tie. Rolled-up sleeves revealed tats of large, feathered wings wrapped around his forearms. Two slender fingers held a suit jacket slung over his shoulder, like he'd been out for a stroll on a beach.

"You clean up pretty good." She chided herself at the lame compliment. *What I really want to say is, you are a mouthwatering chunk of eye candy.*

The way he surveyed her resurrected every detail she'd remembered about him. How his hair had always feathered back on the sides, and that sexy widow's peak gave him a lascivious, bad-boy vibe. And the way he'd transform from a clean shave in the morning to a rugged five o'clock shadow by the end of the day.

"Why are you looking at me like that?" he asked, interrupting her fantasy.

She jerked from her ogling as if a hypnotist had snapped his fingers. "Oh. I was just thinking."

"About what?"

"This is the first time I've seen you out of Nomex," lied Liz. Last year on a project fire, she'd caught him bare-chested coming back from the men's latrine. A definite *yowzah* moment. She recalled having trouble falling asleep in her tent that night.

"I don't wear flame resistant clothing much these days."

"That's right. Sorry." She squeezed her lids shut, regretting her accidental reference as to why he no longer wore firefighting gear. When she opened them, his eyes raked her from head to toe.

I forgot how adorable he is. "Where did you learn to sing like that?"

That impish expression again. "My mother taught me."

"Uh huh. Why didn't you share your God-given talent with us last year, on all those fires?"

"Probably for the same reason you didn't share your God-given talent with your *other* job." His eyes twinkled.

"Touché, got me there. Who told you?"

"Gunnar, Ryan, and I knew from the get-go last year, but I

cautioned them to put a lid on it when I became crew boss."
He chuckled. "No one else knows unless you've told them."

"You knew all along?" Her face heated. So much for
keeping her work worlds separate. "Why didn't you say
something?"

"Figured it was none of my business what my crew did in
the off season."

"Thanks for guarding my reputation." She hastened to
add, "I don't dance because I like it. Some things you do
because you must. Please don't judge."

He raised his brows and shrugged. "I never have. As far as
I'm concerned, when you're in Alaska, you're a firefighter."

She peered at him intently. "Spoken like a true diplomat.
Or do you actually mean it?"

"You're questioning my sincerity? Of course, I mean it."

She wasn't proud of her other job, but it was a necessary
evil, and she needed the money. She worked hard to keep her
Alaska and Vegas worlds separate. Holding things close to her
chest had become a lifelong habit. If people found out, fine.
She'd never let it interfere with her job as a wildland firefighter.

She motioned her champagne flute at a table for two near
the window overlooking the glaciers. "Let's have a seat and
we'll catch up."

"Sounds good. I'll get us some chow." He draped his jacket
over a chair.

"Bring some smoked salmon." She sat in the cushioned
chair across from his.

He moved toward the buffet table, and she observed his
fetching derriere as she drained her glass.

A server leaned down with his tray. "More Champagne?"

She lifted two flutes. "Perfect timing. Thanks."

Jon returned with a plate piled with crab legs, smoked
salmon, and beer-battered halibut. "Figured we could share."
He set the plate on the table between them.

"Excellent. Here's your waiter tip." She offered him a
champagne.

"I've cut back on alcohol." He held up the glass, with a mischievous grin. "I guess one glass won't hurt."

She clinked his flute with her own. "Tell me what you've been up to." Watching him intently, she sipped, then popped a piece of battered halibut in her mouth.

"I'm a certified fire investigator. Finished my training, and I'm all legit."

"Congratulations. You did that when you stopped fire-fighting?"

"First, I took an EMT job at Fairbanks Memorial Hospital to pay the bills and re-group after...after..." He shook his head.

Liz rushed in. "Jon, I'm sorry what happened last season. We've not talked about—"

He held up a hand. "It's okay."

An awkward silence fell between them.

"There's no point in discussing it." He exhaled. "It's a done deal."

The way he said it caused her to lift her chin. "Yes, it's just that—" She stopped herself. *Leave it alone. Let it go.*

"I have a whole new gig now." He sipped champagne, his Adam's apple bobbing. "I traveled Outside for the investigator training, and now I work for the Feds as a fire inspector."

"Alaska Fire Service, I take it." She raised her brows. "'Outside,' as in the lower forty-eight?"

He nodded. "I trained at NIFC, in Boise."

"National Interagency Fire Center. Impressive."

"Yep." A corner of his mouth edged up.

"Should I call you Fire Inspector Silva now?"

"I've been called worse." He gave her his signature, charismatic smile the women of the Aurora Crew knew all too well.

She leaned forward, with her forearms on the table. "Explain what you do when you get to a fire."

"It's not as exciting as firefighting."

"When my dad worked as a cop investigating building and vehicle fires, he'd tell me about it. The process of fire investigation has always fascinated me."

"You should check out the training if you're interested." He paused for a bite of salmon and swallowed.

Since when did Jon Silva eating anything ping her girl parts and make her shift in her seat? *Must be the champagne.* Liz picked up her glass and stared at it, then set it down. "You were saying?"

"First, we look for the answers to where and why did the fire start? We search for the point of origin and the heat source that ignited it."

She liked how he lit up when he talked about it. "You've become a fire nerd."

"Enough about my nerding on fire. Tell me about you." He studied her intently.

She gazed out the window at the glaciers. "I'm starting a new business in my hometown with two co-workers, who are also my roommates."

"In Vegas? What's the business?"

She flicked her eyes up at him. "We're opening a gentlemen's club on The Strip, called Stormy Sapphire, inside the new Amethyst Hotel." She waited for his reaction.

"Oh. Wow. I mean, that's great." He studied his glass as if reading tea leaves.

Not the reaction she expected.

He lifted his glass, and she sensed he forced a smile. "Here's to your success."

She raised her glass and clinked his, figuring he didn't mean a word of it.

Tara breezed over to their table. "Everyone's heading down to the Ptarmigan Bar to go dancing. You guys coming?"

"Down at Hotel Alyeska? Sure. Sounds fun." Liz glanced at Jon to gauge his reaction.

"You'd better get on the tram before nine-thirty, or you'll be spending the night up here." Tara moved off to herd other cats.

"I can conjure up worse places to spend the night." Jon's impish grin had always turned her inside out.

They downed the rest of their champagne.

"Guess I'd better show up." Liz stood, champagne bubbles percolating her brain. She tugged on her gray fleece jacket.

"What a shame you're covering all that up." Jon's scrutiny made a leisurely trip down her body. "You're in the wedding party, so your presence is required."

"So is yours." She slung her daypack over her shoulder. "You're the wedding singer."

"Ha, there's a new title."

"Fire Inspector Silva, the wedding singer," she burbled, the champagne loading her system. "Are you coming?"

He fixed his gaze on her. "I'm not sure the Aurora Crew would appreciate that."

"Don't talk like that. I, for one, appreciate you being here, along with everyone else." She grabbed his bare, tatted forearm and tugged, thrilled at the warmth. "Don't piss me off, Silva."

He glanced down at her hand, then slid her a suggestive look. "I know better than to piss off the daughter of a cop."

"You catch on quick." Liz liked how he paid attention to details about her. She jerked her head toward the door. "Let's go." Touching him sent a magnetic rush through her. She ordered herself to pull free.

He rose from his chair and ambled alongside her, staring at her feet. "What happened back there when you almost did a face plant? You know how hard it was not to crack up in the middle of my song?"

Liz shook her head. "My stilettoes sunk into the ground like missile silos."

His laughter was deep, warm, and rich, tickling her senses.

After tossing back loads of sparkly bubbles, Liz felt no pain on the tram ride down. This time when the car swung as it passed a tall tower, she went with the flow and swayed with it, conveniently tipping back against Jon.

His solid chest pressed rock hard against her back. He rested his palm on her shoulder.

She cursed herself for wearing the fleece, wanting his hand on her bare skin.

Once in the bar, everyone pulled tables together as they'd always done when gathering at a watering hole. Liz sat next to Jon, while everyone discussed the upcoming fire season.

The band played, and Liz tugged him to the dance floor. When they played an oldies but goodies set, he slipped an arm around her waist and clasped her hand to the bouncy rhythm of *Somewhere Beyond the Sea*. He pulled her in tight and sang in her ear.

She had the sudden desire to kiss him. When she turned her lips toward his, he continued to sing along with the band. *What a tease.*

At least Jon had returned to his old, charming self, and that cheered her. She didn't care about anything else right now. Only this.

The band played *The Way You Look Tonight*. Between the champagne and Jon's sexy vibe, Liz didn't want to let go. Tonight might be the only night they may ever have together.

They danced the rest of the slow songs until the band stopped and the bar staff shooed everyone out. On impulse, she bought a bottle of champagne before leaving. Not something she normally did, but she felt like celebrating.

I'm with the only guy who'd ever mattered.

As people wandered out, Rego hollered, "Strip poker in my hotel room!"

Whistles and laughter ensued as Rego's crewmates teased him about stripping to his boxers last year at their crew party.

"Will Rego be dealing you in again?" Jon asked Liz. "As I recall, last time you had two jacks, two queens, and you were down to your bra and blue jeans on a losing streak. I quite enjoyed that."

It surprised her he'd remembered, despite his inebriated condition at the time. "Not tonight. I'm keeping my clothes on," she slurred, willing herself not to sound intoxicated.

Jon motioned at her bottle of bubbly as they sauntered down a dark corridor to a hotel elevator. "You plan on drinking all that?"

"Nope. You're gonna help me." She stopped, aware of

herself swaying in her stilettos. "Whoops... " There went her balance.

He caught her before she went down, his powerful arms holding her up. "Let's get on the elevator." His arm wrapped around her waist as he guided her inside.

"Thanks, Silva." She proudly held out the champagne bottle. "Lookee here, I never spilled a drop. *Damn*, it's so nice to see you again." She rubbed his chest and patted it. "This feels damn nice, too."

She skimmed her fingers along his jaw. "Your whiskers are back. They grow in by the end of every day." She tried winking, without success, and tapped her temple. "I know this from working with you last year. Let it grow up and be a beard. Makes you look hot," she stage-whispered.

He laughed. "Okay," he whispered back.

She sagged against him and peered up, trying to focus. But instead of eyeballing one head, she detected two. Closing one eye didn't help.

"Both your heads are gorgeous. Two heads are better than one. Double the pleasure, double the fun. Ha, I'm a poet and don't know it." She popped the "P" and hiccupped.

He gave her an amused look. "Let's get you to your room."

The elevator opened, and she offered him her key. "Here. Find my room. Four-O-one. No, it's four-O-five. No, wait, it's —aw heck, whatever." She waved a hand dismissively.

"It's on the key card. This way." He took her elbow and guided her along the hallway.

His voice—God, I love his voice. "Will you sing to me again? Boy, this is a really long hallway." Another hiccup.

Jon swiped her key card on the door. "Let's get you some water and something for the headache you're bound to have." He opened the door, perched her on the edge of the bed, and disappeared into the bathroom.

"Silva, want to know something?" She kicked off her heels and stood. Bad idea. The room spun. *Whoa...*she sank back down.

"What do I want to know?" He emerged with a glass of

water and sat next to her on the bed. He opened his palm. "Take these, and drink this."

"Thanks, Dr. Silva. You're a kickass EMT." She tried to wink, but her eye wouldn't work.

"Drink *all* the water," he ordered.

She did what he instructed because it was Jon Silva, *and* he used to be her crew boss, *and* a helluva fire medic, *and* a helluva firefighter, *and* a freaking fire inspector, *and* he was the handsomest guy…along with a bunch of movie stars named Chris or Ryan. She hiccupped.

I like Jon a lot, dammit.

His two gorgeous heads posed a challenge. *Hmm, which to focus on.* "Last year, you called me *your* hero. But the real honest-to-God bottom line truth of the whole fact of the matter of the fact is…" she slurred, pointing at him. "You, my friend, are *my* hero. You always were…" She yawned and felt herself fading.

"Let's get you to bed." He gathered her up, and she angled her arms around his neck. Next thing she knew, he'd pulled down the covers and settled her in.

"Mmm…Jon, come here. Stay with me. Please…stay with me," she whispered.

As her eyelids insisted on lockdown, she sensed him lie down beside her.

"I'm right here," he said softly.

"Good," she mumbled. "Don't go." She yawned.

He held her. Everything would be all right.

Oh God, the room is spinning. I'm so tired…

She drifted off, safe and warm in the arms of the love of her life—only he didn't know it.

And she wasn't sure she would ever tell him.

CHAPTER 3

$\mathcal{J}$on Silva stood in the shower, loving how the spray soothed his scalp. Now that he had time to ponder all that had transpired with Liz—or rather, what had *not* transpired—he thanked himself for two things: Staying sober, and not spending the night in her room. Lord knows he'd wanted to, but his new and improved conscience told him to bail before he changed his mind.

Yesterday, as he'd prepared to sing, he'd zeroed in on the statuesque woman with the honey-colored hair standing next to Tara, staring at him. He'd forgotten the words to his song upon discovering the beautiful woman was Liz. Her hair had grown out to below her shoulders, wavy and pretty. Last year on the fireline, she had super short, dyed-white hair.

And those muscles on her back and arms. *Damn.* Everything about her drove him insane.

Before he'd taken off her dress last night, he made sure she had something on underneath, top *and* bottom. He wouldn't have done it otherwise. *The old Jon would have.*

But not the new Jon.

Great. Now he'd aroused himself and had a chub going on. He had to finish up, shave, and get to breakfast. Mel wanted an early start for their long drive to Fairbanks. He dressed and headed out the door and took the elevator down to the Bore Tide Café, next to the main lobby.

"Hello, everyone. How are we this morning?" Jon strolled in and greeted his former crewmates, huddled over coffee mugs.

Melbourne lifted his ever-present baseball cap from his gray mullet. "The smokejumpers had a fire call from the Alaska Fire Service. Ryan, Gunnar, and the other jumpers caught a five a.m. flight back to Fairbanks."

Jon grimaced. "Ooh, bet that was a bitch. Where's the fire?"

"East of Fairbanks, between the Yukon-Charley Rivers National Preserve and Eagle and Fort Egbert."

"Gunnar left Angela here. I'm giving her a ride to Fairbanks," piped up an equally tall guy next to Jon. "We haven't met. I'm Cohen Tremblay."

"Jon Silva." He extended his palm.

"You're good friends with Elizabeth, I take it?" Tremblay drilled him with a blue stare.

"You mean Liz?" The question took Jon by surprise. "We worked together on the same crew last year."

"That's right. You were the crew boss. I've heard about you." Tremblay stabbed a sausage with his fork.

Jon didn't like the insinuation. "Oh?"

"They told me what happened on the Shackelford Fire last year. I'm on the Aurora Crew now. Gunnar bragged for years what terrific firefighters worked for the U.S. Bureau of Land Management, Alaska Fire Service." Tremblay looked around the table at nodding heads.

"BLM Alaska firefighters are top notch." Jon stirred cream and sugar into his coffee and sipped. Something about this guy rubbed him the wrong way.

"Joined up. Applied and came onboard, as you Americans say."

"Where are you from?"

"Salmon Arm, British Columbia."

Jon grunted. "Canada has some of the best air tanker pilots in the world."

"Yes, we do." Cohen poked at scrambled eggs.

Rego caught sight of Liz at the café entrance. "Harrington, you don't look so good."

Liz plodded toward their table with a pained expression.

Jon empathized with how badly she must feel and quietly high-fived himself for sticking to one glass of champagne. He rode high compared to the hungover, collateral damage around him.

"Good morning, sunshine." He peered up at Liz.

She only shook her head. When the server left with her order of yogurt, granola, and a plea for her own coffee pot, she bent to whisper in Jon's ear. "We need to talk. Now."

Tremblay gave Jon a disapproving look as he rose and followed Liz out to the hotel lobby. Jon hoped he wouldn't have trouble with this guy.

Jon wondered what Liz had to say after getting so shitfaced last night. He'd never observed Liz consume so much alcohol, and it surprised him.

Her ass swayed pleasingly in the perfect shape of an upside-down heart, outlined by her tight-fitting jeans. He'd arrived at this conclusion last year when she'd bent over to cold-trail soil and ashes during mop-up on their first fire.

Liz led him to a burgundy leather couch facing a tall, stone fireplace with an antlered moose head mounted over the gas hearth. She plopped onto the couch and leaned forward, elbows on her slim knees, head in her hands.

"Everything okay?" Jon sat next to her. He instinctively reached over to rub her back, but he thought better of it and instead folded his hands in his lap.

She lifted her head. "I'm sorry I threw myself at you last night."

"Don't be."

"You stayed sober, didn't you?"

He nodded.

"While I made a complete idiot of myself."

"No more than usual."

She gave him a killer look.

"You were funny." He attempted to make her feel better.

"Jon, what happened last night?" She leaned in. "You know, in my room."

"You don't remember?"

She wrinkled her nose. "We left the bar, got on the elevator, and then…" She shook her head. "What happened—in my room?"

"You wanted me to stay and talk. We sat on your bed, and you fell asleep on my shoulder."

"And?"

"I sat with you for a while."

She waited.

"Then you snored." He should probably stop there.

"Silva, come on. You know what I'm getting at."

He felt guilty she had to pry it out of him, but he enjoyed this. As innocently as he could muster, he asked, "What are you getting at?"

"I woke up with my bra and undies still on, but I wasn't sure…"

"About what?"

She let out a heavy sigh. "You know what."

Better to come clean than have her hate him. "I took off your dress and tucked you under the covers." He spit it out fast and waited for the fallout from the took-off-your-dress part.

She stared at him. "What if I hadn't had anything on underneath?"

"But you did."

"Jon, did you—did I—did we…" She twirled a forefinger. Her chocolate eyes searched his face, and she appeared distressed.

"No. We didn't."

She seemed relieved. "You've always been a gentleman. Thank you."

He hadn't expected that reaction, but considering what else

she did for a living, taking off her dress most likely wasn't a deal breaker.

"Let's go eat. How are you getting up to Fairbanks?" He stood and offered his hand.

She took it and let him pull her to her feet. It killed him to let go.

"I'm driving my rental to the Anchorage airport and flying up this afternoon. You?"

"Melbourne's driving us up in his Mustang."

She sighed and gave him a distressed look. "Sorry I drank so much. I rarely do that."

"I did the same last year, and you put me to bed. Now we're even." He stood, looking down at her. "Come on, time to roll."

They stepped back to the café and settled into the booth with the others. Jon saw the way Cohen salivated as he gave Liz the quick up-and-down guy assessment. This potential competition raised hackles on his neck. *Hands off, pal. Don't even think about it.* He wasn't pleased this guy was now on the Aurora Crew.

When everyone finished eating, they rose and tossed off their goodbyes, then scattered to check out of their hotel rooms.

Mel pulled some bills from his wallet and tossed them on the table. "Silva, I need to go check out. Meet you in the parking lot in a few minutes. See you on fires, Liz." Mel touched the bill of his baseball cap.

Jon nodded, his focus on Liz. "Be there in a few, buddy."

"Bye, Mel." She blew him a trite kiss.

"I'll walk you to your car." Jon stepped out to the parking lot with her, dreading the inevitable.

Liz carefully positioned her sunglasses, as if doing so would incur great pain. "Guess I won't be seeing you much this summer."

He didn't appreciate hearing it but knew it to be true. "Probably not. I'll be investigating fires after you fight them. Highly unlikely our paths will cross."

"Have a safe summer. Stay in the black." She winked.

He liked that she told him to do what he'd always reminded their crew. Because the black was safer, where wildfire had already burned, instead of the hazardous, flammable green.

"Thanks, but that'll apply more to you than me, Miss Squad Boss. I go in *after* the fire burns through," he reminded her.

A blue Toyota Camry blinked hello when Liz clicked her key fob. They moseyed over and stood next to the car.

Liz stared off, then back at him and smiled. "Give me a goodbye hug."

He moved close and eased his arms around her, squeezing her tighter than he should. In his mind, saying goodbye justified it.

She squeezed him back and didn't let go. Lord knows *he* didn't want to. But reality bites; she had to go fight fires, and he had to investigate what caused them.

"So long, Silva. Be safe this summer. Don't let the fire gremlins get the best of you."

He let go first. "*You* stay safe. Follow your *Ten Standard Fire Orders* and *Eighteen Watchout Situations*," he cautioned, then turned and strode to Mel's Mustang. He tossed his pack in the back seat and folded himself into the front passenger seat.

As he closed the door, he observed Liz still standing where he'd left her, waving goodbye.

"Goodbye, beautiful. Stay safe on the fireline," he muttered, waving back.

Suddenly, he regretted not having slipped between the sheets to spend the night with her. She'd been so out of it, he would have hated himself. She wouldn't have remembered anyway. The old Jon would have done it without hesitation.

No more deposits into my overflowing bucket of fuck-ups.

Had she stayed awake, she would have made love with him. Of that he was certain. And he would have felt like pond scum.

They'd shared an intense experience together last year when Liz helped Jon escape a runaway wildfire. He respected and admired her as a co-worker, firefighter, and friend. But unease ate at him with her other job.

Last night, she told him he was her hero...that he was wonderful...and a gentleman. And that meant more to his bruised and battered soul than a hundred nights of sex.

Okay. One night of sex.

Jon welcomed the seven-hour drive from Girdwood to Fairbanks. Mel had been unusually quiet on the way, but everyone had partied hard last night, so Jon didn't elicit conversation. Mel kept the mp3 player on, and Jon was content to listen to music. Gave him a chance to mull over Liz. Hard to win her heart when they wouldn't be seeing each other this summer. The thought depressed him, and once more he beat himself up for screwing up on the Shackelford Fire last year.

If not for that, he'd still be the crew boss.

As the Mustang whizzed past the boreal forest of spruce and birch on the Parks Highway, he thought back to the crew party last year at the Snowcastle bar and restaurant in downtown Fairbanks. He'd been the one who drank too much, to mask the torment from nearly getting his crew killed.

He recalled leaving with Liz after their poker game. She'd driven his car to his house, helped him inside, and put him to bed. Then left him a note saying Rego gave her a ride back to the barracks at Fort Wainwright.

All of that after Jon had blithely slurred that Liz was *his* hero and he loved her. He'd meant the hero part after she'd powered him up that steep mountain. The love part had been the beer talking. The next morning, he'd awakened with regret, after saying things he didn't mean.

He'd started over and moved along on a different path. Wasn't easy, but he wanted to stay involved with wildland fire. But not as a firefighter. He wanted, no *needed* to regain the respect of the wildland fire community when he'd blown it after years of kicking ass on the fireline. A desperate desire burned in him to fix what he'd done—redeem himself or whatever the heck you called it after FUBAR—fucking up beyond all recognition.

Then there was Liz. Their timing always sucked. They couldn't seem to catch a break.

In retrospect, he hashed over the whole meaningful relationship thing. He'd never taken time to know the women he'd married; he'd only given his wives lip service, saying what they'd wanted to hear. Never meaning a word. Marriages up in flames.

In all that time, he had not figured out how love worked— as dumb as that sounded. As New Jon, he concluded he had to earn love...but whether he *deserved* love was another story.

He had a fun night with an exotic dancer and didn't have sex. For him, that was progress. Resisting temptation had been a challenge. He'd had a hard-on most of the evening, dancing with Liz, and later in her hotel room.

The new Jon had matured and was serious about getting his act together. No more womanizing or running from relationships. No more telling women he loved them when he didn't mean it.

Later, while lying with Liz—her under the covers and him on top—he told her he might be ready for a genuine relationship. But she'd fallen asleep.

His words had hung in the air, then gently swirled around her.

Like ashes from a wildfire.

CHAPTER 4

$\mathcal{L}$ iz plodded along the women's wing on the second floor of the barracks at the Alaska Fire Service on Fort Wainwright. Despite her exhaustion, it felt good to be back in Fairbanks again. She turned the knob and shoved the door open with her knee.

A lanky, brown-haired woman wearing a T-shirt and shorts glanced up from her cross-legged position on the twin bed opposite Liz's.

"G'day. I'm your bunk mate. McKenzie Quinn. I go by Kenzie."

Liz loved her Australian accent. "Hi, Kenzie. I'm Elizabeth Harrington. Call me Liz." She tossed her day pack and small duffle on her bed and moved toward the woman to shake her hand.

"Good to meet you." She greeted her with a dimpled smile and rows of straight white teeth.

"What part of Australia?" Liz scanned Kenzie's elegant, folded legs and sinewy, solid build.

"Canberra. I'm on a firey exchange with your Alaska Fire Service."

"Firey?"

"What you call a firefighter."

Liz nodded. "Tara mentioned we had a new crew member. When did you get here?"

"Flew into Fairbanks the day before yesterday." Kenzie returned to her task of arranging items on her bed for her fire pack. "I'm assigned to your crew. Met your crew boss."

"You'll like Tara, she's an excellent leader and good to work with." Liz shoved her gear aside and flopped on her back with a forearm over her forehead.

"Heard you were at a wedding." She winked at Liz. "Get a bit pissed, I reckon?"

"Pissed?" Liz peeked out from under her forearm.

"Drunk as skunks, as you Yanks like to say."

"Oh. Yeah." Liz chuckled. "I don't normally drink champagne. Got caught up in the moment."

"Know the feeling." Kenzie laughed. "Met more of Aurora Crew at the dining hall. A guy named Rego who sounds like Al Pacino. And a bloke from Canada."

"Nick Rego. Cohen was the groomsman I was paired with when I saw my—" Liz stopped herself.

My what?

Liz's phone vibrated. Her co-worker and new business partner, Ravish, calling from the club in Vegas. "Excuse me, I have to take this." She rose from the bed and stepped out to the hallway.

"Rav, what's going on?"

"You're hard to get ahold of. Tried reaching you all weekend."

"I attended a wedding. Arrived in Fairbanks a little while ago."

"Thought I'd give you an update. The bank is reviewing our business loan application. It looks like we'll each need to come up with more up-front money."

Liz hesitated. "I thought we agreed on all that before I left? What changed?"

Ravish sighed. "You know how it is with these large corporations. They always want more."

"How much more?" Liz had worked with Ravish at the

club for several years, and when they moved in together, Liz had developed a trust for her.

A pause on the phone. "Fifty grand."

Liz sputtered. "Wait—that's not our agreement. Have you talked to Amethyst Corporation about where our club will be in their hotel? Did we get a first-floor location? Because I'm not paying them a dime more unless that happens."

"I think so, but you must send more money. Thought I'd give you a heads-up."

Liz furrowed her brow. "I want a conference call with them. Can you set it up? I can do it in the evening after I get off work."

"Yeah, I'll try, but they do all their meetings early in the day."

"I don't have access to that kind of cash at the moment." She'd have to borrow it. Her last dance club check went to the Henderson Nursing Home. Dad's care had gone up with the latest loss of physical ability to do things himself.

"We don't either." Silence on the line. "I'll set up an online Zoom meeting with Amethyst Hotel later this week. Do you have access to a computer?" asked Ravish.

"Yeah, I brought my tablet. Sorry I saddled you guys with all this, but I had to get up here for a wedding. Remember, don't tell the club. I fibbed about fire training starting early this year."

"No worries. Trust us to handle things. And you better work on getting more cash."

Liz smiled into her phone. "First, talk to Amethyst. You're a good friend, Rav. Thanks."

"Hey, what are friends for? Love you, got to go."

"Okay, keep me posted. Bye." Liz ended the call.

She entered her room and closed the door as a notification pinged her phone.

Kenzie held up her own phone. "It's Tara. We're to report to fire refresher training tomorrow morning at eight a.m. sharp."

"Okay. I'm exhausted. I need a shower and good night's sleep."

It puzzled Liz why the Amethyst Corporation wanted so much more. She was certain they'd solidified the deal before she left for Alaska. She had pushed hard to complete negotiations so she could get up here for the wedding. Liz had no choice but to trust Jasper and Ravish to manage things while she earned more money for their new business venture. As it stood, she didn't yet have the required amount, let alone more.

She did a rough computation in her head. At her pay grade at the lower end of the general schedule level for a forty-hour work week, plus overtime and hazard duty pay when on direct attack on the fireline, the dollars could add up quick. Plus, Liz earned a little more as a squad boss. Alaska paid a little bit more than the lower forty-eight, but surprisingly, federal fire-fighters weren't paid as much as one might think for putting their lives on the line. But she loved fighting fire.

She crossed her fingers that she could earn the cash.

*J*on relaxed on his living room couch, clicking channels with his remote. He landed on the Audubon channel, his happy place. Felt good to be home.

He'd turned off his phone to block reality. He picked it up and powered it on as an eagle pair locked talons and spiraled through the sky on his TV screen.

Ding. Ding. Ding. The recent call notifications piled up.

He rubbed his stubble and peered at his phone. One voice mail from his employer, the U.S. Bureau of Land Management, Alaska Fire Service, and two from the State of Alaska, Division of Forestry. Fairbanks Memorial Hospital called. Must be short on EMT help.

He scrolled and stopped cold, gaping in disbelief at the last voicemail.

His phone abruptly lit with the same Caller ID, playing the song *Surfin' Bird*. He still hadn't changed the ringtone from his days studying ornithology at UAF. He'd do that one of these days.

"What the hell?" he muttered, eyes glued to the Caller ID.

Roxanne Silva...his first ex-wife. Satan's mistress.

He hesitated, staring at his phone. Against his better judgment, he tapped it, curious as hell.

"Hello?"

"You're the hardest person to get ahold of," said the soft, lilting voice that had sucked him in a decade ago back in Sonoma.

"Roxanne. Wow, this is—how are you?"

"I'm great. It's good to hear your voice again, Jonny."

He recoiled, hating when she called him that. "It's been ten years. What—why—how did you get my cell number?"

"There's this thing called the Internet. You weren't hard to find."

"Where are you?"

She laughed. "Here, in Alaska. I called to say hi."

"You? In Alaska?" More disbelief. Memories of what had led to their divorce crowded his mind.

"I'm in Sockeye Landing, on the Kenai Peninsula. It's pretty here."

"Thought Alaska was never on your to-do list? You were a Cali girl, as I recall." His mouth hung open. Mystified didn't come close to describing the numbness in his brain.

"Things changed. *I've* changed."

Silence while his heart sunk to the floor. "What brings you to Alaska?"

"Remember Tyler, my baby brother? You encouraged him to go into firefighting years ago. He got on a state crew fighting fires. He found a good deal on a lodge, and we became partners. Are you familiar with Coho Lodge?"

"You bought a lodge on the freaking Kenai?"

Her breathy voice. "Knew that would blow your mind."

No shit. A stunning development. "How did you get the capital?"

"My dad loaned it to us. Plus, I had money from my nail salon business, then did some accounting for Sonoma wineries. When Tyler chanced into the lodge deal, we put our money together. I kept my nail salon business and run it on the side."

"Tyler was a good kid and just needed direction."

"He's always admired you, Jonny." She paused. "You married twice after we divorced. How'd that work for you?"

He let out an impatient sigh. "If you know that, then you know how it worked out."

She chuckled. "You never could stick with a relationship. Are you seeing anyone?"

He let it hang there. "Roxanne...why did you call after all this time?"

"I've been thinking about us...the way we used to be. And now that I'm in Alaska, I hoped we'd get together again."

The unpleasant seesaw of revulsion mixed with sympathy flashed back, unsettling his gut. "Not a good idea. I *am* seeing someone," he erupted.

"Who?"

"That's none of your concern."

She laughed. "Oh. So, we're going to play *that* game."

His patience slipped. "No games. Roxanne, I have a lot going on right now but thanks for calling."

"Heard what happened last year on that terrible fire near Fairbanks. Where are you working now?"

"I'm a fire investigator."

"Ooh, sounds impressive. You always could land on your feet when things went south. I can drive up to Fairbanks," she drawled in that alluring tone she used on him years ago.

"Not a good idea." He didn't like where this was heading.

More breathiness. "I'll give you time to think about it. I know this is a shock after all this time. Remember how good we were together, Jonny? You were the best lover and great in bed..."

"That was a lifetime ago. I've moved on and figured you have, too." He paused. "Thanks for calling. Bye, Roxanne."

He ended the call and sat back. *A bit of a shock?*

What an understatement. This was the last thing he'd expected.

He'd honestly forgotten about her, same as he had his second and third ex-wives. Living with Roxanne was like holding the end of a super-charged fire hose. He'd left her and bailed to Alaska for a reason. Flashbacks of their marriage played out in his mind. His finding out about her mental and emotional instability after they'd married. Only then had she told him about her dad's sexual and mental abuse when she was younger. At first, he tried to protect her and help her work through it. Even with eventual treatment, her paranoia made it impossible for him to stay in the marriage. He finally gave up and left Sonoma.

It had taken years for his guilt to fade. And just like that, here it was, back in his chest, aching it again. That's what happens when you unravel the past. Like poking around in a fire to figure out what started it.

Remembering his other voicemails, he tapped and listened. "Jon, this is Keaton Stripling, State of Alaska fire investigation. BLM told me to call you. We're hoping you can join us down here on the Kenai Peninsula to help us investigate fires. I've reserved a room for you at the Alpenglow Hotel in Rockfish."

Jon blanked out on the rest of his message after hearing "Kenai Peninsula." His skin prickled at the thought of being anywhere remotely close to where Roxanne was. With any luck, he wouldn't bump into her down there.

Then again, as the saying goes…Alaska was a small town.

CHAPTER 5

*L*iz and Kenzie took their seats in the second-floor training room at the Alaska Fire Service building at Fort Wainwright. Liz yawned into her cardboard coffee cup.

Tara Waters stood before the group and began the Alaska Fire Refresher Training class. "Good morning. For you new people, welcome to Alaska. And for returning firefighters, welcome back." She distributed *Alaska Handy Dandy Firefighting Field Guides* to everyone in the room. "Make sure you read these."

Tara continued. "First, some announcements. Refresher training goes all week. After that, the Aurora Crew will be available for fire call. Today we'll practice fire shelter deployment, and I want you to know how to use bear repellant." She moved through the room, passing out canisters of bear spray.

The day whizzed by for Liz, and after class Tara approached her. "I'd appreciate it if you'd help Kenzie and Cohen, show them how we do things in Alaska. Okay?"

"Sure. How seasoned are they? Kenzie mentioned fighting her share of bushfires in Australia."

Tara nodded. "They're both experienced. Cohen fought fire in Canada and the lower forty-eight. Gunnar encouraged him to apply to smokejumper school, but you know how people feel about jumping from perfectly good airplanes. Cohen said he'd consider it."

"Can't say as I blame him." Liz inspected her canister of bear spray.

"I've assigned them to your Afi Slayers squad. Tupa and Rego requested to be on your squad, too. That says a lot. You should be proud." Tara patted Liz's shoulder. Last year, Jon had chosen Liz and Tara for two of three squad team leaders on the Aurora Crew.

"I'll go to the barracks with you." Tara linked her arm. "Been dying to ask what happened with Jon after the wedding."

Liz gave her a nervous laugh. "I drank too much."

"You? You never lose control."

"I know, but when I was finally alone with him—I was so nervous and threw back champagne, which hits me hard anyway. I should have known better."

Tara laughed. "Ah, remorse. We all say that the morning after. What happened?"

"Nothing. And that's the way I wanted it," lied Liz, trying to convince herself. "I won't be seeing him again. We've gone in separate directions."

"You never know. Fire is a small world." Tara smiled at her.

Liz shrugged. "It's better this way. I have my life, and he has his. Besides, I love working in Alaska in the summer, but not in the winter. I'm a fair-weather desert rat."

"I didn't want to live here either, but Ryan won me over."

"You two were a match made in heaven. That's not the case with Jon and me." Liz peered at a helicopter lifting off in the distance. "Angela claimed that destiny kicked in for you and Ryan the minute you saw him on that fire near Butte, Montana. Any word from him?"

"He texted. When he and Gunnar demob from the Yukon Charley fire, they're going to the Kenai Peninsula. Dave Doss is already there, helping the state set up an Incident Command Center in Rockfish. He's assigned Ryan to command Air Attack."

"Demobilization from one fire and dispatching to another means fire season has officially started. Ryan will do great. So happy you two found each other." Liz stopped outside her room in the barracks.

Tara turned to her. "Don't give up on Jon. He messed up last year, but he's one of those guys who's a work in progress. Give him time. See you in the morning." Tara unlocked her door and disappeared inside.

"Right. Goodnight." Liz opened her door to an empty room. Kenzie must be out running.

She climbed into her sleeping bag on her single cot and fixed on the mosquitoes dancing on the ceiling in the twilight. *I need to stay focused. The new dance club. A means to an end.* She and Jon had gone their separate ways. End of story.

She wished her gut wouldn't twist and turn whenever she thought about it.

*J*on hurried to the tarmac where Mel had told him to be by 0700 hours Monday morning, for the flight to Rockfish. Mel had one seat left on N74 Juliet, a versatile transport and utility helicopter. He had an AFS helitack crew to fly to the Kenai Peninsula.

Jon climbed into the passenger side and folded himself into the seat. The white flight helmet with headphones and a hot mic hung next to him, and he positioned it on his head, snapping the black strap under his chin.

Mel opened the door and climbed into the pilot's seat. "Got an updated weather report. Winds aloft as we pass Denali Park, then heavy around Turnagain Arm." He gave Jon a lopsided grin. "When isn't it blowing in Turnagain? It sure blew up the fires down on the Kenai. BLM Alaska Fire Service sending you down?"

"Yep. The State of Alaska helped us out last year on those Interior fires. We're returning the favor." Jon observed an air tanker refueling in the distance.

"AFS dispatched the Aurora Crew to the Kenai Peninsula." Mel busied himself with pre-flight checks and donned his own helmet. "Thought you'd be interested."

Jon noticed a windsock flirt with the breeze. "I'll miss fighting fire with them."

Mel flipped a few switches on the instrument panel, then leaned back and rested his palms on his thighs.

Jon looked at him. "Forget something?"

"Silva, what you don't say speaks volumes."

"What don't I say?"

Mel removed his aviation shades. "Liz Harrington."

"What about her?"

"Hard not to notice you both wrapped around each other like pretzels after the wedding. You know the fire world. People rattle on and assume things." Mel had caught Jon off guard by bringing up Liz.

"What are you getting at?"

"I'll say this only once." Mel fixed him in a firm stare. "I've stood by watching you break heart after heart after blowing through two marriages. And that's not counting the first one before I knew you. I haven't uttered a word."

Jon tensed. "No, you've been a good friend."

Mel leaned toward him. "Understand, I'm not judging. But if I find out you hurt Elizabeth Harrington in any way...I will come for you. And I will hurt you. She's a wonderful woman, a good friend, and a damn good firefighter. Don't forget, *she's* the one who got your sorry ass up that mountain last year."

Mel's declaration hit him like a slap. This was the last thing he expected. Now he understood why Mel had been quiet on the drive from Girdwood to Fairbanks.

"I've not forgotten. Hurting Liz is the last thing I would ever do." Jon leveled his gaze. "Hey buddy, I've got to ask...are you in love with her?"

Mel put on his aviator shades and flipped switches. "Let's just say if you hadn't made a move, I would have."

"I plan to make more moves. I'm going to see where she's

staying on the Kenai." Jon glanced at Mel. "Thanks for your honesty."

"Copy that." Mel nodded with a half-smile and powered up the rotors.

So, Mel had deep feelings for Liz. Everyone in fire liked and respected her. She was a strong leader with a cool head and a helluva firefighter, just as Mel said. No doubt Mel could whoop his ass if provoked, despite being half Jon's size. He'd worked with Mel for seven fire seasons before Jon quit firefighting last season. He valued Mel's friendship.

He sat in stunned silence as the rotors rose in pitch to reach flight speed and Mel lifted the helicopter and aimed it south, to Alaska's summer playground, the spectacular Kenai Peninsula. The high-pitched whir of the engine soothed him.

They'd follow the Parks Highway and pass by the mighty Alaska Range, Denali Mountain, and the Talkeetna Mountains. Then fly over Anchorage and head southwest, along the east side of Cook Inlet to Rockfish, midway down the Kenai Peninsula, near the ever-emerald Kenai River.

Jon glanced down at his red long-sleeved T-shirt with "Fire Investigator" above his right breast pocket. He'd make up for last year's screw-up and turn his life around—prove himself worthy of relationships at work and in his personal life.

And prove himself worthy of Liz.

The universe had given him another chance. This time, he wouldn't be an idiot and blow it.

They were both headed to the Kenai and he would do his level best to make sure their paths crossed. First, he had to make changes. Like make up for being an alpha asshole over the past ten years, to just about everybody.

He'd work on that one first.

CHAPTER 6

*J*on entered the Rockfish mayor's conference room in the Kenai-Peninsula Borough administration build- ing. "Good afternoon." He pulled out a chair from the table next to a slender woman with long, chestnut-brown hair.

She glanced up, extending her palm. "I'm Simone West, from the Alaska State Fire Marshal's Office in Anchorage."

"Pleased to meet you." Jon took a seat. "Sounds like things are getting serious."

Keaton took his cue to begin the meeting. Jon had heard good things about Keaton. He respected a guy who knew his shit.

"Good morning, folks. I'm Keaton Stripling, with the State of Alaska, Department of Forestry. We have a unique situation that's developed on the peninsula. The State of Alaska appreci- ates the expertise of the federal Bureau of Land Management to help us with fire investigation. Thank you for being here. First, we'll go around the room for introductions." Keaton motioned at Jon.

"Thanks. Good to be here." Jon dipped a nod. "Hello, everyone. I'm Jon Silva, a fire investigator with the BLM Alaska Fire Service, in Fairbanks. My federal agency appreciates the state inviting us to take part in this multi-agency investigation. We'll help any way we can." Jon kept things brief.

Keaton continued. "Miss West and Mr. Silva, the gentleman to your right, is Kyle Shaw, the mayor of the Kenai Peninsula Borough. He represents all communities on the Kenai Peninsula. Kyle?" He gestured toward the mayor.

"We appreciate the help of our federal friends up north. Your agency is good to work with," Mayor Shaw imparted to Jon. "I've asked Mr. Keaton to head up our KP Pyro Task Force." He picked up papers and passed them to Keaton. "Here, circulate these maps showing the fire locations with GPS coordinates. I'll let Trooper O'Donnell, of the Alaska State Troopers, take it from here."

The trooper shifted in his seat, and his duty belt leather squeaked. Jon's eye dropped to his holstered weapon, a Glock 22. Glocks were handy for law enforcement when seconds counted. Jon preferred a .357 Ruger for bear protection. In all his years working in remote Alaska, he'd never had to shoot a one, *knock on wood*. Most times, he'd scared them off by discharging his weapon, or using bear spray.

"Good morning, I'm Trooper O'Donnell. Our officers have responded to several fires so far along the Kenai River. City and wildland state crews have contained most. We've not had lightning activity, so we think the fires are suspicious."

"All fires are suspicious until investigation determines the cause." Jon took his map and passed the others to Simone.

The trooper nodded agreement. "True. Someone might be setting these fires. They're popping up with increasing regularity." Trooper O'Donnell glanced around the room. "We've requested fire bosses to instruct first responder crews to preserve the point of origin sites for investigation."

"Good, that'll make our jobs easier." Jon tapped his pen on a legal pad. "Which entities have responded to these fires so far?"

"Most have been accessible by road. The city fire departments in Rockfish and Sockeye Landing have responded, along with state forestry crews." Trooper O'Donnell shifted again in his seat.

Jon raised his brows. "We have our work cut out for us."

Simone looked him square in the eye. "If this multi-agency task force determines someone is deliberately setting wildfires, the Fire Marshal's Office will work closely with Alaska State Troopers to track down and apprehend the purported arsonists. It's not the job of land management fire investigators to pursue or apprehend persons of interest in this situation. Leave that to law enforcement."

Jon and Keaton exchanged glances and nodded. "We understand, Miss West." Jon figured the Alaska State Troopers would have the lead on law enforcement actions should the situation turn out to be arson.

Simone looked around the room, her gaze resting on Jon. "Good. We're all on the same page. Thank you, gentlemen."

Keaton took off his cheaters and folded them into his pocket. "Miss West, Mr. Silva, and yours truly are the fire investigation task force. It's time to go to the field. Jon, we've provided you with a state rig, right?"

Jon nodded. "I picked it up when I arrived."

"Mr. Silva, I'll be accompanying you. I have much to review and brief you on. We'll discuss it on our way out to the fire sites this afternoon." Simone held up her briefcase.

Jon scrutinized her. A take charge woman. "Okay, sure."

"Great. I need to change into my field clothes. Meet you in the hotel parking lot in thirty minutes." She straightened to her full height. Only six inches shorter than him, with a killer figure. Hard for any guy not to notice.

"Sounds like a plan." Jon stuck the map inside his manila folder and drove back to the hotel. Once in his room, he assembled items he'd need in the field. He entered the fire locations into his phone navigation app and in his hand-held satellite GPS tracker. When one didn't work, hopefully the other would. Working with devices outside major cities and towns in Alaska often proved to be a challenge. Not all 663,300 square miles had cell coverage, but companies improved it with each passing year.

Jon stepped to the bathroom sink in his room and turned on the faucet. Brown water poured out. He turned it off, then turned it on and let it pour. It didn't clear. "What the heck?" he muttered. He tried the shower. The same brown water.

"Well. This sucks." He gathered the gear he needed for this afternoon's fire site visits, then took himself down to the hotel lobby.

"Brown water comes out of my faucet," Jon informed the woman at the reception desk.

"Oh, goodness, ever since that terrible earthquake a few months ago, the water turns brown sometimes. It comes and goes." She wrinkled her nose and produced two bottles of water. "Here's some glacial water."

Jon lifted the bottles. "Thanks. Any chance of a shower with clean water?"

"Keep checking it. Sometimes it clears up on its own."

"Can you move me to another room?"

"No, sir, we're completely booked."

"Use my shower if you like, Mr. Silva. My room has clean water," said a smooth, feminine voice. Simone stood next to him, dressed in field clothes.

"Uh, thanks." Nice of her to offer, but he'd work it out with Keaton. "Call me Jon."

"All right, Jon. Ready to go when you are," she purred at him.

Oh man, don't need a co-worker hitting on me.

"Let's roll. I have the fire locations." He held up his phone and headed toward the door, putting on his sunglasses.

Simone stepped alongside him. "I'm glad you have an idea where we're going."

"Aren't you familiar with the Kenai Peninsula?"

"Nope. Only been here a few weeks. Transferred up from the Arizona State Fire Marshal's Office."

"For starters, make sure you have lots of bug dope." Jon

glanced down at her boots. "And you have the proper foot gear, so that helps."

He clicked the locks open with his key remote, and they settled into the bucket seats of the new Dodge pickup. Not a bad rig. It had a few bells and whistles and a new car smell. As long as it had good speakers, he was good with it. He liked his music loud.

Simone sat up straight to stretch the seat belt around her. He glanced away upon noticing her hard-to-miss chest protrusions, enhanced by her form-fitting T-shirt. He changed his focus out the windshield and started the engine.

"I look forward to working with you." Simone's slender wrist rested her shades on a tanned face. She resembled the quintessential Angelina Jolie package, complete with full lips. She tilted her head at him. "We'll do well together."

"Glad you think so." Jon stared at his map. He didn't want that certain body part to move. Not for this woman. There was only one woman who could do that merely by him looking at her.

And she is down here somewhere.

He made it a point to find out exactly where.

CHAPTER 7

*L*iz and her crew had flown down in two helicopters and arrived in Rockfish early this morning. They spent the day getting situated in their fire camp on a bluff above the Kenai River. The crew erected four heavy-duty camp tents, three for the men, and one for the women.

"This isn't bad. I've stayed in worse." Liz tossed her gear on a cot in a medium-sized camp tent she shared with Kenzie and Tara. She pulled a granola bar from her pack and gnawed on it.

"I've bunked in far worse down in Oz." Kenzie stood, arms akimbo, assessing their abode. "I reckon we have a bit of privacy. Won't need air conditioning. Twice the mozzies here, in the up over."

"Mozzies?"

"Mosquitoes." Kenzie grinned, slapping one on her hand.

"Little buggers are everywhere." Liz slapped one on her neck as she situated herself in her new digs. A crew van had picked them up and driven them to a large campground outside of Rockfish, perched on a bluff above the banks of the Kenai River.

"I hear this place is a world class salmon fishery." Liz waved her granola bar.

Kenzie nodded. "Reckon so. We should fish for some."

Tara breezed into the women's tent. "Okay ladies, time to go to today's fire information briefing."

The crew piled into the long transport van, and Tara drove them to the Incident Command Center in Rockfish at the state fire headquarters building. Fire crews and overhead staff had gathered on an expanse of lawn behind the building, where they held briefings several times a day.

Liz recognized Dave Doss, chatting with a guy who looked to be the state incident commander.

Tara motioned at long tables set up next to the building. "Aurora Crew, grab a sack lunch, compliments of the State Division of Forestry."

They settled down on the fresh-cut grass, and Liz dug into her lunch.

Cohen sat next to her. "Ready for action?"

"I was born ready." Liz sipped from her water bottle.

He studied her, then bit into an apple. "Is Jon Silva your boyfriend?"

"Boyfriend?" Liz gave him an eye roll. "What? No. He's not my boyfriend. We're only friends."

Several heads turned toward her, and Rego coughed "*Bullshit*" into his hand. Tupa and Kenzie guffawed.

Liz glared at them.

"You were pretty cozy at the wedding," Cohen persisted.

"And this interests you because…?" She raised her brows.

"I'd like to ask you out."

"Like, on a date?" She couldn't believe this guy. "Hello, we're *at work*. There is no going out. I'm not into holding hands and skipping through fireweed with anyone on my crew."

Cohen reminded her of an intelligent pro-wrestler. He was nice enough, and he had a helluva ripped physique, looking every bit a firefighter, tall and fit. She envisioned all kinds of migraines involving herself with someone on her squad.

"I'm serious." He leaned toward her. "Have dinner with me."

She regarded him as if he'd shifted into a moose. "We

already eat, sleep, and work together. I don't date people on my squad."

His glacial eyes sparkled at her. "We won't be working together forever."

"True. For now, we work." Liz gave herself an internal eyeroll. The last thing she wanted was a member of her own squad hitting on her.

"Okay, but when fire season ends, I'll try again."

Liz opened her mouth to say it was a free country, when a voice on the sound system cut in.

"Good afternoon, firefighters." Dave Doss held a portable mic for a sound system. "Welcome to the Kenai Peninsula and today's information briefing. The peninsula has erupted with fires threatening several communities. On the way down, I'm sure you assessed the fuel loads—miles of dry, flammable dead spruce from beetle kill."

"Since south central Alaska and the Kenai Peninsula are in the State of Alaska protection area, the Department of Forestry has operational control of the fires. BLM and Forest Service crews will coordinate with them for staffing and resources. Firefighting protocol works differently down here on the Peninsula as opposed to Alaska's Interior up north. Down here, fires are more road accessible."

Liz munched her sandwich while taking in the white peaks jutting into the sky in the distance. On the helo flight down, Tara had pointed out the four volcanoes at intervals along the west side of Cook Inlet. She gaped at Mount Redoubt, the one that looked like a snow cone.

Hopefully, it wouldn't erupt while they were here fighting fire. What a hot mess that would be. Speaking of hot, dating Cohen would create all kinds of chaos. Liz sighed heavily. She couldn't afford any drama or other complications in her life right now.

I'm here to fight fire, not play with fire.

*L*iz made sure her fire pack contained all essentials for the crew's first fire assignment tomorrow morning. She stepped back, satisfied. Her stomach growled and she looked from Tara to Kenzie. "What are you thinking for dinner?"

"We have a choice of camp food or several restaurants on the main drag within walking distance. Rego recommends the Kenai Kipper. Decent food, and they give fifteen percent off to firefighters. Wear your yellows and show them your ID."

Liz jumped up. "I'm there. Let's go."

"Sounds good." Kenzie rose from her cot.

Tara led the way from their crew camp to the sidewalk along the main drag, also the Sterling Highway that ran through the center of Rockfish. "I finagled a crew van from Dave Doss. We start at oh-seven-hundred hours in the morning, so get to bed early."

"Yes, Mom," Liz teased. "I have my Afi Slayers squad organized. Tupa has his chainsaw, and the rest of us have our Pulaskis, radios, and everything else. We're set."

"Good. I'm counting on you to be good to my old squad." Tara pointed at a red neon fish sign about a block away. "There's the Kipper."

As the three women strolled along in their yellow and green fire garb, a man shouted from a pickup stopped at a light. "Ladies, thank you for your service!" The driver tapped his horn, and the women waved back.

Another guy hung out the window of an SUV, waving his baseball cap. "I'm in love with you!" The light turned green, the vehicles tapped their horns, and sped away.

"The locals are friendly, aren't they?" commented Kenzie, as the women crossed the street to the Kenai Kipper restaurant.

Liz grasped the handle of the large wood door and held it for her crewmates.

It took a minute for her vision to get accustomed to the

darker interior. The hostess motioned them to follow and seated them in a booth near the back.

Tara and Kenzie slid into the seat facing the entrance, and Liz sat with her back to it. She picked up a menu. "Fish, fish, and more fish. I want a plate of something that walks or flies."

Kenzie scanned the menu. "I'm starved. Had a dingo's breakfast. Don't reckon they have wallaby stew."

Tara laughed. "Around here it's moose stew. Wild game isn't normally on restaurant menus."

"Down in the Mohave Desert, I could set you up with grilled roadrunner, barbecued rattlesnake, and tarantula cactus jelly at the Roadkill Café." Liz glanced up to see if the women would take the bait.

"Now you're feeding me a ripper," joked Kenzie.

Tara leaned sideways, squinting. "Isn't that Jon Silva sitting near the door?"

"What? No way." Liz rotated her neck like an owl, but too many people blocked her view.

Tara stretched her neck to gawp. "He's with a woman."

"What do you mean he's with a woman? What woman?" Liz turned back around, heart beating fast, staring at Tara. "I didn't expect to see him again this summer. Who's the woman?"

Tara leaned out from the booth. "Not a firefighter. She's in business attire."

Liz whipped around again, peering up front. All she could see was the back of a head. And she couldn't see Jon.

"The Feds must have sent him to help investigate these fires," mused Tara.

"Who's Jon Silva?" asked Kenzie, squinting along with Tara.

"Our crew boss from last year." Tara shot a glance at Liz.

"In that case, say G'day to the bloke. Or don't you get on well together?" Kenzie's *G'day* drew a quick glance from the server setting salmon burgers and sweet potato fries on the table.

Liz felt like a cornered cheetah. She stared at Tara with a *what-should-I-do* expression.

"You need to go say G'day." Tara smirked at Kenzie.

Who the heck was the woman? Liz wanted a closer view but resisted the urge to glance behind her.

"Maybe you need to visit the loo?" Kenzie sported a mischievous smile.

"Good idea." Liz lifted her chin at a more dignified reason to waltz up front to the entrance.

Tara gave Liz a knowing look. "Take your time."

Liz made a sweet face, then sauntered toward Jon's table. "Well, well, look who the fires dragged in." She pretended surprise in a cheerful voice as she approached. Her breath shortened upon seeing the dark-haired beauty sitting with Jon.

The leggy, heavily made-up brunette fluttered her long, dark lashes at Liz in an up-and-down, condescending assessment.

Liz observed the One Guy Who Mattered with his deer-in-the-headlights expression, like she'd caught him cheating. She and Jon weren't exclusive. He had no hold on her, nor she on him. But his dining with this woman—or any woman, both-ered her more than she cared to admit.

Jon finally made his mouth move. "Elizabeth Harrington, fancy meeting you here."

He'd never used her formal name, and she recognized his fake grin. She knew him better than he knew himself. And far better than the beauty pageant sitting with him.

Her eyes darted to the woman.

Jon gestured at his dinner companion. "Liz, this is Simone West. She's with the State Fire Marshal's Office. Simone, this is Liz. I worked with her on our fire crew last season."

"Hello," intoned Simone.

"Hello," returned Liz. What a bad idea. She wanted to run as fast as her legs would carry her.

She turned to Jon. "How long have you been down here?"

He blew out air. "Came down last Monday. Let's see, today is—"

"Friday," Liz filled in. She edged fingertips into her back pants pocket to appear relaxed. She was anything but. "About a week."

"Uh, yeah, right? Time flies when you're inspecting fires." That fake grin again.

"How many fires have you worked on?" She focused on Jon to avoid his annoyingly beautiful dining companion.

He turned to Simone. "How many would you say?"

"About a dozen," Simone replied in a low voice, like she had it all under control, thank you very much.

Jon glanced up at Liz. "About a dozen," he chirped like a parrot.

This meaningless exchange irritated her. Jon having dinner with this woman irritated her even more. What made it worse —Beauty Pageant appeared disgruntled, judging by her look of disdain.

"Hey, that's great," lied Liz. She glanced at her wrist without the wristwatch. "I have to get back to—good to see you, Silva," she mumbled, hurrying back to her table.

"Where's the Aurora Crew staying?" he called after her.

What do you care? She wanted to ignore him, but idiocy wormed its slithery way into her brain. "At a campground by the river," she carelessly flung over her shoulder.

"Good to meet you," Beauty Pageant called after her in a melodious tone.

The woman only said it for Jon's benefit.

Hmm, I can do things for Jon's benefit, too. Like tell him to go to hell.

Tara eyed Liz coming toward her. "Good grief, woman, you're a thundercloud. What happened?"

"I have to go. Where's my food?" grumbled Liz, glancing at her empty plate. Her stomach gummed up. Food was the last thing she needed right now.

"I had the server bag it for you." Tara gave Liz her sack of food. "Everything okay?"

"Yep," lied Liz, taking the food. "Thanks for getting this to go."

She sensed Tara didn't believe her. At least her boss had

the good sense not to pursue it. Not when Silva at one time had pursued Tara.

Liz shook her head. Who *hasn't* he pursued?

The three women paid for their meal and headed for the door. Liz straggled behind, not wanting to pass by Jon and his date. She pulled out her phone and pretended to busy herself, scrolling like mad.

"Liz," a familiar voice called out.

Cohen waved as he and Rego waited for a table.

Tara and Kenzie greeted their crewmates on their way out the door.

Liz had a diabolical idea. "Tara, you and Kenzie go on back. I'll be along in a minute."

"Okay, see you back at the ranch." Tara and Kenzie left the restaurant.

Liz breezed past Jon's table and made sure Jon noticed as she took Cohen's arm. "Let's get a table," she tossed off loudly.

Cohen gave her a quizzical look. "Thought you already ate."

"I forgot to get dessert." She held up her sack of food and touched his bare arm with his yellow shirt sleeves rolled up. "This salmon burger is to die for," she teased in a sultry voice.

Cohen's manner softened, and he matched her sultry tone. "In that case, I'll order one."

Good. Take that, Silva.

Rego saw his good buddy, Jon. "Silva, you wound up down here, too?" He extended his hand, and Jon shook it. The two launched into conversation, with Jon flipping glances at Liz.

"Come on, there's a table back here." Liz linked her elbow with Cohen's, hoping Jon's stare burned holes in the back of her fire shirt. She slid in next to him, facing Jon's direction.

Rego sauntered back, rolling his toothpick around his mouth. "Wow, what a knockout beauty with Silva." He slipped into the booth across from them. *Thanks for rubbing it in, Rego.*

Liz counted on no one noticing the green rays of jealousy beaming from her eyes like Superman's laser vision. She glanced in Jon's direction.

He didn't pay attention, and it rankled her. Her foot jiggled a million miles a minute under the table, shaking it.

"Whoa, having your own personal earthquake under there?" Cohen peeked under the table.

"Sorry. Restless, I guess."

He chuckled. "Uh huh. Right."

Liz glanced up at Jon and Simone standing and Jon tossing bills onto the table.

She spoke low into Cohen's ear. "I know you know what's bugging me. Will you please do me a favor and put your arm around me?" She knew it was a cheesy, desperate maneuver. But the little green monster had its claws sunk into her like a grizzly on a moose kill.

Cohen glanced in Jon's direction, then back at her. "I'll do you one better."

He lifted his arm and wrapped it around her shoulders, then pulled her to him and gave her a soft, lingering kiss on the mouth.

Liz stiffened, then fervently hoped Jon caught sight of this. When Cohen didn't stop, she pushed him back.

He had a smug look, like a cat with a mouse tail hanging out of his mouth.

"Chrissakes, Tremblay, it's inappropriate to make out with your squad boss." Rego scowled at him.

Cohen shot him an innocent look. "Just helping out a crewmate."

Liz tapped his arm. "You do understand that was for show, right? Don't be getting any ideas."

"Doesn't matter. I liked it." Cohen gave her a lopsided grin.

Jon followed Simone to the door and shot a glance back at Liz before pushing it open.

She leaned into Cohen for more pretending. *Take that, Silva, you jerk.*

"Shame on you, Harrington. You too, Tremblay," muttered Rego, shaking his bald head as he picked up a menu. "You're both going to hell."

"I was heading there anyway." Liz crumpled into a puddle of remorse.

Rego shot her his brown-eyed stare. "Go talk to Silva. Don't play head games. Guys don't like that."

Liz opened her mouth to say women don't like that either when sudden guilt washed over her for involving Cohen in her impulsive jealousy binge. She wanted to crawl under the table and curl up in a fetal position.

Cohen withdrew his arm from her shoulder. "If you want my honest opinion, Silva doesn't deserve you. If he had feelings for you, he wouldn't be having dinner with a beautiful woman. Leopards don't change their spots. I would never do that to a fine lady like you."

"Thank you, that's nice of you to say." Liz forced a smile and stood to go. "I'm going back to camp. I'm pretty tired."

Disappointment crossed his face. "Okay. Get some sleep. See you tomorrow."

She contemplated his sincere blue eyes. Maybe she should take him up on his offer to take her out, since Jon had apparently set his sights on someone else. "You Canadians are polite. Not sure how you put up with us rude Americans."

"You guys aren't so bad…unless things don't go your way."

"Silva might come after you for hitting on his woman," teased Rego.

Cohen fixed a steady gaze on Liz. "You aren't his woman, are you?"

She shrugged. "You saw him with someone else, same as I did. Goodnight, you guys."

"Sweet dreams." Rego pulled out his cheaters to read the menu.

She grabbed her sack of cold salmon burger and headed out the door. Her cheesy maneuver had filled her with remorse, but she appreciated Rego for making light of it.

Rego and Liz had an unfavorable start last year, when Liz considered him to be a misogynistic jerk. He eventually redeemed himself with the women of the Aurora Crew and turned out to be a good crewmate and staunch friend. If Liz got into a jam, she could count on Rego.

Liz hurried from the restaurant back to camp. When she reached her tent, it was empty. Tara and Kenzie were likely at the bathhouse, brushing their teeth.

She changed into her night shirt and laid out her necessities for the morning. Forcing back tears, she checked her fire pack for the tenth time to make sure it was ready to go for fire duty tomorrow.

Jon still chased women. He sure seemed to enjoy Beauty Pageant's company. Seeing Liz had been the last thing he'd expected. He had it written all over him. Why did she ever entertain the notion she and Jon could have something together? Anyway, she was here to fight fire and earn the money for her new business. Period.

She pulled out her phone to do a quick check of her email to see if she had updates from Ravish. Then she scanned her email for a caregiver progress report about her dad. Relieved to see one, she read it and was assured he was okay. He had moments of lucid thought, but his memory was mostly fading. In other words, no change.

She crawled inside her sleeping bag, arranged her travel pillow, and stared up at mosquitoes clinging to the tent ceiling. When Kenzie and Tara returned, she pretended to be asleep. The tears rolled out, and she let them.

Because after tonight, she resolved never to shed another tear over Mister Ho-Magnet.

Screw the oh-so-charming Jon Silva.

CHAPTER 8

The next morning in the hotel cafeteria, Jon finished his continental breakfast as his phone vibrated. He tapped to answer.

"There's another fire further up the Kenai River, between Silverleaf and Sockeye Landing, at the Skilak Road turnoff," Keaton informed him.

"What's the status?"

"Fifteen acres and growing. ICC sent a fire crew. Weather is favorable for containment. I'm meeting with the mayor this morning. Can you take a run out to this one?"

"Yeah, sure, text me the GPS."

"Okay. Keep me posted on what you find."

"Yep. Call you when I get back." Jon tapped to end the call.

Noting recent voice messages, he tapped them. Roxanne called. Twice. She'd called him the day before. And the day before that.

Sighing heavily, he grimaced and tapped the most recent.

Jonny, I heard you're down here on the Kenai. Why haven't you called me? Let's get together. Call me. You have my number. Bye.

He could light up the entire peninsula with the electricity

that lifted the hairs on his neck. He lowered the phone and sat frowning at it, not interested in her previous messages.

Simone strolled in and sat across from him. "Get some bad news?"

He glanced up. "Oh, it's nothing…" He trailed off, shaking his head.

Time to get back in the game. "We have another fire Keaton wants us to check out."

"Can't go. I have a conference call with my headquarters office about a fire I investigated in Arizona before I transferred up here. I'm testifying in a court case."

"Go ahead, I'll handle it. There's a fire crew on it. I won't be alone."

Jon's phone pinged notification. Keaton's text arrived with the GPS coordinates for the fire. He'd have to hike uphill from Skilak Road, but he wouldn't interfere with fire suppression activities.

Simone rose to pour coffee and sat back down. "Who was the woman last night at the restaurant?" Her dark gaze settled on him.

His eyes darted up, then back to his phone. "Someone I worked with last year."

"Hmm." She sipped her coffee, and the corners of her mouth quirked up.

Jon inhaled and glanced at her. "Hmm, what?"

"Couldn't help noticing how you stared when she came to talk to you."

"Oh, yeah?" He pursed his lips and sat back in his chair.

"I was hoping maybe you and I could—you know, we've been working together on all these fires." She took another sip and set down her cup. "We make an excellent team."

"And?"

She shoved her coffee aside and placed her forearms on the table, leaning toward him. "I thought we could get to know each other better. Maybe spend some time together outside of work. Unless there's someone else."

In the old days, Jon wouldn't have resisted Simone's hints

of seduction. She'd been hitting on him since that first day in the conference room, and he'd ignored her advances.

Jon folded his hands on the table. "Simone, I enjoy working with you. You're a top-notch professional, and I've learned a lot from your experience investigating arson."

"But...?" She raised her brows expectantly.

"But...there *is* someone else. I appreciate the sentiment, but I'm not interested in you that way." He shrugged a shoulder.

"And what way might that be?"

He let it hang there.

"Figured you might say that." She sighed and leaned back, assuming a business tone. "You're a fine looking man, Jon. You're intelligent. And masculine. I love strong, intelligent men." Her cat eyes drifted up and down his chest.

He fiddled with a spoon, turning it over and back again. "I'm flattered, but I'm not up for what you're asking."

She cocked a brow. "Oh. I don't normally get turned down." She rose and stood, gazing down at him with a demure smile. "I'll say one thing. Your little firefighter is quite the beauty. Anyone could tell she's in love with you." She bent to whisper in his ear. "I'll bet I could satisfy you better than she can. You know where to find me if you change your mind."

She winked at him and left the cafeteria.

Simone's words jarred him—the "satisfy you" part raised his brows, but the "she's in love with you" observation blew his mind. Why hadn't *he* picked up on that? Because he'd been too busy freaking out over Liz seeing him having dinner with Simone. A business dinner, not a date. How would Liz have known that? *I have to tell her.*

He sat back, stunned, feeling like the dumbest man alive.

CHAPTER 9

*L*iz noticed several white smoke plumes as their van turned right from the Sterling Highway onto Skilak Lake Road. The crew bundled out of the van and gathered their fire tools.

Tara spread a topographic map on the hood of the pickup that had followed the crew van with their gear and equipment. She briefed all three squad bosses, including Liz, on the plan of attack.

"We'll use the highway as an anchor point for the fireline and take it up the hill to the bottom of this mountain." She pointed at the squiggly lines on the topo map. "We want to catch it before it hits the beetle-killed spruce up on this ridge."

Everyone squinted at the endless stands of dead spruce on the mountain behind the foothills.

Tupa shook his head. "Those stands are sitting ducks. If they torch, we won't be able to contain it on the ground. It'll be an air show."

"You got that right," Rego piped up.

Tara nodded agreement. "That's what we must prevent." She launched into her fire briefing about the weather forecast, current and predicted fire behavior, wind direction, humidity, and fuel moisture.

"A camper reported the fire started on this southern end.

We need to preserve that area. Liz, take your Afi Slayers squad up to the ignition source and mark the area with this." Tara tossed her a roll of pink flagging tape. "When you're done, work your way up to us."

Liz caught it and thrust it in her day pack.

"Aurora Crew, stay in radio contact. Follow your LCES, your Ten Firefighting Orders and Eighteen Watchout Situations. Let's do it." Tara led the other two squads up the gentle slope of spruce and willow.

Liz gathered her squad, amused by their expectant faces. Tupa, with his chainsaw on his shoulder, Rego and Cohen with a coil of fire hose on their backs, and Kenzie holding her Pulaski, which she called the axe and grub-hoe, and twin canisters of saw oil and gas.

Pride welled up. "Before we work on our first fire together, I want to tell you what an honor it is to be working with the Afi Slayers from last season." She nodded at Tupa and Rego. "And what an honor it is to work with our new crew from Australia and Canada."

Cohen nodded and Kenzie smiled.

Tupa held out his arm and made a fist. "Afi Slayers—fist in the middle."

They did as he ordered.

"Fusu fa'amalosi. Fight fiercely." Everyone repeated the English words.

Tupa gave them an eye roll. "You're supposed to say it in Samoan."

Kenzie lifted her chin. "I did. You didn't hear me."

He gave her a worshipping look, as if she'd single-handedly put out the fire. "Excellent."

"Okay Afi Slayers, first we need to protect the ignition source. Then we'll build our fuel break uphill. We need to make tracks. Let's go." Liz buckled on her fire pack and grabbed her Pulaski.

She squinted at a new, red truck kicking up dust as it came to a stop on the gravel road behind their crew truck. Liz lowered her sunglasses to double check her vision. "Oh great, look who's here," she muttered to no one in particular.

Jon climbed out and strode toward them.

Tupa boomed out a greeting. "Hey bro, what brings you to our party?"

"Hey, dude." Jon slapped his shoulder. "Aurora Crew is working this bad boy?"

His gaze shot immediately to Liz. "No rest for fire investigators. I'm here to find the ever-elusive point of origin."

Liz maintained her professional mode. "We're on our way up to cordon off the ignition source."

He flashed his signature grin that did nothing for her now. "Great, I'll hike up with you guys." He positioned his hard hat with his chin strap. "Brief me on the way."

Liz motioned to her squad. "You've met Cohen. This is Kenzie. She's on an AFS firefighter exchange with Australia."

Jon dipped a nod. "Good to meet you, Kenzie."

"G'day. I've heard all about you." Kenzie's Aussie accent hit full tilt.

"Ha, I'm afraid to ask."

Liz gave him a solemn look. *You should be, jerk.*

Liz led off and tromped up the hill through black spruce, dense alder, and willow. The rest of her squad followed. She clipped along at a swift pace, not caring whether Silva kept up.

He had no problem matching her pace with his twice-as-long legs. "What do we know about the fire?"

Liz ignored his question and let Tupa and the rest fill him in. She held a low spruce bough for him to step through, tempted to let it go and smack him in the face.

"Winds will stay calm, but heat index will rise. Eighty-six degrees." His boots crackled twigs and branches as he caught up to hike alongside her.

"Thanks for the weather report." Her tone dripped with icicles.

"What's the crew strategy?" he persisted in his chipper voice.

She jerked her head toward the soaring mountain. "The

other two squads are sawing and digging line on the north end to prevent it from reaching the beetle kill."

"Hoping I'd see you today."

"Oh, really." She slapped a mosquito on her neck.

Flames had died down to a low simmer, leaving acrid smoke and black stobs with wisps drifting upward. At mid-slope, they reached where the fire had started.

Jon moseyed around, staring at the smoking, blackened ground. "We need to get flagging around this area." Jon's voice had an authoritative quality she used to like.

Not today.

Liz held the roll of flagging tape. "We as in you, or we as in me and my squad?"

"We don't want lots of boots tramping around the point of origin." He held out his hand, his sunglasses pointing at hers. "I'll do it. Give me the tape."

"No. Tara tasked my squad to flag the point of origin. We'll do it."

Kenzie and the others stood looking from Liz to Jon, waiting for a decision.

"Well, *somebody* do it, for chrissakes," grumbled Rego.

Jon spoke up. "As first responders, you must maintain confidentiality of information relating to the origin and cause of this fire."

Liz glared at him as if he were the one who set the fire. "Of course, we know that."

"How about you and I do the flagging and your squad can join the rest of the crew? Fewer boots to destroy evidence."

Liz opened her mouth to protest but hesitated. She had a few choice words to say to Mr. Stop Telling Me What To Do in private.

She addressed her squad. "Tupa, take everyone up. Silva will help me secure the area, then I'll catch up with you guys."

"Copy that." Tupa whistled for the squad to follow him. "Time to slay flames, boys and girls."

Rego and Kenzie followed.

Cohen turned to her, ignoring Silva. "I can stay and help."

Jon flashed a smile she knew wasn't real. "Unnecessary. We have a handle on it. Go on ahead."

Liz swiveled her head to Jon like a gunfighter. "If you bark one more order to my squad, I'll throw you off this fire. You're no longer crew boss." She glanced at Cohen. "Go ahead, it's okay."

"You sure?" Cohen glared at Jon like he wanted a piece of him.

Jon maintained his confident, unwavering expression.

"Yeah. Go on ahead." Liz motioned her head toward the mountain. "Be there in a minute."

Cohen shook his head and followed the others uphill.

Liz turned to find Jon smirking. "What's so funny?"

"I'm curious to see how you boot me off this fire." Jon displayed a cheeky grin. "You did all that to be alone with me? All you had to say was, Jon I want you."

"What?" She glared at him. "Why would I want a womanizing piece of—"

"Uh-uh-uh, keep it professional. We're working together," Jon cut in.

"You started it." She sounded like a kindergartner.

He flipped her an innocent shrug. "What did I do?"

"If you don't know, then there's no hope for you." She began unrolling the tape. "Let's get this done. I have work to do. Tara tasked me with this, and I'm following her directive."

"Ooh, love it when you talk bureaucratic." He smiled suggestively. "Hey, I know better than to mess with a cop's daughter."

She cocked a brow. "At least you're smart about *some* things."

"Ouch. That hurt." He pulled out a pair of protective nitrile gloves and snapped them on, then put his fire gloves over them. "Here, put these on under your fire gloves." He offered her a pair.

She accepted the gloves and stared at them. "Why?"

"I'll show you why." He waited while she removed her fire gloves and held them out for him to hold while she stretched the nitrile gloves over each hand and slipped her hands inside her fire gloves.

Jon cautiously picked his way around, taking photos. He squatted to finger the dark soil and push aside charred vegetation. "Liz, come here and check out this burn pattern."

She opened her mouth to protest him bossing her, but curiosity won out. She stepped over. "What?"

"Fire burns fastest uphill because it preheats and dries out fuels as it moves."

"What's your point?" She shot him a dour look.

He gestured at a standing, blackened tree, green branches partially intact. "This fire didn't burn hot this morning because the relative humidity had increased. See how the angle of char on the bark is steeper than the slope?"

"And?" She'd be damned if she'd give Jon the satisfaction that he'd taught her something.

He pointed at the undergrowth. "See these leaf curls? They fold in the direction the fire is coming from. It moved this way." He pointed up the hill.

"That's obvious," she mumbled.

"I pointed it out because it indicates a slow moving, light burn." He moved downhill, following the border between green and black. "Check this out. This is the point of origin."

"How can you tell?"

"By the point on the bottom of this V-shaped pattern. Whoa, what's this?" He pressed his fingers to the ground. "Burn patterns are distinct here. Lots of dark scorching." Jon lowered to all fours, his nose to the ashes.

"They train dogs to do that, you know." Liz squatted next to him. "Canine sniffers."

"I have a good nose. Don't need one." He bent and sniffed again. "Smell. Don't stick your nose in it, only the headspace above it."

Liz did, and the pungent odor caused her to snap her head up. She stood, lightheaded.

"Harrington, what's the matter?" Jon stared at her in surprise.

"I hate that smell." Memory crowded her brain. "Smells like nail polish remover."

"That's because it is. Acetone. A common accelerant used to set fires."

"Isn't gasoline the most common?"

"Yes, but acetone is just as flammable. Why do you hate it?"

"Reminds me of my mother." It flowed out of her with such vehemence, Jon gave her a startled glance.

"And not in a good way, I take it?"

She shot him a hard look. "Don't care to talk about it." Her insides lurched, and she closed her eyes for a second to wipe away her unpleasant memory. She had no desire to skip down memory lane with Jon to explain why her mother had deserted her and dad.

"Okay." He studied her for a long moment. "Do me a favor and get the metal container and the spade trowel from my pack, please?" He tugged off his fire gloves with his teeth and shoved them in his pants pocket.

"These nitrile gloves prevent us from contaminating anything. This is vital at the point of origin in case there's DNA or fingerprints."

"On what?"

"Incendiary devices, for one thing."

"Is there one here?" Liz peered at the ground then undid the plastic snaps on his pack. She produced a pint-sized round metal container and the trowel and offered it to him.

"We'll soon find out." Jon took the trowel and teased back the burned litter duff to expose what looked like two burnt twigs. "Here we go. Nothing fancy, just matches." He carefully lifted them out and placed them in a small plastic canister and snapped on the lid. Then he scooped several debris samples into the metal container and replaced the lid.

He sat back on his haunches and raised his brows. "This certainly changes things."

"Someone deliberately set this fire?"

"Too soon for judgment until the forensics lab analyzes the

fire debris samples." He glanced at her. "This is confidential. Don't breathe a word. Not even to Tara or the crew. In fact, I'm glad you sent them off." He stood, scrutinizing the area.

"We'd better get flagging around this area. Here, take the end." She pulled the roll around the outsides of charred spruce and alder. "How much do you want included?"

"Given what we've found, give it a fifty-foot diameter."

"Okay." She picked her way around the burned spruce, making a circle with the flagging tape.

"Careful, don't step into a hot ash pit." Jon wrapped his end around a blackened spruce, tying it off.

Liz closed the circle and noted something pink from the corner of her eye, partially buried in the ashes. She pointed with her boot. "Hey, there's something here."

"Don't touch it." Jon took the roll of tape from her and cut it with his teeth. He tied it around the charred spruce, then bent to examine what she found. He slid his pack off his shoulder and removed another container.

She peered at it. "It's a piece of fabric. From a scarf or something." A distinct shade of pink with blue flecks stood out, as it hadn't charred, which was puzzling.

"Better get this, too." He extracted it with pincers and sealed it in a second metal container. "I'd better take another look around." He combed the circumference of the flagged area, peering at the ground, bushes, and trees.

They stepped in opposite directions around the flagged circle and stopped in front of each other, hiding behind their sunglasses.

Jon placed his hands on his hips like an easygoing cowboy. The way he stood in his red hardhat, all rugged and professional and focused on his work, made her want to forget being pissed at him. Then the image of Simone last night blasted that romantic notion.

"I'd better get up to my crew." Liz shifted her day pack on her back. "Thanks for the fire inspection lesson."

"Harrington, wait." He stared at the ground, then back at her. "I want you to understand something."

"What?"

"The woman I had dinner with last night—she wasn't a date. She's on the multi-agency, investigation task force. We reviewed our finds from the fires we've worked on. That's all. Nothing more." He studied her.

"So?" She summoned every ounce of indifference from her who-gives-a-shit arsenal. "Why are you telling me?"

"I didn't like how that Canadian dude had his mitts all over you last night. And what was with the kissy face? Do you two have a thing going on?"

"Oh my God, kissy face." She snorted. "What are you, five?"

"You didn't answer my question."

The ruse with Cohen had obviously worked. Should she let him think she and Cohen were hot and heavy? She was tempted, but she caved. "I have nothing going on with Cohen —or anyone else."

"Not even with me?"

She blew out an impatient breath. "You tell me. We're always going in different directions—"

"Then how about we move in the same direction?" He shifted his splendid physique.

"Such as?" Her heart exceeded maximum overdrive, and she expected the little sucker to shoot out of her and plop down in the ashes.

"I want to bump into you more than once every ten thousand years. We'll start with dinner tonight."

She narrowed her eyes. "Oh. We will, will we?" She tried to stay mad at him, but her wings of animosity skittered off when he flashed that classic smile that made her want to do naughty things.

Her radio crackled.

"Liz, you copy?" Tara's voice.

Liz lifted it from her holster. "Copy."

"Are you on your way up?"

She locked gazes with Jon.

The radio squawked. "Harrington?"

She keyed hers. "Uh, yeah—right. I mean affirmative. I've finished securing the point of origin area."

"Copy that. See you in a few minutes." Still locked on Jon, Liz returned the radio to her holster. His heat caused hers to inch up her neck.

His mouth quirked up. "You said affirmative. That means you'll have dinner with me tonight."

"I meant affirmative to Tara."

"Then get out of here. We both have work to do." Jon pointed at her. "Kenai Kipper at seven. Your shift will be over by then. I used to supervise this crew, remember?"

She flipped virtual cartwheels. "Sure. Seven it is."

"Text me if you're late. Do you have my cell number?"

"No," she lied. Yes, she did. She still had his number from when he'd called last winter—back when she had her head up her ass. Pride wouldn't allow her to admit it.

"It's time you did." He recited his number, and she pretended to enter it into her phone. "Now get out of here. You're keeping me from my work."

"Excuse me? *You're* the one keeping me from *my* work." She made a face at him, then picked up her Pulaski and moved uphill toward the plumes of smoke, which were now skinny columns. The Aurora Crew had already slowed the fire.

"Now isn't that better than being an uptight ice queen?" he hollered after her.

She turned to see him in a brawny stance, a hand on his slender hip. Her mouth opened to retort, but instead she disgusted herself with wicked notions of unwrapping those scrumptious hips.

"Remember your LCES." He pointed at her. "And no more kissing Tremblay."

"I'll kiss whomever I want." She shot him a teasing smile and headed uphill, raising her arm in a goodbye wave.

When she reached a respectable distance, she paused near a charred tree stump. She bent with palms on her knees, huffing out air.

"Holy hell," she muttered at the trees. "He's so hot, I need a fire to cool me down."

The second Jon explained he hadn't been dating Beauty Pageant, Liz's libido light had switched from red to green. In a nanosecond he'd become Hot Calendar Fire Guy, standing tall and fit on that hill—all fire inspector savvy in his red hardhat and sleek sunglasses. And his dang chest that wouldn't quit and his fabulous ass that wouldn't either...

She practically skipped across the hill to join Aurora Crew, feeling a heat not caused by wildfire.

CHAPTER 10

*J*on knocked on Keaton's hotel door, clutching his change of clothes and shaving kit.

The door opened and Keaton stood in a T-shirt and blue jeans. "Come in, you know where the bathroom is." He sat at his desk, furiously typing on a laptop.

"Thanks, man." Jon moved to the bathroom. He'd called Keaton to use his shower as the water in his room was still a dark brown. He didn't want to take Simone up on her offer—he didn't want or need complications.

He ran the thankfully clear water, stepped in, and pressed his palms on the shower tiles. The spray massaged his back and he reflected on the day's work. He'd spent several hours inspecting the perimeter of the fire and fed his collected data into a hand-held voice recorder.

All the way back to Rockfish, he couldn't figure out why someone would start a fire on the side of a hill along the Sterling Highway. It made little sense.

Jon couldn't believe his luck in winding up at the same fire as Aurora Crew. And working with Liz like old times. He hoped she hadn't assumed he was dating Simone. It must have appeared that way to her in the restaurant. *Damn the timing.*

He finished showering and put on a clean T-shirt, jeans, and athletic shoes. The hotel cleaning service had laundered his stinky, sooty fire clothes, and it was well worth what little they charged him. On the way home, he'd bought a case of bottled Alaska Glacier water. He could at least brush his teeth and have water to drink in his room.

"Hey, thanks, Keaton." Jon wandered out of the bathroom, rubbing a towel on his head.

"Anything of importance today I should be privy to?" Keaton spun his chair around with a topographic map displayed on his tablet.

Jon nodded. "I found traces of an acetone accelerant on the Skilak Fire."

Keaton raised his brows. "Simone and I found the same thing on two of those fires further down on the Kenai River a few days ago."

"Three fires deliberately set?" Jon rubbed his hand across his face. "Let's see that map."

Keaton handed him his tablet, with red dots marking the fire locations. "The two fires Simone and I inspected were close to two different fishing lodges. We found traces of acetone on both. Whoever sets them is careful not to leave traces of anything else. This one's an organized arsonist. Scouts out and pre-selects his targets."

Jon's brow furrowed. "And works nocturnally. Easy to do this time of year when it's light all night. Sets them early morning before people are up. I found a small piece of fabric on the one today, along with debris samples for the forensics lab. Might be irrelevant to the case. A hiker might have torn his or her clothing. Easy to do with thistle and devil's club thorns ready to snag anything passing by."

"Get the debris samples to me first thing in the morning. I'll have them taken to Anchorage for analysis." Keaton rubbed his face.

"Sure thing."

Keaton tossed a pen down and leaned back. "I've been reading why arsonists set fires. Some do it for fun, others for profit. There are even sickos who do it for sexual gratification. One guy watched his fires burn while choking his ferret, ecstatic he'd gotten away with it." He shook his head. "Takes all kinds, I guess."

"Heard that stuff in training. Hopefully, nothing of the sort is going on here." Jon handed back the tablet.

"The Crane Lake Fire that began in the Kenai Wildlife Refuge is edging toward a gated subdivision, called Riverview Estates. Weather report for the next few days isn't good. Hot, dry, windy conditions."

Jon rose to leave. "Thanks for the update, and for your shower. See you in the morning."

"Yeah, later." Keaton went back to work on his laptop.

Jon let himself into his room and perked up to find his phone vibrating. It might be Liz, now that she had his number. He hustled to his nightstand to pick it up.

Roxanne calling again. She'd left multiple messages besides the two she'd left yesterday. He debated.

"Dammit," he muttered and tapped his phone. "Hello, Roxanne."

"Jonny, sweetheart. Why haven't you returned my calls? I found out you're staying at the Alpenglow Hotel, in Rockfish. It's only an hour's drive from my place. I can be there by seven-thirty. What do you say?"

He stood with his mouth open. The last thing he wanted was Roxanne showing up at his door. "Sorry, have plans. Won't be here—"

"I can come later when you're done with whatever it is you're doing. I'll spend the night. Just the two of us, like old times."

"No, Roxanne." He had to put his foot down—just like old times. "I won't be here. I'm staying somewhere else tonight."

"Where?"

"That's not—that's none of your business."

"But I need to see you. I've never stopped loving you. I know you know that—"

"No, Roxanne. I have a life now—I'm seeing other people."

"Who?" She fired it at him like a rocket.

Red flags waved all over the place, making his stomach hurt. "None of your business. We're done here. Don't call me again." Jon ended the call and glanced at his watch. Ten minutes to seven. He'd better get a move on to meet Liz at seven p.m. at the restaurant.

He grabbed his wallet and headed for the door.

*J*on didn't have to study the menu. He had it memorized by now. A table for two appealed to his desire for he and Liz to have privacy. He glanced at the door, then checked the time. Ten minutes late.

He'd silenced his phone and picked it up to scroll through it. Roxanne had called twice since their conversation. He stared at it, deciding to block her number.

"Been waiting long?" Liz ambled up and stood smiling down at him. "You shaved for me."

"Thanks for noticing. Have a seat." His eyes raked her. She couldn't cross a room without wading through the drool of guys who gaped at her. "You didn't text you'd be late." He set his phone on the table.

She cocked a brow. "You aren't the boss of me anymore, remember? I do apologize, though. I had to talk to someone." She inserted herself in the chair across from him.

He wondered if that someone was Mr. Canada.

He watched the server deposit water glasses in front of them. "I'm not just saying this, but you look damn good for a woman who fought fire all day." He fixated on her mouth, then reminded himself to look her in the eye.

"Sweet of you to say." She broke into her beautiful, clean smile. "I could eat ten moose. Or do you Alaskans say mooses when there's more than one? Or meese, like geese?"

Jon laughed and addressed the server poised to take their orders. "She'll have the ten mooses, and I'll have the combo pizza."

"Pizza sounds good." Liz lit up, warming him.

"Make it an extra-large, and we'll split it," Jon instructed.

The server nodded and hurried off.

Liz's shower scent wafted over. He inhaled it, loving how her blue T-shirt hugged those round breasts and the way her clingy jeans emphasized her every curve. He'd always thought she had a kickass shape.

"Did you find anything else at the fire today?" asked Liz, sipping her water.

"Only what we found together."

"I liked investigating the Skilak Fire. Less labor intensive."

Jon watched the server pour water into his glass. "Not the prolonged physical exertion like fighting fire. We still have to pass fitness requirements for our red card. An underground holdover fire could erupt and bite us in the ass. How did you get into firefighting?"

"Dad talked me into it. Said how well it paid and how you get to travel around the country. I was hired onto a handline crew in Nevada, then applied to come up to Alaska."

"I'm glad you did. Your dad is a smart guy." Jon couldn't stop staring. He could easily make love to a piece of blueberry pie and ogle Liz the rest of the night. Or vice versa. A vision flashed—how lovely she'd looked snoozing in his arms the night of the wedding. He wanted that again.

"Today, you said we need to move in the same direction. What did you mean by that?" she asked him.

How can he explain what's been weighing on him? He shifted and cleared his throat. "I've been ruminating ever since the wedding. About you. About us."

"Ruminating? How about a two-syllable word?" she teased, her eyes flickering. "What about us?"

He dipped his forefinger in his water glass and rubbed the rim. "What do you suppose would have happened that night at Alyeska if you hadn't been drinking?" He flicked a glance at her, then focused on his glass. "Would you still have wound up with me if you'd been sober?"

She bit her bottom lip. "I've wanted to apologize for being out of it that night."

"And I've wanted to apologize for doing the same after the Snowcastle party last year."

"I guess we're even. Let's call it a wash." She smirked at him. "You still haven't answered my question about going in the same direction."

"What I tried to say but did a piss-poor job of it—I want us to hang out together more." He annoyed himself at being tongue-tied...not something he stowed in his toolbox of charm.

"Oh, Jon." A sweet scent drifted to his nostrils as she leaned forward, resting her arms on the table. "Are you trying to say you want to be girlfriend and boyfriend?"

He gave her an exaggerated eye roll. "That sounds unsophisticated. Let's call it something else."

"Unsophisticated? I'm a firefighter, not a debutante." She imitated Rego's Bronx accent. "How about we call each other main squeezes?"

"That's even less sophisticated. All right. Main Squeeze it is." He scrutinized her. "Last year, you told me you were twenty-five. Now you're twenty-six."

She guffawed and held up her thumb. "Keep going."

"Wait—you can't age more than a year at a time." He narrowed his eyes. "Unless you lied to me about your age."

She beamed. "I wanted to see if you believed me last year. And you did. Ha, all this time you assumed you were hitting on a younger woman."

His eyebrows shot up. "Okay, come clean. How old are you really? Twenty...seven?"

She laughed and raised her thumb higher.

"No way." He had a hard time believing she was older, with that flawless face and killer body.

"Yes, way. Keep going." She sipped from her glass as the server set the pizza on the table.

"Not a second older than twenty-eight." He lifted a slice and waited for her to raise her plate.

She held it up. "Knew I liked you for a reason. Keep going, buddy."

He plopped a slice onto her plate, then on his own, and counted to thirty-four before she stopped him.

She's older than me? "Don't believe you."

She whipped out her Nevada Driver's License and held it out. "I was born a year before you. Do the math."

"Well, set me on fire." He pursed his lips. "That makes you a cougar."

"Yep. I'll need time to—*ruminate* about getting involved with a younger man." She smirked and took a bite. Took her a millennium to chew and swallow.

He sat back and folded his arms. "How long? We're not getting any younger here."

She leisurely sprinkled parmesan on her pizza, set down the cheese, and sat back in her chair. "Okay, here's the deal. I have two conditions."

"State your case." He chomped the end of his slice.

"You'll teach me about investigating fires."

Not what I expected. He chewed slowly and swallowed. "I can live with that one."

"Second condition. We take this thing slow. One step at a time."

He raised his brows. "Define 'thing.'"

She shot him an exasperated look. "You know—this Main Squeeze thing. That *is* what we're calling this, right?"

"We'll define it however you want—Cougar." A corner of his mouth lifted.

"Don't rub it in. Okay, I'm a cradle robber." She laughed as a slice of pepperoni fell from her pizza and stuck to her lap.

As she retrieved it, a tremendous weight lifted. He relaxed.

She'd gifted him with another chance.

This time, he wouldn't blow it.

CHAPTER 11

*L*iz excused herself for the rest room, while Jon paid the bill. He told her he'd wait in his truck. Had to make a phone call to arrange the transfer of fire debris samples to the forensic lab.

She needed time and space to digest the fact that Jon wanted an actual relationship. His sincerity seemed genuine enough. She didn't want to set herself up for a broken heart. *Why had his marriages failed? What were his ex-wives like? I'll get around to asking him.*

His roundabout way of suggesting they "hang out together more" resonated with her. It hadn't been *what* he said, but his facial expression when he said it. The look in Jon's eyes had reminded her of her dad's the last time he'd recognized her.

A look of hope.

She finished up and strolled outside to look for Jon's red truck in the side parking lot.

Four guys stood next to a parked SUV, yucking it up and laughing. One with a black beard glanced up and grinned. "Lookee here, boys. It's Blaze Diamond."

She squinted at the Nevada hotshot's insignia on his T-shirt, and her stomach flip-flopped. This was the obnoxious friend of the firefighter she'd dated a few years ago. They saw her dance at the club, and the bouncer had kicked him out for groping the dancers.

Oh, great. Don't want my stage name advertised around Alaska. Her heart thudded.

I should turn around.

Too late.

Black Beard stepped in front of her. "What are you doing all the way up here, little lady?"

"I might ask you the same." She glanced around the parking lot. *Where's Jon's truck?*

"We came up here to fight fire," slurred Black Beard's sloppy-drunk buddy. "And you must be here to take your clothes off at the Crazy Moose. Just so happens we're on our way there now. We'll give you a ride." He undressed her with his eyes.

"And we'll have some fun on the way," growled Black Beard, along with sniggers from the others.

Liz's pulse raced. One jerk she could handle. Two might prove tricky. But four...she had no bouncer protection here. She had to manage this on her own.

"Excuse me, I have to go," she stated in a firm tone.

"You ain't goin' nowhere unless it's with us," slurred Black Beard. He moved in close and grabbed her wrist.

A voice boomed out from behind the four men. "Hey babe, there you are."

They turned to confront the tall, brawny guy disrupting their little soiree.

Jon barreled through the group like an army tank.

The men parted to let him through.

Liz dropped her jaw as Jon swooped in and hoisted her up to his elevation. "Did you forget you were meeting your hot boyfriend tonight, babe?"

Who is this guy—Jon's wacky alter-ego?

He lowered her to the ground with his arms around her. "She's a stunner, ain't she, boys? You fellas up from Nevada to fight fire?" His manner was over-the-top boisterous. Surely the men would see through it. Then again, they were pretty soused.

They stared at Jon as if he were high on meth.

"Uh—yeah…" Black Beard eyed Jon like a formidable opponent. "Blaze Diamond is your woman?"

"Hells, yeah. She fires me up like gas on a matchstick." Jon sent Liz a quick look of crazed incredulity as he tugged her close to his side, like a ventriloquist puppet.

Jon's taller, brawnier frame bested the four hotshots, but Liz didn't trust them. They carried switchblades and fought dirty. She'd seen them in action outside the dance club. They sized up Jon like male bears, deciding who was bigger and who'd take a chunk out of who.

"Lucky son-of-a-bitch," slurred Black Beard, looking at Liz like a beefsteak.

Jon displayed his I'm-a-man's-man smile to the firefighters and casually flashed a gold badge. "Move along, boys, you're hanging out in a no loitering zone. We're strict in Alaska about that." He pointed his thumb at a small sign tacked to the side of the restaurant.

Liz suppressed a laugh. *Does Silva know it's a no parking sign? Do these drunks know Alaska doesn't care whether they loiter in this parking lot?*

All she could figure—Jon had to be a Gemini, and this was his rowdy alpha twin.

When the men didn't move, Jon tugged her close. "Give me some sugar, babe. Show me some love."

Jon's arms came around her, and he covered her mouth with such gusto, her brain pulverized to dust. For someone faking a kiss, he rocked it big time. He worked her mouth with his tongue to the point where her knees buckled, and damn if he didn't catch her.

He put on quite a show with his badass macho self, and she didn't know whether to be appreciative or annoyed.

The Nevada firefighters climbed into their vehicle and sped off.

Only Jon didn't stop kissing her.

Instead, he eased her to the side of his pickup and pressed her against it.

The world fell away, and arousal came fast, with a one-two punch. Jon had cranked her libido lever to a high setting, and now *she* didn't want to stop. She pushed off his truck and backed him against the vehicle next to it, wrapping a leg around his.

Anyone watching might figure they were in a power struggle. Jon backed her up against his truck again and pressed his hard body against hers. Neither cared who watched, the fact that it was broad daylight, or that they were going at it like a couple of hormonal teenagers.

His palms found her shoulders and caressed either side of her neck.

Someone yelled across the parking lot. "Hey, get a room."

Liz laughed into Jon's mouth, and he laughed with her, his head bent at an angle. Her breath quickened and they had to stop. After all, this was a public parking lot.

She tried to push him back, but his rock-hard body wouldn't budge. His marathon kiss had turbocharged her with fierce intensity, turning her into a rolling lava flow.

The kiss came to a natural end, and he stepped back with parted lips.

She touched her swollen lips with her fingertips. "My God. If I knew you could kiss like that, I wouldn't have missed out on it all this time."

"Should have spoken up last year on the fireline. Why didn't you step up and say, 'Kiss me, Jon'? Because I would have. In a fricking heartbeat." His gold-flecked, amber eyes glinted in the evening light.

"Right. In front of the whole crew? You were my crew boss. Get real." She brushed back her hair with both hands. "I'm quite sure the Nevada guys believed you, but I could have managed them."

"Not to pop your 'you can handle anything' bubble, but I heard them talking when I came outside. One of them noticed you coming out of the restroom and ran out to tell his buddies. How do you know them?"

"A Nevada hotshot I dated brought that Neanderthal creep into the club."

"They were planning nasty stuff, Liz. That's why I did what I did."

"Why didn't you help sooner? Not that I needed it," she hastened to add.

"Wanted to see how you'd deal with it."

"You think I haven't dealt with these kinds of situations? Get real."

"I didn't like those jerks hassling you."

"I have to admit, you were funny. Tried hard not to laugh." She patted his chest. "You said you were my hot boyfriend. Is that the only reason you kissed me?"

"Harrington, I've been looking for an excuse to kiss you since the day I was born."

"Silva, you're a smooth talker." She laughed as her heart orbited the moon. "Now you're my Hot Boyfriend and I'm your Babe? You laid it on a little thick there, Fire Inspector."

"My other alpha male persona. I have more if you want me to unpack them."

"I'm pretty impressed with that one." She retrieved the metal badge from his pocket and flicked her eyes up at him. "You flashed your Fire Inspector badge."

"They gave it to us at NIFC. Those jerks were too soused to notice."

"Smart move, Silva." She returned it to his breast pocket. "Tell me, was that kiss fake or real?"

"You couldn't tell?" He pushed a tendril of hair from her cheek. "I'll kiss you again, and you be the judge. Racked my brain throughout dinner, figuring out how to do it before the night was over."

Anticipation tingled Liz and she had the sensation of floating off the ground. This Main Squeeze thing was moving right along.

❧

*J*on managed a straight face as he rested his palms on Liz's shoulders. "Blaze freaking Diamond? Seriously?"

Liz's eyes widened. "I swear, if you tell anyone in Alaska my stage name, I will hurt you. And believe me, I can do it."

He raised his hands in mock surrender. "I believe you. My lips are sealed."

"You know what? I don't really care who knows. I can't control fire gossip. I have more important things to think about." She leaned into him and rested her palms on his chest. "Kiss me again. This time for real."

"Copy that, Squad Boss." He threaded his fingers under her hair at the back of her neck as he bent to touch his lips to hers.

Something caught his eye, and he raised his head.

A thin, light-haired woman in a dark baseball cap and sunglasses stood surveying them, gripping the open door of a shiny, black SUV.

He straightened to catch a glimpse before she ducked into the car and closed the door. Dark tinted windows prevented him from seeing inside. For one disturbing moment, he thought it was…no, couldn't be…

Roxanne. Dammit!

"Jon, what's wrong?" Liz twisted to see what held his rapt attention. Her tone switched from sexy to concerned.

He observed the SUV turn onto the street and disappear into traffic. "Nothing. Thought I saw—" He let out air and stepped back, alarmed.

He debated telling her, not wanting his past mistakes to collide with his happy present. Now it seemed unavoidable. "Get in the truck. I have to tell you something." He beeped the doors unlocked with his remote, opened his, and climbed in. He cleared his maps and portfolio case from the passenger seat for Liz to sit.

She climbed in and closed the door.

Jon leaned back and fiddled with his keys. "I have a situation."

Liz waited while he searched for the right words.

"Ten years ago, my first wife and I divorced when I gave her an ultimatum about moving to Alaska."

She turned toward him and steadied her gaze.

He wanted to kiss her again instead of explaining his sordid past. "I filed for divorce and moved up here, and she stayed in California. I gave her what I figured was a fair alimony settlement. Hadn't heard from her since until—" He stopped.

"Until?"

He let out a long exhale. "The night I returned home from Gunnar and Angela's wedding, Roxanne called, saying she wanted to see me again." He shook his head.

"Then what?" Liz asked quietly.

"Her brother got on with the State, fighting fire. He persuaded her to come up and help him run a lodge on the Kenai River. Frankly, I was shocked. She loved California." He stared out the windshield.

"There's something else, isn't there?"

He sensed she knew what lie in his brain faster than he did. Maybe they were psychic.

He nodded. "We had marriage problems because of her mental instability and paranoia." He glanced at her. "It was bad, Liz. She'd go ballistic for no reason, accusing me of things I didn't do—of physically abusing her. I convinced her to get treatment, but she only got worse. Couldn't take it anymore... so I left her." His breathing sped up, recalling those trouble-some times. He had to shove it all back down, like he used to do.

"Oh, Jon." She laid her hand on his forearm. "How long were you married?"

"Two years. We met at Sonoma State University, dated a short while, then married. I was only twenty-one."

"Didn't you sense something was off before you married her?"

85

He shook his head. "Her instability wasn't noticeable when we dated. Only later. She'd been sexually molested as a child by her father."

"Oh, geez, that's terrible. As a youngster she was no doubt powerless. No control over her situation. Had a friend who went through that. It really messed her up." Liz shook her head, furrowing her brow. "I don't wish that on anyone. Is she still calling you?"

He nodded. "She called today, wanting to drive to my hotel from her place in Sockeye Landing. Told her no and stop calling. That was my ex in the baseball cap and sunglasses. She was here, watching us."

"That same woman may have been in the restroom. I thought it odd that she had sunglasses on." Liz's expression changed. "I hope our being together doesn't complicate things."

"You have nothing to do with this. I'll deal with it."

"If you told her to stop calling and she showed up here, she's stalking you. How did she find out you were here?"

An uneven reality dawned on him. "She found out where I stayed and must have followed me here." His skin prickled. How long had Roxanne been tailing him?

"Did you block her number?"

"I started to and then you showed up. I wanted to give you one hundred percent of my undivided attention…babe." He raised his brows.

"Enough babe stuff, Alpha Boy."

He squeezed her hand. "Thanks for being here. With me."

She squeezed back. "I wanted to be here."

"Even if I block her number, she knows where I'm staying. If things continue with her hounding me, I'll need the phone calls as evidence."

"Like for a protective order? Usually, it's the other way around."

"Women harass guys more often than you think. Haven't you seen *Fatal Attraction*?"

"You mean that scorned woman movie from the nineteen eighties where she boiled his rabbit?"

"It still terrifies every American male who even *thinks* about cheating." He shook his head, then flicked his eyes at her. "Not that *I* would."

"Let's hope not. Thank God you don't have a rabbit."

But I have you. A chill tingled his spine. "Told her I wouldn't be staying in my room tonight. She won't be hanging around the hotel."

"You could stay at Aurora Camp. Rego or Tupa won't mind making room for you in their tent." Liz cleared her throat. "And I wouldn't exactly mind having you close by."

Her words cheered him. "Thanks, but I need to meet this head-on. I'm not about to change what I do."

"All right. I'd better get back and get ready for work tomorrow." Her mouth edged up in a crooked smile.

Jon started the truck. Neither spoke much the short distance to Aurora's encampment. He lurched to a stop in the parking lot.

Liz opened her door. "Thanks for having dinner with me and helping with those morons. I'm sure they won't bother me again. Not after you flashed them your badass badge." She teasingly licked her bottom lip.

"Do that again, and I won't let you out of this truck. Sleep fast." He used to say this last year to the crew every night. "Goodnight, Blaze."

She pointed at him, her mouth twitching. "I warned you, Silva. I swear to God. I'll hurt you. Goodnight."

An odd feeling sifted through him when she hopped out, like he already missed her. She closed the door and gave it a couple taps. He wished they could spend the night together. *One step at a time*, she'd told him. He preferred two steps at a time. Or even three.

Liz blew him a kiss as he pulled away.

He caught it with his fist and smacked his palm to his cheek. He was done for. She'd captured his heart.

And not a damn thing he could do about it.

CHAPTER 12

*B*efore the crew van pulled out, heading to the latest fire, christened the Riverview Fire, Liz checked a voice message from Ravish, wanting to discuss recent developments with their business venture. No way would she call her back from the van.

Instead, she volleyed texts with Ravish, who still wanted more money from Liz for her portion of the up-front investment. She didn't need this right now. Frustrated, she turned off her phone and shoved it in her day pack.

Once at their work site, Liz and her Afi Slayers squad positioned themselves along the fireline they'd built. They couldn't allow flames to reach the homes in the gated community of Riverview Estates, along the Kenai River. Two fishing lodges sat on the river, a mile upstream of Riverview Estates, directly in the fire's path. If firefighters couldn't contain the blaze before it reached them, it wouldn't be good.

Earlier, after the fire briefing at Incident Command Headquarters in Rockfish, Tara had informed the crew Ryan O'Connor had arrived. Dave Doss assigned him Assistant Incident Commander and put him in charge of Air Attack for all aviation operations.

Tara hiked up to Liz's location to brief her. "Ryan ordered retardant drops for adjacent areas around Riverview Estates. If winds blow this thing up, the mud drops will at least slow it down. What's puzzling is, this isn't the leading edge of the Crane Lake Fire lightning had ignited in the wildlife refuge. This one started somewhere between the refuge fire and Riverview Estates."

"This is a separate fire?" asked Liz, leaning on her Pulaski.

Rego sauntered over, holding his chainsaw. "Rumor has it someone torched a new one. If that's true, when the Crane Lake Fire joins it, then it'll become one big fire and hide the fact that it was arson."

"Where'd you hear that?" asked Liz.

"A homeowner observed someone setting a new one."

Liz's eyebrows flew up. "Did you talk to him?"

"Tupa mentioned he talked to some guy at the ICC while loading the van." Rego wrestled with the pull start on his chainsaw and gave it a few unsuccessful yanks.

"Thanks, I'll talk to Tupa." She noted Rego growing irritated with trying to start his saw.

He frowned. "Whoever used this Stihl before didn't clean and oil it. The bar and chain are as rusted and dry as a nun's neglected crotch." He flicked his eyes at Tara and Liz. "Oops, sorry, ladies. I'll get this thing running. Have to oil her first."

Tara and Liz exchanged looks, trying to keep straight faces.

Liz nodded understanding. "It's aggravating when things don't work when you need them to. Holler if you need another saw and I'll set you up with a spare from our pickup. Thanks, Rego." She chuckled to herself at his thinking she might be sensitive to what he said. After working at the dance club, she'd heard it all.

She turned to Tara. "I'll get the skinny from Tupa and let Jon know."

"Speaking of which…" Tara elbowed Liz. "How'd it go last night?"

Liz beamed. "We agreed to make a go of it."

Tara gave her a fast hug. "I was hoping it would work out for you two."

"Me, too. It's just…I'm nervous about it. My heart screams

yes, and my brain slaps me upside the head with a resounding no."

"Silva has his faults, but don't we all? Glad you're giving him another chance." Tara smiled and pointed with her radio. "Okay, have your squad hold this south end of the line. The other two squads are positioned along the middle and north ends. Weather forecast is wind and low humidity. Unfavorable fire weather. Right now, our priority is to protect the homes and fishing lodges."

"Right." Liz adjusted her blue hardhat and tightened her chin strap. "I have Tupa cutting trees to create a buffer. It's hard to pick our way around all this downed beetle kill."

"Tell me about it." Tara squinted at an air tanker flying high in the distance. "There's Max. He'll lay down some pretty red mud for us. Stay clear of the drops. You know how embarrassing it is to return to camp with a pink shirt." Tara moved off toward the rest of the crew. Liz placed full trust and confidence in her crew boss's decision making.

Tupa worked further down the fireline sawing scrawny, black spruce. Liz strode down to Tupa and waited while he finished sawing a sizeable, dead one.

"Rego mentioned you talked to a guy who observed a person start this fire. Can you tell me about it?"

Tupa straightened and set his three-foot Stihl chainsaw on the ground. He pulled a bandana from his pocket to wipe the sweat from his brow. "Yeah. Talked to a guy while I loaded the van this morning."

"Yeah?"

"He said he noticed an old, beat-up truck parked on a dirt road bordering his property. A person in a dark blue hoodie sprinkled something on the ground. Then the truck took off."

"Did he tell you the color of the truck?" asked Liz.

"No. He said it kicked up enough dust to hide the fire they'd started before it took off. I figured he'd report it to ICC."

"Did you get his name?"

Tupa made an oops face. "Too early. My gray matter hadn't kicked in yet."

"No worries. I'll make sure Silva knows."

"Yeah, Jon will take care of it." He wiped his brow with his massive palm.

Liz updated him on their strategy. "Keep cutting. Max will make drops with Jaws."

His mouth quirked up. He had a fetching manner when he smiled. "Jaws is badass. Max will get this blaze under control."

Upon hearing "blaze" Liz darted a glance at him. She didn't think Tupa knew about her dance job in the lower-forty-eight. And what if he did? He wasn't the type to judge. He accepted people where they stood, no matter what they believed in or what they were about.

"These homeowners better hope this fire doesn't cross our fuel break. There's a Ready-Set-Go order to evacuate." She scrutinized the beetle-killed trees, ripe for conflagration.

"You got that right." Tupa bent to pour gas into his saw.

"Thanks, Tupa." Liz strode over to check on Kenzie and Cohen, further down the line.

She glanced up at a distant cell tower across the river, obviously there to service the Riverview Estates and adjacent businesses. She crossed her fingers for cell service and retrieved her phone, tapping Jon's number on speed dial. Yes, cell service, but no answer. He must be in a meeting or on his way somewhere. She left him a brief message about the homeowner and shoved the phone in her pocket.

She smiled that this was the first voice message she'd left him.

Liz approached Kenzie and Cohen, working to widen the fuel break. Cohen sawed and Kenzie tossed brush outside of the fireline. "How are you guys doing?"

Kenzie wiped her brow and blew out air. "Stinking hot. Feels like Oz."

Cohen finished his cuts and idled his chainsaw. "You can say that again."

Liz briefed them on what she knew. Her phone vibrated in

her shirt pocket. She smiled at the Caller ID and turned away to chat. "Hey, Fire Inspector."

"Heard your message right after AST filled us in on the Riverview Fire." She loved his voice in her ear.

"We're on the fireline now. Max is dropping mud around the Riverview Estates and the two lodges upriver from it. This is a new fire, not the Crane Lake Fire moving in this same direction."

"That's what the troopers mentioned. I'm heading out to the homeowner's place to see what I can find out. Thanks for the info." He paused. "Am I on speaker?"

"No. Why?" She glanced back at Kenzie and Cohen, busy with their work.

"Don't let the fire get you hot, Blaze," he said in a low, sexy voice.

"Okay, Mister Erotica, stop calling me that." Cripes, he was *incorrigible*. She smiled at the ground.

"Will I see you later?" he drawled.

"Not if you keep calling me that."

"You know how fire is tame one minute and fickle the next," he breathed. Leave it to Silva to make fire safety sound sensual.

"You're such a nag."

"Later, Fire Woman. Be safe out there." He made a kissing noise.

God, I don't need this kind of heat on top of an uncontrolled fire.

She summoned a business tone. "Right. Copy that. Clear."

"This is a phone, not a radio, Harrington." She gave herself an eye roll and ended the call.

Liz turned to find Kenzie grinning, while Cohen fussed with his chainsaw.

"How's the fire investigation going?" he quipped, sharpening his blade with precise, even strokes.

She surveyed the billowing smoke blending with cumulus clouds a few miles away. "Someone is setting these fires. Lightning sure isn't starting them."

"What did Silva say that you wanted him to stop?" Cohen *had* been listening.

"Oh, nothing." She didn't care to discuss this with him at the moment. Or ever.

Kenzie wiggled her eyebrows. "You two getting on now?"

Cohen aimed a blue-eyed, questioning look at Liz.

She ignored him. "Looks that way, Kenz."

"You don't sound too sure." Cohen's candor rankled her. "Silva doesn't deserve you."

She leveled her gaze. "So you've said."

He shrugged. "I've known guys like him. He's a serial marrier and a serial dater. You know what they call him, don't you? Wildland Wolf. Just don't want to see you get hurt, that's all. Besides, you're too good of a kisser." He broke out in a broad smile.

"Oh-h-h, spill it, Yank." Kenzie gave Liz and Cohen a wicked look.

Liz placed her hands on her hips. "You realize the other night was pretend, right?"

"Not on my part." Cohen gave her a solemn look.

"Whoa, Lizzy, you've been busy." Kenzie swung her Pulaski at the ground.

Liz's cheeks grew hot. "No—we just—let's get this fuel break in and thin the understory before the winds kick up." She flung her most annoying look at Cohen. "Wildland Wolf? Seriously? Where'd you pull that one out of?"

Cohen smiled down at his chainsaw and pulled the crank. It roared to life and he set to work felling dry, spindly spruce. Liz and Kenzie each grabbed their Pulaski and hacked at the ground to dig to mineral soil.

Cohen's continual flag waving about Silva irritated her. He hardly knew Jon, so how could he judge him? All right, so Cohen was sweet on her, and that's why he enjoyed discrediting Jon. She didn't need this kind of tension on her squad.

They had a fire to fight.

CHAPTER 13

*J*on's truck rolled to a stop in front of a two-story log home. He grabbed his clipboard with the required forms along with his digital recorder and climbed out of the truck.

The fire that started at the corner of this property had moved on, now heading toward the Riverview Estates, along the Kenai River. The acrid smell of charred ground and residual smoke met Jon as he strode toward the home.

A short, stout man rambled down the front steps and raised a hand in greeting.

Jon flashed his badge. "Good morning, sir. I'm a federal fire investigator, and I understand you detected suspicious activity near your property." He'd worn his yellow Nomex shirt with the agency logo on the sleeve for good measure.

"Glad you're here. Good thing this fire burned away from my house. The smoke still bothers me." The guy waved him to follow him into the house. "Coffee?"

"No, thanks. What can you tell me about what you observed earlier this morning?"

The man recounted what he'd told the Incident Command Center about the truck and person he'd observed at the back of his property. "He acted suspicious. Me and my son drove out to have a look-see." He stopped to blow his nose into a hanky.

"Did you get a good look at the person?"

"No. He had on one of them hoodies they all wear. Then he took off in an old blue truck."

"Can you show me where it was parked? I'll drive," offered Jon.

"Sure." The bow-legged man climbed into Jon's pickup.

Jon drove to the road bordering the man's property. He inched the truck along until the man motioned to stop. They got out and made their way along charred grasses on the side of the road.

"This is where the guy scattered something."

Jon squatted to examine the scorch arrangements. The point of origin became clear by the circular burn patterns. The wind had pushed the fire across the grasses into beetle-killed spruce. He bent to smell the ground.

Acetone. An arsonist had used an accelerant.

He collected his debris samples the same as he had on the Skilak Fire. He photographed the tire impressions on the dirt road left by the truck. Hopefully, the task force could match them to tire impressions from other tires from other fire sites.

"If someone's setting fires, you better catch them before they torch the whole peninsula. We can't afford that in this hot, dry summer." The man shook his head.

"We're doing our best. Thank you for reporting this." Jon drove the man back to his house and he got out and waited until Jon drove off.

Jon pulled onto the Sterling Highway, hit the gas, and was headed back to Rockfish when his phone vibrated. With a hand on the wheel, he answered.

"Hello, Jonny."

He hit the brakes and checked his rearview to make sure no one rear-ended him. "We need to talk. Where are you?" he gritted in a sharp tone.

"Well, where are you?" breathed Roxanne.

"Cut the crap. You should know. You've been following me."

Silence on her end, except for a barking dog.

He didn't have time for this nonsense. "Give me your address. I'm coming out *now*."

"I only wanted to see you—"

He interrupted her. "You'll see me. Give me your address."

"It's the Coho Lodge, on River Ferry Road, in Sockeye Landing."

"Wait until I get the location." He set down his phone and turned into a pullout on the side of the highway and braked to a hard stop. He tapped the map navigation app on his phone and input the location. Up popped the arrow pinpointing Coho Lodge, thirty minutes away.

"Be there in a half hour." Not waiting for a reply, he ended the call and tossed the phone in the passenger seat. It bounced to the floor and lit up.

He banged the steering wheel with his fist. "Dammit, I don't have time for this shit. I'm putting an end to it." Air rushed from his lungs as he put the truck in gear.

He flipped a U-turn and drove like a wild man toward Sockeye Landing.

◆

*L*iz positioned her squad one mile outside Riverview Estates, to connect their fuel break to the road leading into it. Flames marched closer to the Afi Squad's position on the fireline.

Liz's radio squawked with Tara's voice. "Afi Squad, you copy?"

She keyed her radio. "Copy."

"Flames are booking. This thing gobbled a mile in fifteen minutes. Max dropped mud on the left flank, and he's circling back to drop a load along our fire break. Make sure your squad gets clear," instructed Tara.

The BAe-146 air tanker thundered into view. Max had swapped out his DC-10 from last year for this smaller, but more maneuverable air ship, capable of carrying three thousand gallons of fire retardant. He'd flown it up from Boise. "Here comes Superjaws. All clear." Liz shoved her radio in its waist holster, stuck two fingers in her mouth, and whistled. She made a wide gesture with her arm to the rest of *her* squad. "Clear the line for Max's mud drop."

Everyone gathered their gear and retreated toward the Riverview Estates.

Max lined up his mighty air tanker to spray the red-orange quilt over the land as if laying down a carpet for royalty.

When the air tanker approached, the four engines vibrated Liz's insides. She recalled how she and Jon had hunkered down on that steep mountainside last year when Max dropped a load to buy them time to escape.

She and Jon hadn't talked about that day. Unsaid words still yawned between them.

Liz watched the metal gates squeak open to release the Phos-Chek fire retardant on the hottest part of the fire. A plane letting loose fire retardant was a thing of beauty. Max excelled at his dangerous job.

No sooner had the scarlet gel cascaded to the landscape when a heavy wind gust caused a forty-foot flame tower to rise on their left, charging toward the fuel break.

Tupa squinted. "She's running on the left flank."

Flames hitting combustible, dry fuel exacerbated by escalating winds made Liz's stomach turn. Flammable beetle-kill crackled and popped, while ladder fuels seduced the fire to the treetops. Liz's worst fears confirmed as the flames crowned from one tall spruce to the next. An unmistakable freight train sound told her the fire gorged on the brittle, dead undergrowth.

The burn had grown too fast to position firefighters on its perimeter. This was the definitive red flag telling her to get her squad out of harm's way ASAP.

Flame lengths grew exponentially, and the longer she stared at the fire, the more it felt like a grotesque living beast, leering at her with gnarly arms, snaking out to drag her in. She shook off her hypnotic fascination.

Rego piped up. "She's cooking up. Time to Foxtrot Oscar, folks."

"Yep. Time to retreat." Liz gripped her Pulaski and hurried her squad away from the red monster charging toward their fuel break.

"We could have contained it if not for the doggone wind," grumbled Rego as he hiked alongside her.

"That's always the case, right?" Liz led everyone back to the anchor point where their fuel break joined the wide, dirt road. A state fire truck parked near an intersection.

Liz keyed her radio. "Aurora Crew, do you copy?"

Tara responded. "Go ahead."

"Tell Max to make another drop. I'm betting this'll jump our line with these winds."

"I'm betting the same. We'll meet you at the designated safety zone at the road intersection."

"We're already here with another state crew. Afi Squad clear."

Liz's radio woke up. "Aurora, this is Max. Heard your request. Clear for incoming?"

Tara replied. "Copy that. We're clear."

The BAe-146 roared over the leading edge of the fire now blowing through their fuel break. Max aimed his load expertly, and the long, red cloud of retardant descended to the ground.

The state fire truck's radio erupted. "Get helo sling loads in here, get water on these rooftops," barked a voice. More voices dog-piled on the transmission and in a nanosecond the assigned radio frequency buzzed nonstop with air traffic and ground activity.

Ryan's voice instructed helicopters lifting off from Rockfish. He specified location coordinates to sling loads of water to cool hot spots. Lakes and ponds dotted the Kenai Peninsula, but unfortunately the water bodies didn't slow fire. Wind-driven flames simply carved around them and marched on, as long as dried vegetation fed them.

Suddenly, shit got real.

Liz ordered her squad to retreat even further.

The State folks fired up their truck and told them to hop in. The five of them piled in, and the truck drove through the open Riverview Estate gate and lurched to a stop at a row of homes strung along the riverbank.

Tara and the rest of the Aurora Crew pulled up in the van and bailed out. Intense, convective heat slammed them, along with airborne ash and bits of burning trees.

"Eye protection," yelled Tara.

The crew pulled their goggles over their eyes.

"Tara, what's our plan of action?"

"Let me check with city fire." Tara became busy on her radio.

Riverview Estates had filled with city fire department trucks from Rockfish, Sockeye Landing, and Silverleaf, along with ADNR and BLM fire engines. Flashing emergency lights reflected off the dense smoke.

Since their fuel break and Max's mud drops hadn't slowed the charging head as they'd hoped, the reality of these homes in harm's way hit Liz like a grenade.

Police and the state troopers were making sure home-owners had evacuated after their "Go" order. Structural fire-fighters yelled orders in organized chaos as the Aurora Crew scrambled to assist in any way they could. Tara coordinated with city fire, then assigned two of her three squads to help the hose layers get suction pumps into the Kenai River and charge the hoses to pump water onto the homes.

Liz's squad jogged house to house, to make sure all home-owners had evacuated. She scanned the riverbank, and her chest clutched at the sight of the greedy licks of flame that reached the first home and engulfed it. The smoke thickened, and she tugged her bandana up over her nose and mouth, not wanting to ruin a set of perfectly healthy lungs.

Screams erupted in a nearby barn as Liz ran toward a home.

"Tupa, someone's trapped!" yelled Liz, sprinting toward the barn.

When she reached it, she yanked on the handles, and Tupa swung both doors open.

Liz checked the barn. A little llama hugged an inside stall, terrified, his eyes large and bulging. She approached it and tried to get it to move. The animal wouldn't budge. It couldn't be more than a few weeks old. It made an ungodly shrieking noise.

"Tupa! Come help me."

He hurried over to assist. She found a rope and tied it around the baby llama's neck.

"Hold on," instructed Tupa. "There's another little cria in there."

"A what?"

"Baby llamas are called crias," hollered Tupa as he went to fetch the other one.

Liz peered through the open barn door. Smoke filled the outside, limiting visibility. Frantically, she searched for another rope. A lead rope hung next to a stall door. She grabbed it and hurried to where Tupa waited with the llamas. He had hold of the one lead rope tied to the white llama, and Liz tied the other around the black one.

Together they tugged the stubborn animals from the barn into the chaotic fray of sirens, traffic, and firefighters hustling everywhere.

"Where's Tara and the crew?" asked Tupa, peering into dense smoke.

Liz clutched her rope with the little white llama who'd snuggled up to her. She pulled out her radio. "Tara? Where are you guys?"

She barely heard Tara above the commotion. "We're in the van, waiting for you and Tupa. They told us to bug out. Hurry!"

"Okay, hold on a minute." Liz glanced around, disoriented

in the smoke. "Tupa, I can't tell where our crew van is. What should we do with these baby llamas?"

"Take them with us. They'll die if we leave them here." He nodded his head toward the river. "Tell Tara to go, we'll catch up with them later. Come on, follow me."

Liz keyed her radio. "Aurora Crew, go on ahead, we'll contact you later. Time to bug out of here." No time to wait for a response. Her skin broiled, and flop sweat dripped onto her goggles.

Tupa pulled his little llama behind him and trotted to the river, where one boat moored like a sitting duck. Homeowners had moved most boats out of the area ahead of the evacuation order.

"Give me your rope and get in the boat."

Liz's stomach roiled as she glanced at the fast-moving water. No, they can't possibly...this absolutely would not happen.

"Are you out of your mind? We won't fit in that boat with these llamas."

"We don't have a choice, Boss. Get in. I'll drive. The Kenai River current is swift and treacherous. I've been down it lots of times."

She eyed several burning houses while heat, grit, and embers replaced breathable air. They were out of time. "All right. Let's go."

The boat barely fit the four of them. Liz cautiously boarded, and Tupa hefted the white llama and held it out to her. She took the wriggling animal and eyed a cleat on the port side, threading the rope around it.

Tupa offered her the little black llama. "This one's feisty. Be careful."

The black llama wanted none of this action, but she wrestled him into the boat and secured his rope to a cleat on the starboard side.

Two homes exploded with a god-awful whooshing sound, fire licking high.

"Hurry, Tupa!" yelled Liz as she tried to calm the baby

llamas. They screeched again, sounding like a high-pitched, laughing goose.

Tupa jumped into the boat and fiddled with the console, scoping out switches and gears. He started the motor. "Untie us," he shouted, smoke swirling around the riverbank.

Liz fumbled with the ropes and cast off.

Tupa abruptly shifted the gears in reverse, grinding them. He expertly backed the boat away from its mooring dock and clunked it into gear, leaning forward to see in the dense smoke.

A gas tank exploded next to a burning vehicle. The baby llamas tugged at their ropes and shrieked their freaky bird sound. The boat rocked side to side as Liz desperately tried calming them. *If we capsize, how can I save these llamas? Can they swim?*

Oh God, these homes... all lost. She couldn't bear to watch. Disappointment and guilt made her stomach contents rise. She forced it back down. There was nothing they could have done to prevent the homes from burning. An overwhelming feeling of helplessness consumed her as the water's reflection flashed an agonizing red.

Convective heat hit Liz's face as she watched home after home vanish into a conflagration. Her face contorted and tears streamed. She was thankful Tupa couldn't see them as he guided the boat downstream from the destruction. *We failed. We failed to prevent this.*

Low visibility forced Tupa to inch the boat downstream. As they progressed, the llamas became used to the purring motor and quieted, leaning into Liz. She stood between them, rubbing their backs and coughing.

Finally, the smoke thinned, and the emerald river stretched before them. Thank God for no rapids, but the current moved fast, as Tupa had predicted. Buildings emerged from the haze on their starboard side. Liz nearly collapsed with relief. "Is that Silverleaf?"

"Yes," Tupa hollered back. He slowed the motor and expertly eased the boat alongside a dock on the riverbank.

"Grab our lines, please," Tupa yelled at a tall boy standing on the dock, watching.

Liz tossed a stern line, and Tupa threw the bowline. The kid caught both and tied them off.

She let out a relieved sigh. *They made it. Thank God.*

CHAPTER 14

"*H*ello handsome." A tall, smiling Roxanne descended the stairs to the main floor of the Coho Lodge.

Jon hardly recognized her. Her light brown hair hung in waves past her shoulders. She'd thinned down, but her breasts were bigger than he remembered. Her peach-colored lips seemed bigger on her pale skin.

Hard not to notice the black bra showing through the low-cut, transparent blouse. A dark skirt hugged her ass, barely covering it. She'd always had killer legs, but they held no attraction for him now. He reminded himself that under all that beauty was a tiger shark treading water.

"Hello, Roxanne." The past flooded back as she came toward him, with parted lips.

She came in close and slid her arms around him. When she kissed him on the side of his neck, he tugged her arms off and backed away.

"Jonny, it's been a long time." She scrutinized him. "You look terrific. But then you always were a hottie." She smiled in the same beguiling way that had attracted him long ago.

"Come here. Take a load off." Roxanne led him to a sofa in front of a stone fireplace. "Want a cup of coffee? I have blueberry muffins fresh from the oven."

He didn't sit. "No. You know why I'm here."

"Because you were dying to see me." She tapped his arm. "Check this out. I had my nose straightened and my girls augmented." She displayed her side profile and cupped her breasts.

No way would he buy into her manipulative games. "I see that."

"Jonny, I've missed you. Never stopped thinking about you."

"Why have you been following me?" He pressed his lips together in a straight line.

"You wouldn't see me. What was I supposed to do?"

"It's been ten years. Why now?"

"Because ten years have gone by, doesn't mean I haven't loved you all this time." She sat on the sofa and tugged him to sit. "I'm better now. The treatment helped. Don't have symptoms anymore."

Jon remained standing and fiddled with his keys. "That's great, but why Alaska?"

"Tyler talked me into it, saying we could make a ton of money. Isn't it beautiful?" She motioned out the massive picture windows.

He moved to look out at the emerald Kenai River, lazing along below the tall bluff. "Yes, it is."

"Tyler made it fire wise, as you people call it. He leveled every tree within a hundred feet of this place. See how it opens up the view of the river?" She stood and moved over to him.

Jon looked around, noting the vegetation had indeed been cleared. "Where is Tyler?"

"He's fighting fires, earning tons of money." She caressed his arm. "Want to walk along the river? We can laugh about the good times."

He pulled away. "I came here to get some things settled. I have to get back to Rockfish."

"Won't you stay for dinner? I have a salmon fillet—"

A dog barked in the next room behind a closed door.

"Tyler's dog. Wait a minute, I have to let him out." She crossed to open the door and disappeared into the room.

He tapped fingertips on the side of his leg, waiting impatiently. *Don't have time for this.*

"Jonny? Can you come here a minute? I need your help," Roxanne called out from the other room.

He frowned and rose to enter a large sitting room. Roxanne wrestled with the lock on a door leading to a generous back deck. A German Shepherd wagged, waiting for her to open the door.

"This always jams." She threw up her hands helplessly.

He stepped in to help. The lock wouldn't budge and he jiggled it. Finally, it turned. "This is rusty. Get some oil on it," he imparted in an impatient tone, opening the door.

The dog scooted out to do his business, and Roxanne closed the door. "It's hard to manage all of this when Tyler's gone. I need a man here to help." She showed him a cat-eyed, demure look that used to pull him in, but not now.

"Roxanne, we have to talk—"

"No. We don't. You know you want me." She grabbed his hand and shoved it under her skirt, moving it back and forth between her legs. No underwear.

Jon yanked his hand away and pulled back. "Stop. Enough."

"You've always made me hot." She came at him again, wrapped a leg around his, trying to kiss him, her palms massaging his chest.

He pushed her away and headed toward the front door. "Listen to me. We're divorced. It's permanent. I don't want to get back together. Not happening." He gritted his teeth, anger frothing his insides.

He'd be damned if this woman would screw up his life again.

Her doleful eyes filled with tears. "I still love you."

"No, it isn't love. Not after ten years. I don't know what the hell this is, but it sure as shit isn't love." He didn't want a repeat of the past with her accusations of physical abuse. "Don't you get it? I don't love you. That ended when you lied to the cops that I beat you and threatened to kill you during one of your psychotic episodes. Remember?"

She shook her head, and a tear ran down her cheek. "That was a long time ago. I'm a different person now."

Jon fished the truck keys from his pocket. "I'm a different person, too. What we had is over—it's in the past. And it needs to stay there."

"Please don't go. Not like this. Please. I need you, Jonny."

Despite his lingering guilt and sympathy for her turbulent past, he had to be firm with her. "I'll only say this once. Do not call or contact me. Ever. And don't follow me." He hesitated. "I have someone else now."

"It's that firefighter slut, isn't it? The one they called Blaze you mauled in the parking lot last night—those Nevada guys called her a stripper whore." She leaned against the door with folded arms.

Jon stiffened and glared at her, a vein pulsating in his neck. "That woman has more going for her than anyone I know. I mean it—no more contact. Are we clear?" His jaw hurt from gritting his teeth.

Tears streamed her cheeks. If she wasn't so manipulative, he'd be sucked into feeling sorry for her. But he knew better. "I still love you." Her voice shook with emotion.

"Goodbye, Roxanne." Regardless of whether she'd changed for the better, he still hated that she'd infiltrated his world. She resurrected all the mashed-up feelings from their tumultuous time together.

He strode out to his truck and fired up the engine, kicking up rocks and gravel as he gassed it on the road leading back to the Sterling Highway.

Revulsion and guilt washed over him. He had to calm the hell down. He took deep breaths to slow the pounding in his chest. What a mistake to have come here, but he had to tell her to leave him alone. She could never take no for an answer.

She's punishment for all the mortal sins I've committed.

His phone vibrated on the passenger seat. He answered

without taking his focus from the road as he sped toward Rockfish.

"Hello?"

"Silva? It's Tara."

"What's up?"

"Have you heard from Liz?"

"What do you mean? Isn't she with you and Aurora Crew?" He glanced at his wristwatch. "Aren't you guys still working the Riverview Fire?"

"The fire jumped our line. We retreated to Riverview Estates, and the winds brought the burn to the houses. We helped city crews lay hose and made sure everyone evacuated. Liz and Tupa somehow separated from us. I can't raise her on the radio."

The hairs on his neck stood up. "You mean they're still in there? I'll be driving by, I can look."

"Doubt you'll get past the road closures," reminded Tara. "Do you have a radio?"

"Yeah." He reached in the back seat for his Bendix King, turned it on, and set it in the passenger seat. "I have an inspector badge. They'll let me through."

"Okay. We're outside of Silverleaf in our crew van. Keep in radio contact."

"Copy that. Thanks for calling." Jon ended the call and gunned it. He couldn't care less if the state troopers pulled him over for speeding.

Dammit, Liz, why did you separate from your crew? Hopefully, she and Tupa were somewhere safe.

With a heavy heart, he reached across and turned up the radio. He listened as firefighters and aircraft pilots did their damndest to save what they could of the burning homes.

🔥

*P*eople gathered at the boat landing, curious at seeing wildland firefighters with two baby llamas in a boat on the Kenai River.

"I'll untie this white llama and you can lift him out," Liz said to Tupa, as she unwound the rope from the boat cleat and led the llama to starboard. The little bugger screeched so loud, Liz thought her eardrum would burst.

Tupa hefted the white one, and a young father and his son helped Tupa lift it out of the boat, the cria's long neck undulating like a snake. The son held the lead rope, while his dad helped Tupa lift out the feisty black one.

"I have to get hold of Tara." Liz hauled herself out of the boat and pulled her radio from its holster. She squinted at the juice level. Down to the last line. Her insides dropped. "Oh, no."

"What's wrong, Boss?" asked Tupa.

"I left my radio batteries in my big fire pack in the crew van." Liz pulled out her cell phone. Dead battery. "Oh, great. I left my phone charger too. Can't believe I did that," she groaned. "Tupa, do you have your cell?"

"I don't carry it on fires," he replied.

Liz glanced at the father. "Sir, do you have a phone I could use?"

"Sure. Here." He offered his cell.

"Thanks." She stared blankly at the keypad. Jon's number and photo were efficiently stored as a speed dial on her own phone. She hadn't memorized his number. Liz tapped a search for the Alpenglow Hotel and called it. She asked the main desk to give a message to Jon Silva, that she and Tupa were okay.

Tupa stood between the two llamas, holding a lead rope in each hand. "Boss, we need to figure out what to do with these llamas."

"I'll find out." Liz called the ICC for the phone number, then called Rockfish Animal Rescue and arranged for them to pick up the animals. She also requested the ICC to contact Tara Waters of the Aurora Crew to let her know she and Tupa were okay and would soon be back at camp.

She turned to Tupa. "They'll send someone to pick up the baby llamas and give us a ride back to Rockfish. Also, we have to return this boat to its rightful owner."

"The state troopers will take care of it." Tupa squinted at the hull. "They'll retrieve the boat registration number and return it."

Thankfully, the Alaska State Troopers' number was stored on the man's speed dial. Liz called and explained the situation, relaying the boat information. She returned the cell phone, thanking the man.

Twenty minutes later the Rockfish Animal Rescue truck pulled up, and two women climbed out.

Tupa and Liz helped load the llamas into the back of a fenced-in truck bed. "Poor little things look as wiped out we are."

"We'll make sure the animals receive proper care. You guys look exhausted." The women motioned the firefighters to get in the back seat of their crew cab pickup.

Liz and Tupa mumbled thanks and heaved themselves and their gear into the back seat. Liz rested her head back and nodded off on the way to Rockfish. When the vehicle stopped, Liz woke, drool trickling down her chin.

The women unloaded the llamas and Liz and Tupa straggled after them, covering yawns.

Liz stepped to the feisty, black llama, and he nuzzled her palm. "Hey little guy, you had a busy day. We went through a lot together. Bye, cuties." She rubbed his nose, and without warning a lump thickened her throat when she gazed at the big, innocent eyes, framed by long lashes. She turned away.

"Where are you taking them?" asked Tupa, rubbing the animal's noses.

"All evacuated animals are taken to the fairgrounds in Ninilchik on the lower Kenai Peninsula," the woman responded.

"You guys be good." Tupa gave each one a healthy rub.

"Come on, Tupa. We need showers and shuteye so we can do this all over again tomorrow." Liz patted his shoulder. "I appreciate what you did today, taking charge with the boat. Thanks."

He winked. "We got out okay."

When the animal rescue people dropped them off, Liz and Tupa hefted their packs and staggered to their respective tents.

Once they'd cleaned up, Liz and Tupa debriefed Tara on what had happened on the Riverview Estates fire. The three of them assessed the right and wrong decisions Liz had made for the After-Action Report. She knew they'd screwed up in separating from the crew, no matter how noble their reason was for doing so. Tara listened and didn't say much, which bothered Liz.

She repeatedly apologized. Tupa backed her up as best he could, but he wasn't the one in charge. Liz was, and she felt terrible about it.

When their discussion concluded, Liz strolled out to the bluff overlooking the Kenai River. The water rolled along without a care in the world. She settled her gaze on the emerald water, then closed her eyes.

"Thank God for you today," she whispered to the river.

She liked to imagine it whispered back to her...*you're welcome.*

Despite their best efforts, the Aurora Crew hadn't been able to stop the fire with the methods they'd trained for. When the crew had contained the first few fires they'd worked on, Liz had settled into the complacent assumption that they'd contain this one.

That was the danger and disappointment of wildland firefighting. Silva's words from last year rang true: *Never allow yourselves to be complacent.*

Complacency can kill you.

CHAPTER 15

*J*on screeched his truck to a halt on the smoke-filled road outside the gate at Riverview Estates. He hung his head out the window. "Are there any fire crews in there?" he asked two city firefighters in turnout gear standing next to their engine.

"No, sir. No one's in here, except for a few city crews," replied one.

Jon displayed his badge. "I need to get in here."

"Yes, sir." He opened the tall subdivision gate enough for Jon to get his truck past.

He stuck his arm out the window and waved. "Thanks." He hit the gas and motored into the smoking remains of a once beautiful neighborhood along the Kenai River.

Several city fire engines remained on site, spraying water on what few structures remained standing. The fire had burned hot. Several buildings had partially collapsed or burned to the ground.

Jon drove until fire debris filled the road and he couldn't drive any further. He parked and paused a minute, praying for no casualties. Once this area cooled, he and Keaton would be in there doing their official inspection.

A city firefighter gathered a hose to store back on his engine.

"You didn't notice a wildland fire crew in here earlier, did you? A BLM crew?"

Soot covered the firefighter's face, and he looked spent. "The yellows? Yeah, they helped us with hose lays and evacuation. They bugged out with everyone else when the major push cooked up. It blew pretty bad."

Jon nodded. "Two of the Aurora Crew members are missing. A large guy and a smaller woman, about five-two. Did you see them?"

He thought a minute. "One of our guys mentioned two yellow shirts leading a couple of llamas toward the river. Don't know what happened after that."

"Thanks." Jon squinted at the Kenai River about two blocks away. He pulled a mask from his pocket and tightened it over his nose and mouth. Blackened, leveled homes still smoldered and heated his skin as he picked his way through the devastation.

He reached the charred, sullied riverbank, dreading whether he'd find bodies or carcasses. He stopped and froze at seeing a dark lump lying on the ground. His chest clenched as he slogged through the devastation. A burned animal carcass. Maybe a moose.

He trekked further but observed nothing other than charred structures. Burned rubber filled his nostrils along with other unpleasant, chemical smells. The combined stench of seared plastics and wood overwhelmed his senses, despite his mask. He didn't want an asthma attack to kick in, but he felt a headache taking shape.

Jon made his way quickly back to his truck. He pawed through the glove box for an over-the-counter painkiller. He threw back a few capsules and took two puffs from his inhaler for good measure, then drove out the way he came.

Where are Liz and Tupa?

He keyed his radio. "Aurora, this is Silva. Do you copy?" He waited a long while.

His radio squawked. "Copy. Tara here."

"Any news?"

"They're okay. Liz radioed from camp. Her radio died, and she didn't have extra batteries with her. Her cell died, too. They took two llamas to Animal Rescue."

He breathed a sigh of relief. "Good. On my way to Rockfish. Clear."

Tara keyed the radio twice in response.

Thank God.

It didn't sit well with Jon that Liz had separated from her crew. She knew better than that. And worse, she hadn't kept her boss informed.

As the white highway dashes ticked by, he contemplated his concern for Liz, and what it meant in the scheme of things. He recalled how he'd jumped to Liz's defense with Roxanne's name calling. He didn't like the tight ache in his chest, fearing the loss of someone he cared for. Caring for a woman this deeply presented an altogether new experience for him. And he had something to say about it.

He sped to town and turned into the Aurora Camp. After switching off the ignition, he sat back and let out an exhausted sigh. He rubbed his eyes and shook off the bullshit of the day.

He had something to say to Liz before this day ended.

Evening twilight painted the sky pink and purple above the mountains as he pushed open the door and strode toward the women's tent.

&

*L*iz finished explaining to the rest of the crew how she and Tupa had escaped down the Kenai River with the llamas. They gawped with open mouths and bombarded her with questions about how they all had fit in a small river boat.

After the excitement died down, she headed to the bathhouse for a shower. She stepped into a stall, pulled the muslin curtain, and turned on the water. The scorching water felt glorious beating on her head and aching back.

"Harrington, you in here?" a male voice called out.

Hair full of shampoo, she instinctively covered her soapy private parts. "Who wants to know?"

"Who do you think? What other guy were you expecting?" Jon's voice echoed in the steamy bathhouse as he strolled in to where she showered.

"Silva, what the heck are you doing?" She grabbed the shower curtain and draped it under her arm to cover the front of her as she peered around it. "How'd you get in?"

"Through the door. Same as you did." He sank down on a bench next to her shower, holding a bottle of water.

"Excuse me, I'm taking a shower."

He chuckled. "Oh, is that what you're doing in there?"

"Smartass," she mumbled.

"What was that?"

She chose not to respond, and he continued. "Tara called me when she couldn't contact you guys today. I searched for you at the Riverview Fire."

"Why?" she called out through the noisy shower spray. "We got out okay."

"Tupa told me what you guys did, but you should've informed your crew. Heard you had a rockin' river boat ride with a couple of llamas."

She groaned. "Harrowing is more like it. Don't want to do that again."

"I bet not."

"Why are you in here? Couldn't it wait?"

"No. It couldn't, actually. I want to know how you became separated from your crew."

"Didn't Tupa explain?" She stuck her lathered head out at him.

He leaned forward, elbows on his knees, clasping his water bottle. "Wanted to hear it from you."

A dollop of lather dribbled over her eye, and she swiped at it. "It was freaking chaos. The fire overran our line. We had to move back to Riverview Estates. We helped city firefighters lay hose and made sure homeowners had evacuated. The baby llamas became trapped in a barn, and Tupa and I had to get them out." She ducked in to rinse her hair.

"If I were your crew boss, I would have kicked your ass."

"Oh, really?" She popped her head out, droplets running down her face. "Well, you aren't my crew boss now, are you?"

He slipped into his authoritative tone. "Tell me which two of the *Ten Standard Firefighting Orders* you didn't follow."

She sputtered. "Excuse me?"

"Tell me which two." He calmly sipped his water and screwed the lid back on.

She bristled, frowning. "Four and seven. Identify escape routes and maintain prompt communication with my supervisor. Thanks for the pop quiz, Dad."

"Why didn't you follow them? You had a radio. Should have kept Tara informed. Everyone worried about you."

She grimaced and ducked her head back in. "The radio died. I forgot my extra batteries," she called out over the shower spray. "When you say everyone, does that mean *you* were worried?"

Her heart jumped, knowing that's what he meant, but she wanted to hear him say it.

"I searched for you, didn't I?"

"Yes, and I appreciate that. Truly." She rubbed soap on her cheeks and forehead. "I didn't mean to alarm you or anyone else."

"Don't make it a habit." Through the thin muslin curtain, she discerned his shape rise and come toward her.

She held her breath, unsure of what he intended to do.

"Need help washing anything?" He invoked the suggestive tone he'd used earlier on the phone.

"You're only sucking up to me because I'm naked in the shower." She wasn't sure whether to lash out at him or allow him to turn her on by his sudden switch to Mr. Sexy Face. To her dismay, the latter won out. "God, I'm easy," she muttered.

"What did you say?" he called out.

"I said you're sucking up to me after chewing me out."

"I can make magic with a washcloth and shower gel."

"I'll bet you can," she breathed, gulping back her irritation at allowing Jon's cupid arrows to ping her bulls-eye after chiding her. Didn't help when she envisioned his hands sliding across her wet skin. She cleared her throat. "You'd better get out of here before Tara kicks your ass for lurking in the women's shower."

"Lurking?" He chuckled and sidled up close to the shower curtain. "How about a kiss first?"

"After you chewed me out? Hell, no." Liz peered out to show him her grimace and found herself nose-to-nose with him. "Besides. I'm wet...and I'm naked."

"I know." His wink shot straight to her groin like a pinball.

"You're twisted." She ducked back in because her nipples hardened at the thought of kissing him right now.

Tara's voice called out. "Silva, get out of here before we all get in trouble."

Liz rinsed herself. "Don't say I didn't warn you."

"Harrington, don't get separated from your crew again. And no more forgetting radio batteries." He double tapped her shower curtain and sauntered toward the door. "Stay safe so I don't have to search for your wayward ass again."

"What? You—you—" spluttered Liz, trying to spout a retort. Instead, she inhaled water and coughed out a lung.

"Bye, ladies," Silva called out to Tara and Kenzie, waiting with their towels. "Harrington, do something about that cough."

The door slammed shut.

"Next time, wait until I'm out of the damn shower!" Liz rasped after recovering from her choking fit. "Where does he get off?" she fumed.

Kenzie's brows rose. "Hoo-eee. Jonno's a looker. He belongs on our Australian Firefighters Calendar."

"With an axe planted in his chest." Liz huffed out air. "He acts like he's still my crew boss."

She wrapped a towel around herself and stepped out, then bent to twist another towel around her head.

Tara smirked at her. "Silva's in love with you in case you

haven't noticed. When I told him you were showering, he wouldn't take no for an answer."

"Uh uh, that's not it. He wanted to rub in the fact that I screwed up today. Once the situation became FUBAR and we found the trapped llamas, all rational thought left my brain." Liz straightened. "We should have informed you right away what we were doing."

"Thanks, I appreciate that. You reached safety, and that's what matters." Tara began undressing. "What did Jon say?"

"That if he were my crew boss, he would have kicked my ass."

"Good. He saved me from having to lecture you." Tara tossed her towel over her shoulder.

"I'm sorry, Tara." Liz reached for her clothes and dressed. "It won't happen again."

On the way back to the tent, she realized the extent that she and Tupa had inconvenienced people by rescuing the animals.

"Silva, you were right, dammit," she muttered. "But I won't give you the satisfaction of telling you."

Jon had taken time from his busy investigation schedule to search for her.

In her mind, his actions spoke louder than words.

$\mathcal{B}$right and early Monday morning, Simone West stood at the front of the long conference room in the Kenai Borough mayor's office. She appeared pert and crisp in her jacket and skirt, better suited to an Anchorage high-rise than a tiny, first-floor conference room in Rockfish.

Jon sat back in his chair and thumbed through the pages of his notebook, reviewing the last several fires he'd determined were human caused. He kept the lightning-caused fires under a separate tab, but tracked them anyway, in case subsequent evidence might prove otherwise.

"Mr. Silva, please brief us on what you have so far," proposed Simone to the mostly male room, her glasses perched on her nose.

Jon took the front podium with his laptop he'd pre-positioned before the start of the meeting. He moved through the still photos and a few videos, panning to the points of origin on the fires he, Keaton, and Simone had investigated. His laptop images projected onto a large screen on the front wall.

"Here's what we found at the Skilak, Kalifornsky, and Riverview Estates fires. We identified acetone accelerant at the points of origin for all three." Jon clicked on a map with the locations of each fire relative to the small towns along the Sterling Highway and the Kenai River. He pointed out for those unfamiliar with the area that the U.S. Department of Transportation had designated Sterling Highway as a National Scenic Byway.

"There's not only a pattern of what's been used to set these fires, but where they start. Except for the Skilak and Kalifornsky fires, the points of origin have been close to structures, either homes or businesses. The Skilak Fire started near an electric transformer, which the Aurora Crew contained before it traveled anywhere." Jon clicked through images of the fire sites and evidence photos from each.

"We've received the results from the State fire forensics lab in Anchorage. The lab confirmed acetone as the accelerant used in the Skilak and Kalifornsky fires. However, the arsonist wanted the Riverview Estates fire to burn hot and used gasoline as the accelerant. Whoever sets these is careful not to leave other evidence, but we did find a torn piece of fabric near the point of origin at the Skilak Fire."

Trooper O'Donnell spoke up. "Any other evidence?"

"I took photos of tire tracks at two of the sites. Maybe a single tread pattern will emerge common to all the sites."

Jon continued. "I've met with Dave Doss, our BLM Incident Commander. He's assisting the State of Alaska IC on these fires, to make sure he briefs all firefighters about preserving the areas of origin."

His cell vibrated. Dave Doss. "Pardon me, I have to take this. Keaton, please finish up for me, if you would."

Keaton gave him a quick nod and moved to take over.

Jon stepped out of the room and wandered down a brightly lit fluorescent hallway.

"Dave, what's up?"

"We have another one. Near the Swiftcurrent Lodge in Sockeye Landing. This is bad. There are two more lodges nearby, plus all the businesses grouped together for fishing and rafting Kenai River trips. We're throwing all we have at this one. Ryan O'Connor has his firefighting aircraft dropping mud and helos slinging water."

"Okay, let me know when it's safe enough for us to get in there. Any idea on the point of origin?"

"Just returned from a recon flight. Area of origin is in the spruce forest below the Swiftcurrent Lodge. Fire burned straight up the hill to the lodge before first responders arrived. A total loss. Now we're trying to protect the town. Have to go. Later." Doss ended the call.

Jon pulled up a map of Sockeye Landing on his phone. Found the Swiftcurrent Lodge. Three fishing lodges were in proximity to the narrow canyon carved by the Kenai River. Most structures were close together in this area.

He pulled up an aerial photo map, expanding it with his thumb and forefinger on the screen. Curious, he pulled up the Coho Lodge outside of Sockeye Landing. The fire had burned south of it. He peered at the terrain. The lodge sat on a hill overlooking a gravel pit below—a natural firebreak.

He wasn't overly concerned about Roxanne's welfare, but he wouldn't wish her to be in harm's way. Her lodge wasn't in immediate danger unless the wind did an opposite shift and took the fire downriver.

He strode back to the conference room. "We have a fire at Sockeye Landing threatening the entire town. ICC has launched a full scale, direct attack to save homes and businesses."

Everyone reached for their phones. The mayor's cell rang, and the meeting dissolved into people scattering out the door in all directions.

Jon turned to Simone and Keaton. "Doss will inform me when it's safe to access the area. Access is bad on that twisting, two-lane highway and tall mountains on either side limiting air activity."

Keaton jangled his keys. "My brother has a river rafting business there. Going to go check on him. I'll be in touch." He left the room.

Jon moved to the front to pack up his laptop.

Simone stood with folded arms. "Keep me informed.

When the IC calls, let me know ASAP, no matter what the hour."

"Okay." As he gathered his things together, he noticed her studying him. "I'm going to catch lunch, then head over to the ICC for their midafternoon fire briefing."

He picked up his laptop case and slung his jacket over his shoulder, heading for the door.

"Jon." She spoke softly, like a faint bell ringing. "Have you thought about my proposition?" She moved in close. "Can I change your mind? Gets lonely at night in my hotel room."

Her hand brushed his chest, and he glanced down at it. "Simone, you're a beautiful woman. If you would've said this to me a year ago, I'd be in your bed right now." He gave her a rueful smile. "I'm not that guy anymore. I'm not interested."

"That little firefighter sure has you wrapped, doesn't she?" Simone moved closer and breathed in his ear. "I envy her." She lifted her brief case from the conference table and sashayed out the door.

He shook his head as he followed her swaying, tight-skirted ass down the long hallway, her spiked heels clicking on the tile.

Two women have propositioned me two days in a row. And the one woman I want to proposition me hasn't.

The old Jon would have taken both up on their offer in an Anchorage minute. And the new Jon figured Roxanne and Simone made him want to be a better person.

But not for *them*—for that one little firefighter they both envied.

❦

*J*on pulled into a parking spot at ICC headquarters and switched off the engine. He dove into the burger, fries, and chocolate shake from a quick drive through. He'd skipped breakfast after his shower and ran short on time for the meeting.

His phone vibrated. A buddy from Fairbanks called to say he had reservations for a weekend stay at Steller's Jay Lodge across Kachemak Bay and couldn't make it. Would Jon like to take his place since he owed Jon a favor for a fishing trip?

Hell's, yeah. He could finagle a couple days off the third weekend in May, depending how investigations were going. It fell on his birthday weekend, and he deserved a break. Yes, he'd take him up on his generous offer.

With that all settled, Jon inhaled his burger as fire crews assembled for the fire briefing. He kept an eye out for the Aurora Crew to catch a glimpse of Liz.

A brilliant idea whacked him on the head. *I'll ask Liz to go along.*

Might be a long shot, but maybe he could pull it off.

He recalled when Aurora Crew began their rotation schedule and figured the end of their three weeks would fall on that same weekend. Liz would be due for her two days off.

Jon danced his thumbs on his phone to text her, chancing the spotty cell phone service on her fire location. He approved what he typed and hit send. Hopefully, she'd get his text sooner. rather than later.

He finished eating and climbed out of his pickup, sucking down his shake. There was a spring to his step as he waved a greeting to Dave Doss on his way to the state Department of Forestry building.

He hoped the next two weeks would go fast. And nothing better screw this up…unless Liz declined his invitation.

What if she turns me down?

CHAPTER 17

*L*iz studied the long line of fire vehicles parked along a dirt road near Sockeye Landing. IC Dispatch had assigned the Aurora Crew to the new Swiftcurrent Fire. It had already torched The Swiftcurrent Lodge and now charged north along the Kenai River toward town.

The Aurora Crew arranged their hose lays to prevent the flames from reaching the rows of rafting businesses, restaurants, and fishing lodges that stretched along the narrow canyon on either side of the Sterling Highway. Tara instructed the three squads on Aurora Crew to set up their pump operations along the Kenai River to get water on the hot spots.

Liz ordered her Afi Slayers squad downstream to distance themselves from the other two squads. Tupa carried a small pump to the riverbank, and Cohen set down a catchment tray to set it in. "Attach that foot valve to the suction hose. Stick the suction hose in the water and give it eight inches minimum depth to fill it," instructed Tupa.

Cohen did as ordered, and Tupa reached for the other end of the suction hose to connect it to the pump intake and tightened it with a wrench. "She's ready. Get the water thief fastened to her and connect the discharge hose. Then prime the pump and get her going."

Liz liked that Cohen and Tupa worked well together, thankful that her squad got along without drama.

Tara made her way to the Afi Slayers Squad. "Keep cutting trees in this dense stuff and douse the hot spots. This canyon's too narrow and dangerous to dig line."

Liz scrutinized the landscape in the dense smoke. "Yeah, escape strategy here could get tricky. We used the river last time. We may have to again."

"Lucky for us there's three six-man river rafts in the back of our equipment truck. One of the raft guides loaned them to us in case we needed them." Tara pointed her thumb toward the vehicles.

Kenzie unspooled a section of hose. "Wouldn't mind a quick river run after work."

Tupa came up behind her. "Ever navigate rapids?"

Liz had noticed Tupa hovering near Kenzie in recent days. He'd been shy around the pretty and capable Australian at first, but Liz noticed he'd taken a special liking to her. Others on the crew teased him, when in fact Tupa was painfully shy with women...except Kenzie.

"Oh yes, class four and five rapids. My old man's a river guide down in Oz."

"Your dad runs rivers?" Tupa raised his brows. "Me and my cousins mostly run the Kenai."

Liz hated to break up their tender moment, but they had to get busy. "Okay folks, let's hit these hot spots." She helped Kenzie and Rego carry their hose lay equipment further up the riverbank.

Rego set up the portable water pump and fittings, and Tupa filled the small gas engine on the pump.

Kenzie motioned to Liz for an aside. "Does Tupa have a girlfriend?"

Liz glanced at her in pleasant surprise. "Not that I know of. Are you interested in him besides a crewmate sort of way?"

Kenzie looked thoughtful. "He acts tough and rugged, but I sense a gentle bloke in there."

"There is. I've seen that side now and then. Tupa holds

things close to his chest, but he's an onion worth taking the time to peel. His family is from Samoa, and they live in Anchorage. There's a sizeable Samoan population in Alaska."

"Ha, he's from my neck of the woods, give or take six thousand kilometers." This seemed to delight Kenzie.

"MacKenzie, let's get this hose up and pissing," called Rego.

"Yep. Thanks, Lizzy." She moved off to help.

Liz eyed the three-foot flames slowly burning between the road and the river. They had to prevent the flames from climbing up and crowning the spruce.

She stepped away to see how Tupa and Cohen were faring with their hose pump operation, when she caught sight of a red SUV slowly coming toward them on the dirt road.

A tall woman with a light-colored ponytail climbed out and came toward her. "Good morning. I'm helping today with lunches and snacks for the firefighters." She extended her hand. "I'm Rhiannon and have a catering business in town. We're helping firefighters by donating our services."

"That's great, thank you." Liz shook her hand. "I'm Liz."

Rhiannon opened the rear door of her vehicle and pulled out a plastic bin full of sack lunches. "Your crew boss told me to distribute these turkey sandwiches and chocolate chip cookies to you guys." She reached in and offered several of them.

"Wow, thanks." Liz took a sandwich and unwrapped it. "So, they let you through the road closures?"

"Oh, yeah, I have a pass to come in here. Caterers have passes." She held out an ID card on a lanyard around her neck, then reached into the rear seat of her vehicle. "Care for a Gatorade or a soda?"

"Gatorade, thanks." Liz motioned to the rest of her squad. "Feel free to pass out lunches to the others." Liz motioned toward Tupa and Cohen on the riverbank, busy pumping river water into their hose.

Rhiannon complied and stepped over to the guys.

Liz couldn't help noticing how Cohen's face broadened

into a toothy smile as he accepted the food the woman offered. The two of them talked and laughed like they'd known each other all their lives.

Kenzie stepped over to Liz. "Look how Canada Boy is getting on with Food Chick."

Liz nodded as her radio sounded. "Afi Squad, do you copy?"

She keyed her radio. "Copy, Tara, what's up?"

"The IC wants us to demob from this location ASAP. The fire's crowned downriver and racing through the canyon in our direction. We're gathering our equipment and heading to the North Fork Road on the other side of Sockeye Landing."

"Copy that. On our way." Liz shoved her radio in her holster and finger whistled for her squad. "Come on guys, we have to pack up and relocate."

She glanced at Rhiannon. "Nice meeting you, thanks for the food."

"Oh here, take the rest of these for your crew." Rhiannon tossed the sandwiches and small chips packages into a grocery bag. "Might as well take these, or they'll go to waste."

Cohen appeared next to her. "I'll take that. Thank you. Hope to see you around sometime."

Rhiannon gave him a flirtatious smile, climbed into her red Toyota Forerunner, and drove off.

Liz's squad disassembled their equipment and loaded it into the crew pickup. Rego drove the truck while Tara drove the crew van. Smoke limited visibility as Tara crept the van onto the Sterling Highway. They proceeded through the road-block and turned north.

"Tara, what's the plan?" asked Liz.

"Doss says there's been a significant push of the fire to the northeast. He wants Aurora Crew positioned on the north side of the Kenai River, near Sockeye Landing on a patrol to monitor the fire to protect cabins and businesses. And we're to find and extinguish spotting from the main fire. He has four engine crews there working to reduce fuels around structures."

Tara inched the crew van through the dense smoke on the

highway, with Rego following close behind in the pickup. It took forever to wind around the tight curves with all the fire traffic and cross the Skilak Lake bridge. She turned left onto North Fork Road and followed it a mile or two, then parked behind a green Forest Service truck and a yellow state truck. Their tan crew van with the Bureau of Land Management triangle logo let everyone know they were present on this fire.

Tara gave all three squads their marching orders. "We're here for the duration, folks. Hike in three miles and set up our spike camp. Doss wants us to patrol and douse spot fires and reduce fuels."

They'd brought their large fire packs in case they had to make a spike camp instead of commuting to and from Rock-fish. Rego had the crew's camping equipment in the back of his truck with the rest of their necessities. The crew hefted their gear and hiked up a gentle slope to an open bench area. From there, they had a vantage point of the surrounding terrain.

As Aurora Crew began their ascent on a game trail through the spruce, Liz glimpsed a vehicle pull up behind theirs and turn off its lights. The haze prevented her from seeing who it was. Probably some fire management officer making the rounds.

As the crew made their way to their respective position to patrol and monitor the fire, Liz's mind drifted to what Silva might be doing right now. No doubt on the other end of this fire, doing his investigation thing.

A twinge poked her chest that Jon no longer supervised the Aurora Crew. She respected Tara's leadership, and she'd become a good friend. Jon had left a gaping hole when he'd resigned from the Aurora Crew. The guys often remarked how they missed his lighthearted humor, leadership, and savvy about firefighting.

Liz missed his calm voice of certainty.

She reflected on their interlude last night when she'd show-ered, despite his annoying her about following firefighting orders. He did it because he cared about her. She chuckled at his wanting to kiss her before he left and figured that was his motive for bugging her in the shower.

Who knew when it came to Silva? He could charm his way through a swarm of murder hornets.

She looked forward to seeing him again. In fact, she couldn't *wait* to see him again.

Liz smiled the rest of the way to their crew camp.

❧

*L*ate Monday afternoon, Jon and Keaton drove up a one-lane dirt road to what remained of Swiftcurrent Lodge. Jon shifted into four-wheel drive to get up the steep, rutted road.

"My brother's river rafting business burned." Keaton gripped the wimp handle on the right of the windshield to steady himself in the lurching truck.

"Oh, man, I'm sorry. Did he have insurance?" Jon peered up at the smoke as he crept the truck past a gravel pit with two burned-out rigs parked in it.

"Yeah, but it's still a pain in the ass," growled Keaton, shaking his head.

"I can imagine. Doss reported several businesses torched in this one." Jon rounded a curve, and the smoking ruin of Swiftcurrent Lodge came into view.

He parked the red truck, and the men climbed out into the smoky haze. He lifted his air purifying respirator mask over his head to cover his nose and mouth, and Keaton did the same. The last thing Jon needed was his asthma kicking up, though he'd worked hard to control it since last fire season's debacle.

They picked their way over to the twisted, smoking ceiling beams, collapsed and hanging diagonally to the ground. Jon shook his head at the waste of the beautiful log architecture.

Whenever Jon first entered a fresh burn, his neck hairs rose at seeing the blackened remnants. No insects crawled or flew. No birds or voles moved. Nothing but smoke tendrils lifted from an occasional, lingering glow. Charred black wiped clean all hum of life on the forest floor.

The deafening silence chilled him.

They wandered around the large log building and noted not all the smaller log cabins had burned. Only the ones nearest the main lodge. It never ceased to amaze Jon how wildfires picked and chose their paths of destruction.

Jon examined and photographed the tire tracks in the small parking area. This lodge had mostly burned by the time city fire crews arrived. It torched fast and hot. Whoever did it had intended it that way.

A caretaker oversaw the place, but he hadn't been by for a while. The lodge was a ruined disaster, and adjacent vegetation had carried the fire upriver to Sockeye Landing.

Jon noted a darker, scorched area and bent to smell. Gasoline dominated the headspace above the charred ground where the cabin wall had collapsed. He waved Keaton over.

"Smell the gas?" Jon grabbed his trowel and containers to gather soil and fire debris samples. "There was enough gas poured on this fire to jumpstart the Trans-Alaska Pipeline."

Keaton held out an empty gallon-sized paint can. "Stick the charred pieces in here."

Jon scooped them up with his tongs and inserted them in the can. He squatted and picked through the soil. A cigarette butt with burned stick matches fastened to it caught his attention. "Found the ignition source. An incendiary delay device."

Keaton squatted next to Jon and squinted. "A good, old-fashioned, hot start ignition device. This one has six matches. Someone made sure this ignited. This cig must have burned at least six to eight minutes before torching the match heads."

Jon scrutinized it. "Yeah, by the time this ignited, the fire setter was long gone."

Keaton pursed his lips. "This may be the arsonist's signature device. We'd better tell Trooper O'Donnell to have the troopers step up their search. We have to catch this jerk before he torches the whole peninsula."

Jon lifted the device with tongs and inserted it in his

container. "If we're lucky, there'll be saliva DNA on the cig butt. Maybe a fingerprint. Arsonists often assume their fires destroy ignition evidence. Not always the case."

"Not when fire moves away from the point of origin and seldom burns back on it. Like this one did."

"We need to get this up to the Anchorage forensics lab on the next flight or with a fast raven." Jon grunted as he stood to seal the containers and label them.

Keaton glanced around. "Do we know whether anyone noticed anything unusual in the last twenty-four hours?"

"Not that I know of. The troopers are visiting homes and businesses that are still standing to question people."

Jon stared off at the woods. A movement caught his eye in a partially burned copse of spruce and birch. Thick branches and brush prevented him from seeing who or what it was.

A twig snapped. And another. Then someone crashed through the brush.

Jon yanked off his respirator mask and yelled. "Stop! Want to talk to you for a second." He lowered his goggles over his eyes and entered the dense brush, pushing back scorched alder branches to ramrod his way in.

Someone in blue moved beyond a dense thicket.

Jon picked his way through the char but couldn't catch sight of the person. He stopped and bent over, with palms on his thighs. "Damn," he muttered.

Keaton came up behind him. "Did you get a look at him?"

"Nope. Someone was watching but didn't want to be seen." Jon slowed his breathing. "Let's go, I'll do the paperwork and get these samples turned over to the lab."

A car engine fired up, and music filtered out an open window. Fleetwood Mac.

Jon looked toward the sound as the vehicle took off. He worked his way through the rest of the burn to the dirt road.

Keaton followed and stood on the road next to him. "Who do you suppose it was?"

"Hard to say, but here are their tire tracks." Jon stooped to

131

study them and took photos with his phone. "Let's take an impression."

"Couldn't hurt." Keaton retrieved a sack of dental stone powder from his day pack. He poured some inside a clean, plastic bag and poured in water from his water bottle. He sealed the bag, squished it up to mix it, then smoothed the pale pink mixture gently onto the tire tracks to capture an eighteen-inch mold.

While they waited for the mold to set, Jon's brain kicked into overdrive. They didn't have a whole lot to go on so far, so hopefully the tire track imprint would help. He had a hunch the fire setter had returned to the scene of the crime to watch them.

Arsonists loved visiting the aftermath of their destruction.

CHAPTER 18

*L*iz and the Aurora Crew had prevented the spot fires from taking hold on this end of the fire by extinguishing hot spots up to 300 feet from their containment lines. Each day, they patrolled a six-mile wide and two-mile deep area in case wind carried burning debris out front of the main fire. They'd extinguished three fires so far, beating them with spruce boughs and dousing them with piss-pump bladders on their backs. ICC had trucked up an ATV so they wouldn't have to hump supplies the three miles from the highway.

Doss sent firefighters to tow a large woodchipper and drop if off for them to dispose of brush piles from fuel removed from their secondary containment lines. Anything to reduce the amount of fuel load was a pro-active move to prevent a worse burn. Tara assigned Liz and her squad to reduce the brush piles left from building fire lines on the north end of the Swiftcurrent Fire.

Liz tried texting Jon, but intermittent cell service made it a painful, drawn-out process. Cell gnomes loved messing with people and phones in rural Alaska. Sometimes Liz's phone would receive a text, but she couldn't send one. Liz volunteered to drive the ATV to the highway to pick up delivered supplies from town. She had a better chance of picking up a cell bar or two next to the Sterling Highway.

The first text from Jon arrived the day after he sent it.

Heard you're on the Swiftcurrent Fire. Call if you can. MS.

Liz sat on the ATV on the shoulder of the Sterling Highway, frowning at one cell bar. On a good day, she'd get two bars by tramping in circles and raising her phone up and down like an extraterrestrial tribal dancer, to sneak a text through. Not today. At this rate, it would take geologic time to find out anything.

Can't call, only text. What's MS?

His response popped up right away.

Main Squeeze, duh. When are your days off? Have an invitation for you.

Curious, she texted back.

Invitation to what?

Several days later, another Jon text.

To spend a weekend with me at an ocean resort.

When? At the end of fire season? Liz's heart skipped a beat. It had taken the better part of a week to get those few texts squeezed through this dead zone out here in the boonies. Might as well be chiseling hieroglyphics on rocks. She danced her thumbs across her screen.

Mexico or Hawaii? This is taking forever!

His response popped up right away for some miraculous reason.

In Alaska. Must get there by boat.

She responded like lightning as she waited for firefighters to unload water containers from a supply truck.

Bummer. Thought you had a Lear jet.

Texts flew thick and fast. Better make the most of cell service while the getting's good.

What do you say? Yes??

Liz hesitated, her thumbs hovering over the keypad. She glommed onto the last word. "Geez, I should play a *little* hard to get," she muttered, slowly tapping the letters.

I'll think about it.

She tapped send before she could change her mind. No response. Either she'd annoyed him, or an eagle had crapped on a cell tower.

I do have to think about it. She wanted to see him, but was she ready to go off with him for an entire weekend? That kind of thing screamed commitment.

She hopped on the ATV and drove the crew's water and fresh food supplies to Aurora's camp.

After dinner, Tara announced, "Aurora Crew, Dave Doss agreed to a crew rotation. We're heading back to Rockfish tomorrow morning since our three weeks are up. Another crew will relieve us."

A communal cheer went up all around.

Liz had pondered Jon's invitation since reading his text. Now that they'd be heading back to town, her feelings locked horns with her logic, knocking around her brain like two heavyweights. Logic argued involvement with Jon would complicate her life.

She motioned at Tara with her head in a *"time for a confab,"* same as they did last year when the need arose. The two women set off along a pond on the other side of their camp. Liz waited until they were out of earshot of the crew.

"Jon asked me to spend the weekend with him at a resort." Liz waited for the response she knew she'd get.

"Woohoo! It's about freaking time." Tara hugged her shorter friend. "You two have danced around this far too long. No pun intended."

Liz laughed. "Right. I'm not sure if I should go."

"Wait, I thought you wanted this?"

"My exotic dancer brain can't help wondering if he expects sex in exchange for a free mini vacation?"

"What if he does? You're both adults." Tara brushed red tendrils away from her face. "Lay your cards on the table. Ask him. If there's one thing I've learned about relationships, honesty is the best way to start one."

"I'm not sure I even want a relationship. I have plans set in motion that don't include a guy in Alaska."

"I was the same way if you recall." Tara let out a sigh. "Keep your options open. You never know what could happen."

"This'll be the first time we've spent longer than a few hours together." Liz thought a minute. "I haven't been with a guy in so long, there's cobwebs on my girl parts."

Tara guffawed. "Seriously? I figured you to be the most experienced when it came to guys. You're around them all the time in both jobs. I guess I assumed that because—"

Liz finished for her. "Because I'm an exotic dancer. Everyone assumes that." She shook her head. "I've not let any guy closer than a one-minute relationship. I haven't been inti-mate with anyone in a long time."

"How long?"

"Since velociraptors roamed the Earth." Liz motioned at the landscape.

"Oh, come on, you've never shared that." Tara glanced around as if the surrounding wildlife strained to hear her every word. "Okay, listen. Start with an icebreaker. Before…you know." She twirled her finger.

"We may not get that far. I mean, we've only kissed."

Tara laughed. "You sound like pre-teen Barbie. Hello, this is Jon Silva we're talking about. I can't believe I'm giving *you*, of all people, birds and bees advice."

Liz leaned in. "Hey, I'm an expert at the honeybee dance. I flaunt my body parts at guys for a living, so I do have a clue. I know Slot A goes into Slot B."

"And sometimes into Slot C." Tara's devilish expression made them both dissolve in laughter.

Tara wiped her eyes. "Okay, back to the icebreaker. Come up with something that'll get both of you to relax. It'll make all the difference."

"You mean an icebreaker like, let's go around the room and share? Good evening, my name is Elizabeth Harrington, and when I'm not fighting dangerous wildfires in Alaska, I take off my clothes and wiggle my boobs in guy's faces." She stuck out her chest and batted her eyelashes.

Tara giggled. "Perfect! Do that to Jon. Remember last year when I spent my first night with Ryan?"

"How could I forget—you forgot your name or what planet you were on the next day. I had to steer you around." Liz smirked.

"Ryan and I were both nervous. I went all cowgirl. Pulled off his belt and twirled it like a rodeo queen and let it fly. His belt buckle cracked the window, and we howled. And the rest, as they say, is history."

Liz threw up her arms. "When it comes to matters of the heart, I'm shy. I know that's weird coming from me."

"Matters of the *heart?* You sound like a Jane Austen novel." Tara stopped walking. "What are you afraid of? Are you having second thoughts because Jon was your crew boss?"

Liz grimaced. "It's hard to picture myself having sex with someone who's done my performance rating."

"Afraid he'll give you another one for your sexual prowess?" Tara smirked and leaned in. "What did he give you last year?"

"A level five—outstanding."

Tara gave her a devilish look. "So, give him one back."

"For what—oh, you're badass." Liz laughed, picturing herself naked with a clipboard, glasses perched on her nose, evaluating Jon's sexual performance. She laughed till tears ran. "Thanks, Tara. Now I won't get that out of my head."

Tara's expression changed to solemn. "Seriously, you need to do this. Go with open arms. Let yourself get all mushy and gooey. Don't hold back."

Liz summoned the courage to speak her truth. "I'm terrified to love for the first time. Scares me to death."

"How do you think I felt last fire season? I was petrified, falling for Ryan. Screw complications. This might be the only boat that lands at your port." Tara pointed for emphasis. "Get in the damn boat, Liz. Get in and sail off with Jon Silva."

Liz thought for a long moment. "All I can envision is how complicated my life will become."

Tara stared off in the distance, and her eyes became misty. "My mom told me something a long time ago, just before she died. She said, 'Be resilient with love, and you'll have no regrets.' At the time, I was too young to understand. When I fell for Ryan after being burned by another smokejumper, I finally understood."

"We've always had a buffer—working on fires around other people. What if Jon tires of me like he did his wives, and God knows how many other women?" She flicked her eyes at Tara. "Worse yet—what if I tire of him?"

"Now you're overthinking it. You're a firefighter. You take risks for a living. Take another one. If you don't, you'll wonder about it the rest of your frigging life." Tara rested her palm on Liz's arm. "Go easy on our boy. What happened last year crushed his spirit. You've resuscitated it—I've seen the way he looks at you. If you and Jon are meant to be, it'll work out. If not, call it good and walk away."

The independent part of Liz hated to admit she needed help making this decision. In the past, she'd not had a bestie like Tara to confide in. Trust hadn't normally resided in her wheelhouse, and she was grateful for Tara's friendship. She'd become Liz's Spock, mistress of logic.

"Thanks, I appreciate that. You make it sound easy." Liz laughed. "Guess I have been overthinking it."

Tara paused. "The thing about loving someone for the first time—it makes you feel anything is possible and gives you the desire to be a better person. Be fearless. Grab hold and don't let go. I promise you won't regret it."

"You sound so sure." Liz let out a long sigh. She'd never been one to make impulsive decisions. Tara was right. If she didn't go, Jon might take it as rejection and lose interest.

If it turned out they weren't compatible, then nothing lost, nothing gained. And if they were...well, she'd take it one step at a time. This was one thing she couldn't plan.

If she didn't go, she might regret it the rest of her life.

And wonder about it forever.

*L*iz felt close to normal after showering. The crew piled back into the van, and Tara drove them to the barbecue. Liz stood in line, holding out her paper plate to the server dishing up food under a row of white canopy tents.

Rhiannon plopped a juicy steak on her plate. "Hey, what's up?" chirped Rhiannon.

Liz startled at seeing her. "Oh, hello. You're serving us more food."

"Your crew de'mobed from the Swiftcurrent Fire, huh?"

"Uh, yeah. How'd you know?"

Rhiannon pointed at a white board near the state forestry building. "ICC posts the crew fire assignments over there." She switched her attention to Cohen, next in line behind Liz and Kenzie.

Liz glanced back at Rhiannon, who smiled and chatted with him. They both had their phones out, tapping away.

Kenzie elbowed Liz. "I'll bet coin they're exchanging phone numbers. Friendly girl, yeah?"

"Looks that way." A twinge pinged Liz even though she'd resisted Cohen's advances. Of course women would be attracted to her friendly, hunky crewmate. As his squad boss, she felt big sister protective.

Rhiannon seemed to pop up everywhere, like so many of the locals, eager to help out with the firefighting effort. One of those small town, enthusiastic community volunteers.

Kenzie led the way to sit on the wide expanse of lawn and Liz sat next to her. They dove into their food.

Liz cut into her steak and popped a bite in her mouth. "Oh, this is divine." She let out a moan, then practically inhaled the rest.

"Going back for more?" asked Kenzie after consuming her own plateful.

"I'm eating like a logger. I can't help myself, it's delicious." Liz rose and sauntered back to the food line.

"There you are." Rhiannon materialized in front of her. "I

wanted to ask you—would you like to go fishing for Kenai King salmon? We can catch enough to feed your whole crew. Fires are keeping all the fishermen away. There's tons of fish."

Liz stared at her in surprise. "Geez. Um, I'm not sure when I'd have the time."

"It'll only take a few hours. We can do it one evening after you get off work. That is, when you feel up to it."

Liz looked at her. "Give me your cell number, and we'll figure out a time." She waited expectantly.

Rhiannon hesitated. "Instead, let me have yours."

Liz had a policy of not giving her cell number to anyone but close friends. "Uh, I'm sure we'll see each other around."

"Sure, we'll figure something out," said Rhiannon. "I want to show you our Peninsula hospitality."

"I appreciate that. Thank you." Weird to get celebrity treatment, but some locals really appreciated the firefighters.

"Have to run, see you later." Rhiannon hurried off and disappeared into the parking lot.

What a strange woman. Maybe she doesn't have many friends and latches on to firefighters for company.

As Liz stood at the back of the never-ending line for more delicious food, her phone vibrated. She took it from her pocket. Ravish calling from Vegas. She groaned and tapped to answer.

"Hey Rav, what's up?"

"We have a situation. Amethyst has raised their rental occupancy price, and if we still want our club in their hotel, we have to fork over three hundred grand more to hold our space to get in the front door."

She gasped. "Can they do that? What about our contract we signed with Amethyst, Inc?"

"They voided that contract and drafted a new one. We have to come up with the additional bucks, or we're out."

"Rav, you and Jaspar will have to get the two hundred grand, and me one hundred grand. I'll need the rest of the summer to pull that together."

"Uhh…Me and Jaspar don't have it. You'll have to pony up half. One hundred fifty thousand."

"Wait a minute, that's not the amount we agreed on. We stick with our original agreement. We each pay one-third."

"Better reconsider if you want this venture to fly. You're up there making the big bucks."

Liz cut her off. "Wait a minute—"

"I'll give you the weekend to think about it. Later." Ravish ended the call.

Liz stood staring at her phone when a baritone voice sent shock waves up her spine. "Harrington, you're back in one piece."

She turned to behold Jon, standing there, all masculine and brawny. Instinctively, she had an impulse to hug him but restrained herself. "Hello, Mr. Inspector. We no longer have to text in geologic time."

"Good old hit-and-miss cell service. You look like you've lost your last friend." He smiled, and she noted the short growth of a beard and mustache.

"Weird texts from friends." She waved her hand dismissively and shoved her phone in her pocket, along with her unpleasant conversation. She gestured at his face. "You gave up shaving."

He grinned. "You'd commented on my nightly shadow. Figured I'd give it a go."

"Looks good on you." An understatement. It absolutely amplified his masculinity. Made her want to climb him like a dance pole.

"How was the Swiftcurrent Fire? You guys spike-camped for quite a while."

"We did." She gawped at the tanned, gorgeous face, his dissolve-your-panties widow's peak, and the aviator shades that screamed covert counterspy, rather than fire investigator.

Goosebumps feathered her arms despite the warm sun. She glanced away to get a grip on her turned-on self. "It's good to be back in civilization."

"And civilization is glad to have you back." He lifted his plate to a server for a steak.

Liz lost interest in eating—too many butterflies competed for space in her stomach.

Jon motioned his plateful of food toward the far end of the lawn, devoid of people. "Let's sit over there."

She grabbed a bottle of water from an ice cooler and followed.

He lowered himself to the grass, sitting cross-legged.

She dropped down to the cool grass and sat facing him, suddenly feeling shy.

He cut a piece of steak and popped it in his mouth, studying her.

She tilted her head. "Why are you looking at me like that?"

He swallowed his steak. "Waiting for you to say yes."

"To what?" She knew damn well what, but she wanted him to say it.

"Don't give me that. You know what." He cut another piece of steak and tugged it off his fork with his teeth.

Everything she'd confided to Tara jumped front and center. Should she, shouldn't she...*Get in the boat and sail away with Jon Silva.*

Liz shifted her gaze to the only guy who'd ever mattered. "Yes."

He studied her. "Yes?"

"Yes."

"Wow. I expected all kinds of no." He shoved another piece of steak in his mouth. Chewed slow and swallowed.

The way the steak moved down his throat had her eyeballing him like a dark chocolate, hot fudge sundae. "You've —um, underestimated me."

"When you texted you had to think about it, I took that as a no."

"When I texted I had to think about it, that meant I had to think about it." She fiddled with the lid on her water bottle, heart galloping.

"I won't ask why. But good. I'll ask why later." He slanted his Silva heat at her. "Now that we have that settled, what time can you be ready tomorrow? It's a three-hour drive."

"Liz!" Tara hollered across the lawn, waving her over to catch a ride back to camp.

She waved back and stood. "Four-thirty p.m. at the earliest. We'll be retrieving and cleaning up fire equipment tomorrow."

Jon lifted his slightly bearded face. "Four-thirty it is. I'll be in the parking lot."

She smiled shyly. "It's a date, then."

"Our first official one." He stood, holding his empty plate.

"See you tomorrow, Silva." She turned to go.

"Elizabeth." He hadn't called her that since last year, during the first roll call.

She turned around.

"Don't be nervous. We'll have fun. Trust me." His heat rushed at her again.

"Okay." She turned her dazed self toward the parking lot, not wanting to leave him just yet.

He'd knocked it out of the park with his suave, relaxed manner the way he always had, the sun reflecting those badass shades of his. No one in a million-mile radius could compare with this guy.

Her mind zig-zagged in all directions like pyrotechnics gone wonky. She felt good about her decision to go with him.

Screw complications.

CHAPTER 19

*J*on left the hotel and pulled into the campground parking lot, overlooking the Kenai River. His heart ticked up at Liz coming toward him with her pack over one shoulder.

He beamed at her, eager to get started on their road trip. "Ready for some relaxation?" He took her pack and tossed it in the back seat of the crew cab.

"I'm always up for a few days without breathing smoke." She headed to the passenger side and swung into the cab, closing her door.

Jon sunk into the driver's seat and started the truck. "Where I'm taking you, there'll be less of it, hopefully."

"Where is that exactly? You've been mysterious about where we're going."

"Trust me, you'll like it. Better than hanging around crew camp for your two days off."

Jon focused on getting to Homer in time for the dinner reservations he'd made at Land's End Resort. He drove the two-lane highway faster than normal. They'd make the dinner reservation, provided not many slow drivers impeded his progress.

Liz hadn't been to this part of Alaska. He left her alone to absorb the magnificent views of Lower Cook Inlet and the majestic volcanoes on the other side: Mt. Iliamna, Mt. Redoubt, and Mt. Spurr, snow clinging to their summits. All had erupted within the past couple of decades, raining ash over Southcentral Alaska.

"Oh, look at this!" Her eyes grew wide as they crested the final hill above Homer. A panoramic view of Kachemak Bay and Lower Cook Inlet came into view. Blue-gray mountains bordered the bay on the other side, marching out to greet the Gulf of Alaska.

"It gets better." Jon aimed the truck downhill into the coastal berg of Homer, the southernmost town on Alaska's mainland.

"No way. How could it?" She ooh'ed and ah'ed the remainder of the drive to the Homer Spit, a narrow jut of land extending six miles out to where Cook Inlet met Kachemak Bay.

Jon loved this unique landscape, where massifs met the sea. He drove to the end of the Spit, pulled into a modest parking lot, and cut the engine. He welcomed the wood carving of a mermaid perched on top of a sign, *Land's End Resort.*

"We're eating dinner here before crossing the bay." He smiled at her wide-eyed and open-mouthed expression from the relentless, spectacular scenery along the Lower Kenai Peninsula.

He led her inside the entrance, a nondescript casual entryway to the main lobby. "We're having dinner in the Chart Room." He motioned to the hostess, who waved them to a table next to the expanse of windows overlooking a 180-degree view of the ocean.

When they settled in and perused their menus, Liz peeked around her tall menu at him. "This is magnificent. Do you come here often?"

"As often as possible." Jon scoped out his favorite specialty. "Seafood fettucine. I highly recommend it." He noted the time. He didn't want to rush their meal, but they had a water taxi reservation in an hour and a half.

"Everything okay?" She nodded at his wristwatch.

"Better than okay," he murmured as the server poured their white wine into two generous glasses.

Liz raised her glass. "Thank you for inviting me this weekend."

"Thank you for accepting my invitation." He clinked hers and sipped. As the chilled wine moved through him, he hoped the next few days would be good ones. He set down his glass. "Any news from down south about your new business?"

She heaved out a sigh. "Money. It's always about the money. How much each of us is investing." She frowned and sipped her wine.

"How committed are you to this Vegas deal?" He wished she wasn't heading in that direction. Chrissakes—Vegas. Anything could happen down there.

"I still have to come up with my share. That's why I'm here fighting fire."

He forced a smile. "I hope it works out for you." *No. I don't. I don't want you working anywhere near that volatile environment.*

All he wanted was a break from both their work responsibilities. He couldn't wait to be where the ocean reigned as monarch over everything. He'd spend time with Liz with no interference. No arson, ex, or co-worker to interfere. Nothing except the two of them.

His battery needed recharging.

He couldn't think of a better person to charge it with than Elizabeth Ann Harrington.

🔥

*T*he last thing Liz wanted on her mind was anything work-related in this gorgeous place, surrounded by Alaska's beautiful coastal waters. Small boats motored into the Homer Harbor, and the *Tustamena* marine ferry eased into port. A wide rainbow arced from the Homer Spit to the mountains across Kachemak Bay, as if arranged by design.

She loved having dinner with Jon in this beautiful restaurant, with the panoramic view of the emerald waters of Kachemak Bay and the blue waves of Lower Cook Inlet. She had questions to ask Jon now that they were alone. One in particular gnawed at her. "Do you recall last year when we made it up to that ridgetop? You said something I've always wondered about."

"What?"

"That you loved Tara." She surveyed a purse seiner separating waves as it glided into the harbor. "Is that still true?"

He sipped his wine and leaned back, gazing at the incoming seiner. "Much has happened since then. You know how it is when you're first attracted to someone. You test the waters, see if you have a chance. And when you don't, you move on."

"Tara fell in love with Ryan the minute she saw him on that Montana fire. Had nothing to do with you."

"I figured that out in the end. No, I don't love Tara. She's a friend." He stared at her for a moment. "Tell me about your Nevada hotshot boyfriend."

She shrugged. "Nothing to tell. Only went out a few times. Those Nevada firefighters you kindly helped me with—they're friends of his who saw me dance. When guys find out I'm an exotic dancer, they automatically assume they can get a piece of ass. Nothing could be further from the truth with me anyway."

He studied her. "Why do you dance?"

"It pays exceedingly well. I make more in a night of tips than I do in one firefighting shift with hazard pay." She eyed him directly. "I don't let it define me."

"Make sure when you make the money, it doesn't make you."

Her eyebrows rose at his comment. She fished her phone from her pocket, swiped her photo gallery, and tapped a video. A large fishing boat glided past as she waited for him to finish watching it.

His expression at seeing her dance in an onstage ballet

performance tingled her with satisfaction. *Now he sees what else I can do.* She tapped to end the video.

His jaw dropped. "Wow. What are you doing in a dance club when you can dance like that?"

Liz was used to this question but preened at his accolade despite herself. "I've auditioned for lots of professional dance companies."

"And they didn't hire you? Who the hell *are* these people? Are they blind?"

"Competition is fierce." She set her phone on the table. "I had to take a job that paid good money."

He shook his head. "You should be at Carnegie Hall with that kind of ability."

She didn't care to blather about her failures and why she'd been desperate for cash. "Let's hear about you and why your three marriages ended."

His eyebrows shot up. "We're doing this now?"

"No time like the present."

He let out a long sigh. "You know about Roxanne. Number Two was a blind date my friends set me up with when I moved to Fairbanks. We moved in together, then got married. Things were great until her first winter. She left for the lower forty-eight, filed for divorce, and I never saw her again."

"And Number Three?"

"Found her on a dating app." He sipped his wine. "By that time, I'd been working on my ornithology doctorate. I found a birder woman who'd always wanted to come to Alaska. While chasing a green honeycreeper in Mexico, she found another birder guy. They never found the honeycreeper because they were too busy hooking up in an Acapulco hotel room."

"Geez, that must have sucked." She gave him an inquisitive look. "Does Roxanne want to get back with you?"

He shook his head. "I told her not to contact me again."

Uneasiness niggled at her. "But she's mentioned it?"

"She means nothing. If she did, I wouldn't be here with you."

Hearing him say it eased her fears. And it helped to know

he didn't cause all of his divorces. Still, three marriages was a bit of a red flag—for anyone. She'd keep an open mind as Tara advised.

The server brought their food, and they ate heartily.

Jon glanced at his watch. "We'd better go. We have a water taxi to catch."

"I'm done. Let's go."

He tossed his napkin on his plate and reached for his wallet.

"You aren't paying for this. I'm paying my share," Liz stated emphatically.

He winked and rose swiftly, moving toward the cashier.

By the time she made her way to him, it was too late.

He strode toward the truck. "Put on a jacket. You'll need it."

She jogged to keep up with his long stride. "I'm not cold."

"You will be. Trust me." He climbed in the truck and cranked the engine.

She hopped in and tugged a fleece pullover from her pack.

Jon drove a short distance along the Homer Spit road and pulled into the harbor parking lot. He cut the engine and looked at her.

"Grab your stuff." He hoisted his duffle over a shoulder and headed to a metal ramp that led down to the boat docks. "It's low tide, so be careful. It's a steep trek down."

Liz hoisted her pack to her shoulders. She clung to the railing, stepping gingerly along the steep incline, letting the steel teeth grip the soles of her athletic shoes.

They reached the bottom, and Jon turned right and headed toward a boat with *K-Bay Water Taxi* on the hull. He called out to a guy in tall rubber boots, swishing buckets of water on the dock.

"Two of us." He gave the boat captain some bills and swung himself on board the beefy, thirty-eight-foot boat with a small wheelhouse at the stern. He offered his hand to help her in.

Once onboard, Jon steered her toward a bench seat in front of the wheelhouse.

She had never been in a boat on the ocean, and her heart galloped.

He leaned in. "You're going to like this."

The two outboard motors fired up, and the boat backed out of the slip and stayed at no-wake speed until reaching the mouth of the harbor. The skipper opened the motors, lurching them forward. After passing gulls on the rocks with heads tucked under wings, the boat arced and aimed across the bay.

She checked the zipper on her life vest and gripped the edge of her seat.

"Don't worry," yelled Jon over the noise of the motors. "It's only four miles across."

She nodded, thankful for the calm seas and sun glinting on glassy waters as the boat sped smoothly across. Her reflection in his shades smiled back at her, her hair blown back. She leaned sideways and tucked into him for warmth and composure.

He nudged her shoulder with his, the way friends do when sharing a special moment.

As the boat clipped along at a smooth pace, Jon pointed at a large boat towing a smaller one behind it. "Purse seiner," he shouted above the motors.

She nodded and noted a group of kayakers in the distance making their way across the bay. She turned her head and thought she glimpsed something break free of the water near the kayakers.

Jon pointed. "Whale!"

Of course she missed it. She'd give anything to see a whale.

Each time Alaska showed Liz a new jaw-dropper, she'd top herself with another grand display to take Liz's breath away.

The mountains loomed taller as they neared the remote side of the bay. The boat traversed a rocky coastline, passing a wide mud flat, then turned into a narrow inlet. The motors slowed as they approached a large log building with several smaller ones, lined up on a series of cedar boardwalks. The captain maneuvered the boat to a stop next to a large cedar dock.

A young woman waited on the dock, ready to catch the bowline Jon tossed. She caught it with ease and tugged the boat close, snaking the ropes around a large cleat. The captain tossed her the stern line, and she did the same.

Jon spread his arms wide. "Welcome to Steller's Jay Lodge."

"Are you freaking serious?" Liz's jaw dropped. The majesty of the mountains bordering the private narrow inlet and emerald water lapping the gravel shore had her gaping. It was nothing like her desert world, that was for sure.

They hefted their gear, and she followed Jon along a large cedar platform to a rectangular log building with geranium and lobelia baskets on either side. He pointed at a garden with tall, eye-popping blue flowers.

"Blue Himalayan Poppies do well here. They grow better in Alaska than anywhere else. Wait here, I'll get us checked in." He ducked inside.

"Okay." She wandered the boardwalk that paralleled the shoreline, taking in the boats and noting sea kayaks stacked along one side of a dock platform. She inhaled the salt air mixed with spruce and hemlock and the sweet smell of pristine rainforest.

A pungent fish smell wafted from a boat docked with a fresh catch of halibut. The deckhands hoisted large white coolers from the boat up onto the dock. A large, white fanned-out fishtail stuck out of one.

Jon came up behind her. "We're set. This way to our cabin." He led her to the last one on the end. He hesitated and turned to her. "This has two separate beds."

"Sure thing." She hadn't necessarily fretted over it, but now that he'd mentioned it, she was good with having an option.

He unlocked the decorative wood door with a stained-glass window of a bright-eyed otter and her pup. The door swung open, and they lugged in their gear.

The beauty of the Lower Kenai Peninsula held her captive,

and she'd shoved aside thoughts about their sleeping arrangement. Jon had offered an option by mentioning two beds. This should prove interesting. One thing was for sure.

At long last, they were alone.

CHAPTER 20

*J*on fished two bottles of water from his duffle and stuck them in the small fridge in the corner. He sank onto the couch after closing the window curtains.

"I know it's early, but we need some shut-eye. I have lots of fun planned for tomorrow."

Liz turned around after taking items from her pack and sat on the loveseat. "Like what?"

"It's a surprise. How do you like it so far?"

She scrutinized the cozy cabin, her gaze resting on the stone fireplace with a large black bear rug in front of it. "I love it. Never been to a place like this on the ocean. I've only been to Lake Tahoe when Dad took me with his cop buddy families."

"Tomorrow we'll do some sea kayaking, then motor up the coast for lunch at Halibut Cove."

"That sounds fun."

He sensed her awkwardness. Time to grab the elephant and toss him out for the night. "I asked you here because I enjoy your company. I'm not expecting anything else…like what you think other guys might expect…" He trailed off.

"Thanks. I appreciate that." She grabbed her toothbrush and other essentials and headed for the bathroom.

There was only one bedroom with a queen bed, and the

foldout couch was in the main living area. Jon made a quick decision. The gentlemanly thing would be to give Liz the bedroom, and he'd take the fold-out couch. He winced at the idea of the cross bar gouging his back.

Off came the cushions, and he unfolded the full-size bed. He fluffed the pillows and tossed his duffle on the bed. Thankfully, Risa had sheets and blankets already made on it.

Jon hauled Liz's pack into the bedroom and arranged it on the luggage rack in the corner. He then breezed out to the kitchen sink to brush his teeth.

"Where's my stuff?" asked Liz.

He turned to the delicious sight of her in a clingy night shirt that hit her mid thighs. "In the bedroom, where you'll be sleeping."

"You're sleeping out here?"

Was she disappointed?

How was a red-blooded Alaskan guy sharing quarters with a gorgeous exotic dancer—also a kickass firefighter—supposed to respond to that? He motioned at the foldout bed with his toothbrush. "Figured you'd want your privacy."

She made a joyful noise. "How sweet of you but I can sleep on the foldout. I don't mind—"

He lifted the toothbrush away from his teeth. "Nope. Done deal. You're in the bedroom."

"I don't care what they say about you, Silva. You *are* a gentleman." She padded into the bedroom with those sexy bare feet. And he wasn't even a foot man.

He grinned that he'd scored points with her, foamy toothpaste dribbling down his chin. He wiped it with the back of his hand.

She padded back out, tugging the hair tie to release her ponytail.

For him, she was a slow-mo scene in a movie: *Hair falling— cascading—to below her shoulders. She shook it loose and combed it back with her fingers as her night shirt rode high on her thighs…*

With her back to him, she moved to the picture window,

gazing at the emerald bay and mountains framing it in the twilight.

He studied those tanned, muscled dancer's legs. Firefighter legs. They'd driven him insane at the wedding in that titillating dress. He would have gladly handed over his left nut to get her out of it. And he had...except she'd been ten sheets to the wind. Turned out he had a conscience.

He admired the graceful lines of her neck that drove him wild. And her perfectly heart-shaped ass made his tiller move without the captain steering.

"When I first came to Alaska, I couldn't get over how the all-night summer twilight lowers the dimmer switch on the stars." She turned toward him. "I remember you saying the first time you watched fireworks on the Fourth of July in Fairbanks, you said they were invisible and why bother?"

"It's the winter skies that are spectacular. I save my wad for New Year's." He ducked his head to busy himself with whatever the heck he'd been doing...oh yeah, brushing...to avoid gawking at the nipples poking through her thin shirt.

Jon finished up, wanting to flee before he'd trip over his hard-on. He beelined for the bathroom and shut the door. "Sweet Jesus, this'll be a long night," he muttered, glancing down at himself.

No way would he undress and prance out there in his skivvies with his tiller pointing at Liz. He did his damndest to visualize making love to a halibut—or a sea lion—anything but *her*.

When his rudder begrudgingly deflated, he exited the bathroom fully clothed.

Liz had curled up in an armchair, reading a fishing magazine. "Aren't you getting ready for bed?" Her mouth twitched. "Are you shy about undressing in front of me?"

"Me? Shy?" He huffed out air and gave her an eye roll. "Right. I don't think so."

"Then show us whatcha got," she teased. "Strut your stuff, Slick. Hey, I'm in my nightshirt."

"I see that. Hey, I'm not the stripper—" He stopped short, and heat crawled up his neck. "Sorry. Didn't mean…"

"Oh Silva, I'm not made of sugar. You didn't insult me." She tossed the magazine onto the end table next to her and stood. "I'm tired and calling it a day. Goodnight, Shy Boy."

She hesitated, then disappeared into the bedroom. The bed springs squeaked as she settled herself in for the night.

I hope I didn't insult her. He stood there, nonplussed. "Goodnight."

He undressed except for his fitted shorts and crawled into the foldout. The pesky bar poked the middle of his back, and he winced. He tried to get as comfortable as he could in the all-night twilight and closed his eyes.

Liz was only a short distance away, but she may as well have been on the moon.

His sexual tension was taut as a fishing line with a salmon shark snuffling on the end of it. He wanted more than anything to sneak into the bedroom and crawl into bed with her.

No way could he assume that would be okay. It had to be what *she* wanted. They were still on Main Squeeze terms… whatever that was.

"Jon?" Her voice floated out to him, soft and quiet.

His eyelids popped open. "Yeah?"

Her bed creaked as she changed position. "What's your favorite song?"

"All of them." He sounded smartassy. "I mean, I don't have only one."

"If your spaceship stranded you on Mars, like the Watney guy in that Martian movie, what's the one song you could listen to over and over? That poor dude only had disco."

He let out a sigh. "Hmm, that's a hard one."

"Pick one and sing it."

He racked his brain. "Since we're near the ocean, how about this?"

Took him a few tries to find the pitch for *Beyond the Sea.*

Could have found it faster if he had his guitar, but he'd left it home after the wedding.

He finished the song, and all was silent for a while.

She yawned. "You have a lovely voice. Thank you."

"You're welcome." Her words heartened him. He sang softly in a cappella...*Dream a Little Dream of Me.* The Mama Cass version.

When he finished, Liz's petite little snores drifted out to him.

Not a terrible start to the weekend. Could have been worse. Not everything had to be about sex—thought New Jon.

But Old Jon thought, *it sure does help.*

*L*iz woke up refreshed after a glorious night's sleep.

"Good morning, Risa and Spencer," Jon boomed out as he and Liz entered the large dining area. They'd piled the table with breakfast goodies.

"Jon, I've missed you." The woman gave him a tight hug. "You got in late last night."

Liz raised her brows at the invigorating reception by this pretty woman. She stood beside Jon, smiling.

"Hi, I'm Risa. You must be Liz." The woman offered her hand.

Liz shook it. "Yes. You have a spectacular place here."

"I'm Spencer," piped up a short, stout guy, somewhere in his thirties. "Welcome to Steller's Jay Lodge. Let us know if you need anything."

Jon gave him a guy hug and slap on the shoulder. "Still have *Sea Monster?*"

"Yep. She's moored out behind the big boat. We stacked the sea kayaks in their usual place on the dock. Tomorrow will be a good day to paddle out to Gull Island. You finish that bird doctorate?" Spencer stuffed a bite of blueberry pancake in his mouth.

"Not yet. You can take the man away from the bird, but

you can't take the bird from the man. Or something like that." Jon made a bug-eyed face that made Liz laugh.

Jon and Liz sat at the long pine table and made fast action out of blueberry pancakes, coffee, and fresh fruit.

"You make this table, bro?" Jon ran his fingers along the sleek side.

Spencer sipped his coffee and nodded. "It was a long winter."

Liz took an instant liking to Risa, and they chatted nonstop. "Jon's talked about you. Don't worry, all good things. He told us about the kickass squad bosses he chose last year on your fire crew." Risa winked at Jon, who only smiled.

Liz's heart kicked up a notch on that one.

Jon finished up his breakfast. "Okay Harrington, down that coffee. Time to hit the water. It's best at high tide."

"I'm ready." High tide, low tide. She knew nothing about ocean tides. Only that the moon dictated them.

Jon winked and jerked his head. "Come on, let's go."

Back at the cabin, Jon called out a checklist. "Bug dope, rain gear, portable phone charger, sunglasses, water bottles. And life vests." He pulled one large and one small vest hanging from the pegs by the door, unzipped them, and held the small one out to her.

She took the red and yellow life vest and zipped it, then made sure she had what she needed in her small day pack.

"And we need these bootylicious rubber boots." He perused the lineup of tall mud boots and plucked out an extra-large and small pair. "We'll be in tidal waters getting in and out of the sea kayaks. Plus, these keep the no-see-um flies from chewing up your ankles."

Liz was so far out of her element, she locked on to Jon's every word. She was a desert rat. Granted, she'd acclimated to Interior Alaska, but this was a whole different ball game.

They strolled along the boardwalk to the dock platform in front of the main lodge.

Jon poked around the rack of sea kayaks and chose a wide,

blue tandem one. "This one is the most stable. Grab the other end."

They lifted it off the rack and rested it on the dock. Jon tossed in their gear and tucked it into the rear cargo space.

Jon nodded at the kayak. "Grab your end, let's get her in the water." They carried it down the metal ramp and over to the gravel shoreline at the water's edge.

She inspected the water, squinting at a blanket of yellow washing up onshore. "What is that?"

He glanced at what she pointed at. "Spruce pollen. Trees have to reproduce, like everything else." He held the kayak secure for her in ankle-deep water. "Get in front. I'm heavier, I'll sit in the stern."

She gingerly stepped in and lowered herself to a sitting position. Jon offered her a white kayak paddle, then shoved off and inserted himself with the grace of a swan alighting on the water. The kayak rolled gently from side to side as Jon settled his tall frame into the stern.

"This kayak doesn't have a rudder. I'll be the rudder and match your strokes. Watch how I do it."

She twisted to observe how he dipped the paddle, lifted, and rotated it from side to side.

Jon had Liz practice paddling to get the feel of the kayak. "We'll paddle around the inlet until you're comfortable before heading out."

"Okay." She found it was easier than she figured and liked the immediate response of the boat.

"Good job. Knew you'd be a quick study." He sounded pleased, and it reassured her. "Ready for more?"

Apprehension twisted her chest. This proximity to the ocean's surface made her think of *Jaws*. She tamped back those disturbing visuals. "What if it gets rough?"

"It's supposed to stay calm all morning, and there's no wind." His calm manner reassured her.

"Okay. Let's do it."

They paddled along the narrow inlet that opened into the larger bay. Jon steered them toward Gull Island, an enormous pair of rocks jutting out of the water a quarter-mile offshore. As they neared the island, thousands of seabirds were in the air and on the water.

He pointed his paddle at a colorful group to their right. "Horned puffins."

The puffins wore little tuxedoes with yellow and orange beaks. Her anxiety lessened as she took in all the birds.

Jon pointed up. "Those are kittiwakes. The long-necked dark birds are cormorants, and the others are murres. We'll circle so you can see their nesting sites."

She was awed by the cacophony of chattering birds flying to rock walls and landing on tiny precipices.

As they paddled around the rocky island, the powerful stench of bird droppings penetrated her nostrils. She glanced furtively overhead, hoping no birdie presents dropped on her.

"Reeks a little, doesn't it?" shouted Jon over the din of shrieking gulls. "The puffin nests are in those rocks. They're always on alert because of eagles." He pointed his paddle at an eagle with wings set, circling the rocks.

Seabirds floated peacefully on the water and abruptly took off. A loud commotion broke out, and Liz spotted an eagle torpedoing a gull as the bird perched on a rock. It knocked the bird over, and the eagle savaged the gull as it lay there screaming.

"Oh my God, it's eating that seagull alive! Do something!" She'd not witnessed nature's brutality since a rattler gobbled a roadrunner next to her house in Vegas. She loved Jon's ornithology world but hadn't signed on for cannibalistic bird murder.

"Survival of the fittest. That gull messed up. He should have been on his game."

She spluttered. "How can you be so cold about it? You're a bird lover."

"Hey, it's a bird-eat-bird world. Everything has to eat." He shrugged, his life vest rising with his huge shoulders. "Want to head back now?" The bird rookery was incredible and being on the ocean like this was unlike anything she'd experienced. But she preferred land that stayed still.

"No more birdicide." She forced her rubbernecking away from the cannibalizing eagle.

Jon gave her a cool look. "Birdicide is when they hurl themselves at the rocks."

She looked at him, horrified. "Seriously?"

He grinned, then turned around and paddled.

"You bullshitter!" She splashed him with her paddle.

He cringed. "Harrington, behave yourself."

As they paddled toward the inlet leading to Steller's Jay Lodge, something whooshed to her right. A mighty spray of water whizzed high into the air, then suspended for a moment, like fire retardant. As it dissipated Liz caught the bright bend of a rainbow in the spray.

"Jon, look!" Water splashed Liz as she snapped her gaze to see a long flipper slap the water again, soaking her. The knobby, uneven dorsal fin arced as it rolled into the water. The whale dove, raising a black and white mottled fluke in slow motion high in the air. Water dripped off the bottom of the massive tail as it vanished into the deep.

"Humpback! Virtuosos of the deep!" hollered Jon, pointing with his paddle.

The rest of her words caught in her throat. She let out the breath she didn't realize she'd been holding. She'd never seen anything like it.

"That one was close," Jon yelled out over the fracas of seabirds, attracted to the surfacing whale.

She found her voice after swallowing it. "That was...that was..."

His exuberance was contagious. "Should have seen your face."

She beamed. "Should have seen *yours*."

"Fifty tons of whale just soaked us." Jon whooped and laughed like a little kid seeing his first spaceship.

They paddled back to the protected inlet and Steller's Jay

Lodge and glided onto the gravel beach. Jon climbed out and held the boat for her to step out.

Thankful for the mud boots, she plopped a foot in the water to stabilize before hauling herself out. She and Jon each lifted an end and carried the kayak up the few stairs to the dock platform.

"How about a faster ride?" he tossed at her.

"I'm still in shock from the first one."

He laughed. "Weather is moving in tomorrow. I want to show you Halibut Cove while I can."

"Okay." Getting back on the ocean wasn't what she wanted at the moment, but she reminded herself she was Jon's guest, and he was excited to show her his other favorite world.

Jon steered her to a white Boston Whaler skiff with *Sea Monster* in blue on the back of the transom. He tossed in their gear and helped Liz climb aboard, then jumped in and took the helm. "Untie us from the cleats and cast off, Harrington."

Liz leaned over the side of the skiff to undo the ropes.

Jon motioned her to a cushioned seat in front of the captain's chair and cranked the motors. He maneuvered the skiff away from the dock at no wake speed until they reached the mouth of the inlet. Once out in the bay, he opened up the motors and pointed the boat north along the coast. The boat skimmed still, calm waters while a lazy mist of fog hovered over Homer across the bay.

After motoring a short distance, Jon turned the boat into a narrow inlet. Halibut Cove was a collection of mostly homes and art galleries nestled behind the rocky east coast of the bay. Quaint houses on stilts lined the shores between stands of spruce and hemlock. A series of boardwalks made of word connected everything well above the tidal waters.

Jon eased the boat over to a nearby dock, where they tied it off and left the boat. He led Liz along a series of walkways that fronted several art galleries, everything from octopus ink paintings to encaustic wax seascapes and fused glass in every kind of sea creature imaginable.

She'd spotted a beautiful glass puffin Jon had admired in

one shop. On impulse, she told him she forgot something and to wait for her on a bench. She ran back to the shop, bought the puffin, and meticulously inserted it in her day pack.

When she returned, Jon stood at ease while three women surrounded him, laughing and flirting.

As she approached, Jon's face lit up. "Good talking to you, ladies. Don't forget what I said about the Kenai Fjords tour out of Seward."

"And we won't forget the lovely man who told us about it." The redhead gave him a dimpled smile, eyeing him like a buttery, blueberry scone.

Liz knew that mouthwatering look and shocked herself at the temptation to hurl the woman off the boardwalk. Instead, she linked Jon's elbow in a classic *he's-mine-hands-off* move. "Ready for lunch?"

He grinned at the women who eyeballed him like a pack of she-wolves targeting a mate. "Have a good rest of your trip, ladies."

"If all Alaskan men are like you, we sure will," the redhead purred. She and the other two she-wolves wiggled their asses in the opposite direction.

"Phew, cool me off." The redhead fanned herself as they moseyed away.

Liz marveled at how Jon seemed oblivious to them. Maybe he was used to women fawning over him.

They returned to the boat, and Jon motored a short distance to a dock with a sign that read, "Parking for The Saltry only." A guy on the dock took the bow and stern lines Liz tossed and tied them off.

"Harrington, you're a good deckhand." Jon removed his life vest and straightened, the sun highlighting every luscious part of him. He stepped out of the boat, helped her out, then guided her up the metal ramp to the restaurant.

"Have a seat." Jon motioned to an outdoor table on the spacious balcony overlooking the cove.

When they settled in, a server asked what they wanted for beverages.

"It's five o'clock somewhere, right?" Liz smiled at the lanky guy she figured was a college student, judging by his *Alaska Pacific University* T-shirt.

His mouth lifted in a flirtatious smile. "It is in the lower forty-eight on the east coast. You're good to go."

"In that case, I'll have a chilled Riesling."

Jon declined because he had to drive the boat. He ordered bay oysters to share, and each ordered the seafood chowder with salmon and halibut.

"You'll have your fill of halibut and salmon by the time the weekend's over." He tilted his head and leaned back, studying her. "Do all guys flirt with you?"

"Do all women flirt with you?"

"Women become strangely infatuated with Alaskan men when they tour around up here."

"Why do you think that is?" she asked innocently, knowing full well why.

"The stereotype. The whole romantic adventure thing… bush pilots, mushers, men in the wilderness, yaddayadda." He sipped his water. "You don't strike me as the type to fall for all that."

"Depends on the guy." She smiled as the server set the wine in front of her. "How do you know Risa and Spencer?"

"From UAF in Fairbanks. I needed roommates to help pay my mortgage. We lived together a couple years. Then Risa's parents passed and left her the lodge, and they moved down here."

"Are you paying for our stay?"

"My buddy prepaid it."

"In that case, I need to pay—"

"It's taken care of." Jon nodded at the server, setting a plate of oysters on the table.

"Then at least let me get this meal." She eyed the oysters. Not her favorite, but she wouldn't insult Jon by not trying one.

"I won't argue." He plucked an oyster, dribbled it with melted garlic butter, then emptied the shell's contents into his mouth.

"Good, because you wouldn't win." She raised her wine glass. "Here's to eagle bullies and whale surprises."

Jon toasted with his water glass. "Way cool, you have to admit."

She inhaled the aroma of the steamy chowders the server set in front of them.

"You know what these are?" He nodded at the oysters. "Aphrodisiacs."

"I've heard that." She picked one up, scrutinized it. "So. What are your long-term plans?"

He gave her a surprised look. "Long-term plans? What is this, a job interview?" He paused. "I don't know, finish my ornithology doctorate. Get more fire investigation experience."

"If you had your pick of anything in the world, what would make you leap out of bed every morning?"

"Playing guitar and singing." He stared off at the cove.

"Not firefighting?"

"That was another life. Firefighting taught me life is a gift and time is precious."

"Ditto," said Liz.

"What about you?" he asked.

"Owning a dance studio. And owning a winery."

Jon stared at her as if she'd shifted into a mermaid. "A winery? It's a ton of work. Keeping grapevines alive, nursing them through drought, hoping they don't burn in a wildfire, like what happened to several vineyards last year."

"How do you know about all that?" She sent him a long look.

"My parents ran a winery in Sonoma. I grew up in a vine-yard. Believe me, I know the work involved."

"I didn't know that about you. You've never mentioned it." Her brain whirred with that bombshell. "Just like you never mentioned your musical talents."

He shrugged. "My folks left the vineyard to my brother and me. I didn't want to stay in California, so he runs it. When I landed in Alaska, I didn't want to leave." He settled back in his chair. "Tell me about this dance studio."

"Just something I've always thought about."

"What's involved?"

"Upfront money, like anything else." She studied her wine glass. "The Vegas business will get me there. Along with money I've saved from fighting fires and dancing."

"Ah." He stayed quiet for a long while.

She sensed he held back what he really wanted to say.

He downed the last of his water. "Ready to go? We can check out a stream where red salmon spawn. Get in on some salmon sex."

She angled a brow. "Those oysters did a number on you."

He chuckled. "Hey, it's fun to observe a little fish sex now and then."

"That's twisted." She smirked.

They finished their meal, Liz gave her credit card to the server, and Jon left cash on the table for a tip.

Once they settled onboard the boat, Jon told Liz to sit on the bench behind the captain's seat, as the seas had kicked up in the usual afternoon chop. He swung the Boston Whaler out to the open bay and took it slow on the way back.

The Boston Whaler took the four-foot waves in stride. Now and then, the bow slid down a five-footer, splashing her. The water was frigid, but no way would she complain.

Jon slowed the boat abruptly, and Liz peered ahead. A wall of white enveloped them. "Fog. Don't worry, I've got this," Jon yelled.

She nodded but tensed as the boat entered the heavy fog bank. The creepiest feeling she'd ever had in her life was not being able to see where they were going while riding the rough seas. She clutched the gunwale hard.

Don't panic, Jon knows what he's doing.

Her heart sped, and she glanced nervously from side to side, unable to see the next wave slosh against the hull.

Jon peered at the compass and fiddled with a small monitor. He glanced back and winked at her, then tapped the screen. "Chart plotter. Don't worry, I know where we're going." He didn't look rattled in the least.

What choice did she have but to trust him a hundred percent? She knew nothing about oceans. *Give me a desert, and I can get us anywhere.* She chose to suck it up like she'd been a subarctic mariner all her life. *I fight fire for chrissakes.*

Liz squinted out the port side, knowing the coastline of rocks was close. She'd studied them as they'd motored past earlier. Rocks jutted up from the ocean like barnacled fingers trying to break free of the sea.

Sure enough, dark things loomed out of the fog. The dreaded rocks. *Oh, no.*

"Jon? Uh, Jon?" She pointed left, then hung on as the boat took waves that sloshed her legs.

He nodded and again pointed at the chart plotter. Obviously, he knew the rocks were there.

Liz closed her eyes, clutching her seat so hard, her fingers numbed.

"Harrington, we're here." Jon grinned at her as she opened her eyes.

They'd left the fog bank and were at the mouth of the inlet leading to Steller's Jay Lodge. She breathed a sigh of relief as Jon motored them along the narrow inlet and parked the boat at the dock.

Liz climbed out of the boat, drenched. "Captain Silva, great job out there," she gushed.

He grinned as he shut down the motors and flipped switches on the dash. "That's why God made compasses and chart plotters." He stepped from the boat to the dock.

She took in his mariner vibe—rosy cheeks and new beard and mustache. Her heart turned inside out. "If you don't mind, I'll jump in the shower to clean up a little."

"Knock yourself out. I'm taking a quick walk before dinner."

"To get in on some salmon sex?" She gave him a coy look.

He laughed. "I get my thrills where I can," he teased, unzipping his day pack and lifting out a revolver.

Her eyes bugged. "Whoa, I didn't know you had a Ruger with you."

"You know your guns."

"I know that's an SP 101, double action .357 magnum revolver."

Jon gave her an adoring look, as if she were Venus descending in a cloud of gun smoke.

"It's a cop-daughter thing. He taught me about firearms. I take it, this one's for animals?"

"Most black bears here run from humans. They have plenty to eat with the salmon and low tide pickings. It's the sows with cubs you have to watch out for. I use it to scare bears, not shoot them. This wouldn't do the trick anyway." He popped out the shell chamber to check the loads, then snapped it back in. He returned it to his day pack and slung his pack over a shoulder.

"Enjoy your bear-aware hike. Hope you won't need your Ruger."

"Enjoy your shower." He gave her a salacious smile and strolled off the boardwalk.

She scrutinized his hind side as he moved along the dirt path and disappeared into dense alder and spruce. The more time she spent with him, the more her dam of resistance leaked.

What'll I do if the dam breaks?

Retreating to the cabin, she heaved her day pack onto a chair and peeled off her wet clothes. She stepped into the hot shower, letting the pulsating, delicious water beat on her head.

"Ahhhh…" she groaned, breathing in the soothing steam.

Visions of Jon cavorted in her brain. She loved his little-boy wonder look when the whale had surfaced…how hot he'd looked driving the boat like a steadfast sea captain, commanding waves with his *I've-got-everything-under-control* style.

He sprung to life in her mind as she glided soap along her skin. An ache pulsed down low. No guy had ever made her feel this erotic. She traversed a slippery glacier, falling for her former crew boss. She envisioned him wreaking havoc on her body as she smoothed her palms over slick skin, loving the trickle of water between her fingers and between her legs.

Trickles led to rivulets, which could result in a raging torrent.

If this dam breaks, I'm a goner.

Thoughts of Jon had erupted into an erotic sensation as she closed her eyes and climbed a precipitous slope. Swells of pleasure burst from Girl Parts Headquarters…wave after delicious wave. She astonished herself at the intensity of her insides contracting and pulsating…in a shower all by herself.

*Oh, God. My damn dam burst…*and all she did was think about Jon Silva.

Yep, she was a goner.

CHAPTER 21

*J*on's phone had vibrated all morning. He should have left the stupid thing at the cabin but wanted to take photos of Liz.

He followed the dirt path that led to another cove and roamed a long, gravel beach. There was better cell reception on a rocky point, called Otter Rock, with a clear line of sight to the cell tower in Homer. As much as he wanted to distance himself from work, he still had to keep in touch with Keaton for the two days he'd be gone.

Once at Otter Rock, four cell service bars showed on his phone. He scrolled through his messages. A few from Keaton. And Roxanne. Two from Simone, relaying info she'd found investigating two suspicious fires south of Rockfish. And her sultry tone…*See you when you get back. My offer still stands. Bye.*

The woman was persistent, he'd give her that. But she was too big city for his taste. Another lower forty-eight metro girl wanting a romantic fling with an Alaskan guy so she could post it on social media. He'd read the posts: *"Had a fantastic adventure with a daring, muscled Adonis-of-the-North. He scooped me up with one arm, and I was breathless as he cruised through glistening snow on his sled pulled by a team of huskies…"*

When in reality, the Alaskans he knew—both men and women—were wildly passionate about slaying fish, hiking, boating, snowboarding, snow machining, and living the Alaskan dream with a dash of crazy mixed with good humor and lust for adventure.

In the old days, he would have taken Simone up on her flirtations.

He was a different man now, tired of the same-old, same-old of telling women what they wanted to hear to have sex with them, like a man whore. Then afterwards, the emptiness and loneliness…life going nowhere. He was so done with that pointless lifestyle.

He scowled at a text message from Roxanne and reluctantly tapped it.

I miss you. I still love you. We need to talk.

Her issues weren't his problem. He heaved out a heavy sigh, poised to delete the rest of her voice messages, but something in his gut told him not to.

Instead, he tapped his photo gallery to see Liz's startled expression when the whale had surfaced, her horrified expression when the eagle chowed down on the gull, and her awe at everything else. He'd taken the photos without her noticing, to capture her sense of wonder.

He admired her inner beauty. He wanted her; not just sexually—he longed to share himself with her. He was easy and relaxed around her. Didn't feel tense and uptight like he did around some women. She understood him. She was kind, funny, and intelligent. He respected her brevity and integrity as a firefighter. Her approval meant more than all the women he'd ever been with rolled into one.

And that killer body of hers frankly did him in. _Big time._

After what happened last fire season, he'd believed she was too good for him and he didn't deserve her. He recalled her tenacity in reassuring and consoling him when he'd plummeted to rock bottom last year. She'd seen him at his worst and hadn't judged him for it.

No woman had ever done that.

He shared a cabin with her last night and didn't have sex. Most guys would accuse him of being one match short of ignition and undeserving of his share of testosterone. He figured he deserved a Congressional medal of honor for his self-discipline.

As he moved along the boardwalk near their cabin, he set his sights on the lovely vision coming toward him, fresh and glowing.

She smiled and waved.

And that alone warmed his guilt-ridden, undeserving heart.

*L*iz always tingled when Jon came toward her with his easy stride. This weekend had presented him to her in a different light. The guy brimmed with such diverse skills and talent, it blew her mind. She knew none of this when they'd worked together last year.

"Being on the water sapped my energy. I'm a new woman after my shower." *If he only knew.*

"The ocean has a way of doing that." His eyes roved her, and she noticed.

She brushed her hair back with her fingers. "Our cabin is equipped with a blow dryer. Haven't used one all summer."

He tilted his head in that cagey, Sam Elliot way. "You're pretty with your hair down."

"Thanks." Warm fuzzies skipped around a variety of her body parts.

"Heading to dinner in the main lodge?"

"Yep. Dinner's at six, right?"

He nodded. "I'm going to clean up first. Go on ahead and I'll be there in a flash."

"Okay." She turned to enjoy the finer assets of his backside, as he ambled to the cabin.

A baked bread aroma hugged her nostrils as she opened the door to the lodge. She continued through the large living room to the dining area, with floor-to-ceiling windows framing the emerald bay.

Risa greeted her. "Did you enjoy your excursions today? Jon told us a humpback broke water next to your kayak."

"I'd never seen a whale, let alone one that close."

"I'm so glad you had a good day on the water. You have perfect timing, we're getting supper on the table." Risa motioned to an empty chair, and Liz sank into it, admiring the ornate oak table that stretched on forever. Risa bent to whisper in her ear. "Did you know today is Jon's birthday?"

"What?" Liz drew back, surprised, her neck and face heating. "No, he hasn't mentioned it." *Why didn't he tell me?*

Risa gave her an eye roll. "Of course not. It isn't his style. I baked a cake, and we'll sing him Happy Birthday after dinner."

"Sounds great. Thanks, Risa." Liz combed her brain for what she could do for Jon's birthday present. She remembered the fused glass puffin she'd purchased earlier at the art shop in Halibut Cove. She'd wrap it up and give it to him.

Two older couples sat at the table.

"Hello, my name's Liz." She reached for a bottle of white wine and poured some into her glass.

All heads turned toward her. "You saw a humpback? We love watching them off the California coast," commented one of the older women Liz guessed to be in her seventies.

"Yes, it was fantastic." Liz passed a bowl of biscuits to the woman.

Risa set a large platter of beer-battered halibut and salmon in the center of the table, while Spencer set down salad. "They hang around Gull Island bird rookery this time of year. Lots of food there."

"Tell us about the whale," said a gray-haired guy with glasses.

Liz explained their experience. "…and then my boyfriend —I mean my friend, Jon—"

"I heard my name in vain," a deep voice cut in behind her.

Heat shot up her neck at Jon catching the "boyfriend" comment. For some reason, it embarrassed her, like she was being presumptuous. She avoided looking at him as he pulled out the chair and sat next to her.

"Wine?" Spencer stood behind them, holding a bottle of chardonnay.

"Fill it up. I'm not driving anywhere." Jon leaned sideways toward Liz, while Spencer filled his glass. "Hey, girlfriend," he drawled in her ear.

She hastened to explain. "Slip of the tongue—"

"I liked it," he whispered out the side of his mouth, patting her thigh under the table.

"Here's to not driving," the ruddy-faced bald guy said, clinking his glass with those around him.

The woman with snow-white hair picked up a biscuit. "How do you two know each other?"

"We're firefighters. I am, but Jon isn't. I mean he was, last year," she hastened to clarify. "Jon was my crew boss last season. That's how we met."

"You don't fight fires now?" the woman asked Jon.

He wiped his mouth with a napkin and leaned back. "Not anymore. I'm a fire investigator."

Liz knew how torn up he was after what happened last year, though they hadn't discussed it. She'd always sensed his anguish over it and had become good at reading him.

"Jon is here from Fairbanks investigating the fires, and I'm here with my crew fighting them. We had a few days off." Liz artfully led the conversation away from why Jon left firefighting. She felt mama-bear protective whenever the subject came up.

"We noticed the smoke when we landed in Anchorage, and on our drive down to Homer." The woman looked at Jon. "How do you investigate a fire?"

"We figure out the point of origin, the cause, and collect evidence. I'm on an interagency task force with state and federal agencies." He dipped a breaded, halibut chunk in tartar sauce and chomped it.

"Jon's good at investigating fires because of his many years of expertise fighting them."

He squeezed her leg, sending her appreciation for the compliment.

"You're proud of your boyfriend, I can tell." The woman smiled.

"I am." And she was.

Jon was amused at the boyfriend comment, judging by the twitches working his mouth.

Everyone finished eating, and Risa emerged from the kitchen carrying a cake in the shape of a puffin, with lit candles. Spencer and Risa led the room in singing Happy Birthday as Risa set the cake on the table in front of him.

"Make your wish and blow out the candles, Slick." Liz sat back and studied him with a curious intensity.

He blew out each candle.

Liz leaned into him. "What'd you wish for?"

Jon made a face. "I can't tell you that."

"Why didn't you mention it was your birthday?" She elbowed him in the side.

He shrugged. "Didn't want to make it a big deal."

"It's a big deal to me." His not telling her hurt her feelings.

Risa's voice called out. "Okay all, come into the living room, and we'll entertain you."

People rose from the table with their beverages and drifted into the large grand room.

Risa picked up two acoustic guitars and moved to Jon and Liz, sitting together on a loveseat. She offered one to Jon. "Are you still our featured soloist?"

Spencer piped up. "Yeah, do you still remember our Jitter Beans set from Fairbanks?"

Jon laughed. "Jitter Beans. The only place with a decent mocha north of sixty degrees latitude."

Risa nudged Jon's knee with the guitar. "Will you sing?"

"He sang at our friend's wedding and serenaded me to sleep last night." Liz winked at him. "Silva, you're wanted onstage."

He lifted his brows in resignation and rose, slipping the guitar strap over his shoulder like any seasoned performer.

She was still peeling back his layers. On all the fires they'd worked together last year, he'd never mentioned singing or playing the guitar.

Plucking strings to tune them, Jon wandered to the piano where Risa played scales. He twisted the guitar's tuning pegs until they matched the pitch of Risa's piano notes.

A fire crackled in the large stone fireplace and the room grew quiet as the three of them prepared to play. Jon glanced at Spencer. "How about our Greatest Generation medley for our California friends?"

Spencer nodded at Risa, who began playing a Frank Sinatra classic, *I've Got You Under My Skin*. When Jon sang the first few notes to Risa's accompaniment, a strong sense of déjà vu waved through Liz as she curled up in the comfy loveseat with a glass of wine. His eyes reflected the flickering flames, the way they did last year when the Aurora Crew gathered around their evening campfire for dinner.

Liz observed the pleasant faces enjoying Jon's soothing voice and Risa's piano playing. No one seemed to notice they hadn't played together in a while. When they finished, the room erupted with applause.

"You give Old Blue Eyes a run for the money, Mr. Silva," called out the gray-haired woman. "And you're much better looking."

"Thank you."

Liz reveled at how well he took compliments. She'd noticed it when he supervised the crew, accepting compliments firmly and graciously.

He sought Liz's gaze, and she loved the way his eyes crinkled on the edges. Squint lines from working outdoors for so long.

Spencer nodded acknowledgment as Jon strummed a familiar introduction and they sang harmony on *Wildfire* by Seafret. When he switched to the higher key change toward the end, his voice on those passionate high notes shot shivers up her spine. She tingled all over. Music had an intense emotional effect on her.

Only my favorite group in the entire universe. Had she mentioned that to him?

As the song progressed, Liz became entranced at the sound of their combined male voices. She loved Seafret's music. Jon must have observed her listening to it on her phone last year at fire camp. What else had he observed when they worked together?

"Okay folks, one more. I don't want to upstage what Risa and Spencer have planned."

Jon launched into the song he'd sung for the wedding, *Now and Forever*. He angled his body toward Liz, singing like he meant it.

She hadn't expected the emotion he poured into each note. He sent his song to her, his message clean and strong, emptying her mind of all else except him. The kinetic energy between them crackled with such intensity, she swore every person in the room sensed the static charge.

When he ended the song, she placed her hand on her heart, the way people do to show performers how much they love their performance.

The room exploded with applause. Jon jokingly poised to toss her his gold guitar pick, like a rock star would do to a front row groupie.

She formed a catcher's mitt with her hands, and he tossed it at her. Perfect catch. She pressed it to her chest in groupie fashion, then tucked it into the pocket of her jeans.

His heated look tore open her dam of arousal, and a tsunami rushed in. She couldn't breathe. They'd made an electric connection all right. Enough to generate their own lightning.

Their own inferno.

Was she that shallow? That all it took was for Jon to sing a love song and she'd swoon like a weak-kneed groupie? Apparently.

Blessed be the shallow minded.

In that precise moment, Liz decided what else to give Jon for his birthday.

CHAPTER 22

*J*on experienced something extraordinary singing those last two songs—an emotionally hot moment when he exchanged gazes with Liz. He'd known since last year that she liked Seafret. So, choosing one of their songs tonight was no accident. He hadn't expected such intensity of feeling when he sang—he'd meant every word.

Judging by the look on Liz's face, he'd chosen well.

As he rested the guitar in its case, Liz approached. "That was beautiful."

He studied her, loving her honest sincerity. "Thanks."

"Want to call it a night?" The twinkle in her eye shot juice to his groin.

He was more than happy to take her up on it. They said goodnight and aimed for the door, bumping into each other in their haste to leave. He sensed she was on his same channel.

When the door closed behind them, she threaded her fingers with his. "I've been dying to kiss you—"

Jon's light flashed green. The rest of her words fell into his mouth as he pressed his lips to hers, kissing her deeply. He wanted to finish what they'd started that night in the restaurant parking lot.

She dipped her tongue into his mouth with such vigor, he rapidly became aroused.

Jon lifted from her lips. "You said I'm your boyfriend. That's a step up from a Main Squeeze. I liked it." He loved his hands on her.

"Admit it, Silva. You've had a Princess Charming complex ever since I rescued you on that badass fire."

"Technically, you didn't rescue me. You helped me climb up a mountain."

"Not to split hairs, but you couldn't have climbed it without me and Tupa."

"True." He brushed her hair back behind her shoulder. "What's a Princess Charming complex?"

"Where you develop a crush on your rescuer." She observed the preening, rolling otters, then slid her gaze back to him. "Come on, let's go to the cabin. I have birthday presents for you."

She didn't have to tell him twice.

*L*iz waited for Jon to close the cabin door. He turned around, smiling that impish charm of his that had electric-charged her from day one.

"What's my present?"

"Wait here." She moved to the bedroom to retrieve the glass puffin, snatched her red fire bandana, and wrapped it around the glass. A joyful glow moved through her as she sauntered out of the bedroom and offered it to him. "Happy Birthday."

He unwrapped it and broke out in a wide grin. "The puffin from the art shop. When did you get this?"

"When you were flirting with those women who wanted to consume you for lunch."

"Hey, *they* were flirting with *me*." He held the sparkling glass up to the window, tilting the glass as the low-setting sun brought the colors to life. "A puffin cake, and now a puffin. Did you and Risa collaborate?"

"I didn't know she'd made you a puffin cake. I'm ticked at not getting the memo about your birthday."

"Didn't want you to feel obligated." He tilted it toward the light, reminding her of a little kid seeing a shooting star for the first time. "This will fit in with my mish-mash of bird stuff."

She took the piece of glass from him and set it on the table.

"Hey, wait—I was looking at it."

"I have another birthday present. I'm thinking you'll like this one. And it's not out of obligation."

"I liked the first one." He lifted puppy dog eyes, framed by dark lashes.

She dragged a chair from the tiny kitchen table, placed it in the center of the room, and led him to the chair.

"Sit," she ordered.

"What are you going to do?"

"Sit and be patient. I'll return with instructions."

"For what?" He plunked down with folded hands, an ankle on one knee. He nodded at the fireplace. "Am I allowed to light a fire?"

A little ambiance couldn't hurt. "Sure. Knock yourself out."

When he rose and moved to the fireplace, she tossed the red bandana under his chair, then retreated to the bedroom. Grabbing her day pack, she stepped into the bathroom.

Once she closed the door, her heart sped as she peered at the mirror. *Am I out of my frigging mind? He was my crew boss. If I do this, there's no going back.*

This could be a stupid move, but it was the first time she'd ever *wanted* to dance for anyone. At work she danced for money on autopilot, without emotion. This was different...she wanted to do this for Jon.

Her bells and whistles were back in Vegas, and she had little to work with. Pawing through her pack, she fished out the black lacy bra, and matching thong Angela had given her for a bridesmaid gift.

She tugged the hair tie down her ponytail and let it fall to her shoulders. It felt odd to put on this lingerie at a remote resort in Alaska, she thought, tucking each ample breast inside the lacy pushup bra.

Her neck and shoulder muscles felt tight, and she rolled her head and shoulders to loosen up. After a final once-over in the mirror, she pulled up the playlist on her phone. This called for a special song, not dance club music with the relentless, pounding beat. The song Jon sang earlier popped up, and she selected *Wildfire*, by Seafret.

She opened the door and tip-toed to the doorway of the cabin's main room in her bare feet. She studied Jon, last-minute doubt freaking her out.

If this goes south, I'll blame it on Tara.

He had binoculars trained out the picture window, but he must have sensed her leaning against the door frame because the binocs swiveled to her like a periscope. His mouth fell open. "Holy hell!"

He leaned forward in disbelief as his eyes traveled up and down her muscled, toned body, as if watching a vertical game of tennis.

"Are you flirting with me?" He stared at her, slack jawed, at the sudden appearance of her breasts spilling over the lacy pushup bra.

She moved to him, took the binoculars, and set them on the table. She then sucked in a steadying breath and moved to the front of him, assuming a straight-backed dance pose, phone in her hand.

He jerked upright and gawped like a teen at his first topless joint.

Liz had seen this expression many times, but never as cute as it was on Jon.

Straining to keep a no-nonsense demeanor, she assumed the serious persona that was part of her act. "The same rules apply here as that famous strip place in Anchorage you Alaskan guys go on about."

"The Devil's Club," he recited robotically.

"Right. Whatever." She leaned in and fixed him with a stern stare. "No touching. Only watching. I can touch, but you can't." She cupped his chin. "Copy that, Fire Inspector?"

"Love it when you talk fire." His hooded gaze drifted to her cleavage. "Are you going to—"

"Shh, no talking. Copy?" She displayed her *Do-as-I-say-or-you're-dead-meat* look, then in classic, Scarlett O'Hara fashion, she cocked a brow with resting witch face. Inside she felt as if she'd congeal into a ball of goo and melt into him.

The only way to pull this off is to maintain control of the situation. Just like at the club.

"Uh, copy." He took a deep breath, then shifted, his hands covering his expanding body part.

She bit her lip to control the urge to laugh. When she reset her resting witch face, she leaned in close. "If you tell anyone —and I mean *anyone* I did this—you'll regret the day you were born. Understand?" Each word she emphasized, slow and deliberate, in case he was hard of hearing.

Her bountiful breasts in the black, push-up bra were eye magnets, and he goggled at them.

Poor guy was in shock. *Get the fire hose ready.*

Liz snapped her fingers and formed a V, pointing them at his eyes, then back at hers. "Yoo-hoo, up here. Nod once for yes," she ordered, enunciating as if he were deaf.

He nodded once.

This was getting funnier by the second. She choked back her amusement at his still-as-stones posture and stunned expression. Adorable, for someone used to running a fire-fighting show.

But this wasn't a fire. Not yet anyway.

She tapped the song on her phone and propped it on an end table. The easy tempo allowed her to move slowly as she undulated and rotated her hips...then bent to rub his muscled thighs. She eased his knees apart and skated her palms along the insides of his thighs, stopping short of his tender man parts.

He sucked in air, his fingers twitching as he lifted his gaze.

I can't look him in the eye, or I'll get distracted.

She slid her palms up his arms and around his biceps. He was utterly delectable sitting there doing what he'd been told.

A salmon-colored sunset angled in through the window. A light designer couldn't have matched its radiance along with erogenous, fireplace flames bathing Jon in a sensual afterglow.

It made her hot.

She'd bet blackjack winnings this was exponentially more erotic for her than it was for him. Never had she felt like this when doing a lap dance.

Not like *this*. Her normal, bone-splitting confidence teetered. She hoped she wouldn't mess up.

Lap dancing was all about making the patron feel they were the most important person in the world. In the past year, when dancing for faceless men, she'd sometimes envisioned Jon in their place, to get through the difficult shifts. Now here she was in the flesh, dancing for him—no longer selling a fantasy. What she felt for him was real.

Arching her back, she leaned in and brushed her breasts lightly up his rippled stomach to his chest. Goose bumps shot up like daisies on her arms. She swung a leg over and straddled him.

His intense expression was priceless, and his breath caught; they didn't call this exotic dance for nothing.

And she was good at it.

She hooked her feet around the chair legs...arched and leaned back, snatching her firefighter bandana from under the chair. Enjoying this, she snapped the bandana taut and slipped it around the back of his neck...and tugged him to her ample cleavage.

"Blindfold me," she whispered, preparing herself for the grand finale.

He hesitated. Wordlessly, he did her bidding and slowly tied it around her head.

She sat backwards on his lap, pressed her back into his

chest, and rested her head on his shoulder. His stubble grazed her palm as she cupped his cheek and puffed hot air on his neck.

The temptation to kiss his neck and devour him like a vampire was irresistible, but she composed herself.

What was he thinking? In her experience, most guys couldn't form coherent thought by this point. When she'd asked him to blindfold her, his baffled expression threw her off-center. Not what she'd expected.

Maybe this wasn't a good idea after all.

She stood and brushed a hand lightly across his shoulders as she stepped around his chair. Her foot caught one of his flamingo legs, and she tripped.

His hand shot up like a reflex and caught her under one arm before she went down.

Damn!

Jon said nothing, but he didn't let go. Instead, he grasped her other wrist. "You don't have to do this for me," he said softly.

She froze with her mouth open. *What? He didn't like it?*

His words slammed her. This had been a mistake—an enormous lapse of judgment on her part. Regret spiked her, recoiling her stomach.

He stood and untied her bandana.

Her chest heaved from exertion as heat crawled up her neck. She squeezed her eyes closed. "Jon…"

Realization smacked her like a spruce limb. All she'd ever wanted was for Jon to see the person beneath her tough fire-fighter and squad boss façade. And now she'd sabotaged herself by mingling her dance and fire worlds. Something she swore she would never do. Self-loathing caused a tear to roll slowly down to the corner of her mouth.

He lifted her chin. "Open your eyes."

Humiliation suffused her, paralyzed her.

"Fire Woman. Look at me."

She forced her lids open, blinking back tears.

"Can I touch you now, Tiny Dancer?" he murmured.

She nodded, her face contorting.

He moved close and cradled her cheeks. "You don't have to dance for me. You won my heart a long time ago." He pulled her tight into his arms.

Liz searched for something to say and instead buried her head in his chest. Her trust in him had been a long time coming. The feelings she'd shoved aside for so long, her denial of him, and how he'd shared his world with her...tangled up and streamed out in a torrent of soul-shaking sobs. Years of endless, frustrating failure and self-disappointment rolled out in wordless emotion.

"I wanted to do something special for your birthday," she choked out.

"I get that." He kissed her forehead and tightened his hold, stroking her hair. "Don't cry, Fire Girl. Please don't cry." He moved his palm tenderly around her back, squeezing and caressing.

The music stopped, and she didn't care. She was desperate for him to keep holding her. She'd gotten used to filched gropes and touches, but she hadn't been touched like this. Such tender caresses from a man whose tough exterior commanded respect in the way he approached his work and what he demanded of himself.

God, how she'd missed the compassionate embrace of another human being...and longed for his.

Jon lifted a hand to dab her sopped cheeks with her bandana.

She let herself dive into his pools of amber—but hadn't prepared herself for what she discovered there. A tenderness she hadn't seen before.

"Fire Woman, you have skills," he said softly, smoothing his palms over her bare, sculpted back. "Your lap dance expertise is up right there with your stellar firefighting ability."

She swallowed and gave him a half smile. "It was a birthday present—and an icebreaker. Tara's idea."

"Icebreaker for what?"

She gave him a *get-with-it* look. "What do you think?"

Understanding crossed his face, and he chuckled. "Oh. Well. You of all people don't need an icebreaker. Don't get me wrong, I loved it. What guy wouldn't? But it just didn't feel right—like it cheapened what we have."

"And what is that exactly?"

He lifted a strand of hair stuck to her cheek. "I know you as Lizzy, the lion-hearted, tough, badass firefighter and squad boss—saver of men who screw up on fire. Not an exotic dancer. It's hard for me to see you that way."

"With dancing, I play a role like any onstage performance. It's not me, it's the fantasy I'm selling. Tonight? That was me. It's the only time I've ever *wanted* to lap dance."

"Do you have any idea how hard it was to leave your hotel room the night of the wedding? Do you have any freaking idea?" He up-talked at the end to emphasize his point.

"I wanted you badly that night. I was shy and nervous and drank too much because of it." She peered up at him. "Right now, I'm sober. And I'm already dressed—or rather undressed, for the occasion."

"For my birthday?"

"More like the occasion where you make love to me." Their vision locked, and her heart took a perilous leap.

His eyes darkened, searing her with want. "I've always imagined your body under the Nomex. But this…" he brushed his fingertips down the side of her rib cage and dragged them along her bare hip. "This is beyond anything I envisioned."

"I have to stay fit for both jobs."

"I see that." He brushed his lips across hers, tasting them tenderly, deliciously.

Relieved at not having blown it, Liz was where she'd wanted to be since meeting him for the first time. She could pinpoint the exact moment when their eyes had first met and they'd sparked across the training room, at the Alaska Fire Service. Just like that song her mother used to sing about seeing someone across a crowded room, from an old movie musical.

Had she known then what she knew now, she would have crossed the room and kissed him, and to heck with everything else. But circumstances and real life had complicated her world. Now she had a second chance.

It was time to uncomplicate things.

CHAPTER 23

She loved his mouth on hers. He tasted like red-velvet puffin cake and merlot with a smidge of garlic.

He took hold of her bare derriere and lifted her, and she locked her legs around his waist. She wouldn't stop kissing him while he carried her into the bedroom. Her aim was to make up for lost time. No doubt it was his, too.

He set her gently on the bed and tugged off his shirt. "I want you to be absolutely sure about this." He stood there in his low-slung jeans, revealing that well-defined guy arrow that aimed south.

"I'm beyond absolutely sure." She admired the wing tats that spiraled his forearms, and the flame tat that crept over his left shoulder to his chiseled back.

"Told you before. I won't tangle with the daughter of a cop." His voice grew husky.

"I like your style." She rose to her knees on the edge of the bed, moving her palms around his rippled stomach, dipping into every solid muscle. Carefully, as if exploring unfamiliar terrain to fight a fire, she navigated his body, moving her hands along his waist, fingers tracing the mellow indent on each side of his hip.

"I liked that you did what I told you to do. Turned me on, big time," she murmured, kissing his chest. "Because I always had to follow your orders when you were my crew boss."

"Glad you did. I wouldn't have enjoyed firing this cute little ass." He reached around and caressed her bare cheeks. "Oh God, I've wanted to touch these for so damn long."

He palmed her shoulders and slid them down her arms, the same way she'd done to him. He bent to exhale hot air on her neck.

She made a sharp intake of breath. "Copycat."

"I don't have to copy your moves. I have my own. Now it's time for you to do what I say."

Liz gave him her stink-eye. "What if I don't want to?"

"Do you trust me?"

"Didn't used to," she drawled, as if there were an unexplained puzzle behind her words.

"That's what kept us apart. That and my stupidity." He kissed her neck and skimmed his lips over the tops of her breasts, still in their lacy, pushup bra. "Do you trust me now?"

"Getting there." Her thoughts became shipwrecked by his scrumptious mouth roaming the length of her, kissing every inch along the way. He stoked the embers of flame rising inside her.

She let it burn. No way did she want *this* fire contained.

He shot her a mercurial smile that sent her pulse racing. "My turn to tantalize you."

"Is that what I did?" she purred, knowing full well what she freaking did.

He traced her clavicle with his forefinger and traced the curves of her breasts, gentle like an artist's delicate brushstroke. He swept his lips over her mouth, testing and tasting, then slipped his fingers under her thong, lightly massaging her.

"Oh-h-h-h… " Her body arched at the incredible sensation of him knowing precisely where to touch.

She spoke into his lips. "I want to unwrap you like a chocolate truffle. Off with your pants."

"That's what all the women say," he teased, lifting a packet from his pocket before she unzipped and yanked his jeans down with the force of an ocean wave. "I like a woman with determination." He kicked them away.

She eyed his form-fitting, dark gray boxers. "Oh, I'm determined, all right."

"Finish it," he breathed, sloping his dark heat at her.

With pleasure. She settled her hands on either side of his waist and tugged down his boxers, freeing the rest of him. He was more than ready for her. Admiring his muscled anatomy, she reached around and cupped his fabulous ass, incredulous at how firm it was.

"Let's get rid of this." He unclasped her bra, letting it fall.

Self-conscious for reasons she couldn't fathom, she wrapped her arms around him to draw him close.

"No." He pulled away from her. "I want to look at you. And please get off your knees. I'll *never* ask you to get on your knees for me."

He stood her on the floor and kissed his way around each breast, then skimmed his lips along her neck and up to meet hers.

She whispered into his lips. "Haven't done this in a while."

"Me neither. Doesn't matter." Twilight glinted in his eyes as he edged her back on the bed and eased off her thong.

He tore open a packet with his teeth and moved on top of her. She kissed him as he eased in gently, a little at a time, supporting his weight on his elbows.

Her nails dug into his rear, leaving marks she hoped wouldn't scar him for life. She let herself smolder as he began to move.

"Oh, Liz…" he breathed out, his lips searing a path along her neck.

She matched him stroke for stroke. Their combined power jumped the legs of the poster bed across the wood floor. The brute force of two firefighters making love made her giggle.

He laughed with her. "Whoa, Harrington, slow down. We'll wind up in the ocean." He replaced his forceful movements with a slow, gentle intensity.

Her need for release erupted like magma from a volcano.

She blew apart, and her senses shattered. Torrents of emotion orbited wave after wave of pleasure that had her trembling. She swore this was the most mind-shattering, unforgettable climax ever recorded in the annals of human evolution.

In my evolution, for dang sure.

She let out a shuddering breath, while Jon burned himself into her.

After he released, he collapsed on her until his breathing slowed. His chest heaved in perfect synchronization with hers. Their hearts conversed in their own language, with a rapid one-two beat.

She kissed him, then curled into the curve of his body.

His arm came around her, and he pressed her against him. "That was incredible, Harrington."

"Ditto, Silva," she groaned out, satiated in a way she never knew possible.

He waited while their breathing calmed.

"When did you decide to dance for me?"

"When you unicorned me with your last song. I'd never lap danced outside of the club."

"Unicorned you? In that case, I'm honored." He propped himself up, leaning on an elbow. "Where did you get that hot costume?"

"It's lingerie. Bridesmaid gift from Angela."

"I'd love to see the rest of your lingerie…with you in it."

She chuckled. "Happy Birthday, Silva. I miss fighting fire with you."

"Me, too. Mind if we talk about that?" He quirked his brows, his eyes probing hers.

This discussion had been a long time coming. She held a forefinger to his lips. "No more words. Make love to me again…and again…and again…" Words meant thought, and that was the last thing she wanted right now. Their touches were their words.

He moved over her. "I can't get enough of you."

She sensed him ready again and welcomed him inside of

her. Afterwards, she drifted off in his arms, wondering how she'd ever slept without his comfy body melded to hers.

They both wanted this, needed this—the intimacy to lie naked with each other, their vulnerabilities and underbellies all raw and exposed.

Trusting one another.

A long time coming.

CHAPTER 24

*J*on rose early to get a jump on the day since he and Liz were driving back to Rockfish to return to their work worlds. He quietly dressed, letting her sleep, and slipped out the door. He texted Keaton to check on the status of their arson investigation, then aimed to get coffee and find out what Risa had for breakfast.

Keaton texted back there were no new breaks in the case. Just two new starts south of Rockfish that fire crews managed to put out. He did say Dave Doss and Ryan O'Connor had managed full containment of the Swiftcurrent and Riverview Estates Fires, but the Crane Lake Fire that had crept along for days in the Kenai Wildlife Refuge was now heading toward the Sterling Highway.

Simone and Keaton handled the workload during Jon's absence, but Keaton said he'd be glad when Jon returned, so Simone would stop hitting on him. He followed his text with a winking smiley face. Then sent another.

That woman is perpetually horny.

This one made Jon laugh out loud.

The steady rain pooled on the cedar as Jon strode toward the lodge. The gray overcast shielded the mountains and fog hovered over the bay as wind slapped waves onto the gravel beach. He'd become so preoccupied with Liz, he hadn't thought to check the weather. Or maybe it was more that he hadn't wanted to. He enjoyed this quality time together with her. He'd always figured if they could get time alone, things would work out between them.

He only wished he could change her mind about her other job in the off-season.

He opened the door to the main lodge, welcoming the heat from a cheery fire in the hearth. Voices hummed in conversation at the breakfast table.

Risa greeted him as she poured a coffee. "Hey, Jon."

"What's a guy around here have to do to get coffee and a muffin?" he greeted the two older couples at the table.

Spencer breezed in, dripping in his rain gear, holding up a large bucket of blue mussels. "Mike the Mussel Man boated these over from Halibut Cove before the gale kicked up this morning."

"Fantastic, we'll have them for dinner tonight." Risa took the bucket into the kitchen.

"A gale? How long is it supposed to last?" asked Jon.

"NOAA marine forecasts say up to thirty-six hours. Wind gusts up to forty-five knots with thirteen-foot seas. There's a small craft advisory." Spencer took off his raincoat and hung it on the rack next to the front door. "Let me guess, you both have to work tomorrow morning."

Jon raised his brows. "Yep."

"Sorry, buddy. You aren't going anywhere for a while."

"I'd better tell Liz."

Risa sailed out of the kitchen with a tray holding two steaming coffee mugs and a small plate of fresh-baked blueberry muffins, covered with plastic wrap. "Here, Jon, take this to your cabin. Figured you and Liz might want a private breakfast." She squeezed his hand.

He smiled appreciatively, that Risa knew this time with Liz was special. "Thanks, Rees. You're the best." He took the tray and headed to the door.

Spencer opened it for him. "I can tell it's killing you to stay longer."

"Breaking my heart. Thanks, bro." Jon feigned a sad face as he exited the lodge and headed back to the cabin, secretly elated. A hard, cool rain splashed off the plastic wrap covering the tray.

He welcomed this kind of weather when he didn't have to travel. Storms forced things to slow down. As he sloshed along the saturated boardwalk, he pondered last night's long-awaited change in his relationship with Liz. He perceived it as a breakthrough and valued his time alone with her.

Last night when she'd appeared in the doorway mostly naked—he had an erotic sensation picturing her—he didn't know what to think.

When she'd turned on the music and gave him marching orders to sit and not touch her, he figured things out quick. And it blew his mind. A mixed bag of bring it on mashed up with she didn't need to be doing this—struck a dissonant chord, like wrong notes in a song.

In his humble opinion, her dance ability seemed wasted. When she'd lap danced, he loved the turn-on and admired her incredible expertise—oh God, how he loved it—but he didn't see her that way. He must be nuts. What red-blooded male would tell a woman to stop lap dancing for him? *Cripes.*

He vowed never to tell any living male he'd stopped a lap dance. Men everywhere would question his sanity. Nope. That little detail must remain between him and Liz.

The wind had picked up, blowing his drenched hair. He reached the cabin and opened the door. Balancing the tray with both hands, he kicked it closed.

"Jon?" Liz called out to him from the bedroom.

"Coffee and blueberry muffins." He set the tray on the kitchen table and removed his dripping jacket. He shook the droplets from his hair and ran his fingers through it.

She emerged from the bedroom in the thin night shirt that had driven him insane their first night. Her nipples poked through as she padded over to him, smiling, hair all messed up. She moved into him and wound her arms inside his jacket and around his back.

"Ooh, you're all wet." She tugged his face down to hers, nipped his lower lip, and slipped her tongue into his mouth.

Instant boner. What an idiot he'd been not to make his move sooner. Like a year ago.

God, I love this, I love...wait...am I ready for the L word? One step at a time, one step at a time...

Moaning, he broke the kiss. "It's pounding down out there."

"I see that. You taste like coffee. I want some." She let go and took the mug he offered.

"We can't leave yet. There's a severe storm, and no boats are crossing the bay."

"You're kidding." She wandered to the big picture window, a lovely vision in daylight. The bay had morphed into a white froth of pissed-off water. Waves crashed onto the gravel beach, and boats bounced on their moorings. "I hope the otters are okay."

"Being stuck here isn't an issue, but you're worried about the otters?" He stood next to her and put his arm around her waist, watching the storm with her.

"We have to stay here another day?"

"Yep."

"Gee, that's unfortunate."

"Yeah. Isn't it though?" He viewed their forced proximity of this weekend as nature's way of saying they belonged together.

"Okay, Tiger, in that case let's be bed buddies. We need more sleep, don't you think?" She gave him an innocent look and led him to the bed they now shared. She stopped next to it and pulled off her shirt. Standing naked in front of him, she cradled his face to plant a solid kiss on his lips, turning his knees into jelly.

Damn. Now he understood how Delilah had weakened Samson.

She helped him undress, and they fell into bed, mauling each other. Jon made love to her as many times as he could. Not once did she tell him to stop. Afterward, she spooned into him, all warm and soft. He treasured the freedom of moving his hands over her at will, marveling that he could now touch her in this intimate way.

The last time he'd been this relaxed and content was...well, he couldn't remember. All he knew was, everything was good now. The woman of his dreams was in his arms, and it felt right.

She felt right.

Jon pressed Liz tight against him, and she mewed a cute little moan, her body molding perfectly to his. One of his favorite songs, *Feels Like Home*, rolled around in his thoughts. He hummed it softly until drifting off, the wind whistling around them.

CHAPTER 25

*L*iz's eyelids fluttered open to rain slapping the windows of their cozy cabin. Jon slept next to her, lying on his side, facing her. She wanted to touch him but not wake him. Instead, she settled for studying his scruffy jaw she could nibble on forever.

She noticed their clothes neatly arranged side by side on wall hooks, a hint of their intimacy. His shirt and jacket tucked next to hers. She wanted more of this. Afraid of wanting more, but dammit, it felt good. Natural. Like they belonged together.

She was punch drunk with infatuation after their first official sleep-together. Not what she'd expected.

They'd made love most of the night and slept a good part of the day, like a couple of slugs. She chuckled, recalling his expression when she'd sashayed out in her underwear. What she assumed would end in disaster hadn't. Her emotion had roared into an inferno that lasted the night, and today she rode high on euphoria.

Where do we go from here? When they leave this beautiful nirvana, what then? She didn't want to spoil it by thinking about it. This time with Jon was Shangri-La. Nothing would ruin it if she could help it.

She reached out to caress the strong tendons in the back of

his neck, then ran her palm around his shoulder winding up on his pectoral. She traced the lines around it.

Jon shifted position, and his lids eased open. He ran his fingers lightly over her face. "Isn't it great to lie here all comfy cozy in this hella storm?" He slid his palm up the side of her leg, dipped it at her waist and eased his other hand between her legs. "Don't hate me, but I want you again."

She pressed close, loving that he was ready for her. "Why would I hate you for *that*?"

He made leisurely love to her, taking his sweet time with every kiss, lick, nip, and caress.

And then they did it all over again and lay back, panting.

Liz groped for her wristwatch on the nightstand and squinted at it. She groaned at the late afternoon hour. "I have to call Tara and tell her we won't make it by morning."

"Text her instead. I can never get enough cell bars to make calls from here. We have to head out to Otter Rock for better reception."

"Where's that?"

"A short hike over to the next cove."

She rolled back to him. "Mmm, I don't want to leave this bed with you in it."

He traced his fingers over the curve of her ass. "Me neither. Kiss me, Fire Woman."

They made love for the thousandth time before getting up and going to dinner at the main lodge. She could make love with him a thousand times more.

🔥

*J*on had his fill of mussels, judging by the stacks of shells on his plate. He noticed Liz liked them too, along with sourdough bread and homegrown vegetables from Risa's garden.

Spencer finished turning the crank of a bucket full of homemade custard ice cream. Risa spooned it into bowls, and everyone helped themselves and took seats around the room. The California guests had stayed another night, too.

Jon noted Liz had taken a liking to Risa. They'd talked non-stop through dinner while he'd caught up with Spencer.

"Tonight, I figured we'd dance to work off the ice cream," announced Risa. "Ladies and gents, we have a special treat, a professional dancer in our midst. Liz has agreed to show us some ballroom dance steps."

Jon drew back in surprise. "You never mentioned you did ballroom dancing."

"I worked at a dance studio teaching classes a few years back."

He pointed his thumb at her. "Hey, this woman can dance, she's brilliant." He bit his tongue before saying *and boy, can she lap dance, but she's too talented for it.*

"Oh, please dance for us," the white-haired woman called out to Liz, and others joined in.

"Do that dance you showed me on your phone," suggested Jon.

Liz stared at him and stood. "Risa, do you know any Sarah Brightman songs?"

"I have some of her sheet music." Risa moved off to find it and situated herself at the piano. "Spence, roll up the center rug."

Jon rose to help him roll it up and drag it to the side of the room.

"You going to dance in those?" Jon motioned at the flip-flops she'd worn to dinner.

"Probably not a good idea. Thanks, Slick." She wrinkled her nose at him and kicked them off. As she moved to the center of the room, she reached up and put her hair in a messy ponytail.

The room was full of expectation, and she glanced shyly at the guests. When she caught Jon's eye, he nodded encouragement.

"I performed this while studying dance at UNLV years ago.

Hope I still remember it." She assumed a professional stance and arched her back, arms forming a perfect oval.

Risa played the intro, and Spencer joined in with his cello.

When Liz took her first steps, Jon became captivated—she was the most intoxicating person in the room. Her twirls, spins, and moves with such disciplined muscle control aroused him so much, he became hot for her all over again.

When she finished, the room erupted in applause. Liz picked up her flip-flops and sat next to Jon, her chest heaving. A jubilant, rosy glow filled her cheeks.

"Wow, Harrington." He put his arm around her and squeezed her shoulder. "You blew my mind."

She beamed, and her exuberance excited him. "Thank you."

Risa came over and squatted in front of Liz and Jon. "At dinner, you mentioned you'd love to have your own dance studio."

Liz laughed. "Only every day of my life."

"I have a friend in Fairbanks who's selling hers. She's moving to the lower forty-eight. It's large and has a solid clientele." She smiled at Jon, then at Liz. "I'm not sure what your situation is, but if you're interested, I could get her info for you."

Liz looked like a caribou caught in headlights. "Oh, gosh. I'm not sure…" She trailed off.

Jon maintained a neutral expression. No way would he pressure her into doing something she didn't want to. Because they were intimate now, didn't mean she had to change her plans for him.

"No pressure. If you're interested, let me know. It's an excellent opportunity. I don't mean to be pushy, but when I watched you dance tonight—you should be on a Broadway stage and running your own studio."

Jon nodded agreement and kept his mouth shut.

"Thank you." Liz blushed. A rarity, Jon noted.

Risa joined Spencer at the piano, and they played a waltz. "Come on, all, get up and dance," Risa called out.

The couples took to the floor.

Jon offered her his hand. "Want to cut a rug like we did at the wedding?"

She gazed at him as if he were the only guy in the world. "I'd be honored."

He loved how she eyed him like a succulent piece of shrimp. He pulled her up, then swung her close. "You're a damn talented dancer, Harrington," he breathed in her ear.

"And you're a damn magnificent lover," she breathed back. "Thank you so much for this weekend. It's been…indescribable." She hugged him.

"My sentiments exactly."

He kissed her, not caring who noticed him touch his lips to hers.

CHAPTER 26

$\mathcal{L}$iz lit a fire in the hearth of their cozy cabin, while the wind whistled, and rain walloped the windows. The flame responded to her careful control.

"I love it when I can command fire."

Jon came from behind and nuzzled her neck. "And I love watching you dance. I want a selfie to remind me of our weekend. Back up, baby." He lifted his phone.

"Make sure you text it to me." She backed into him as he held the phone at arm's length.

He goosed her behind to get her to laugh and took several more photos. He then turned her lips to his and kissed her while he took more.

"I have another reminder for you, but you must promise not to show *anyone*." Liz produced her phone and tapped a boudoir photo album, taken last winter to promote the dance club. She tapped her favorite: Wearing a lacy white thong with a full-length faux fur coat opened to expose her bare breasts, as she arched against a dilapidated horse wagon, surrounded by snow.

She held out her phone, and his eyes nearly snapped out of his head.

"Good God, woman." He snatched the phone and used his thumb and forefinger to zoom the screen, zeroing in on her standout nipples. "Good Lord, check these babies out." He pulled back to examine them in situ.

"You're such a perv." She lightly slapped his arm. "A bunch of us drove up to Truckee to do this shoot with a professional photographer."

"In the Sierra Nevada? Must have been cold. Your nipples have hard-ons."

"Yours would too, at ten degrees." She snatched the phone back and sniffed. "I suffer for my art."

He grabbed at it. "No, I'm not done!"

"Hold on, Horn Dog." She retrieved another photo of herself lying on her stomach, propped on elbows facing the camera. The high camera angle emphasized her bare ass. Another naked photo had her standing sideways to the camera, a cowboy hat dipped forward, her body in an erect dance pose.

He took the phone from her. "I've always thought your perfectly shaped ass looked like an upside-down heart."

"How long have you thought that?"

"From day one. Can you sext me these?"

"Make a pinky promise and swear on your grandmother's grave you won't show these to a blessed soul. Or I *will* hurt you, Slick."

"Pinky promise. I'm the only one who will see these. I'll guard them with my life." He gaped at them, mesmerized, as if beholding a pot of gold.

"Stop drooling on my phone, Silva, it's not waterproof," she said, delighted he enjoyed her photos. She snatched her phone and texted the photos to his .

He lifted his head with the hooded desire that sent squiggles up her spine. "God, now I want you all over again." He motioned at the sizable black bear rug in front of the fireplace.

"I take it Alaskan guys fantasize about having women on bear rugs next to fires."

"Yep. We're not complicated."

"You're a cliché." She offered him a cat-eyed look.

"And proud of it. Make yourself comfortable on yonder rug, and I'll pour us a Disaronno on the rocks."

"You're a high roller, Silva. All right, I'll be your cliché tonight." She wandered into the bedroom and removed her clothes. On impulse, she pulled her yellow fire shirt from her pack and put it on, buttoning the lower two buttons. She swaggered back out, wearing only the shirt.

Jon lounged on the bear rug with their drinks. He fixated on her, eyes darkening. "Look at you, sexing the Nomex. Come here, Squad Boss."

"Always been curious—why did you make me a squad boss last year?"

"You want the truth, or the company line I told the fire bosses?"

She sauntered over and stood over him. "What do you think?"

"Told them you're strong, smart, and you had terrific leadership skills. I liked your take-no-shit vibe and knew the guys on the crew would listen to you. Back then, I wasn't aware of your *other* skill sets. Not that it would have made a difference."

Licking her lips in a teasing manner, she lifted her bare foot and rubbed his swollen crotch, making him moan.

"Get down here, Harrington."

The black, silky fur and sparkle of the fire heightened her want of him. After all, it was fire that had brought them together in the first place. She kissed him slow, soft, and sensual. When she drew back with her fire shirt half-open, his expression changed to raw desire.

She broke out in smiles, letting her heart bump around.

Jon set down his empty glass and skittered it across the hardwood floor. He eased her fire shirt off one shoulder and kissed her smooth skin. He unbuttoned her shirt and slipped it off.

She lowered herself to the luxurious rug and tugged him down on top of her. "I want you inside me."

He looked surprised. "What? No foreplay? What happened to the timeless art of seduction? You greedy little minx," he teased.

"Don't make me suffer, Slick." She fumbled his pants open and pushed everything low enough for him to enter her.

"I want to hear you call my name again." His voice dripped with arousal as he took his time to kiss her all over. He reached her stomach and inched his way down until he landed on her one spot.

"Jon!" she cried out. She clutched his head and tugged him up to her.

"Knew I'd get you to yell my name." He nipped her neck and buried himself inside her as much as physics would allow without sending them both to the emergency room. It didn't take long for each of them to shoot their fireworks.

Afterward, they intertwined like pretzels while she rubbed his muscled back. His gentle touch had catapulted her libido to the stratosphere so many times this weekend she lost count. She felt squishy from sex, her bones so pliable, she could wrap herself around Jon like putty.

This is the way it's supposed to be for all humans, thought Liz. If the whole world could pair up and retreat to a far-off place to make love for an entire weekend, how much better everything would be.

Her only regret was having missed out on this for so long. No point in chastising herself. She was with him now in the most intimate way two people could be. Grateful for this hard-won haven of safety and calm, she felt cherished.

She marveled at how they fit together, like two puzzle pieces. This weekend had been perfect.

Liz couldn't have asked for a better time with the one who mattered most.

CHAPTER 27

*E*arly Monday morning, Liz woke Jon to get dressed, reminding him they had to make phone calls to their employers. Rain still poured, but not as heavy. Wind hadn't let up though, and the latest forecast projected low pressure would weaken and move out by late Monday afternoon.

Liz recalled Jon saying they must hike out to a rocky point called Otter Rock, where they'd get cell reception. They put on their rain gear to take the short hike through the alder and spruce.

Jon led her along the gravel beach, stepping around seaweed and bull kelp left by the storm surge at high tide. The wind blew sideways as they put their heads down to hike to the point, the length of a football field.

She pointed at the length of rock stretching into the bay, protecting the cove. "It resembles an otter on its back," she called out against the crashing of waves on the gravel shoreline.

"Cool, huh? We need to make this fast," Jon yelled back. He grabbed her hand and tugged her along. Her shorter legs were no match for his long ones, and she practically had to jog to keep up.

Once on the point, the wind intensified, and rain pelted their skin. The tall grass bent sideways, along with everything else. Williwaws skittered white froth across the wave crests, like ghosts dancing on the waves.

They fished phones from their pockets and squinted at them.

Jon turned his back to the wind, phone to his ear to call Keaton.

She did the same and tapped speed dial for her crew boss. "Hello? Tara?"

"Hi, are you on your way back?"

"We're still stuck across the bay and can't get a boat ride back to Homer until the storm calms. Jon said you guys contained the Riverview Estates and Swiftcurrent Fires."

"Yes, but now they're worried about the Crane Lake Fire moving out of the refuge toward the Sterling Highway. The storm hitting you guys down there is expected to move up here tomorrow. The forecast sucks for fire. Think you'll make it by tonight?"

"Depends on whether we can get a water taxi to get us across if Spencer can't in his boat."

"Okay. See you when you get here, tonight or tomorrow."

"Liz, let's go," shouted Jon. "It's getting worse out here."

Tara chuckled. "I hear Silva. Are you enjoying your time off?"

Liz could tell, Tara was dying to know the details. "Yes! I'll fill you in later. Uh—thanks for your tip on icebreakers." She smiled into the wet phone.

"Ha, you and Jon—really?" sputtered Tara.

"Harrington, let's go." Jon moved along the beach at a fast clip.

A wind gust caught her phone, determined to steal it. "Whoa! Okay, must go, Tara. I'll keep you posted." She ended the call and shoved the phone in her raincoat pocket, hurrying after Jon.

A dark movement caught her eye off to her left. "Jon, it's a little bear cub. Oh, and there's another. Ahh, they're so cute!"

The cubs bounded along without a care in the world. They rollicked and romped on the gravel, one chasing the other in the sideways pelting rain, oblivious to the gale blowing around them.

She caught up to Jon and tugged his arm. "Did you see—"

"Watch out!" screamed Jon, reaching under his raincoat.

It happened fast.

A mama black bear ran full bore at them on the long gravel beach, ears back, clacking her teeth, the cubs bawling after her.

"Liz! I forgot my gun!" Jon's phone flew from his grasp as he slipped on a slick bed of kelp. His legs flew out from under him, and he slammed down hard on the wet gravel. "Dammit!"

The bear closed in fast.

"Oh God! Oh God!" Liz frantically dug in her day pack for her bear spray canister. Fumbling it out, she pulled back the orange safety tab with her thumb and aimed the nozzle at eye level with the sow.

Liz sprayed, but a gust of wind blew it to the side. *No!*

The sow kept coming. This was no bluff charge. Oblivious to the blowing storm, she had cubs to protect.

Liz sprayed another long burst, moving it side to side, praying some of it would reach the bear's nose and eyes despite the howling wind.

The wind won. The bear kept coming.

"Stop, bear!" She sprayed at point-blank range and squeezed her lids closed in case the spray blew back on her.

The bear let out a sharp bawl and skidded in the gravel. Liz opened her eyes to see her swing her head back and forth, pawing her nose.

"Come on, let's go!" Liz grabbed Jon under his arm.

He shook away her hand. "I can get up. You've done enough." He pushed to his feet, and they took off running.

His words stung her, but this wasn't a good time to ask for clarity. Not with a pissed-off mama bear on their heels.

The rain and wind howled around them, flapping their rain jackets as they jogged away from the beach and circled around back to the lodge. Liz glanced furtively over her shoulder, but mama bear didn't follow.

"Good thing you had your bear spray," huffed Jon.

"Tara gave these out in refresher training."

"You saved the day. Again." His hard expression was unreadable, and she was curious at the change on his face.

He stepped ahead, leaving her to follow—and wonder what she'd done wrong.

※

*L*iz noticed Jon hadn't said much on the way back to the cabin. Or when they'd packed to go as soon as the bay waters calmed.

Something obviously bothered him. Because she sprayed the bear? *It shouldn't matter who sprayed the bear! At least one of us did.* Better than the alternative of getting mauled in the middle of a gale.

Jon sat in the armchair, staring out the window at the gray overcast and low-hanging mist. The rain had let up.

Liz dragged a chair over next to him. "Time for a conclave, Slick."

He gently squeezed her thigh. "I know."

"You're quiet. Did I do something wrong?"

He shook his head. "You did everything right. That's the problem."

"You're not making sense. What did you mean when you said I'd done enough back there on the beach?" She sent him a confused look. "I sprayed the bear to protect us."

"I should have had my gun. You had to save my sorry ass yet again." He stared out the window.

She studied him for a long moment. "Oh. So that's it."

When he didn't respond, she breathed a long sigh. "I wondered when we'd get around to this." She folded her arms. "You're still toting baggage from last fire season, aren't you?"

"What's that supposed to mean?"

"Meaning it's time to get over yourself and your tough guy ego. You act like I emasculated you when I helped you up that stupid mountain. And again, today on the beach."

"Not true. I'm glad you helped me," he mumbled.

"It bothers you that a woman half your size helped you, doesn't it? All you can think about is how you screwed up." She leaned toward him. "You resigned from firefighting too soon, before Alaska Fire Service completed their incident report. Last year wasn't your fault."

"Yes, it was."

"Haven't you read the amendment to the After-Action Report from the Shackelford Fire last year? The one Ryan O'Connor did for Dave Doss, the IC of that fire?"

"What amendment?"

"Don't tell me you didn't read it. Ryan emailed it to the crew at the end of last fire season."

"Never opened my emails after I left AFS." He shook his head, staring out the window.

"You don't know that ICC owned up to sending you the wrong coordinates for us to go to the left flank?"

"I still put us in the fire's path."

Liz threw up her arms. "Enough with the self-flagellation. ICC sent you the wrong GPS coordinates. You entered the lat and long numbers *they* transmitted. The error was theirs, not yours." She pulled her phone from her shirt pocket and tapped her email. "I downloaded the amended report last winter when Ryan emailed it." She gave him her phone.

He finished reading and leaned back. "You can split hairs any way you want, but you seem to forget the minor detail that I falsified my fitness results. I had to resign before they fired me."

"Yeah, about that. Why did you falsify your medical?"

He shrugged. "I fought fire for six years before I had asthma. Then the Feds required a pulmonary function test as part of our fitness requirements. I didn't want to stop fighting fire."

"You went to all that trouble to stay fighting fire? And you wound up quitting anyway. Geez Jon, you and your damn ego." She threw up her arms and dropped them to her sides. "It's time you pull up your big boy boxers, own it, and move on. We've all messed up one time or another. Get over yourself."

His eyes flashed. "Let's analyze what *you* do to stay fighting fire. You take your clothes off and dance for horny guys."

He may as well have slapped her. Hard. It got old explaining her other job.

"I can't believe you fricking said that." Liz flew off her chair and stood glaring down at him. She pointed a thumb at herself. "This is Liz talking, not Blaze Diamond. I am *not* my dance job, and I am *not* that lifestyle. I detest that lifestyle."

He stared out the window. "Then why do it?"

"Whoa, let's back up the truth trolley, Slick. You don't like that I work as an exotic dancer, do you?"

He swiveled his head to her. "No."

"So. You're judging me after all." She spoke through gritted teeth. "You have no freaking clue."

"No. *You* have no freaking clue." He raised his hands and dropped them. "Why don't you ask me why I don't like it?"

"Okay, I'll bite. Why?"

"I had friends who did business with dance clubs in Vegas —one wound up dead, and the other maimed for life by some badass. I don't like that you're involved with them because they have vicious people. Not to mention other random predators. Google what happened with a serial killer in the early nineteen eighties, that targeted exotic dancers and prostitutes in Anchorage."

"What are you insinuating?" An angry heat traveled up her neck. She felt her cheeks flush.

He stood to make his point. "What you do and where you do it is dangerous."

She sputtered up at him. "So is fighting fire."

"Why have two dangerous jobs when one is enough?"

"That's not the reason you don't want me doing it. You look down on it—like it's a low-life job. Do you believe I am what I do?" she fumed.

"I've partied in Vegas. I've seen the sleazes in those clubs and how they are with dancers. I would fucking lose it if I caught some dicklick treating you like that. It was bad enough seeing those Nevada hotshots treating you like a...like a..." He trailed off.

"Like a what, Jon?" She waited.

"With such disrespect," he muttered, staring out the window.

"I'm an expert at dealing with pond scum. Had you not intervened that night at the restaurant, you would have seen that."

"You shouldn't have to put up with losers like that. If guys treated you like that in fire, they'd be out on their ass." He shook his head. "Don't you understand? You're too good to be working in a Vegas strip joint. You're wasting your God-given talent."

She stepped close and narrowed her eyes. "*You* sure enjoyed my God-given talent as I recall. You don't like what I do because it's not a socially acceptable occupation for your girl-friend." She fingered air quotes around "socially acceptable."

"No! Because it's dangerous! Wait, back the hell up. So, we agree you're my girlfriend? We seem to dance around this all the time."

"I might be the dancer, but you're the one tap dancing around the bushes." She whirled on him. "What the heck else am I after this weekend? Your personal prostitute? A free resort stay in exchange for sex. How convenient for you." Her words tumbled over themselves in her haste to get them out. "FYI, exotic dancing and the sex industry are two separate things. There's a ginormous difference. I sell fantasy, not sex."

"I never said that. You're twisting things..." he protested.

She marched over and yanked her jacket from a wall hook, then stomped back over to him. "You're the first person I've had sex with in three freaking years. Speaking of God-given talent—you've done nothing with yours as a singer. Oh, wait—that doesn't fit with your tough, Alaska-macho image, does it? You know what they call you? Wildland Wolf!"

She tugged on her jacket and beelined for the door. She paused to glare at him. "And I'm not a stripper. I'm a professional dancer and a damn good firefighter." She opened the door and rushed out. She wouldn't let him see her cry.

"Wait, Liz! Come back here—that's not what I meant."

Everything blurred as she hurried outside, slamming the door behind her. He invited her this weekend just for sex, assuming she'd put out? She shouldn't have lap danced for him. Big mistake.

She should have guessed all of this was too good to be true.

Jon Silva was no different from the rest.

❧

*J*on couldn't believe how such a fantastic weekend could end in disaster. His own bruised ego had gotten in the way. Liz hit the nail on the head that last year still bothered him. The bear incident only triggered things to burst into the open. Then he'd blown it with his comments about her dance job.

Why couldn't she understand his concern for her safety, wanting her out of that volatile environment?

The storm had calmed enough by mid-afternoon so Spencer could boat Liz and Jon across the bay to Homer. They'd unloaded their gear and tossed it in Jon's truck for the three-hour drive to Rockfish. Neither of them had uttered more than a few words since they'd left Steller's Jay Lodge.

As they drove north, Jon noticed the air quality diminish. More smoke, more fire. The radio reported smoke had settled into the valleys at night, and storm winds had blown up several fires.

He gave Liz a sidelong glance, and his stomach tightened at her insistence to ignore him.

She'd positioned herself as far from him as she could, staring out the side window, chin in her hand. He wanted to sort this out, but not while driving. As they drove through the tiny town of Ninilchik, Jon turned right into a parking area for a coffee shop and cut the engine.

"Do you need to use the restroom?" he asked.

214

She shook her head and stared out the window, flipping his gold guitar pick between her fingers. The one he'd tossed to her back at the lodge.

"That pick belonged to my favorite guitarist. Eddie Van Halen."

Her eyes grew round in disbelief. "Nah, get out of here."

He grinned. "Truth. I caught it when he tossed it out after one of his last gigs."

"He's gone now." She scrutinized it. "You should have it back."

"No. I gave it to you. It's yours."

She held it out to him. "I can't keep this. It's irreplaceable."

"So are you." He pulled the keys from the ignition and leaned back in his seat. "I don't like how we left things back at the lodge."

Her fingers drummed her thigh as she stared out the side window.

Jon fiddled with the keys. "I didn't explain myself very well."

She wouldn't look at him. "Yes, you did. There isn't anything else to say. I can't afford to quit dancing because you don't approve of my doing it."

"I didn't mean it the way it sounded. I worry about your safety, that's all."

She swiveled her head and gave him an icy stare. "You know full well I can take care of myself. And others when necessary."

"I admire that about you." And he did—but he had to learn how to stop tripping on his ego.

"Admire? Interesting choice of words." She sat staring out the windshield.

"I know you better than you think. We're a lot alike. We hold things close. Level with me." He set the keys on the dash. "Because these keys aren't going into the ignition until you do."

"There's a reason I keep my two work lives separate." She let out a sigh. "It's hard to explain."

"Try me. I won't judge. I promise." He reached across and laid his hand on hers.

She drilled him with her stare. "First off, I need to know if the reason you invited me this weekend was only for sex."

Her words threw him. "How can you say that after—after everything? God Liz, no. If that were the case, I would have jumped in bed with you the first night at the cabin."

She stared down at the guitar pick in her hand. "Loyalty runs deep in my family on my dad's side. He retired from the force with a generous pension. His health insurance covered things until Alzheimer's took hold of him at fifty-nine years old. Too young for Medicare. It wasn't a gradual onset. His set in fast, and I had to get him into skilled nursing care. His pension wouldn't cover the costs. I wanted him to have his own room, so I had to come up with twice as much." Guilt tugged at her each time she thought how she'd visited him less and less.

She glanced at Jon, and he nodded, listening.

"When I graduated from UNLV, I auditioned my ass off with every major dance company in the U.S. I tried the New York City Ballet and West Coast dance companies in L.A. Even tried the movie business. Dad paid for me to fly to Moscow to audition for a Russian ballet company. About that time, I noticed Dad forgetting things. Big things. It got worse— to the point where I couldn't leave home. He needed me.

She continued. "I auditioned for Cirque de Soleil and the casinos as a showgirl, but I'm too petite. In high school, we used to joke about working at slut central—the dance clubs. But the pay is incredible. What I make with tips in one night pays for one day of Dad's nursing care."

"Wish you would have told me before." Now he under-stood. He felt like a douche for having judged her. "Breaking into professional dance sounds tough."

"Like I told you, I prefer to keep my two jobs separate. The professional dance arena is brutal. Impossible to break into unless you know somebody. My Vegas connections didn't mean squat in the ballet business. So, my friend's dad bounced at the Iris and helped me land the dance job."

"Seeing you dance on that video and at the lodge...I don't understand why the pros didn't hire you. I'm sorry. I had no idea."

"Not like I have a choice. He's my dad. And he was a kickass cop. He was even shot in the line of duty and recovered, only to lose his memory. I hate this effing disease. Last time I visited, he didn't remember me. I cried on the plane all the way to Alaska."

She glanced up. "And then at the wedding, I saw *you*, and my world righted itself." Her voice broke a little.

He held her hand. "Liz—"

She interrupted. "You need to understand something. When I took the dance job at the Iris, I made it clear what I wasn't willing to do. I don't dance for high rollers in the V.I.P. rooms for private sessions. You wouldn't believe the celebrities and politicians I've lap danced for, men *and* women. I could blackmail any number of people." She paused to take a breath and control her rising tone. "I've never had sex with patrons. Ever. I don't do the guilt-ridden bullshit that keeps other dancers awake at night. I'm old by striptease standards, and because of my professional dance training, they keep me on the main stage, like a topless prima ballerina."

He nodded, trying to understand with all his heart, forcing himself to stay quiet. She'd never opened up like this.

"A friend of Dad's helped me get hired with a Nevada fire crew, and I fell in love with firefighting. Discovered an opportunity to apply to the BLM Alaska Fire Service, and this is where I earn the rest of my income."

"I wish you would have told me sooner. I wouldn't have given you such a hard time about it." He felt like a doofus all over again. "You must work at the dance club until your Dad can get on Medicare?"

"Either that, or I run my club and hire the dancers." She lifted a water bottle and sipped. "Then I can stop dancing and focus on managing the new club."

"You have to do what you think is best, I suppose."

"I know what I'm doing. I grew up in Vegas. You don't have to worry about me," she informed him in a defensive tone.

He wished he could believe her.

CHAPTER 28

*L*iz had a mash-up of relief and uneasiness that she'd opened up with Jon. After this weekend, things had changed, and she trusted him more than she had before. It meant a great deal to her that he knew the why of her actions. What she did in her other job felt like a yawning abyss between them now. Maybe getting involved with Jon was a bad idea after all and this was just an Alaskan fling.

The deep stir in her stomach and chest told her it was more than that. Time would tell, she supposed.

When Jon dropped her off at Aurora Camp, they'd parted on civil terms, but she hated the tension. She'd kissed him on the cheek and thanked him for the wonderful weekend. She had to force herself to step out of the truck when she really wanted to throw her arms around him and hear him say everything would be all right.

How could they continue their relationship with her plans and ambitions? Jon lived in Fairbanks. No way did she want to live on that frozen iceberg. She was on the trajectory of an investment in her own business. Her golden ticket out of dancing.

Her brain ached from these overwhelming thoughts. She couldn't ignore the fact that Jon had persisted in hanging in there with her since last year.

Liz organized her gear in the women's tent, thankful to be alone. Kenzie and Tara must be at dinner. Her phone pinged notifications. She checked her voice message from Ravish:

Jasper and I decided that since we're doing the work putting this deal together, you'll get twenty percent, not thirty-five percent of the profits as we originally planned. Plus, we need two hundred grand more to stay in this venture. Sorry, but that's how this will roll. If you want to stay in, those are the new terms. I'll email you the new contract. Sign it within the next three days.

A text followed with photos.

Perhaps this will motivate you.

Two naked photos of Liz filled her screen from the same boudoir photo shoot she'd shown Jon.

Send the money. Or I must send these to your Alaska fire bosses with a link to the Iris where they can see more of you. And I'll send them to Henderson Nursing Home so your dad can see them, too. You don't want these going public, do you? Smiley face.

Air whooshed from her lungs as she dropped to her cot in disbelief. How could they do that? Could they break the first contract agreement she'd signed and replace it with another?

Tara opened the door to their tent. "Welcome back. Good timing. The Crane Lake Fire blew up, and we can't spike camp anymore. It's too volatile of a situation. Doss declared it a project fire, with several state and federal agencies involved in committing resources to fight it."

Liz surveyed Tara and Kenzie, their faces dark with soot and ash. "You guys look beat."

Kenzie plopped onto her cot with her boots and all. "What a ripper of a day. Those strong winds made a shitstorm." She rested her forearm over her face.

"How was your long weekend with Jon Boy?" asked Tara, eyes gleaming. "You two make progress?"

"Yes and no." Liz stared at her phone.

Tara sat beside her. "That doesn't sound good. What's wrong?"

Liz tapped her phone text and held it out to Tara.

Tara read it and glanced up, horrified. "Oh no, can they do this?"

"It's extortion. Or blackmail. Whatever it's called when people threaten you because they want more money. What am I going to do?" Liz's eyes watered. "If these photos go to the Alaska Fire Service, I'm done. They'll terminate my employment."

Tara stared at her. "Okay, breathe. Remember last year when Hudson trashed my reputation on social media? He called me names foul-mouthed sailors wouldn't repeat."

"Yeah, but naked photos of you weren't in the mix. I should have known these would leak out in a bad way. Down south, we call it sextortion—revenge porn."

"Are those photos on your dance club web page?"

"No. I only allowed my boss to upload partially nude photos. Wouldn't allow full frontal or topless photos like the other girls. I even bought the rights to the photos from the photographer."

"Then how did Ravish get hold of them?"

"She must have downloaded them from my laptop files after I left. It's a crime to post or distribute explicitly sexual images online without that person's consent," explained Liz. "That still doesn't stop people from doing it when they want something. Ravish knows this. She's smart. She's not threatening to post them online, she's threatening to text and email them to my fire bosses and employer in Alaska to skirt around that law."

"With Internet and social media, people can wreak all kinds of havoc. Gosh, I'm so sorry."

Kenzie held out her hand. "Let's see those photos."

Liz gave her the phone.

"They're in good taste. Not like the smut mags my brothers read, where a woman's insides leap off the page at you. Don't sweat it. Naked pics fly around all the time. Everyone and his dingo are on a nudie calendar."

"I don't want Dave Doss or Ryan and the smokejumpers to see them. I don't want Jon to see them—" Liz choked back the rest.

Tara put an arm around her. "Don't worry, we'll put our heads together and think of something."

"Thanks, Boss, I appreciate it." She gave Tara a squeeze. "Think I'll take a walk. I need some air." Liz ducked out of the tent and headed toward the steep path that led from the bluff down to the riverbank.

She stood fixated on the swift, emerald water, wondering how she could lay fast hands on some cash. Her paychecks deposited every two weeks. Her next one wouldn't arrive in her account for another week. She pulled out her phone and frantically tapped her username and password to her checking and savings accounts. It had taken her several years to build up a healthy sum of a hundred grand.

Zero. Zilch. Nada. The number of zeros jumped off her screen in a bitter reality. Instead of five, there were three— zero-point-zero-zero.

Ravish and Jaspar not only had threatened her, they'd robbed her blind.

&

*J*on unlocked the door to his hotel room after the long drive from Rockfish and instantly sensed something amiss. What clued him in were the black bra he tripped on as he stepped into his room and matching thong a few feet away, leading to his bed.

The bed with his naked ex-wife on it.

He stopped, stunned—not only seeing a naked Roxanne stretched out on his bed, but how in blazes did she get into his hotel room?

"Come lie with me. We'll have some fun." She patted the bed with a seductive look.

Instant heat flashed up his neck to his face. "How the hell did you get into my room?"

A smug smile formed as she flipped a key card between her fingers. "I took this from your pocket when you came to the Coho Lodge."

He hadn't noticed his second key card had been missing. It hadn't exactly been on his radar the past several days. He stooped to pick up the scattered underwear and threw it at her on the bed. "Get dressed and get out."

She sat up and brought her knees to her chest. "Before you get all worked up, you'd better listen to what I have to say."

This had gotten officially out of hand.

"Get dressed." He tossed her clothes at her and stood glaring, cursing himself for being an easy mark. Obviously, she'd been planning to do this ever since he talked to her at Coho Lodge.

Roxanne dressed, then tossed her intimates on the nightstand. "Who do you suppose this is?" She tapped a photo on her phone and held it out.

He stood, glaring at her. "Why should I care who it is?"

"Oh, you'll care." She pushed herself off the bed and came toward him, holding her phone.

She tilted her head. "Who does our son looks like...you or me?"

CHAPTER 29

"*T*he winds are back. The line won't hold," yelled Liz, assessing the progress the Aurora Crew had made on creating another fuel break for the Crane Lake Fire. She had difficulty acclimating to her first day of work after the long drive back from Homer last night.

They'd been on this fire since early morning and hadn't stopped sawing trees and clearing them. Liz had fatigued to the point where a headache had taken hold. She drank more water from her canteen.

Several fire crews stretched along the perimeter of the Crane Lake Fire that had moved through the wildlife refuge and now headed toward the Sterling Highway. The radios squawked nonstop with aerial fire activity, marine tankers dropping mud, and helicopters slinging loads of water on the hottest spots. Despite their efforts, air attack hadn't slowed this mammoth.

The storm that had stranded Liz and Jon at Steller's Jay Lodge, moved north and blew up the Crane Lake Fire. "We have to retreat, it's overrunning everything we've done today," announced Tara to the crew. "The NorthStar crew is relieving us. We'll be back here first thing tomorrow morning."

Liz and the crew had to hike the two miles out to the Sterling Highway to their transport van. Her feet were two globs of raw meat and her popped blisters stuck to her socks.

Whenever she thought of her finances, her gut ached. She hadn't had time to call the bank or do much of anything. As per usual, no cell service was available at their remote location. Limited cell service was a pain in the ass.

A loud shriek startled Liz as she stood to zip up after relieving herself behind a blackened alder. She froze, peeking around the burned brush. Another shriek made her jump. Cautiously, she stepped around the charred vegetation and caught movement next to a clump of burned lupine and cow parsnip.

Enormous dark wings flapped on the ground. An eagle. She moved toward it. The enormous bird eyed her and froze, ready for a fight. Its head feathers stuck out in a comical punk-rock hair-do, and she laughed out loud.

"You poor thing. You're hurt." She wished Jon were here. He'd know how to handle this.

Upon hearing her voice, the bird flapped in the ash and soot, creating a cloud, and Liz had to back up. The raptor's tail feathers were no longer white. It resembled a California condor more than an eagle, except for the beak.

She used a soothing tone. "Hey buddy, it's okay. Let me see what's wrong."

The eagle eyed her like prey, but it was fear. As rulers of the skies, she recalled Jon saying eagles didn't know fear. A grounded eagle was another story.

"Yeah, we're all walking wounded. Join the club," she mumbled as she moved around the bird.

Liz was no bird expert, but she could tell it had a broken leg. She kneeled and tried to stretch out a wing. The eagle shrieked, and she sprung back. "Okay, okay, I need to see your leg."

"Elizabeth?" Cohen called out a short distance away. "We're heading back to the van. Where are you?"

"Over here," she shouted.

Cohen appeared and stood next to her. "Wounded bird, huh? What's wrong with him?"

"Broken leg, I think. We need something to put him in. Empty my pack. I must keep his wings next to his body. Then I can set him in it without losing an arm." She offered him her pack.

"Think he'll fit? He's too pharaonic." Cohen emptied her pack contents on the ground.

She gave him a blank look.

"He's too big."

"Oh. Only one way to find out." She grabbed the roll of pink flagging tape she and Jon had used on the fire. "Hold him while I wrap this around him. Watch those talons. They'll slice you like a knife."

The traumatized eagle's razor-sharp talons were nothing to screw with. She noted the bent, pointed beak that could pierce a hole in her the size of Alaska.

The eagle pecked at Cohen and he jerked back his gloved hand with the speed of a frog's tongue. "He wants me for lunch."

"He thinks you're trying to kill him. Good thing we have these thick gloves," muttered Liz as she wrapped the tape around the bird. One wing escaped, and she folded it against the eagle's body before he could outsmart her again.

"He's a stubborn one." Cohen helped her hold the wings.

"Who knew eagles were so dang strong?" Liz pulled off a long section of tape and severed it with her teeth.

The eagle's beak opened as if to say, *Come near me, and you're shredded meat.*

"Hold him for me," she ordered.

Cohen moved the eagle onto its belly and held the wings close, while Liz wrapped the tape around it and tied it off.

The eagle let out a shriek that threatened to break her eardrums.

"Should have put in my ear plugs. These things are drum splitters." Cohen rubbed his ears.

"Worse than the llamas," Liz grumbled. "Roll him gently

on his side. I'll wrap his talons, and maybe he won't break the other leg."

"There is no gently." Cohen gritted his teeth as he wrestled the struggling bird.

After she finished, she glanced at Cohen. "Help me get the eagle in my pack."

"He'll bite your head off."

"I won't put it on. I'll carry him at my side." She scrutinized the bird, whose tousled head feathers looked as though he'd sizzled himself on an electric line.

"Here, do this first." Cohen bit off a short piece of flagging and wrapped it around the eagle's beak and tied a tidy bow. "Hope we don't get arrested for BDSM with an eagle—binding and gagging it like this."

Liz shot him a sly grin. "Why, Cohen, is there something you're trying to tell me?"

"Hey, I don't…I'm not into—" he spurted, cheeks glowing red.

She laughed. "Too late, Tremblay. You dug your hole. Don't worry, I won't tell anyone if you're into a little kink." She winked at him, which flustered him even more.

"Okay, in my pack he goes." The eagle fought hard, and it was like trying to get water to flow uphill as the two firefighters wrestled the huge raptor into her pack. On the way, talons dug into the underside of her bare forearm. Not a good day to have rolled up her shirt sleeves, but the heat called for it.

The crazed eagle resisted being inserted into Liz's pack, his crazed head turning from side to side, unable to open its beak to shriek. A razor-sharp talon raked her forearm on its way in. "Ow! Dammit, you birdbrain!"

"More like a Birdzilla. Did he claw you?"

She glanced down at her forearm and wrinkled her face. "Yep. Should have rolled my sleeve down. It'll be okay. I'll get the eagle to Silva."

Cohen gave her a sharp stare. "Why Silva?"

Liz rolled down her sleeve to cover the two talon scratches.

"He's an ornithologist," she stated matter-of-factly. "He's handled birds of prey, including eagles."

"You act like he's Superman."

He is to me. She ignored his comment.

"What's this?" Cohen stooped to pick up something. He straightened and held up a gold guitar pick.

Liz snatched it from his fingers. "This was on the ground?" *How did that happen?*

She thought back to last night, when her nose fell out of joint with Jon on their drive back to Rockfish. It had been one of Jon's prized possessions. His giving it to her had significance.

He pointed. "Yes, with the rest of your things."

"Thanks." She dabbed her finger in her mouth to wipe the dirt off the pick. When she noticed Cohen studying her, she shoved it in her back pocket like nothing weird had happened.

He stepped toward her. "This may not be an appropriate time to say this. I was hoping when fire season ends, maybe you and I could have a committed relationship." His azure gaze targeted hers.

His words threw her. "Oh Cohen, geez. I can't think about relationships right now, let alone committed ones." She barely knew him outside of their working together, let alone that Silva had gobbled up the prime real estate in her heart. "I thought you liked Rhiannon?"

He raised his brows and shrugged. "She's a friend."

Birdzilla's head poked up, looking around with that trussed-up bedhead and the cute pink bow on the side of his beak. She speculated at how many exotic-dancer-firefighters had rescued batshit crazy eagles today…and how she almost came unglued over a guitar pick. Not to mention she hadn't a cent to her name because her loser roommates had drained her accounts and threatened to send her nude photos to her fire employer.

She shrugged. "Cohen, I'm sorry—I just can't. You're a terrific guy. It's nothing personal."

"But?"

"But there's a lot going on in my life right now…" She shook her head, unable to finish.

"Was hoping you'd give me a chance." He looked crestfallen.

She reached up to pat his shoulder. "Truly, I'm sorry."

"Don't apologize. I know you're in deep with Silva." His voice had a disheartening tone. "I see it in your eyes and hear it in your voice. How you stare off at nothing—I wish it were me you were dreaming about. If you were mine, I'd treat you like gold." His sincerity poked a guilty hole in her chest. "You aren't a woman a man forgets."

"You're sweet. Thanks for the compliment. Any woman would be lucky to have you." She took his hand and patted it. "I wish I were that woman, but I'm not."

She had to admit, on a scale of one to ten, Cohen snagged a solid nine-point-five with his windblown hair and rocking firefighter's body. He had a gorgeous smile and fun personality, but she preferred Jon's sass and quick humor. And how they seemed to be on a psychic channel. She had the sudden desire to talk to Jon. She wanted things to be the same as their glorious weekend.

Coming back to reality sucked.

Cohen motioned his head at the crazy-looking eagle, with its goofy bedhead feathers poking out of her pack. "Well, we'll always have Birdzilla. It's been an honor rescuing eagles with you, despite you breaking my heart."

"Thanks, Cohen. Even if we BDSM'd the poor thing."

His mouth quirked up. "Don't let word get around. I have a reputation to uphold." He squatted to tie the rest of her stuff to the top of his pack with flagging tape. He glanced up at her. "At least give me credit for trying."

She nodded, smiling. "I do. And I'm flattered."

"If things go south with Silva, you know where to find me."

Tara strode up at a fast clip. "What's taking so long—" She stopped to gawk at the scruffy head poking out of Liz's pack as she held it at her side. "Oh, you have company. What's his deal?"

"A broken leg but his wings seem okay. We had to bind and gag him to get him out of here." She smirked at Cohen.

He caught the joke reference and gave her a conspiratorial wink. What a good sport after she'd rejected him.

Tara laughed. "All you had to do was toss something over its head, and it would have calmed down. Then pick it up and carry it. Don't you have your rain poncho?"

Liz and Cohen exchanged annoyed looks. "Guess we'll do jail time for maltreatment of a national symbol," said Cohen.

The three of them burst out laughing, while the eagle glared at them like crazy humans.

Liz wiped away tears of laughter. "When we get to the highway, I'll call Jon. He'll know where to take him. It's after hours. State agencies are closed."

"Good idea. As long as we deliver him to Alaska Department of Fish & Game or a licensed bird rehab facility, we're good." Tara grinned at Liz. "Let's go, everyone's waiting. We have a live concert to go to tonight, down in Ninilchik. Salmonfest, where Rabid Fish will be playing. We could all use the break."

"That sounds fun." Liz was down for some live music.

First, she had to take care of Birdzilla.

CHAPTER 30

*J*on tapped his phone's speaker. "Hello?"

"Silva. I have a wounded eagle," said Liz. "Where should I take it?"

Road noise came from his speaker.

"What's wrong with it?"

"Broken leg. Wings seem okay."

"Where is it? How are you transporting it?"

"I have it bound and gagged in my day pack in the van."

Some things Liz did left him speechless. "I'm afraid to ask."

Liz breezed past it. "Long story. Can you meet our van at Aurora Camp? We'll be there in half an hour."

"Sure." Jon ended the call and leaned back in his hotel room chair.

He blew out air, glad she finally called. They'd left things messy and unfinished. He wanted to apologize for being a judgmental dickhead. The fresh development Roxanne had sprung on him didn't help matters. She'd lied so much in the past, he couldn't help thinking she was toying with him.

And lying about a son? If her son was his, why would Roxanne wait ten years to tell him? After she showed him the photo, he'd numbed with shock. Her parting shot was informing him he'd never see his son unless he agreed to marry her again. They'd argued, ending with him ordering her to get out. He'd made certain he had both room key cards before escorting her out the door.

Angry and desperate, he'd gone to Keaton's room for a shot of whiskey to calm down. Jon confided the whole shitshow to Keaton, who sat nodding understanding. Jon had warmed up quite a lot to Keaton. He'd cautioned Jon that since Roxanne had a history of lying, not to assume she was telling the truth.

Now he'd been summoned to transport Liz and a wounded eagle.

Should I tell Liz?

No. Bad idea. Liz wouldn't like the part about a naked Roxanne in his hotel room. How would she react? Hell, he still wrestled with the possibility that he might have a son. And if so, his cunning ex thought she could leverage the boy to get Jon to remarry her? That was ludicrous.

He snorted. "Yeah, that'll happen," he muttered.

If he *was* his son. Jon would find out on his own.

He shook his head as he grabbed his keys and headed for his pickup. Didn't need this snag while trying to put his life back together. Finally, he had a good woman in his life, and he couldn't afford to let anyone screw that up.

No, he wouldn't tell Liz. Not yet. Why had drama from his past suddenly slammed into his present? What did he do to deserve this?

You screwed up last year. The universe is paying you back.

Smoke hung heavy in the air as Jon pulled into the crew camp parking lot. He reached behind him and grabbed an old worn pair of men's leather gauntlet gloves he still carried around with him. He'd volunteered at bird rehabilitation centers, handling raptors like peregrine falcons, ospreys, red-tailed hawks, and eagles.

Aurora Crew unloaded their van as Jon rolled to a stop in the campground parking lot. Liz and Cohen came toward him, hefting a large cardboard box between them.

Jon stepped out of his truck.

"So, you're the big bird expert," quipped Cohen.

Jon's temper still percolated on high. Tremblay was the last bastard he wanted to see right now. "Nope. Strictly a Kermit the Frog man," he deadpanned.

Liz laughed, as Jon hoped she would.

Cohen didn't. Instead, he folded his arms and narrowed his eyes. "Funny. You're a funny guy."

"Yeah. I got more." Jon grabbed hold of the box, and the two men glared daggers at each other.

"Geez, you guys, chill. Silva, help me load this eagle in your truck. Where do you want him?" Liz looked up.

"Back of the passenger seat." He waited for her to open the rear door, then he eased the box onto the seat. It jiggled as the eagle knocked around inside.

Liz turned to Cohen, who stood watching. "Thanks for all your help."

"Sure. Let me know how it went when you get back."

"Aren't you going with the crew to the Salmonfest concert?" asked Liz.

"Nope, I'm staying in camp. Birdzilla wore me out. Along with other things." Cohen shot Jon another death stare and strode back to help Aurora Crew unload the van.

Jealousy sprang from Jon's chest like an alien, and he clamped down on his tongue. *The hell she'll let you know, asshole.*

"Get in, let's go," Jon spouted, more gruffly than he'd intended. He'd never been good at covering his sour moods, and he wasn't doing a good job of it now. He climbed into the driver's seat and slammed the door, eyeing Cohen and the others unloading their gear.

"Thanks for all your help? What exactly was he helping you with?" grumbled Jon.

Liz hoisted herself into the passenger seat and followed his line of sight. "You don't like him, do you?"

He started the engine and flashed her a fast, fake smile. "I like him fine."

"Liar," she said.

He ignored her comment, backed up the truck, and pulled

onto the Sterling Highway. "Bird Treatment Center's twenty miles south."

She peered out at the smoky air. "Are you still bothered from what we discussed back at the lodge?"

"Which part?"

"You know which part." She let out a sigh. "I hate arguing with you."

"I hate arguing with me, too." He stared straight ahead, wanting to change the subject. One shitstorm at a time, thanks. He'd investigated another arson fire today and was in no mood to babble about his angsty problems.

He summoned as much cheer as he could muster. "Tell me how you found the eagle."

Liz explained how she'd found it. "Fire traumatized that poor bird."

"You're lucky you still have eyeballs in your head. And damn lucky a bear didn't beat you to the bird."

"I've had enough of bears, thanks." She stayed quiet until they stopped in front of a large one-story building of the Bird Treatment & Rehabilitation Center.

Jon felt like he teetered on a high wire with the tension taut between them. He shut off the engine. "You want to come in or stay here?"

"Come in."

"Okay." He climbed out and lifted out the cardboard box. "Get the door, please."

Liz closed the truck door as he muscled the box to the one-story building, then held the door for him. A woman met them and wrote down Liz's information. She motioned them to follow her to the back of the building where they housed the birds.

When they arrived at a large cage enclosure, the woman opened the door for Jon to carry in the box.

"I used to work at the Bird Center up in Fairbanks and the Raptor Center in Sitka. I'm an ornithologist and experienced with raptors," explained Jon.

The woman nodded. "Then you know what you're doing."

Jon turned to Liz. "Stay out here in case your eagle goes ballistic."

He put on his gloves and opened the box. The eagle had calmed, but that wouldn't last long. He waited to give him time to adjust before taking him out, then eased his hands in to lift the enormous bird.

"This is a female. She must be fourteen pounds at least, with an eight-foot wingspan." Jon carefully rested the eagle on a small table.

"How do you know she's a female? Because she's strong and determined?" asked Liz, smirking at the woman.

Jon caught the innuendo and gave himself an eyeroll. Women. Always making sure guys knew how strong they were. And right now he needed that strength to lean on.

"Females can be a third of the size larger than males and tend to weigh between ten to fifteen pounds more. Females typically have a wingspan of up to eight feet. Males have a shorter wingspan at six feet." Jon slipped easily into avian science mode, which always impressed Liz. He liked to think so, anyway.

He shot her a cool look. "In case you were wondering, this characteristic of females being larger can be seen in all birds of prey. The scientific term is 'reverse sexual size dimorphism.'"

Liz nodded. "Ah, sexual dimorphism. I thought as much."

The woman appeared amused, and Jon noted her mouth twitching.

He ignored Liz's smartass comment and glanced at the woman. "Let's cut this flagging so one of us doesn't lose a body part. I'll take care of the beak and wings, and you do the talons."

Jon pulled out his pocketknife, and the woman fished one from her pocket and thumbed open the blade.

"Ready? Go." Jon deftly situated the blade under the flagging and cut upwards away from the eagle. He did the same with the wing tape.

The bird immediately flapped her wings to fly. She couldn't get traction for takeoff with the broken leg.

The woman ushered Jon out of the enclosure and closed the door. "Thanks for bringing her in. I'll email you forms to fill out. Email them back, and I'll keep you apprised of her progress."

"Sounds good. Thanks." Jon placed his hand on the small of Liz's back as they stepped outside. Felt good to touch her. He was so damn lost right now.

They moseyed back to the truck and Jon opened the passenger door and stood next to it.

"Thanks, Silva." She gave his fire vest a tug, smiling up at him.

He took off his sunglasses and hung them on his collar, then cupped her chin. "Hey, are we okay?"

"I hope so. Aren't we?"

"I hope so, too." He kissed her in a tender way, not lusty in the least.

She kissed him back the same way, so she couldn't be too terribly upset.

He finished the kiss, his voice hoarse. "I want us to be where we were last weekend. The good part."

"Me, too. Can we be together without talking about anything real? She gave him a cat-eyed look. "Unless it's sexual dimorphism. Which isn't the case with you and me."

He grinned appreciation for her humor. "Thank God for that. I like your petite self. Want to go to my hotel room and make love until we pass out?" He wanted her badly right now. He needed comfort and figured she did, too, after fighting fire and wrangling Birdzilla.

Her eyes turned feral. "How fast can you drive?"

Green light, go. He drove like a madman and lurched to a stop in the hotel parking lot. They bailed from the pickup like they were racing to a fire and stampeded inside the three-story hotel.

She hurried after him to the elevator and put her arm around his waist as they stood waiting for the elevator to open. When it did, they stepped in, and the door closed.

Liz pressed against him, a corner of her mouth lifting. "Remember last time we were in an elevator?"

"I had to hold you up."

"And then you put me to bed. Want to do it again?"

"You read my mind." He liked how she calmed him—she'd always given him hope when things had gone south. His arms encircled her, and he held on tight.

She slid her arms around his neck, and he bent his head to give her the healing, makeup kiss they both desperately needed. He needed her forgiveness for acting like an ass. When a guy seeks redemption, he can't be proud.

The elevator opened, and a man cleared his throat.

Jon broke the kiss to see Keaton with raised brows, his typically neutral expression one of amusement. "Hello, I'm Keaton, Jon's cohort. The State guy."

"We won't hold that against you," Jon said with a smirk as he stroked Liz's shoulder.

Liz dipped her chin. "Pleased to meet you."

"So, this is the cute little firefighter you jabber about." Keaton held open the elevator door. "Heading out to eat. Want to come with?"

"Nah, we're both tired." Jon steered Liz out of the elevator, feeling beat to shit, but not too tired for their planned activity.

"Hang in there, buddy." Keaton patted the back of Jon's shoulder as the elevator closed.

"What did he mean by that?" asked Liz.

"We had another arson case today." Jon waved it away, knowing Keaton referred to their earlier conversation. He had to tell her about his son. But not now. God, not now. He had everything to lose by telling her.

Jon kept his arm around her as if she'd somehow vanish as they headed to his hotel room. It occurred to him that in all this time, she hadn't been there yet, and how odd that was.

He waved his key card, and the door unlocked. He pushed it open, they wandered in, and he let it slam shut.

Liz wasted no time. She pulled her fire shirt over her head

and tossed it on the floor, standing in her tank top, Nomex pants, and fire boots.

His eye went immediately to the bloody scratches on her forearm. "Hot damn, Harrington, the eagle did that?"

She scowled. "Birdzilla of the North."

"We have to take care of this so it doesn't get infected. I've had these before." He led her by the hand to his bathroom.

Jon opened his first aid box and cleaned the two jagged scratches with bottled water and soap. He dabbed them dry, then offered her a clean washcloth. "Stick this in your mouth and bite down, this is going to sting." He held up a bottle of hydrogen peroxide.

"You're a sadist now, huh?" she teased, eyes locked on his as she bit down on the washcloth. She squealed when he poured the chemical liquid over the pair of scratches. They both watched it turn into white, fizzling foam.

He shot her a look of reproach. "You squealing in pain isn't a turn-on for me. The talon didn't go deep. You don't need stitches."

"Thanks, Doc." She eyed him with trust in her eyes, and it undid him.

His other brain woke up and nudged his zipper.

Jon finished dressing her wound and instructed her on how to take care of it for the next few days.

"Now, where were we?" Liz traipsed out of the bathroom and stood next to her yellow fire shirt crumpled on the floor. "I believe I was right here." She gazed at him with want in her eyes.

"Yeah. Here." He sauntered to her and ran his palms deliciously under her tank top to unclasp her bra as he covered her mouth with his. His need was ravenous.

She moaned a little as he meticulously lifted off her tank top and bra and let them fall. He cupped her breasts, his tongue deep inside her mouth. He broke the kiss, backed up, and devoured her with his eyes.

"You're sexing the Nomex again, Harrington. You know

how I like that." He said it low and slow. "Let's get you out of those pants."

She unzipped and he unsnapped, and they both tugged her pants down. Liz laughed. "Fire pants won't come off till the boots do, Slick."

"Love it when you talk fire. You know what that does to me," he breathed, picking her up and carrying her to his king-sized bed.

She gave him reckless kisses on the way, and when he set her down, they both clawed the laces on her boots, as if vying for a blue ribbon.

He won. "I can strip a stripper faster than the stripper can strip." He gave her an impish look. "I don't want you mad at me again."

She chortled and fell back on the bed, prone in her red bikini undies. "How can I be mad at you when you make me laugh?"

Jon pulled off her boots, plunked them to the floor, then removed her fire pants, leaving on her red undies. He had his own clothes off in record time.

"I'm sorry if what I said before hurt you. I'd never do anything to hurt you." He ran his palm up and down her bare thigh, his thumb massaging her sore thigh muscle.

Her chocolate eyes watered, and he swam in them.

"I'm sorry, too." Her eyes commanded him to continue.

Right now he had to have her. He craved intimacy and being with her comforted him. If she only knew how much he relied on her for inner strength—she didn't know it, but he depended on her right now.

He couldn't remember ever making love with such tenderness. He moved slowly, taking his time to appreciate and kiss her, caressing her smooth skin. Her body made him hard as granite, admiring every muscle that shaped her. Even the bandage on her arm gave her a badass vibe.

He kissed where her neck met her shoulder. "Trapezius." He moved his lips down. "Clavicle. And a beautiful one," he murmured, kissing his way down her arm. "Deltoid." He kissed it. "Bicep." Kissed that, too. "Tricep." He kissed his way around her bandage.

"Mmm, so this is what foreplay is like with an emergency medical technician," she groaned out.

"That's right, baby. There are five hundred and fifty muscles left to keep me busy until morning."

"I won't be able to stay awake. You'll have to carry on without me."

"I'll manage somehow." He pretended to sob, and she giggled.

He traced around her bikini undies. "Did you wear racy red just for me?"

She gave him an irritated look. "Hey, no slut shaming. I didn't know we'd be doing this when I dressed for work this morning. I happen to like red."

"Fire colors. They're hot." He trailed his lips on a decadent trip down to them. He tugged them off, then repeatedly kissed where they'd been.

"Oh-h-h..." Liz practically levitated from the bed. "Jon, I want you. Get in here."

More than happy to accommodate, he lifted himself over her and covered her mouth with his. He sheathed himself, then eased in thickly inside her, slow and reverent, like entering church. No, more like going home.

This was no lust fest. It was amorous desire. He took her slow and easy. More than anything, he wanted to please her. This felt right, like when a lyric and melody matched perfectly when he composed a song.

When she crested, she shouted his name how he hoped she would. He followed, with his grand finale so intense, he moaned her name in return.

Jon didn't want to leave her cozy warmth, but he had to use Keaton's shower. He preferred doing it while Keaton was away from his room, to avoid getting hooked into investigation talk.

Twilight had settled in as he gathered his stuff to go shower. He sat on the edge of the bed, studying Liz in the evening's rosy afterglow. If only she could stay the night, but he knew it was easier for her to get up and leave with her crew in the morning.

She opened her eyes and clasped his hand. Kissed it. "Where are you going?"

He bent to nuzzle her neck. "I have to shower while Keaton's gone. Want to come with?"

She traced the widow's peak V on his forehead. "I'm too tired. How about I lie here, and you can give me a sponge bath when you get back?" she purred.

"Ooh, I like that idea." He bent and dipped his tongue between her parted lips. "Relax, and I'll be right back. Clicker is in the nightstand drawer if you want to watch TV." He gathered his stuff and paused at the door. "I'll order takeout for us."

"I'll await your return with bated breath," she teased, blowing him a kiss on his way out.

He still had to figure a way to tell her he might have a nine-year-old son.

CHAPTER 31

*L*iz rolled over and stretched out her arm to open the drawer of the nightstand. Her fingers probed for the clicker but closed around something else. She pulled back her hand. A black bra unfolded from her fingers, along with a black thong with the initials "RS" embroidered in light blue.

They sure as heck aren't mine. A magnitude ten earthquake tremored her insides. *God, please let me be hallucinating.* Then the reality of a nightmare dawned.

Liz shot out of bed like it was on fire. *What is this? Who is RS?*

Her brain whipped two and two together, and she hurtled back to Earth as truth reared its ugly head. *Roxanne Silva?* Was Jon having sex with his ex on the side? Confused and bewildered, she stared at the traitorous, lacy underthings, then dropped them as if they scorched her hand.

She scurried around, confused, gathering her undergarments and fire clothes, not wanting to be there when Jon returned. Her intense fury could cause her to hurt him physically, though violence wasn't her way.

I have to get out of here.

With trembling fingers, she dressed and fumbled on her

boots, not bothering to lace them, then numbly put her hair into a messy ponytail.

She riffled through Jon's corner desk for something to write on. Her vision blurred with brimming tears.

Has he been seeing Roxanne this entire time?

She picked up a yellow legal pad, noting two words of interest at the top: *Tell Liz???*

Damn him. He'd been debating whether to tell her he was enjoying his ex as a side dish? Tears spilled onto the paper, forming blurry, blue pools. Good. Let him see how he'd hurt her.

She found a pen and scrawled: *You didn't have to tell me, chicken shit. I found out on my own! WTF? You ARE a Wildland Wolf!*

Tears blinded her as she carelessly tossed the tablet on his bed. She plucked the black bra and thong from the floor and threw them on top for good measure. Pain stabbed every cell in her body. She groped for her phone and hit speed dial for Tara. No answer. Too distraught to leave a message, she tapped Rego's number. He didn't answer either. Neither did Tupa or Kenzie.

"Dammit, why aren't they picking up?" she muttered. Then she remembered they were all at the concert. She'd have to walk back to camp, and she was exhausted.

Wait, Cohen said he was staying at camp tonight. She hovered her finger over his number. After his suggestion of wanting to pursue a relationship, she was reluctant to ask him to come get her. It was only a ride. On impulse she tapped his number.

He answered. "Liz?"

"Hi, I need a ride back to camp. Can you please come get me at the Alpenglow Hotel?"

He paused. "Sure. I'll be there in ten."

"Thanks." Liz shoved her phone in her pocket, appreciating he didn't ask questions.

Jon's phone lit up and vibrated on his desk. *Roxanne.*

Liz stared at it, tempted to heave it in the trash. Instead, she tapped the speaker icon. "Hello, Roxanne."

She waited for the caller to speak.

She didn't.

"Jon's not here, what do you want?" Liz punched each word with intensity.

Silence. A dog barking. Then a whisper. "Who's *this*?"

"Someone you don't want to tangle with." Liz spoke in an even tone, holding it together as her heart disintegrated into ashes.

Roxanne ended the call before Liz could say anything else.

Liz stood frozen, staring at the phone until it blurred. She scrolled through Jon's recent calls. Teardrops fell on his phone when Liz scanned through dozens of calls from his ex. And because she was her father's daughter, she took a photo of Roxanne's phone number with her cell phone.

Oh, God.

Heart thundering, she tapped the message icon and read the last text where Roxanne blathered how much she loved him.

Liz couldn't bear to read the rest.

"No-o-o-o!" The shock was too much. Her chest clenched, and it hurt like hell. She wailed and pressed palms to her heart to stop the dreadful pain.

She pitched Jon's phone on top of the other presents she left on his rumpled bedsheets and beelined for the door.

As she stepped onto the elevator, she glimpsed Jon proceeding barechested down the hall, with damp hair and a white towel around his neck.

"Liz! Where are you going? Wait—"

She wanted to throttle him but squeezed her eyes shut as the doors closed, her finger fumbling for the lobby button. When the doors opened, she exited the hotel as fast as she could. The crew van sat idling in a front parking space, with Cohen at the wheel.

Desperate to control herself, she faltered. *Get a grip. You're Cohen's squad boss. Now act like it.* Weakness wasn't an option. She felt anything but strong at the moment.

Cohen hastened from the van and came around to her. "What's wrong? What happened?"

His genuine expression of concern undid her. She stared at him, shaking her head. "I should have listened to you."

He moved to her and pulled her into a tight embrace.

She laid her head against his chest and sobbed.

"What the hell did he do to you?" he muttered in her ear.

They stood next to the van, while Cohen consoled her.

Jon hadn't broken her heart.

He'd shattered it.

🔥

*J*on couldn't figure out why Liz had left. Maybe something happened back at Aurora Camp and she had to get back? He debated following her. Instead, he went to his room and peeked out the window.

Shock didn't begin to describe seeing Liz in the arms of Tremblay. What the hell? He watched in disbelief as the dude held her like she was his. *No dickhead, you don't get to have her.*

Liz seemed upset, crying about something. Did something happen to her father? Cohen wiped her tears, then opened the passenger door for her to get in. He got in and they drove off.

Jon stood mystified. They made passionate love not even an hour ago. The best ever, in his humble opinion.

When he turned and noticed the rumpled sheets on his bed, he was even more baffled. He picked up and read what she'd written on his legal tablet. *What's this Wildland Wolf shit?* He stared at the black bra and thong crumpled on the bed. With thumb and forefinger, he lifted them and noted the RS initials.

Roxanne left them here last night. Why hadn't he noticed them before? *How did Liz see these, and I didn't?*

His eyes darted to the open drawer of his nightstand and TV remote on the floor. He twisted, remembering he'd told Liz the clicker was in the drawer if she wanted to watch TV. Roxanne must have stashed her bra and thong in it.

"Dammit!" he erupted, pitching the intimates at the headboard.

Did Roxanne think this would turn him on? No, she was shrewd. She did it for other reasons. Roxanne must have figured Liz spent time in his hotel room. She'd gambled on Liz discovering them before Jon did.

The gamble had paid off for Satan's Mistress.

He beat himself up for not noticing one of his key cards had been missing. He had to get his act together, pay closer attention to what he did, now that he knew the lengths Roxanne would go to get what she wanted.

This was the last straw. Roxanne would pay for this. He wasn't sure how, but it was time he wised up with this situation.

For starters, he wanted a paternity test for the son she claimed was his. The boy in the photo had dark hair like his, but Jon had observed no other resemblance.

First, though, he had to talk to Liz. He tapped her number. No answer. He left messages and texts. She didn't return them. Now what? Too late to drive over to Aurora Camp, everyone would be in bed.

Liz had fire to fight in the morning when Aurora Crew went back on the fireline. And he had a fire investigator meeting first thing tomorrow morning.

He made one last call before going to bed.

"Hello, Jonny. Figured you'd call," Roxanne said with a yawn.

He chose his words in a careful, measured tone. "If you come anywhere near me or Elizabeth Harrington, I'll have you thrown in jail. I'm getting a protective order. Don't contact me." He tapped to end the call before she could say another word, then blocked her number on his cell.

No way would he let Roxanne have the upper hand. He'd track down her son to find out whether or not he was the father. The last thing he'd do was allow her to blackmail him. Why did she want to marry him so badly again? Roxanne did nothing unless it served her own agenda.

His family's money. That must be the reason. She'd made a

grab for it when they divorced, but Jon hired an attorney that prevented it.. Contrary to her claims she had changed—no, she hadn't changed at all.

He recalled Simone mentioning that she'd hired a private investigator a few years back to dig up dirt on a cheating husband. After their meeting tomorrow, he'd ask her about it. He'd find Roxanne's son and arrange a paternity test.

What bothered him most not knowing exactly how much leverage Roxanne had.

That was about to change in a big way.

CHAPTER 32

*L*iz had set her alarm early to make phone calls before going on shift. First to Ravish, who wouldn't answer. She'd checked her bank account again. Nothing. Her own fault for leaving her username and password on her desk back at the Nevada apartment. Liz kicked herself for her reckless stupidity.

She called the bank and explained that her roommates found her username and password to steal the money from her account. She didn't have a vast amount but had saved what she could from her dancing and firefighting paychecks.

The bank told her they could protect her savings account, but they weren't sure about the checking. They told her to report it to the Las Vegas Police Department. Liz still knew some of her dad's officer friends, and she called two of them, Officers Lundgren, and Murray. Both stated they would open a case on the theft and see what they could do.

Helps to know cops. They would do what they could to help her. Only problem was, she couldn't leave fire and fly down right now. She'd have to rely on others to help her out. She preferred to handle it herself, but what choice did she have?

She couldn't believe Ravish would do this to her, after the last three years of living and working together. Liz thought they'd become good friends. She wasn't a BFF like Tara, but Liz talked her boss into hiring Ravish, then offered to share the apartment she'd found in the Vegas suburb of Henderson. The only thing was, Liz disliked Jasper, her boyfriend, immensely. She wondered if Jasper had convinced her to drain Liz's accounts and blackmail her with the photos.

Liz beat herself up for leaving her username and password on a sticky note with her laptop. She'd been in such a rush to get to Angela's wedding, she hadn't given it a thought. And now she'd paid for it. Literally. The last thing she figured was that Ravish would screw her over.

If her dad were lucid, he'd admonish her. "Serves you right, Lizzy. I taught you better than that." She heard his voice in her head.

Liz prepared to go out on the Crane Lake Fire. The weather forecast predicted an ongoing pattern of storm tracks with high winds, a firefighter's worst enemy. Winds tracking from the Bering Sea and Gulf of Alaska could be fierce, even in the summer.

Heavy smoke had settled over south central Alaska and Anchorage's air quality readings were off the charts, causing all kinds of problems for its active outdoor population. The municipality issued the first dense smoke advisory in its history —so bad, it hid the Chugach Mountains. Health advisories were in effect from the Kenai Peninsula all the way up to Talkeetna, in the Mat-Su Valley.

Limited visibility affected everything from small plane travel to offshore commercial fishing operations. Visibility was so poor along the Sterling Highway, the Alaska Department of Transportation used pilot cars to lead strings of traffic north and south.

The Crane Lake Fire so far had burned 150,000 acres, with no signs of slowing. Four hundred and eighty-seven fire-fighters had contained seventeen percent of it with crews from all over Alaska. More were on their way from the lower forty-eight.

Dave Doss stated the highest priority was protecting the

three communities of Sockeye Landing, Silverleaf, and Rock-fish, and all the businesses and homes in-between. The confla-gration had the potential of wiping out countless homes, along with the economy of the Kenai Peninsula, if they couldn't get it controlled.

Aurora Crew's job today was to cut a 60-foot wide, two-and-a-half-mile long saw cut line, eliminating all the black spruce to make a wide fuel break to prevent the fire from advancing to the highway, where it could cut off ground trans-portation to and from the peninsula.

Ryan O'Connor had directed air attack operations all day on the radio. He'd been in the air, flying reconnaissance to observe fire behavior. Now the weather system had trapped smoke on the valley bottoms, making it too difficult for aerial observations.

The news media hit the Peninsula in full force and camera crews were everywhere. Reporters tagged the situation on the Kenai Peninsula as the most catastrophic fire in Alaska's history. Tara instructed the crew not to talk to news reporters without first clearing it through her.

Liz was so preoccupied with her problems, she didn't remember the drive to the fire. One minute she'd climbed into the van, and the next minute she stood on the fireline, with her day pack and Pulaski. The night before lodged in her mind, like a disc stuck on whir, playing a bad movie. *Why hadn't Jon been honest about seeing his ex-wife while having a relationship with me?*

She knew he felt guilty about how their marriage had ended. Was it pity sex? No matter how she cut it, the whole thing sucked.

Tara plodded up to Liz, both spent after a day of removing and stacking spindly black spruce trees. "If this fireline won't stop this fire, I don't know what will. Ryan has Air Attack hitting this hard, but the wind gusts keep pushing it."

Liz eyed a charcoal sky growing ever closer along with the black smoke roiling up from never-ending blooms of fire the crew had difficulty slowing. "I understand the Pioneer Peak Hotshots are relieving us."

"They're on their way now. Time to go." Tara motioned everyone to the van.

Liz stared off in the distance at the flames, thinking that caring deeply for someone can scorch a person's heart and soul, just like fire. She numbly whistled at her squad.

Tupa and Kenzie gathered the tools and began shuttling them next to the Sterling Highway. Liz had observed them working together all day, as if something connected them at the hip. It made her feel good, and she smiled. She had nothing else to smile about at the moment.

Her chest tugged each time she thought of Jon. Why hadn't he been honest with her? What happened to trusting each other? In love's cruel aftermath, her memory was rebranded with pain.

How could he be having sex with Roxanne and me at the same time?

What was wrong with people? How could Ravish have stolen from her? Too many questions, and no damn answers. She desperately needed time to think. Hard to do while working on an eighteen-person fire crew she lived, ate, and worked with every day.

She dozed on the ride back to Rockfish, tired of breathing dense smoke and helplessly seeing flame gobble spruce after spruce, mountain after mountain. When the van lurched to a stop, she straggled to the women's tent and sunk onto her cot.

Liz was so tired, her nerves throbbed. She gave Kenzie a weary look. "Kenz, carry me over to the camp mess tent, so I can gobble a gallon of ice cream."

"You're not yourself today, Yank. What's going on?" She looked concerned. "Cohen mentioned you're crossways with Jonno."

"The story of my life when it comes to him."

Kenzie patted her shoulder. "Blokes get messed up sometimes. You'll get things sorted."

"Not this time. He freaking blew it." The sound of finality made her wish it weren't so.

"Let's go get a toastie. You'll feel better with a full belly." Kenzie winked.

Her stomach knotted. "A toasted sandwich sounds good, but all I want is raw cookie dough and a truckload of dark-chocolate-fudge-moose-tracks ice cream."

"Off your duff, mate. Let's go." Kenzie pulled her up. "There's a saying in Oz—don't sweat the petty things, and don't pet the sweaty things."

Liz laughed at her friend's attempt to cheer her up. The two women sauntered over to the long, rectangular mess tent Aurora Crew shared with several other crews.

Liz's phone vibrated, and she fished it from her pocket. Jon calling. He'd only called ten times today. And as many texts:

Call me please. Need to talk to you ASAP.

"In your dreams, buddy." She silenced her phone and jammed it into her pocket.

The women loaded their plates with food.

Liz plastic-wrapped hers. "I'm taking this for later. Not in the mood for conversation."

"Catch you later. Seeya back at the ranch." Kenzie dove into her second hot roast beef sandwich.

Liz smiled at Kenzie sounding more Alaskan than Aussie. As she stepped out of the mess tent, Rhiannon came toward her, carrying a crate full of vegetables.

"Hello, Liz," chirped Rhiannon.

"Oh, hello." Liz was in no mood to chat.

"The kings are running thick and fast." Rhiannon nodded toward the river. "You can see their red backs when they gather in the eddies next to the riverbank."

"Salmon are spawning now?" Liz stopped to be polite, but she was reluctant to expend energy on conversation.

"Do you want to go fishing for Kenai Kings tomorrow? We have a spot where the river isn't as fast, and they practically jump in your net." Rhiannon wore a *Sockeye Landing Caterers* baseball cap, with her hair piled under it. "The current is too fast to catch them here. We'll get enough king salmon steaks for your whole crew and grill them in the mess tent."

"I'm putting in ten-hour days, and am pretty wiped out at

the end of them. Tomorrow will be the same." Liz was too weary to make plans for tomorrow.

"It'll only take an hour and a half at the most. I'll pick you up here. We have to hit the king run while we can. Your crew can help us clean them," explained Rhiannon, smiling.

How could this person stay perky all the time, wondered Liz. "It does sound like fun, and I do need a break. But I'm not an experienced fisher person."

"You don't have to be. I'll show you. I'll meet you here tomorrow after I finish work."

She could use a break away from the crew. "I'll see how I feel. Give me your cell number, and I'll text you."

"Nope, don't need it. I'll be here in the parking lot tomorrow." Rhiannon gave a little wave and continued to the mess tent.

"Rhiannon!" a male voice called out.

Liz turned around to see Cohen striding toward Rhiannon. He gave Liz a nod as he stopped to talk to the woman. They launched into animated conversation and Cohen took the crate from Rhiannon and carried it into the mess tent for her.

Liz raised her brows. She didn't know what to think of Cohen. He'd consoled her after she bailed on Jon last night and had seemed sincere, despite her rejecting his suggestion of a relationship. Now he was cozying up to this woman. What did she expect?

Nothing anyone did or said made sense to her right now. She suddenly felt out of sync with everything around her. On the way to the women's tent, she wandered along the bluff overlooking the Kenai River. She tried to sort through everything, but when she did, her brain ached.

Her biggest regret was allowing herself to fall for Jon, despite her initial concerns about it. The very thing that had attracted her had been his biggest downfall—how he charmed women. Three divorces had been a red flag from the beginning. She should have heeded that little detail. Cohen's remark played in her mind, that a leopard didn't change its spots.

Apparently not. Jon hadn't changed his old ways. Not when his ex's underwear populated his hotel room.

She couldn't think about how FUBAR her life was right now. *I wish I could talk to Dad or Jon about it.* She corrected herself —*Oh yeah, Dad doesn't know who I am and Jon is the enemy now.*

She dragged herself through a shower and crawled into her sleeping bag, too tired to cry herself to sleep.

CHAPTER 33

After Jon had showered and dressed the next morning at the crack of the all-night, Alaskan dawn, he needed to see Liz to explain himself. She hadn't responded to his calls. Not that he blamed her after what she'd found in his room.

How could he convince her he hadn't had sex with his ex-wife?

Aurora Crew would be pulling out of camp at 7 a.m., as they had every morning prior, from what Liz had told him. He jumped in his pickup and pulled into the lot, only to find the van had already left for the Crane Lake fireline.

He had to relieve himself, so he headed for the men's restroom. As he strolled to the crew camp, someone called out.

"Silva." The voice didn't sound friendly.

Jon abruptly stopped and turned around in the parking area adjacent to the Aurora camp.

Tupa, Rego, and Cohen piled equipment into a truck, when Cohen stopped and came at Jon like a fire engine, moving into his personal space. "You have some nerve showing up here."

Jon stood his ground and straightened to his full height. "Don't remember asking for your approval."

Tremblay wasn't the least bit intimidated. He was shorter but matched Jon's brawn. "I had to go get Elizabeth the other night because of whatever you did to her. She wouldn't tell me what. Took a while to calm her down."

"None of your damn business," gritted Jon, his fuse diminishing by the second.

"It is when I'm the only one who's always there for her—which is more than I can say for you. Anyway, she's gone on fire. You're too late."

"You've been dogging her from day one," growled Jon, straining for what little patience he had left for this guy. He held up a hand. "This isn't a good time for this discussion."

"No? Alright, we'll see who the better man is and which one of us deserves her." Cohen turned to go, then turned back around. "I've known guys like you. You're players. Users of women. You gather them like firewood, burn them, and move on to the next. Tell me, did Liz find you with one of your whores?"

Jon's temper slammed down. "Motherfucker!" He shoved Cohen hard, causing him to stumble back.

"You're a real tough guy, aren't you?" Cohen recovered and rushed at Jon to throw the first punch.

He knocked off Jon's sunglasses. Jon's arm shot up to block Cohen's fist. His other hand balled into a fist and caught Cohen's right upper cheek, sending him to the ground.

"Dammit!" Cohen rolled to his side and yelled, holding his eye.

"What the hell, Silva?" Rego charged over, with Tupa on his heels. "What's with you two?"

Tupa grabbed hold of Jon as he was about to pounce on Cohen, while Rego tugged Cohen to his feet.

Jon shook loose from Tupa's grip. He pointed at Cohen. "I came here to see Liz. Not get into it with you. Be careful with your accusations. You don't know squat about me and Harrington."

Cohen glowered at him. "I know more than you think."

"Keep your grubby mitts off Liz," growled Jon. He stooped to snatch his sunglasses. "We'll settle this later. Count on it." He stomped off toward his truck.

"Anytime, loser. I'll be here!" Cohen called after him.

Jon wanted nothing more than to tear into this dickhead, but he'd only make things worse. He didn't need this right now, before his investigation task force meeting.

Smoke hung in the air as he drove faster than he should have to the mayor's building. When he climbed out of the truck, he noticed his vest pocket had torn from his early morning tussle. He fumbled with his fire inspector badge to pin the flap in place, smoothed his tousled hair, and hurried to the conference room.

Dammit, he hadn't expected to confront Tremblay. A shitty start to his day. He didn't need his nose out of joint right now.

The meeting had started with the usual reports in a round robin as Jon breezed in to take a seat at the long conference table. "Sorry I'm late," he mumbled.

Trooper O'Donnell gave him a curt nod and led off. "We haven't made leeway on an arson suspect. People have reported suspicious behavior here and there, but no leads so far. Except maybe one."

He clicked through the slides on his laptop, with images projected on the screen at the front of the conference room. "We obtained video and still images from a surveillance camera mounted on a utility pole next to the one lodge that didn't burn in the Swiftcurrent Fire."

He clicked to the first photo. "This vehicle parked here for fifteen minutes before the fire started. We made out the plate info with magnification."

Jon leaned forward and squinted at the image. He recognized the black SUV with tinted windows. It prickled his spine.

Trooper O'Donnell clicked through the rest of the photos with vehicles owned by employees. "The SUV is the only vehicle where we can't get hold of the owner. Belongs to a Tyler Kettleman."

The name clanged a gong inside Jon's brain. *Roxanne's brother.* The vehicle she'd driven the evening she'd followed him to the restaurant.

Could his morning get any worse? He debated whether to

admit he knew the owner but chose instead to keep his mouth shut. Soon as this meeting ended, Jon knew where he had to go.

Jon asked the trooper, "Have you talked with the owner?"

"His sister said he was out fighting fire."

Wheels spun in Jon's head as people discussed their concerns about the Crane Lake Fire and its threat against the three Kenai Peninsula communities along the Sterling Highway.

When the meeting ended, Jon caught up to Simone as they left the building. He'd lost count of the brush fires he needed to stamp out in his personal life.

"Have you changed your mind?" She smiled in that beguiling way of hers.

He chuckled. "You're persistent, I'll give you that. I need a favor. Can you put me in touch with a private investigator in the lower forty-eight?"

She raised her brows. "Trouble down south?"

"You might say that. Need someone in northern California."

Simone opened her bag and lifted her wallet, pulled out a card. "This guy will hook you up."

He took the card and examined it. "Rattlesnake Smith? Sounds like a gunfighter."

"Not his real name. It's an alias. Too many people are after him. He's good at what he does." Simone winked.

"Thanks, appreciate it." He twirled the card in his fingers as they headed to their vehicles. "I'll catch up to you and Keaton later. I have someplace to go first."

"Wherever it is, be safe. Word is, they'll be closing the Sterling Highway due to dense smoke and fire burning toward it."

"Not to worry. Safety's my middle name."

She rubbed his shoulder. "You know where I'll be if you need—someone to be with."

"Right." *Not likely.* He knew who he needed.

He stopped off to run up to his hotel room to get his Ruger. The one he'd forgotten the day Liz sprayed the bear. He'd stashed it in his nightstand drawer. Now he stood staring down at the empty drawer.

Shit!

His stomach clamped down at the sickening prospect that Roxanne had taken his Ruger.

He flinched, then grabbed his keys and raced to his pickup.

I must get it back.

🔥

*L*iz's stomach hadn't calmed down since leaving Jon's hotel room two days ago. It only worsened as she took in the information at the morning fire briefing at the Dept. of Forestry headquarters. She lost herself in her work to stay sane. She had a sense of control on the job—unlike her personal life, which had gone up in flames. She may be done with Silva, but life had to go on.

The Crane Lake Fire had made another run, parallel to the Sterling Highway and jumping across the 60-foot fuel break Aurora Crew had created yesterday. The fire had grown in intensity, tossing spot fires in front of the main head. Now it had set its greedy sights on Silverleaf. The southwest corner of the fire had not only reached the Sterling Highway, it had crossed it twice in the last twenty-four hours.

The Alaska State Troopers had issued a "Go" evacuation order earlier that afternoon, and evacuated Silverleaf, except for the city fire departments, wildland crews, and law enforcement.

Aurora crew hiked up a steep slope on the fire's right flank. They set to work cutting spruce and brush, tamping out flames with spruce boughs.

Liz's radio squawked. Tara's voice. "They've closed the highway to travel between Sockeye Landing and Silverleaf. Smoke is dense. Zero visibility."

"Copy that." Liz blew out air. "We're continuing to mop up on this end, to make sure all hotspots are out."

"Good," replied Tara. "We're doing the same on our end.

Dave Doss has ordered controlled ignition operations to reduce the energy component of the main fire."

"Hope it works." Liz eyed the flames in the distance. "Wind speed is picking up."

Tupa, Rego, and Cohen had stayed behind to load hoses and other fire gear in a pickup that arrived later. They hiked up to join Aurora Crew.

Cohen marched up to Liz, his Stihl chainsaw over his shoulder. "Your precious Jon Silva is a rat bastard barbarian. He plays you like his cheap guitar."

Liz paused, her canteen halfway to her mouth. She took in Cohen's purple shiner, and her jaw dropped. "What do you mean? What happened?"

"I defended your honor. That's what happened." He tossed off a stern look and strode along their fire break to saw trees.

"He and Silva got into it this morning back at camp." Rego shook his head. "I don't understand what's gotten into Jon. I've never seen him so quick to punch someone's lights out."

Tupa stood next to Rego. "They were fighting over you, Boss."

"Oh. Thanks for telling me." Unwanted guilt seeped through her. Now what had she caused? Just when it couldn't get worse, it had. Life had a way of not only smacking her down, but kicking her in the gut on the way to rock bottom. Then kicking her some more for good measure.

I'm here to fight fire, not mediate a love triangle. Cohen told her he wanted a relationship, and she was tempted now, after discovering Jon still banged his ex. She despised him for it.

A sudden explosion lifted all heads, catching everyone by surprise. Liz's radio squawked. "Afi Slayers, get out of there," ordered Tara. "Fire hit a propane tank next to a cabin, and it's heading your way."

"Copy that." Liz noted the flame towers coming toward them and shoved her radio in its holster. "Afi Squad, we need to bug out now," she shouted to Rego and Kenzie.

"I'll fetch Tupa and Cohen." Kenzie jogged off.

Liz noticed a sizeable spot fire burning toward Kenzie. As

soon as the realization hit her that Cohen and Tupa were also close to it, someone screamed.

She tore off running, her boots twisting and turning in the clumps of vegetation as she leapt over downed skinny spruce trees.

Liz reached Kenzie, Rego, and Tupa, to see them attempting to lift a tall, burning spruce off Cohen. He was face down on the ground, moaning.

"Tupa, saw the tree in half. We have to get it off him," ordered Liz, her heart thundering. "Rego, Kenzie, help me get this fire out."

They'd already set to work beating the flames on the fallen tree. Kenzie had the water bladder piss pump on her back, spraying them.

Tupa's chainsaw bit into the tree next to Cohen, careful not to come in contact with his body. Finally, the tree lifted a little when Tupa cut it in half.

Tupa and Rego hefted one end, while Kenzie and Liz dragged Cohen from under the flaming tree.

Rego and Liz kneeled, one on either side of Cohen.

"Roll him over. Gently," ordered Liz.

They eased Cohen to his side, and he moaned.

"Talk to me, buddy," urged Rego, his brow furrowing.

"Not dead," Cohen croaked out. "Just feels like it."

"You're okay, Cohen," Liz reassured him, palpating her hands along his arms and legs, feeling for injuries. Blood ran down his face. His hardhat had prevented head injury, but it had a sizable dent on top.

Liz eyed the encroaching flames, and her pulse raced. Another snap and whump as another tree hit the forest floor. "Time to GTFO, folks," ordered Liz.

"Tremblay, we have to hot-shoe out of here, buddy." Rego grabbed Cohen's arm and slung it around his shoulder. "Tupa, grab his other side."

Fire debris rained down on their hardhats as the five of them hustled out of the woods from the advancing fire as fast as they could.

Liz caught sight of the rest of her crew up ahead. Tara ran toward them when she observed Liz's squad helping Cohen.

"Burning snag fell on him," panted Liz. "He needs an air evac to a hospital. Don't think he broke bones, but he needs to get checked out."

Tara keyed her radio and asked Ryan to send her a medevac chopper.

Once they reached the highway, the guys set Cohen on the ground next to it. Liz squatted next to him and removed his hardhat. Thankful his hardhat had done its job, she checked his scalp, waving away mosquitoes. She plucked one from his swollen cheek and smiled down at him. "So, you duked it out with a spruce."

"The tree outsmarted me. Jumped off the stump when I cut it, and it attacked me."

She forced a smile. "The attack of the killer trees. I'm sure it's a movie." She patted his shoulder. "We'll get you fixed up, don't worry. You'll be fine."

"Thanks." He closed his eyes.

"Try to stay awake, okay?" Liz tried to control the tremor in her voice.

"Yeah," he mumbled.

Her chest knocked as she kneeled next to Cohen, feeling responsible for what happened. She cared for Cohen. Not romantically, but in a brotherly way.

Mel landed with Juliet, and two paramedics hopped out with a portable litter. They ducked under spinning rotors and carried the litter and set it on the ground next to Cohen.

Once they had him loaded onboard, Liz and the crew backed away as the forceful rotor blades whipped up stinging clouds of dust. Tupa helped carry and load Cohen inside Juliet, then ducked out of the way.

Everyone backed away from the rotor wash as Mel lifted Juliet and disappeared into thick smoke. Liz breathed a prayer of thanks that Mel was the pilot transporting her squad member to the hospital in Rockfish.

Tara announced to the crew, "Time to stop for the day.

NorthStar Hotshots are here to relieve us. Let's get to the van before they close the highway, and we sit in a line of traffic."

She waved the crew to their van and pulled Liz aside. "Tell me what happened."

"The spruce jumped off the stump when he cut it, and he couldn't get out of the way. None of us saw it happen. Tupa cut it in half so we could free him. It's all my fault." Liz shook her head, guilt gnawing at her.

Tara gave her a sharp look. "Why do you say that?"

"Cohen said he tangled with Jon back at camp. Jon came to see me this morning and wound up giving Cohen a black eye. He didn't have his head on straight when he stepped onto the fireline. I should have calmed him down first. He was distracted by what happened."

"Not your fault. Don't beat yourself up. He'll be okay." Tara climbed into the van.

"I hope so." Liz wanted to run. Get away as fast as her legs would carry her. She needed a distraction. "Would it be weird to go fishing with Rhiannon, the food lady? I don't know her very well, but I really need a break to clear my head."

Tara plopped into a seat and shook her head. "Not weird in Alaska. Up here it's not that unusual for people to invite acquaintances on fishing trips. People do it all the time. Besides, you know her well enough. She's all over the place providing food to firefighters."

Liz sank down beside her. "True. Yeah, I may take her up on her king salmon fishing offer."

"Have fun. Don't wear yourself out after working all day," cautioned Tara.

"Right, Mom, I won't." Liz gave her friend and crew boss a grateful smile, then leaned back and nodded off for a quick nap on the way to Rockfish.

When they arrived back at camp, Liz barely had time to unload her stuff, clean up, and stuff a few things in her day pack. She tossed in two bottles of water, her pocketknife, a light jacket, and her phone. This time, she made sure it was fully charged.

Rhiannon waited in her pickup and waved as Liz emerged from the women's tent. She must be crazy to be going fishing right now. Tara had assured her that it wasn't unusual in this neck of the woods to go salmon fishing with someone she hardly knew. In the smaller towns, it was no big deal.

As tired as she was, Liz desperately wanted to distance herself from the stress of the day. She longed to let her troubles slip into the emerald waters of the Kenai, as she stood on its banks, catching colossal salmon. She'd make up for today's close call by gifting her crew with grilled king salmon steaks.

As Cohen's squad boss, she felt responsible for his accident. Especially upon learning he and Jon had come to blows because of her. She'd find a way to apologize to Cohen. For now, she needed a diversion from her multitude of problems.

Liz opened the door to the pickup and hauled herself into the passenger seat. She smiled at Rhiannon. "Okay, let's go. Take me to slay salmon."

"Slay. I like that word." Rhiannon nodded and gave her a broad smile, backed up the truck, and kicked up gravel as she revved the old pickup out of the camp parking lot.

CHAPTER 34

efore Jon pulled out of the parking lot, he contacted
Simone's Rattlesnake character in Phoenix while he
still had cell service. He rousted the guy out of a massage and
the dude referred him to another private investigator in Sacra-
mento. Jon called, and the P.I. agreed to take care of obtaining
the paternity test. And it would cost him. Jon didn't care. No
way could he travel to the lower forty-eight right now to do it
himself.

He told the P.I. he'd call back with specific information
when he obtained it. Surely, Tyler would know the whereabouts of Roxanne's son. He needed to get hold of Tyler.

Once he'd wrangled that gnarly situation, he peeled out
onto the Sterling Highway, closures be damned. Screw it—he
had to beat the state troopers to Coho Lodge. He needed
answers.

And he wanted his gun back.

He turned up his Bendix King radio to listen to highway
closure info. Jon gunned his pickup. Two miles south of
Sockeye Landing he turned onto the road leading to Coho
Lodge, leaving dust in his wake.

Jon lurched his pickup to a halt in the small parking lot in
front of the main lodge. The black SUV and a red Toyota
4Runner were parked out front. He sat a minute to see if

anyone moved around inside the impressive main lodge. Couldn't help but marvel at the large spruce and red cedar logs used to construct it. The red cedar logs, he guessed, were thirty inches in diameter. He admired the log trusses and ridgepoles that braced the roof.

Jon admired Alaskan log construction and had always thought about building his own log home someday. Too bad his ex owned this. It was the type of place he'd love to stay in to go fishing. The Kenai Peninsula was the last place anyone wanted to be right now, salmon or no salmon—agony for Alaskan anglers while kings were running. If he didn't have all this work to do, he'd have a line in the river.

Convinced no one occupied the lodge right now, Jon pulled a pair of blue nitrile disposable gloves from his fire investigation kit and snapped them on. The last thing he wanted was to leave fingerprints anywhere since he intended to enter the premises. He grabbed his digital camera and climbed out of his pickup. First thing he did was inspect the SUV. He took photos of both vehicles, including plates, and tire-tread patterns. He peeked inside both and tried the door handles. Locked.

Smoke pallor penetrated everything, giving the place an eerie vibe. Jon stepped up onto the covered porch and peeked inside. No movement. He tried the front door. Also locked. He moved off the porch and circled the building, checking for signs of life.

Nope, no one home. Jon wondered what Roxanne drove, since the black SUV and red Toyota Forerunner were there.

A small log building tucked behind the main lodge drew his attention. He loped over to it and tried the door, surprised that it opened. A "Roxy's Nails" sign hung in the front window. He remembered her saying she'd brought her nail salon business with her to Alaska.

Jon stood in the small building, examining the layout. The usual nail salon supplies, he supposed, stacked on shelves, and a nail polish display rack of every color on the planet. He leaned in and squinted at a unique teal color he'd noticed

Roxanne wearing when she planted herself in his hotel room. *Metallic Mermaid.*

The sharp, pungent smell made him straighten and take notice. The unmistakable stink of acetone. A tiny utility closet on the far wall caught Jon's eye. He moved to it and opened the door to three shelves containing gallon jugs of nail polish remover—enough to torch the entire state of Alaska. A lower shelf contained cartons of Marlboro cigarettes and boxes of wood stick matches. The same brand of cigarettes and type of matches found on several of the fires.

Roxanne didn't smoke. Neither did her brother.

Realization rushed at him like a wall of flame. He choked and staggered back, disbelieving.

My fucking ex-wife is the arsonist?

Jon's neck hair raised with enough electricity to light up the entire Peninsula. He rummaged around for his gun, yanking out drawers and riffling through boxes on shelves. No Ruger.

He whipped his camera into motion, photographing everything.

Jon fished out his phone, his finger hovering over Trooper O'Donnell's number. He hesitated, knowing he shouldn't be here. O'Donnell had warned him not to involve himself should he find the arsonist.

I have to know. I must get inside the lodge first to see what's there! He circled the lodge until he found the back door with the jammed lock he'd helped Roxanne with that day he was here. He jiggled the doorknob, trying to recall how he'd unlocked it last time. Frustrated, he kept fiddling with it.

It finally clicked open, and the door swung in. At least he didn't have to break in, but he was still entering illegally. The hell with it. He was in no mood to wait.

"Roxanne?"

No response. He stepped into the main lobby. He yelled again.

Nothing. Good. Made things easier.

Jon headed for the office behind the reception counter, looking for his weapon. Not finding it, he zeroed in on a laptop. While he waited for the computer to power up, he spied a map of the Kenai Peninsula on the wall, with stick pins in certain locations. One tiny label caught his eye: Swiftcurrent Fire. He lifted the camera and photographed it.

He turned to the laptop and sat down, hoping it wasn't locked. Roxanne had never been one to secure anything. That hadn't changed.

A photo icon on the desktop snagged his eye, and he clicked it. Up popped random photos of Jon driving, eating, going to or from his pickup in the hotel parking lot. Another of him and Liz kissing in the restaurant parking lot, and he and Liz eating. His neck prickled.

He photographed all of it, recalling that ten years ago he'd predicted Roxanne's mindfuck would backfire on her someday.

It seemed someday had arrived.

He skimmed through photos of Liz at various fires. What jarred him were candid photos of her at Aurora Camp, walking to and from the mess hall and bath house. His stomach twisted. Roxanne had been stalking them but targeted Liz.

Icebergs spiked his spine, and he went numb.

Jon pawed through the desk drawers. Mostly random junk, except for a few grocery receipts. One for two cartons of cigarettes. He took a photo of the cigarette receipt and laid it on the desk.

Adrenaline pumping, he ducked out to peer out the windows. Still, no one around. *Better hurry in case someone shows up.*

Jon clicked on more files, frowning at spreadsheets of surrounding lodge businesses, and the ones that had burned had red lines through them.

He found photos of Aurora's Crew roster and a list of their fire assignments by date and location. Roxanne must have gone inside the state forestry building to get all this info from the Fire Situations Unit rooms.

She'd been tracking Liz's whereabouts.

The clincher—a photo of Liz standing with her Pulaski in

hand, talking to her Afi Slayers Squad… on a *fire*. How did she come by that photo? His breath caught at an image that eviscerated his insides. A photo of Liz with a bold, red circle and a solid bar through it. The image damn near nailed his heart to the wall.

He lifted an empty CD cover of Fleetwood Mac lying open on the desk. He pressed the CD button on the laptop and pressed play. Stevie Nicks sang *Rhiannon*. Roxanne's favorite song. Realization hit him with a one-two punch to his stomach. Nausea pushed up.

He remembered Liz saying a woman named Rhiannon had brought them food on the Swiftcurrent Fire. Jon sprang to his feet, feeling like he'd imploded. He knocked the chair over in his haste to race outside and down the steps, leaving the door gaping open. With trembling fingers, he retrieved his phone and tapped Liz's number.

Pick up. Pick up! No answer.

He tapped Tara's number. "Tara, I need to speak to Liz."

"G'day Jonno, Kenzie here. Tara's busy at the mo, I caught her phone."

"Kenzie, is Liz there?"

"No. Tara said she took off with that weird woman. The one a few roos short of a paddock if you ask me."

"What weird woman?"

"The caterer woman who feeds the firefighters. Rhiannon. Liz said something about going salmon fishing on the Kenai River."

"Rhiannon?" The trees, the lodge, the woods, his truck rushed in, then out again. He slowed his breathing to function. "Did Liz say where they were going?"

"Somewhere on the Kenai River. Don't know where."

"Thanks, Kenzie." Jon couldn't tap Trooper O'Donnell's number fast enough.

"O'Donnell."

"Hey, it's Jon. I found out who the arsonist is. And she has my—my girlfriend."

"She? The arsonist is a she?"

"My ex-wife, Roxanne Silva. She goes by an alias, Rhiannon."

"Your ex is the fire setter?" A long silence. "Wait—not that caterer woman who makes those delicious chocolate chip cookies?"

"I know, it's crazy. I'm as shocked as you are, believe me. I'm at her place now, the Coho Lodge in Sockeye Landing. Arson evidence is all here. You boys need to get here, pronto." He hastened to add, "I didn't break and enter. The door was unlocked."

"Doesn't matter, Silva. As far as you and I are concerned, you weren't in there before we were, got it?" Trooper O'Donnell let out an impatient sigh. "Thought I made it clear you fire investigators were not to involve yourselves directly with the arsonists."

"Yes, sir, you did. However, when I identified the black SUV in the surveillance video, I knew something was up with the ex-wife and her brother. I apologize for not telling you, but I needed answers on a personal level."

"We'll need a search warrant from the district judge in Kenai. I'll prepare an application and an affidavit and fax it over," mumbled O'Donnell. He paused. "If the arsonist has the same last name as you, this isn't gonna look good for you, Jon."

"I know. I'll deal with that when the time comes. First, we need to find Elizabeth Harrington. I believe she's in danger."

"Your girlfriend? How do you know?"

"My ex has been stalking me and Liz. She pretended to be someone else and somehow persuaded Liz to go with her. I believe she'll harm her. Can you dispatch troopers to search for them? They're in an old blue truck. Don't have the plate info."

"This certainly changes things. All this time we've been looking for a male. Where do you suppose they are?"

"Liz's crew mates said she was going fishing on the Kenai River."

"With the arsonist?" Disbelief was evident in Trooper O'Donnell's tone.

Jon knew the whole thing sounded ludicrous and let out a heavy sigh. He reiterated, "The arsonist posed as someone else and befriended Liz, who's a firefighter on the Aurora Crew."

"Let me get this straight. Your ex-wife, also the arsonist, kidnapped your firefighter girlfriend. And you happen to be the fire investigator of the fires your ex sets and your girlfriend fights." Trooper O'Donnell paused. "Am I missing anything?"

"No sir, that pretty much sums it up." Jon exhaled, resigned. "We need to find them." O'Donnell made it sound contrived. Jon had to admit, the whole thing did sound whacked.

"The Kenai is a long-ass river. Can't you zero in on a location so I know where to send my cruisers?"

"I'll contact her brother. He might know."

Another pause. "Gotta ask you this. You're not—you're not involved with the arson, are you, Jon? You aren't one of those fire investigators who start fires, like in past wildfires in the lower forty-eight?"

"Chrissakes, O'Donnell, hell no! Look, you need to get over here ASAP. The evidence tying Roxanne Silva to the arson fires is all here. I'll call the brother, see if he knows where his sister might have taken Liz. I'll wait here for you, but please, hurry."

"All right." Trooper O'Donnell ended the call.

Jon tapped Dave Doss's number. He had to find Tyler Kettleman.

Liz's life was in unbelievable danger, and time was running out.

CHAPTER 35

*L*iz tried once more to fasten her seat belt, without any luck.

"You should get this fixed," she mumbled. She peered through the cracked windshield of the beat-up pickup. "The State and Feds have been wrangling over closing this highway. We may not be able to access your magical fishing spot."

Rhiannon flashed her an irked look. "I'm not worried. I go around these closures all the time." How odd that Rhiannon wore a dark hoodie on such a warm day.

Liz raised a brow. "The closures are for public protection."

They passed fire vehicles parked on the left shoulder with lights blinking, and crews walking in single file along the roadway. "There's the Midnight Sun Hotshots," remarked Rhiannon.

"Right. How do you know that?" Liz craned to catch a glimpse as they sped by, her suspicious nature kicking in.

"I know a few crew members. Two I know more intimately, if you know what I mean." Rhiannon broke out in a smug smile, her insinuation clearly messaged. "Your Aurora Crew and Midnight Suns are on the same rotation schedule."

Liz's curiosity increased by the second. "Your finger is

certainly on the pulse of what's going on. How do you know our schedules?"

Rhiannon gave her a side glance. "The catering business I work for has a contract with the state firefighting division to provide meals for firefighters. They tell us where the crews are assigned, and we drop off the food. Like that day on the river when I dropped off lunch for your crew."

"Oh." Liz figured that made sense, but it bothered her the woman insinuated she'd had sex with firefighters. She wasn't sure why it bothered her, but it did.

Rhiannon drove like an unseen force propelled her. They blew past Silverleaf and fire smoke thickened as they neared the wildlife refuge.

Suddenly, Rhiannon braked and turned right onto Kenai Refuge Road. They drove fifty feet, and abruptly stopped at an orange-and-white road barrier with a BLM fire truck parked nearby. Two firefighters in yellow shirts stood next to it.

"Damn," muttered Rhiannon. "This was open yesterday."

Liz slid her window down to talk to the firefighters. Before she could speak Rhiannon threw the truck into reverse, then lurched it forward onto the highway. She drove a short distance and braked hard.

Liz heaved forward, bracing her hands on the dash, then thudded back against the torn seat. She shot Rhiannon an incredulous look. "What are you doing?"

"Almost missed the road." Rhiannon swung onto a rutted dirt road that had seen better days. Another orange-and-white barrier stopped them. Rhiannon slammed the brakes, then leaned back. "Help me get this barrier off the road." She had an edge to her voice.

Liz looked at her as if she'd sprouted devil horns. "No way. It is there to keep the public out. We shouldn't go past it."

Rhiannon stared upward as if deliberating something. She adjusted her baseball cap, sighed, and looked directly at Liz. "I really need your help to move this. It's heavy."

Liz shook her head. "We need to get out of here. Can't you access the river another way without going past a closure?"

"No. This is the only way in. Come on. You want salmon, don't you? We won't be there long." She flashed an urgent smile at Liz.

Against her better judgment, Liz shoved open her door and got out. She stepped to the barrier and grabbed the end of it. It pulled back easily. "This isn't heavy," she mumbled, glancing behind her as she tugged the plastic structure to the side of the road.

Liz heard a strange sound and looked up.

Rhiannon stood in front of her, holding a revolver.

Liz did a double take, unable to comprehend. "Why are you pointing a gun at me?"

"Get in the truck. You're driving." Rhiannon motioned the gun at the driver's side door. "I said get in."

Liz stood, stupefied, her mind searching for a logical reason. What was this woman going to do? Was Liz being kidnapped? Did the woman expect a ransom for her?

None of this is logical. None of this makes sense.

"Not telling you again. In the truck!" Rhiannon's voice rose, her mouth a tight straight line.

"You can't do this!" cried Liz in disbelief. "We'll be driving toward the Crane Lake Fire."

"I don't mind shooting you and leaving your body here for the fire. Because that's what'll happen if you don't get in and drive." Her eyes shifted to a cold, hollow stare.

So, this is how people disappeared in Alaska—accepting invitations from lunatics.

Liz's hackles raised to red alert as she climbed into the uncomfortable driver's seat and took the wheel. "Why are you doing this?"

Rhiannon took the passenger seat, pointing the gun at Liz. "Just drive."

Liz sputtered. "This is insane! You're insane!" *Crazy. Weird. Nothing made sense.*

"Say that again and I'll blow your head off! Drive until I say stop," snapped Rhiannon.

Liz shifted into gear and jounced the truck along the rutted road. "I noticed no fishing gear in your truck." She glanced at Rhiannon with narrowed eyes. "So where is it?"

Rhiannon smiled an evil grin, sending chills through Liz's veins.

I better pay attention to my surroundings. Liz made a mental note of a large clearing to their right in the yellow-gray haze.

After driving another mile, an old, dilapidated cabin emerged from the haze on the left. It sat back a few hundred feet from the road.

Rhiannon lifted the gun and gestured it at the cabin. "Pull in here."

Liz's stomach twisted. "Why are we here? Tell me what's going on!"

"Shut up and get out. Don't piss me off." Rhiannon waved the gun again.

Liz thought about opening the door and bolting through the woods. Not a wise choice with a fire thundering toward them. Plus, she didn't want to get shot. She opened the door and hesitated, staring down at the overgrown driveway. No tire tracks except theirs.

"No one's been here in years," muttered Liz, her heart hammering at what this woman intended to do.

"That's right." Rhiannon got out and herded Liz onto the porch. She fished a key from her pocket and held it out to Liz. "Open the padlock. Do it!" she snarled.

Liz's shaking hand wrestled the key into the beefy padlock. It unlocked and Liz glowered at her. "If you're kidnapping me for ransom, you won't get away with it. People will look for me. My boss knows I'm with you."

Rhiannon snickered. "Shut up and open the door."

Liz removed the padlock and Rhiannon yanked it from her hand. Liz grunted as she pressed her shoulder to the door, and it gave way. Dust shook loose and a dank, musty smell filled her nostrils. The last thing Liz wanted was to go inside a deserted, dark cabin. She peered inside, trying to adjust her eyes to the dark. "This place stinks."

"That's why you deserve to be here." Rhiannon shoved Liz

inside, followed her in, and slammed the door, leaving the place dark and eerie.

Slivers of daylight edged in between gaps in the rotted boards nailed over a narrow, dirty window. The cabin stunk like dead bats and slimy things—humid and rancid. A ramshackle wood table and broken chairs crowded one corner. In another stood a rusted, potbellied wood stove, and a crude wood bunk without a mattress.

Liz peered at Rhiannon standing in front of the door, pointing the gun. "Why am I here?"

"Why do you think?" Rhiannon unzipped her hoodie and tugged it off with one hand. Careful to keep the gun pointed at Liz, she let it fall to the floor. She stepped forward, into a narrow shaft of light.

The world spun away as Liz zeroed in on Roxanne's pink blouse with the blue flecks. Her heart thundered in confusion until an unnerving reality broke out as instant sweat on Liz's forehead. "You're not Rhiannon." Liz glowered at her. "You're Roxanne Silva."

Roxanne let out a sardonic laugh, and her demeanor changed, as if she'd been possessed. "Pathetic little tramp. Took you long enough to figure it out."

What a freaking volatile situation. Liz kicked herself for getting sucked in. "Jon and I found the little gift you left behind when you set the Skilak Fire." Liz motioned at the torn hem in her pink blouse.

Roxanne glanced down and lifted the sheer hem to the light, scrutinizing it. She smirked at Liz. "You can't prove anything."

"You went to all the trouble of creating a fake identity just to lure me on a fake salmon excursion? I'm flattered."

"Ha, you fell for it. Why else would I pretend to be friends with a sleazebag stripper? You people disgust me." Roxanne regarded her with animosity and folded her arms. "Want to know how I kept track of your crew schedule? Your buddy, Cohen. He's terrific in bed, by the way. He sure likes your slutty ass, though I can't imagine why."

"Liar. Cohen doesn't have time to lay women. And he won't be doing it anytime soon. He's been injured."

Roxanne laughed. "Gee, that's a shame." Her tone could slice ice.

Liz's revulsion rolled out of her mouth. "Don't you care what happened to someone you supposedly had sex with?"

Roxanne shrugged. "Not really. He was a means to an end. We hooked up that night after I saw you at the mess tent. Something else you should know. My husband and I had a glorious time in bed while you were out fighting my fires," she taunted, smiling.

Liz flashed back to Roxanne's bra and thong in Jon's hotel room. She didn't know what to believe right now. She didn't know whether Jon had sex with his ex or not. One thing was certain, this woman was capable of lying—capable of anything, after torching thousands of acres and now holding her at gunpoint.

"*Your* fires? You narcissistic witch! Jon is no longer your husband, remember?" Liz wanted to lunge at her and wallop her with her fists, but she had to maintain control and strike at the right moment.

"Of course I set the fires. My brother needed the work. I loved watching you people fight the good fight. Plus, I had to get rid of my competition. Coho Lodge will be the go-to tourist place on the Kenai from now on." Roxanne appeared pleased with herself.

"Well, aren't you the clever one?" Liz needed to record this on her cell phone, but how could she pull it off without Roxanne seeing her? *Create a diversion.*

"Jon still loves me, and we're getting remarried. Has he told you we have a son?" Roxanne chirped.

"Yeah, right." The news jolted Liz, but this chick could be concocting all kinds of bullshit. She had to stall for time.

Liz wandered over to a dust-caked, linoleum counter and eyed a grimy dish rack of old dishes. With lightning speed, she reached for the dish rack, whirled around, and heaved the whole thing at Roxanne.

Roxanne squeezed her eyes closed and crossed her wrists in front of her face to deflect the airborne plates. One knocked her baseball cap off and another hit the gun, but it didn't fire.

Liz fumbled her phone from her pants pocket, tapped the red "Record" icon, and shoved it back in her pocket, praying it had turned on. There wouldn't be a second chance.

"You little bitch, you'll pay for that! What's in your pocket?" Roxanne recovered and charged at Liz, but she jumped out of the way.

"This!" Liz reached for her fire knife and flipped open the short blade with her thumb. It seemed puny compared to Jon's Ruger, but it was all she had. *Oh God, Jon. Where are you?* She needed to contact him, but how?

Roxanne guffawed. "What are you going to do, stab me? Ha, like that'll happen." She waved the gun around then aimed it at Liz's face, eclipsing her paltry pocketknife.

Liz fixated on the muzzle, recognizing the Ruger. "You stooped to a new low, stealing Jon's gun." *Think. Think.* What had her dad instructed her when someone pulled a weapon?

"I've always held the winning cards and controlled your puppet strings." Roxanne's casual tone made Liz want to strangle her.

"You set fires for control? That's twisted. Then again, you arsonists always show up to admire your handiwork."

"Arsonist?" Roxanne laughed again. "Sounds badass. I like it. I prefer to call it cleansing the competition. My lodge will be the most successful business on the peninsula."

"Hard to run a business from prison." Liz hoped her phone captured all this. Even if Roxanne shot her, hopefully fire investigators would find the phone with her confession—*if it survives the wildfire burning toward them.*

"Mmm, don't think so, sweetheart. Fire destroys evidence, remember?"

"Not always," gritted Liz. She thought of Jon, and her heart ached. Her eyes stayed on the muzzle as she stood gripping her knife. She thought of lunging at Roxanne but feared getting shot. Or she could pitch the knife if she could hurl it at the speed of light.

"When we remarry, I'll make sure I inherit the trust fund from Silva Vineyards." Roxanne *did* sound like Satan's Mistress, just like Jon said.

Liz guffawed. "You're out of your mind if you think you'll get away with a lame black widow crime. Jon's too smart for that fatal attraction bullshit," she snorted.

Roxanne's eyes flashed, and her hand twitched. "We'll see who's smarter." She lurched toward Liz, to backhand her with the gun.

Liz had anticipated the move and jumped out of reach, but Roxanne managed to knock the knife from Liz's hand, catapulting it across the room.

"I'm done toying with you. Time for a firefighter to die by fire." Roxanne held the gun out with a straight arm as she backed to the door and yanked it open. "So long, Blaze Diamond. Can't wait to see Jon's face when I tell him you're dead."

Roxanne exited, pulling the door closed. Liz stumbled on the dishes and pans she'd heaved at the crazed woman as she raced to the door. By the time Liz yanked the door handle, the sound of a padlock had clicked into place. It may as well be a guillotine dropping onto Liz's neck.

A hollow panic seized her. *How could I be so stupid to let this sociopath suck me in?*

Liz sunk to her knees in hopeless despair as regret and self-loathing ripped her insides to shreds.

CHAPTER 36

*J*on waited in his truck, frantically tapping Dave Doss's number, his nerves taut as hell.

"Dave, it's Silva. I need to contact a Tyler Kettleman, state firefighter. Can you please locate him for me ASAP? This is a family emergency. Something happened to his sister." A little white lie, but he'd atone for it later. If Jon had his way, he'd toss Roxanne overboard in the Gulf of Alaska to let the crabs and bottom dwellers go to work on her.

"Sure, Jon, I'll track him down and have him call you."

"Thanks, Dave. There's more to it, but I'll explain later."

"Copy that. Later."

Jon ended the call as an Alaska State Trooper's cruiser swung in, sun glistening on the white hood. Trooper O'Donnell parked it next to Jon's rig and climbed out.

He opened his door to brief the trooper. "I photographed the evidence. Acetone jugs and incendiary device materials are in that nail salon building out back." He pointed. "Seize the computer and map on the wall. It's all evidence. I know it sounds bizarre, my ex being the arsonist. She did it for profit, and for spite against me."

O'Donnell held up a clipboard with a legal document containing the district court heading and the Alaska seal. "Obtained the warrant." Trooper O'Donnell raised his brows.

"If your ex is the arsonist and she has your girlfriend, no telling what she'll do. Don't handle it yourself. That's our job. I don't want fire investigators pursuing or apprehending arson suspects. Are we clear?" His eyes pierced Jon's.

"Yes sir, crystal." Jon couldn't make any guarantees but no way would he let O'Donnell know that. Not where Liz was concerned. "Please keep me posted. You have my cell."

Jon climbed in his pickup and gunned it. He bounced along the gravel lane and spun out as he turned onto the Sterling Highway. He wondered how many times he'd sprayed gravel, peeling out to get on this road.

His phone sounded as he left Sockeye Landing. Roxanne's brother. He pulled off in an RV parking area, thankful he was still in cell range.

He answered. "Tyler, thanks for calling."

"Has something happened to Roxy?"

"Your sister is in serious trouble."

"What kind of trouble?"

"You need to be straight with me. Do you understand?" Jon cleared his throat. "Do you know your sister is an arsonist?"

Silence.

"Tyler, you better come clean with me, man. I don't have time for bullshit. Roxanne has my girlfriend, Elizabeth Harrington. She took her somewhere, and I think she means to harm her. I have to find them before Roxanne does something stupid."

"Your girlfriend? What do you mean, Roxy took her?"

"I need you to tell me where Roxanne might have gone. She took Liz fishing for kings on the Kenai River. Have you taken Roxanne fishing on the Kenai?"

"Yeah, a couple times."

"Where? Which roads?"

"The Kenai Refuge Road. We have a fishing hole eight miles in, but the road's closed. They won't get in."

"Any other roads?"

"There's a spur road half-mile north of the refuge road that winds up in the same place."

Jon glanced up at a trooper cruiser zipping past, lights flashing. He hoped they were heading out to search for Liz. "What would she be driving if not the black SUV or red Four-Runner?"

"My old blue Ford pickup. It's the only other rig we have." Tyler sounded anxious, and for good reason. Things weren't looking good for him right now.

Jon flashed to the homeowners' photo of a blue Ford pickup with the person in a hoodie.

"Tyler, you must level with me. If you cooperate when the Alaska State Troopers question you, they'll go easier on you." Jon wasn't sure about that, but he needed the truth. Who knew when he'd get the chance to speak with Tyler again? "Do you get what I'm saying?"

"Yeah."

"Are you aware Roxanne has been setting wildfires?"

More silence. "I know about one. Uh, maybe two."

"Did you know before or after she did it?"

Tyler exhaled fast. "After. She always joked about setting fires so I could earn money fighting them. And she hates the competition with our lodge. She joked about torching their lodges, but I didn't think she'd actually do it."

That fit with what Jon had found in the lodge office. "Which fire did she tell you about?"

"The Skilak Fire. That's all I know."

"Thanks, Tyler. One last thing—does Roxanne have a son? If so, where is he?" Despite his urgency to find Liz, Jon had to glean what he could now in case Tyler landed in jail.

"You mean Dusty? He's with our parents in Sonoma. Why?"

"Who's his father?"

"Roxanne said you were. She swore me to secrecy, that I'd never tell you about him."

"She slept around those last months before our divorce. The math doesn't add up for me to be the father."

"Geez, Jon. Honestly, I don't know."

Jon had no choice but to believe him. "Okay. Thanks for your help."

"Will Roxy go to jail? Will I?" Tyler sounded innocent.

Jon prayed he was, for his sake. "I can't speak to that right now. But if you stick to the truth, things will go easier for you. Don't lie to protect your sister. Not for something this serious."

"Uh, Jon? Um—you don't think I set any fires, do you?"

"The troopers have video of your vehicle parked at the Swiftcurrent Lodge the morning it burned. Even if Roxanne had been driving it, they'll be contacting you. I have to go. Thanks, Tyler." Jon tossed his cell in the other seat and thrust the truck in gear.

Enough monkeying around. I've got to find Liz.

Jon peeled off the gravel shoulder, kicking up a cloud of dust that mixed with fire smoke. He eyed the upcoming highway sign, *Only You Can Prevent Wildfires.* Smokey the Bear wanted motorists to know *Fire Danger is EXTREME Today!*

He blew by the sign so fast, his draft sucked the pants off Smokey the Bear.

🔥

*L*iz squinted at the cracks between the boards covering the window. Roxanne held a red gas can, splashing gas on the rotting, log walls. A glop hit the window, and Liz pulled back, horrified.

Roxanne plans to torch the cabin.

Liz had to do something fast. She'd be damned if she'd die in this bumscrew never-to-be-found bodyville.

As the stench of gas filled her nostrils, she reached in her back pocket and fished out her phone. The red "Record" button still blinked. She tapped it off. Only one bar for cell service. The recording function had drained her battery. Only fifteen percent juice remaining.

Fingers shaking, she tapped the speed dial for Jon. "Please! Answer it!" she cried out loud.

Her call pulsed his phone once, then her phone died. She tried again. Nothing.

No! How will I notify Jon? Oh God.

My pocketknife! She dropped to all fours and brushed her hand in a wide arc on the rough wood floor, frantically searching for it. Shoving plates and pans out of the way, she heard a metallic clink on a pan. She found the knife, snatched it, and stood, heart thundering, thankful for the dull slivers of daylight so she could see.

Liz heard Roxanne step around the decrepit shack, sloshing gas on all four walls. She paused in front of the narrow window and raised a flame starter. "Let's see you put this one out, fire-fighter."

Whoosh! The spaces between the logs generously allowed the pungent stench of gas to fill the small cabin. Smoke seeped in as the flame took hold.

"Run fast, you pathetic loser—I'm coming after you!" raged Liz as terror turned her stomach inside out. She shook so hard, her knees knocked.

"You'll have to come back from hell to do it," taunted Roxanne, laughing.

Smoke penetrated the cabin, crowding her brain's chaos, and nausea pushed up. Her stomach rolled at a sudden rush of sorrow for herself and Jon if she were to die here.

Liz glanced around wildly, then darted about, yanking out drawers and rummaging them for anything to help her escape. Her only way out was through the impossibly skinny window if she could pry off those boards.

She squinted at the rusty nails holding three wide boards over the narrow window. She clutched the top board and pulled. Nailed tight. Couldn't budge it. She needed a tool. She plucked her pocketknife from her pants, unfolded the short blade, and stumbled to the boarded window. Wedging the knife under one end of the board, she pulled with all her strength. It gave a little, but at this rate she'd be dead by the time she pried off one end.

"Screw this!" She whirled in a panic. "You better hope to

God I don't get out of here!" yelled Liz. She involuntarily sucked in a breath and choked out a coughing fit.

Muffled laughter from outside, then Roxanne yelled back, "Let's see you put this one out."

"Murdering skank!" Liz shouted.

More laughter as flames crackled, eating flammable, rotted logs.

Roxanne's truck started up and zoomed away.

Seeing was impossible in the smoky dark. Liz remembered a pot-bellied stove in the corner to the right of the door. Where there's a wood stove, there had to be tools. She fumbled her way over and felt behind the stove. Her hand contacted a long wood handle.

An axe! She lifted it for laser-quick inspection. More rust than metal, but better than nothing. She prayed the thing wouldn't disintegrate when she whacked the boards.

Her eyes watered and sweat flopped as she raced back to the wood countertop. She flung the axe on it, then climbed on top, hoping the rotted counter wouldn't cave in. Smoke plagued her lungs, and she gagged and coughed. She swung the rusted blade at the top board repeatedly, hard as she could.

Crack! The board split along the grain.

Liz wormed her fingers between the boards and yanked. Half the top board broke off in her hand. She feverishly hacked at the middle and bottom boards with the axe. The bottom board broke apart, but the middle one was stubborn and wouldn't give.

"Dammit, come on!" she screamed at it. Fear of burning to death spiked her adrenaline to the max.

Smoke sucked her oxygen as she tugged at the remaining board that blocked her escape. The burning, nasty stench caused her to gag and cough even more. She tugged the obstinate board with all her might from the grimy window, scratching and scraping her fingers. Splinters pushed in deep.

Liz grabbed the axe and brought it down hard on the last board. It broke off. She raised the axe and swung with all her might at the glass, but she only cracked it. Another swing, and the rusty axe head flew off into the smoke.

"No-o-o-o!" she sobbed, desperate not to give in to the terror determined to paralyze her.

"Break, you sucker!" Grunting and roaring like a crazed brown bear, she repeatedly rammed the glass with the blunt handle until it shattered, and she doubled over in a coughing fit.

Fumes fused with spirals of smoke as the fire roared and licked, consuming rotted wood.

Coughing out a lung, she sat and leaned back on the counter to kick the remaining glass shards with her boots until the opening was large enough for her to squeeze out.

The pop and hiss of the fire as it engulfed the shack let her know she was out of time. She couldn't inhale without choking.

Praying she wouldn't impale herself, she stuck her head through the narrow window, gasping for oxygen.

Six feet to the ground.

Fingers of flame danced up the outside wall below the window. She had to dive out headfirst. Hell, it was no different than dangling upside down on a pole, only minus the pole.

She squeezed her head and torso out the small window. Glass shards tore her shirt and stabbed her right side as she muscled herself through the tight fit. "Ow, dammit!"

Liz grimaced from the pain and launched herself out with one last push. She splayed her hands to break her fall, hitting the ground hard. Flames licked at her clothes. *Where's my Nomex when I need it?*

She ducked her head and rolled away from the flames, wincing as a rock gouged her side. Coughing, she labored to stand and backed into a birch. She glanced down at her torn shirt. Blood ran down her side. She winced as she untucked her shirt, wadded the bottom, and pressed it against her side to stem the bleeding. Her lungs heaved from exertion as she watched the blaze consume the shack—without her in it, thank God. She wasn't sure what sucked more, the wildfire smoke outside or putrid smoke inside that dank shack.

At least I'm out of that death trap.

Liz felt for her phone. Gone. Must have fallen out. She stumbled forward to look on the ground and spotted it where she'd fallen. She dived for it. Flames licked at her as she grasped it and backed away, heat searing her face. The phone was hot to the touch.

Dead battery. *Oh God.*

Liz stumbled to the road, disoriented. Sharp pain stabbed her side, and she knew not to touch the open cuts with dirty fingertips. She kept direct pressure on her wound, recalling Jon's first aid training last year up at Chinook, Alaska, on Aurora Crew's first fire assignment. *Jon, I need you badly right now. I'm so sorry for getting pissed at you.*

Which way had they driven in? She remembered turning left to park in front of the cabin.

Holding her side, she turned right and half ran, half jogged along the rutted road, pain preventing her from sprinting. Every muscle screamed from the strain. At this rate, her only hope was to reach the Sterling Highway and pray to God it wasn't closed. She had to find someone to call the state troopers and give her a ride to Rockfish. And tell the troopers to find Roxanne.

Smoke cloaked her like a silent monster, reminding her a catastrophic wildfire was gaining on her.

CHAPTER 37

*J*on blew past the sign for the Kenai Refuge Road, squinting at the smoke. He slowed and crept the truck along so he wouldn't miss the turn. Seeing a break in the spruce, he slammed his brakes, jerked the steering wheel to the right, and stopped at an orange-and-white road barrier. Two firefighters stood next to their rig, parked off to the side.

He slid his window down and stuck out his head. "Hey, fellas. I'm searching for an old blue pickup with two women in it. One's real pretty, honey-colored ponytail—"

"Yeah, we saw them," one guy interrupted him. "They turned in, saw the road closure, and took off like someone was after them or something."

"Which way did they go?"

The firefighter pointed in the direction Jon had come. "That way."

"Thanks, boys." Jon reversed the truck and headed back.

"Dammit." He gritted his teeth and peered out the wind-shield, forced to slow to fifteen miles per hour along the narrow, two-lane highway. He activated his hazard lights. Hopefully, anyone coming up fast behind him would see the blinking lights in this godawful smoke.

He made a superhuman scan of the dense spruce edging

the highway, looking for a space between the trees, indicating the unmarked road. Another orange-and-white road barrier met him as he swung his truck to the right. This one was halfway across the road, as if someone moved it in a hurry.

Jon swung around it. The washboard road jiggled his truck as the ruts pulled his tires left and right. *God, Liz, where are you?*

His phone lit, and the *Surfin' Bird* ringtone played. He slammed on his brakes and picked it up.

Liz calling!

The song stopped, and the light went out. "Wait, wait…" He tapped it, but the call had dropped. *Dammit.* His recent calls menu had snagged the Caller ID, not the location. He tried calling her back, without luck. He tossed his phone in the seat and took off down the road.

An old blue truck barreled toward him, kicking up dust. Jon slammed his brakes and waited for it to get closer. Roxanne at the wheel. No Liz. He threw his truck into park and clambered out with his arms spread wide for her to stop. She swerved around him, leaving him in her dust, then turned into the clearing off to his right.

He jumped into his truck and followed her in. She skidded her shabby vehicle to a stop, and he pulled up to the left of it.

Roxanne was out of her truck by the time he killed the engine and bailed out. Holding up a radio, he sprinted around the hood of his truck to confront his ex. "Tell me where Liz is, and I won't call the state troopers."

He stopped short when Roxanne lifted his stolen Ruger and pointed it at him.

"Your stripper is dead."

CHAPTER 38

*L*iz made her way down the road for what seemed like forever, clutching her slashed side. She reached the clearing she'd noticed on the way in, and stopped to assess the dense smoke.

She rested next to a clump of alder, her lungs ready to explode after jogging nonstop. Each time she coughed her right side burned with pain. She lifted her arm to inspect her wound. Blood caked her side where the window shards snared her when she'd squeezed out of that hellhole. She'd managed to stem the bleeding while she forced herself down the rutted road, careful not to twist her ankles.

Shouting came from the clearing. A man and woman arguing. Liz peeked around the alder, peering into the yellow haze, disbelieving. Roxanne's blue truck parked next to a newer red one. *No, it can't be—Jon's pickup? What the heck is going on?*

She fought an impulse to dash out and pummel Roxanne for leaving her to die. What was Jon doing there? She ducked back behind the alder, parting the branches to scrutinize the situation.

"What did you do with Liz?" Jon's voice sounded dangerous.

She'd not heard him use that tone before.

"Get in the truck!" yelled Roxanne.

"Where did you take her? Give me my gun!" Jon moved into view, his hands out front in a defensive posture.

Roxanne returned his menacing tone. "I said get in the truck."

"You've gone too damn far this time!"

Roxanne waited for Jon to get back into the truck, then she climbed into the passenger side, pointing his gun at him.

Liz fought panic. *Is Jon's whacked out ex going to shoot him?* A flash of wild grief tore through her.

She wasn't sure what Roxanne planned to do, but Roxanne had no qualms about leaving Liz to die in a fiery cabin. This made her a dangerous killer—along with the moniker of arsonist. Liz no longer sympathized with Roxanne's abusive past. Not when it came to destruction of lives, property, and her beloved wildlands.

Liz had to get in close and do something. *But what?* Roxanne presumed her to be dead. At least she had *that* going for her. Liz's only option would be to sneak up to the back of Jon's truck and pray to God Roxanne wouldn't see her.

She had no other choice.

Her side stung, and she pressed her torn shirt against the wound. She fixated on Roxanne's head inside the truck. Hopefully, she wouldn't notice Liz sneaking up behind them.

She stooped low and crept from her hiding place to the middle of the clearing. She scooted up behind the tailgate, careful to stay low. Muffled arguing came from inside the truck. Liz couldn't make out what they were saying.

I must get Jon's attention.

Liz crouched down, wincing at the pain in her side. She inched to the left, behind the tailgate.

If Jon would only check his driver's side mirror.

"What do you mean Liz is dead?" Jon shouted, a heaviness centered in his chest.

"She died in a cabin fire. I couldn't get her out." Roxanne shrugged.

Jon's heart stopped as he stared down the barrel of his own gun. "You'd better be lying. Tell me where she is, or this won't end well for you."

"You have no say in the matter." She wiggled the gun. "I'm in control now." The self-satisfying way she said it sent chills up his spine. He wanted to wipe that smug smile off her face.

Jon fought to maintain a relaxed demeanor, but his insides twisted, and his brain hammered. He switched on the ignition and put the truck in gear. "I'm going after Liz, so start talking."

Roxanne raised the gun and pointed it with a straight arm. "Cut the engine. We need to talk. We aren't going anywhere."

"That's debatable." He glanced at his side-view mirror, his hand resting on the ignition keys. He blinked.

Am I hallucinating? Sure as hell hope not...

His heart launched in a Mach One trip over the moon. There was Liz, crouched near the rear fender, waving like a wild woman.

Chrissakes, she's alive! Joy mashed up with disbelief and dread —she was still in danger.

"You have a decision to make. Either you marry me again or pay me a million in cash."

Jon held back a guffaw. Instead, he gulped. "You're doing this for money? Of course, you are—your alimony dried up." He now had a precarious balancing act—keeping Roxanne occupied while Liz planned to do God-knows-what from the back of his rig.

Keep her talking. He glanced at his side mirror. "Why would I marry you after holding me at gunpoint? You know I don't have that kind of cash. We settled finances in the divorce agreement. I paid you alimony for the first ten years, as the court specified. I met my commitment. I'm done."

Roxanne narrowed her eyes. "You can get it. Your family has the money."

Jon flashed her a venomous look. "Ever since our parents died, my brother Rick's worked his ass off to keep the winery from going under. Wildfires destroyed our vineyards, and Rick had to start over. I know you know that."

She tilted her head. "You have a trust fund."

"Not giving you any money. Not after this. Arson is a felony. You're going to prison."

Roxanne laughed. "Hardly, Jonny. I'm the one with the gun."

"The name is Jon. Stop calling me that." He stole a quick glance at his side mirror. *Where's Liz? What is she doing back there?*

"I said turn off the engine." Roxanne waved the gun at the ignition.

Jon shut off the truck. He leaned back, staring straight ahead, focusing on his peripheral vision to catch movement to his left. *Distract Roxanne, keep her talking.*

"Why did you set the fires?"

"I got off watching you show up and tromp around. And I had to get rid of the lodge competition. Too hard operating our lodge with other lodges stealing our business."

He snorted. "Give me a break. *That's* the reason you burned half the Kenai Peninsula? You burned others out so you could get their clients?"

"Tyler needed the work, so I created the work for him. That's how I did it in California."

He shot her a look of incredulity. "You set fires down there, too?" His chest thumped as he squeezed the bottom of the steering wheel. Arson was the last thing he thought she'd be capable of.

"Of course, idiot. Tyler made us a ton of money fighting fires around Sonoma."

"If I find out you set the fire that destroyed our vineyard —" Jon's jaw dropped at the sheer lunacy of all this. He couldn't believe his ears. "You're crazy if you think I'll give you money, let alone marry you again."

She raised the gun to his face. "Don't you *ever* say I'm crazy. Take it back. Apologize." Her tone rose, growing louder with every word, yelling the last.

He held up his hands. "Okay, sorry. Calm down. Lower the gun." He stole a fast glance at the side mirror. Liz hunkered next to his rear fender, waving frantically.

Jon had to stall. He pretended a coughing fit.

"You still haven't gotten rid of that annoying asthma?" Roxanne said, contempt in her voice.

Jon pretended an obnoxious production of hawking up a loogie. He opened his door and leaned out to spit, tilting his head toward Liz. He jabbed his thumb back toward his truck bed. *Get the flares in my toolbox!*

He closed the door and wiped his mouth with the back of his hand.

"That's disgusting. You haven't changed." Roxanne leaned back against the passenger door, holding the gun with both hands.

Jon eyed the weapon. "What happened to you falling all over me for sex?"

"Because that always worked with you. You used to do anything for a piece of ass."

"I'm not that guy anymore."

"You banged that little stripper whore. Now she's a pile of ashes."

No. She isn't. Jon ignored her comment and managed to keep a neutral face.

"I have photos of your tire treads that match the treads at the fires. I have a phone video from a homeowner who watched you set the Riverview Fire." Should he mention he'd gone through her computer? No, she might shoot him.

She picked up his digital camera and handed it to him. "I suggest you delete those photos. And let me see you do it." Roxanne raised the gun to his chest. "Delete, dear husband."

"Not your husband anymore." He leaned in and glared. "Put the gun down."

He had to think of something, and fast.

CHAPTER 39

*L*iz couldn't figure out what in God's name Jon pointed at. Something in the back of his truck? She was no Vegas magician. How could she pull off a presto act without Roxanne seeing her?

More arguing from inside as Liz sneaked to the back of the pickup and crouched low, peering up at the tailgate handle. Could she lower it without attracting Roxanne's attention? No choice but to risk it. Hell, she was a firefighter. Risk-taking was in her DNA.

She couldn't sit idle, with a lunatic pointing a gun at Jon. She glanced behind her at the ominous smoke cloud coming toward them. The smoke grew heavier, filling the air with ash and particles.

Now or never.

She braced herself, with her feet apart, then grabbed hold of the tailgate handle and lowered the tailgate all the way down. She crouched below the open tailgate to contemplate her next magic act.

Jon slid his window down, most likely for Liz's benefit. She peeked around the left bumper, hoping to catch Jon's eye in the side mirror.

He spoke in loud tones and sounded pissed. "How did you learn to start fires?"

"You should know. You're the hotshot fire investigator," taunted Roxanne.

"You used stick matches rubber-banded to cigarettes. What'd you do, Google it on the dark web? Why didn't you use *road flares*?" He damn near shouted the last two words.

Liz scrunched her face. Why would he suggest ways to start fires to an arsonist? Was he out of his frigging mind?

"*Flares* are easier." He emphasized the word again, drumming his fingers on the outside of his door. He casually hung his arm out the window, pointing his forefinger at the truck bed.

Liz lifted and saw the toolbox. *The flares are in his toolbox!*

As she summoned the nerve to hoist herself onto the truck bed, Roxanne opened her door. "I need some water."

Liz froze.

"I have water right here," Jon said quickly and reached behind his seat to grab a bottle. At the same time, he hung his left arm out the window, motioning Liz to the truck bed.

Roxanne closed her door, and Jon set a bottle of water on the consul between their seats.

"Close your damn window. It's too smoky," ordered Roxanne.

Jon studied his side mirror as he closed the window.

If ever a time presented itself to invoke Liz's ballet skills, it was now. Maybe all the ballet she'd studied had prepared her precisely for this moment—to slither onto the bed of a dusty pickup and belly crawl to the toolbox like a stealthy, ballet ninja without being detected.

She placed her hands on the tailgate and pushed herself up onto it, keeping her weight on her biceps. She slowly lowered her body face down on the dusty rubber mat of the truck bed, holding back a sneeze—praying she wouldn't blow it. Once she suppressed her sneeze, she inched forward on her elbows, like a Navy SEAL. All she needed were sleeve tattoos and black grease smeared on her face.

Took forever, but she reached the toolbox. Jon talked nonstop to hold Roxanne's attention while Liz unlatched the lid and groped inside with her fingers. Two flares lay on top, along with a wrench. She clutched all three and eased the steel toolbox closed. Grunting, she inched backward on her elbows, wrench in her left hand, flares in her right.

She eased off the tailgate and crouched down. Now what? Throw one flare, use the other as a weapon? She gave herself an eye roll. *Yeah, that would work against a gun.*

She thought of a cop strategy she'd heard countless times when her dad and his buddies told their war stories about going after bad guys. *Create a diversion, then move fast.*

Liz moved to the right side of the rear bumper and hunkered. She shoved a flare in her back pants pocket and pointed the other away from her. She pulled off the top and rubbed the top flint against the flare, striking it like a match. Nothing. Nada. She struck it six more times. It wouldn't light.

This better not be a dud.

She'd give anything for a cigarette lighter right now. An arsonist would have a cigarette lighter, right? Does a moose drop nuggets in the woods? Roxanne undoubtedly had one in her truck. Too risky. *I have to light this.*

In exasperation, Liz glanced around. She snatched a sizable rock and struck the flare like a crazed pyromaniac.

It caught and fired up! Ecstatic, she felt like Tom Hanks in *Castaway*. She had to act fast. She stood tall and hurled it over the length of the truck, aiming for the hood. She waited till it landed, not caring whether it rolled off.

"What was that?" yelled Roxanne.

Everyone exploded into action.

Jon bailed out of the driver's side door as Liz sprang to the passenger door, opened it, and yanked Roxanne out of the truck.

*J*on rounded the front of the truck in time to see his Ruger go airborne, then bounce off the blue truck and skid to a stop on the ground between the two vehicles.

By the time he reached the women, one of them had snatched the gun. He couldn't tell which, as they'd locked onto each other, wrestling for control of it.

As Jon took hold of Roxanne to pull her off Liz, he noted Roxanne had ended up with the gun.

Shit!

"What are you doing here? You're supposed to be dead!" screamed Roxanne.

"Surprise!" Liz clutched Roxanne's wrist, but Roxanne grabbed Liz's ponytail and yanked her close. She wrapped an arm around Liz in a cross-chest hold and pressed the muzzle of the Ruger against the side of Liz's neck.

Jon's world imploded in a full-blown panic.

"Don't move, or I'll put a hole in your neck," Roxanne threatened through gritted teeth, her chest heaving.

Liz's eyes bulged, and she panted like a frightened rabbit.

"You're going to watch her die!" screamed Roxanne, tears streaming. "If I can't have you, she won't either."

Jon took a step, eyes hard on hers. "Roxanne. Put the gun down. Let her go." He noticed dried blood along the side of Liz's shirt, but that was the least of her problems at the moment.

Roxanne tensed and pressed the gun harder against Liz's neck.

Liz shook her head, her eyes begging him. "Jon, please. Don't."

His blood turned to ice, and adrenaline hurtled through his veins as his brain fired afterburners, trying to plan his next move.

An unmistakable freight train sound usurped everything.

The oncoming wildfire was a mile from the clearing, tossing debris. Some distance away, a tree snapped.

Roxanne flinched. Jon took advantage of her split-second distraction and lunged for the Ruger. He yanked the barrel away from Liz's neck and tugged her away from Roxanne.

"Run, Liz!" grunted Jon as he tussled with his ex for control of his weapon. He made sure Liz bolted a safe distance away as he pried the gun from Roxanne's fingers.

He was strong, but Roxanne was cunning. She brought her knee up hard, square in his balls. The wind left his lungs, as if sucked by the oncoming fire. Before he dropped to his knees, he attempted to wrench his weapon from Roxanne.

The gun fired.

Jon felt excruciating pain and fell to the ground.

CHAPTER 40

*L*iz jumped at the jarring report of the gunshot and spun around to see a dazed Roxanne staring down at Jon, his Ruger in her hand. Jon lay on his side, moaning and bleeding. A puddle of red formed on the dirt.

Rage coursed through Liz's nervous system, like a torrent. She took full advantage of Roxanne's stunned surprise at having shot Jon. Liz went ballistic, ramming her solid body into Roxanne's. Her side wound reminded her this was a bad idea. Anger super-charged her as she knocked Roxanne to the ground, seizing the gun. Liz straddled her, gripping the revolver just the way her dad had taught her, left hand supporting her right. She aimed it at Roxanne's face.

"Get off me, you whore!" Tears streamed from the sides of Roxanne's eyes.

"Five rounds in this Ruger say you're not in charge. I am." She shot Jon a worried glance. "Talk to me, Slick."

"Shoot her if she moves," grunted Jon as he pushed to stand, blood saturating his side. He limped to his truck and returned with a roll of silver duct tape.

"You'll both regret this," hissed Roxanne, glowering at Liz.

"You shot me. You're done," muttered Jon. He half-fell onto Roxanne's legs to wrap duct tape several times around her ankles, then tore it with his teeth. Groaning, he held his side and inched over to Liz, sitting on the ground. He took the gun from Liz and held it steady on his ex.

Liz pinned Roxanne's wrists to the ground, wincing at her own pain.

Jon motioned with the gun. "Roll her over and put her wrists together."

Roxanne twisted a hand free, and Liz caught the fist as it swung at her.

"Dammit, roll her over, Liz!" growled Jon, his face racked with pain.

She shot him a disastrous look. "Dude! I'm not a fricking octopus. Give me that thing." At lightning speed, she let go of Roxanne, snatched the Ruger from Jon, and aimed the muzzle at Roxanne's face. "Press your fire-setting wrists together, or you'll be chewing on a bullet," she spit out, emphasizing every word to make sure the woman understood.

The corners of Roxanne's mouth lifted. "You won't shoot me, you spineless whore."

Liz moved the gun sideways to the left of Roxanne's head and pulled the trigger. Everyone jumped, including Liz, as dust and gravel sprayed their faces.

Eyes wide, Roxanne slammed her wrists together.

"Jesus, Harrington." Jon's eyes bulged out of his head.

Liz fixed a killer gaze on Roxanne, her voice rigid. "Next time, I won't miss. Roll over and suck dirt."

Roxanne rolled to her stomach, and Jon zapped Liz an *I-don't-believe-you-said-that* look. He grabbed his ex's wrists and wrapped duct tape around them several times. Roxanne rolled onto her side.

Liz picked up the weapon and stood, once again pointing it at Roxanne. "You locked me inside that putrid, burning cabin and left me to die. And you've injured both of us. I should put a bullet in your head." She punched out every word through gritted teeth.

"You're the one who deserves to die," hissed Roxanne.

Jon pushed to stand and placed a hand on Liz's trembling shoulder. He pushed the muzzle toward the ground with the other. "Stand down, Officer Harrington. I'll take this now." He closed his hand over hers and rubbed it with his thumb, easing his Ruger from her quaking hand.

"Roll over and suck dirt? Seriously?" he groaned, rolling his eyes. "Cop kids," he muttered, shaking his head.

"It got the job done, didn't it?" quipped Liz.

"Let me go!" Roxanne cut loose a string of vulgarity that would make a smokejumper blush. Nothing at the exotic dance club came remotely close to the exorcist movie rolling out of her mouth.

"Nice language. Tell Liz I didn't have sex with you." Jon scowled at her. "Tell her."

Roxanne sneered. "I told her you're still a good lay."

"You're done here." Jon tore a piece of tape with his teeth and slapped it over Roxanne's mouth, then stuck on a few more for good measure.

Roxanne's muffled protests drew no sympathy from Liz.

She squatted next to Jon, pain biting her side. "Let me see your wound."

Blood soaked the side of his shirt. She sucked in air and wrinkled her face.

"We need to stem the bleeding," Jon croaked out, his face contorted with pain. "Bandana is in my pants pocket."

Liz found it and pressed it to his wound. "Hold this," she instructed, pressing firmly.

He did as she ordered. "I don't think the bullet hit anything vital, like liver or kidneys, or I'd be bleeding out. Check to see if there's an exit hole in my back."

Liz lifted his blood-soaked shirt. "Yep. There's a hole on the side of your back."

"Good. Went clean through. I have an extra T-shirt in my truck. Get it and tear it into strips. And grab my cell and radio. Please." He grimaced and Liz knew he was in pain.

Yellow smoke thickened as Liz hurried to the truck, gathered the items, and sunk down next to Jon. She offered him his cell and radio, then retrieved her pocketknife to tear holes in his spare shirt. She tore it into strips, then kneeled next to him.

Jon eyeballed the knife in her hand, then flicked his eyes up at her. "Remind me never to piss you off while you're holding a weapon. Here, tie these strips around my waist. Firm, but not too tight."

She stretched them around his waist to hold his folded bandana firmly in place over the bullet hole. "You've lost a lot of blood."

"Nah, just looks that way." He nodded at her side. "We're both wounded in the same spot. How'd you get yours?"

"Glass cut me when I crawled out the window. After your ex locked me inside a burning cabin." She glared at Roxanne.

Jon called out to his ex. "Attempted murder along with arson. Kiss your ass goodbye."

Roxanne lay still, glowering back at him.

Liz finished tying the strips into secure knots. Jon didn't look good, and it alarmed her. "You can't drive with that wound."

"You'll have to." Jon tapped his cell and winced. "Crap, no service."

Liz rolled her eyes. "As per usual." She nodded at the old blue pickup. "What about her rig? Won't you need it for evidence?"

"Nothing we can do. Let's go." He sighed and his face wrinkled with pain. "I feel queasy. And dizzy as fuck."

Liz held the water to his lips, and he took several sips.

"I have an idea. Let's see your radio." She handed him the bottle of water and keyed the Bendix King. "Aurora, this is Harrington. Anyone copy?"

Tara's voice. "Copy. Where are you?"

"With Silva on a spur road one half mile north of Kenai Refuge Road."

"I won't even ask why you're in a closed area. You know the highway is closed. Fire's burning on both sides of it. Are you okay?"

"For the most part. I'll fill you in later." Liz didn't want to explain their injuries. Tara would only worry. "Where are Tupa and Rego? Are they still shuttling equipment between Sockeye Landing and Rockfish?"

"They're at Sockeye Landing. Told them to stay there until the highway opens."

"Can you have Tupa radio me? We need their help to shuttle vehicles." She didn't have time to explain about Roxanne, either. The less Tara knew, the better for the time being. No time for lengthy explanation.

"Are you in immediate danger?"

"Not really, but we could use the help," lied Liz. She noticed the color of the smoke had changed to charcoal. It must have hit a dense stand of timber. Hopefully, the birch will slow the flames.

Tara paused. "According to my GPS, they're fifteen miles from your location. I'll have them contact you. Be sure to check in with me later. Aurora clear."

Liz keyed her radio. "Thanks, Tara." She glanced at Jon and noticed blood had leaked through the shirt strips.

Jon looked up at her. "What if they can't get here?"

"Then we leave the blue truck, and your ex will come with us."

"Oh, lovely." Jon made a face, then reached to open the bloody hole on the side of Liz's shirt. "That's a deep, jagged gash. You need treatment. Get some gauze from my med kit and bring me another water bottle."

"We don't have time—"

"Do it. Please."

With a furtive glance at the billowing smoke in the distance, she hurried back to the truck and returned with his medical kit and more water.

"Lift your shirt and hold still." He unscrewed the lid and poured it over her wound, saturating her jeans. He tore a piece of duct tape off with his teeth and taped the gauze in place. "That'll hold it for a while. We use duct tape to hold planes and vehicles together, so this'll hurt like hell when they rip it off."

"Oh goody, I can't wait," she mumbled.

The radio squawked with Tupa's voice, saying he and Rego would be there in ten minutes. As soon as Tara had relayed they needed help, Tupa said they didn't hesitate to brave the driving conditions. Liz was thankful she could depend on her squad to help her no matter what, just as she would do for them.

Jon glanced at Liz. "We have to get Satan's Mistress into her chariot. Can you drag her over and lift her in? Sorry I can't help."

Liz's anxiety eased with Jon's ability to still crack jokes. "Yeah. Got zip ties?"

"What am I, a serial killer?" He gave her an annoyed look. "Use duct tape to strap her to the seat." He moaned as he lowered his back to the ground and closed his eyes.

Liz grabbed Roxanne's feet and dragged her to the passenger side of the blue truck. She wrestled her into the seat, then wrapped duct tape around her and the seat at least four times. That woman wasn't going anywhere. She slammed the door on Roxanne's muffled protests, then scurried over to help Jon into the passenger seat of his pickup.

Flames leaped into the crowns of the trees about a mile from the clearing, just as Rego and Tupa rolled to a stop and climbed out of their truck.

"Thanks for coming, you guys. Tupa, can you drive Roxanne's truck to Sockeye Landing and turn her over to the troopers? Rego, you need to follow in case this POS breaks down." Liz gave the blue pickup a doubtful scan.

Tupa glanced around. "Who's Roxanne?"

Liz suddenly realized no one on Aurora Crew was privy to her and Jon's world the past few hours. She led Tupa to the blue truck and pointed.

He raised his brows. "That's the Rhiannon lady who gives us food. Why is she duct-taped?"

Liz talked fast, as they were running out of time. "Her real name is Roxanne Silva, Jon's ex-wife. She's the arsonist and tried to kill us. Come on, we have to get out of here."

Tupa stared at Liz. "You're messin' with my brain."

"I know." She pointed at Jon in the passenger side of his truck. "Silva will fill you in. I have to get us ready to go." She eyed the flames, thanking God the clearing served as a natural fuel break to buy them time to get out.

Liz slammed the tailgate in place, then hurried to the blue truck and reached through the driver's side to retrieve her day pack. She blew Roxanne a kiss. "Have fun in prison." Hopefully, she wouldn't see this woman until she testified in a courtroom. She fully intended to file an attempted murder charge or two.

Roxanne shot her an evil stare with muffled screams of rage.

She hurried back to Jon's truck, tossed her day pack in the back, and climbed into the driver's seat.

Tupa and Rego had stunned expressions as Jon finished briefing them. Rego was slack jawed. "Holy shit. Your ex sets fires, we fight 'em, and you investigate 'em. In other words, it's SNAFU."

"Situation normal, all fucked up." Tupa nodded.

Jon managed a lopsided grin. "More like a clusterfuck. Tupa, it's important you get Roxanne to the state troopers in Sockeye Landing. Not only did she set the fires, she tried to kill Liz and me."

Rego's Bronx accent kicked in. "Shit, Silva, what did you do to piss her off? I know all about scorned women. I wrote the survival manual. Even though one of them could suck-start a snow machine. Good thing you don't have a rabbit."

Liz cut in. "I told him the same thing. Okay, guys, we have to GTFO before this fire wants a piece of us." This was no time for idle chat.

"You okay, Boss?" Tupa's expression of concern warmed her.

"Yep. Silva saved me. And if we don't get the heck out of Dodge, we'll all need to be saved."

Tupa did something out of character. He gave Liz a quick hug through the window. "Careful, Boss. See you in Sockeye Landing. Keep your ears on."

She patted the radio on the consul. "She's tuned into your frequency. Thanks, Tupa, you're the best. By the way, don't remove the tape from Roxanne's mouth, unless you want to hear words that'll make you blush."

Tupa nodded, stuffed himself in Roxanne's truck, and shoved the seat back. It was a tight fit for his gargantuan frame.

Liz called out to Rego. "Right behind you."

"Copy that." Rego folded himself in the crew equipment truck.

Everyone cranked their engines, and Tupa led off, followed by Rego. Liz brought up the rear with Jon's agency rig. The small procession reached the Sterling Highway and turned right just as the flames reached the clearing.

Smoke limited visibility, and they couldn't haul ass as Liz had hoped. Twenty-five miles per hour was the max in smoke so thick she could slice it with a Pulaski. She focused on the solid white line to her right to keep the vehicle on the road.

She glanced at Jon. "How are you doing, sport?"

"Thirsty," he huffed out, leaning against the door.

Liz reached behind her for two bottles of water and offered one to him. "Drink all of it."

"You must be spent. Fighting fire all day, then this." He took a long pull on the water. "Mmm, this tastes good. Thank God we're out of that fucking clearing." He leaned back. "I could use a painkiller. Do me a favor, hand me my first aid kit."

She reached behind her for the white plastic box and handed it to him. "How's your side?"

"Hurts like a sonofabitch." He rummaged through his kit and squinted at two bottles of acetaminophen. "Damn, there's only nighttime meds."

"Take them anyway. You need to rest until I get you to a doctor."

"I need to stay lucid in case you need my help."

She gave him a dour look. "I think I can handle it. Take two. Do you trust me to get us there?"

"Knowing you, yes."

"Then take four."

He popped the PM caplets, took a pull on his water bottle, and closed his eyes. "Thanks for what you said back there. You got it wrong, though. *You* saved the day."

She shook her head. "Roxanne would've pulled the trigger, and you prevented that. She hadn't counted on me surviving her first murder attempt." She smiled out at the smoke. "You took a bullet for me, Silva. Just like the Secret Service. There's a new gig for you if you get sick of fire."

"Thank God you escaped from that cabin." Jon turned his head to her. "You're like Wonder Woman. Only sexier."

She reached for his hand. "Sorry I was so upset with you after I found your ex-wife's—" Liz cleared her throat. "Intimate gifts in your hotel room."

"I'm sorry, too. She stole my hotel key card, planted those things in my room, and stole my gun."

She squeezed his hand. "And I'm sorry for being a flaming idiot for getting sucked in by her friendly Rhiannon bullshit."

"Now that we've apologized to each other, we can have makeup sex when this is over."

"Always working the angles, aren't you, Slick?" She grinned. "Depends on how well you mend."

Liz squinted, realizing she'd lost sight of Rego's taillights while she and Jon were yakking. She tried to speed up but had to slow in near-zero visibility.

"Here. Check in with Rego." She handed him his radio and did a double take at beads of sweat on his forehead.

Driving had sucked up her full concentration, and she hadn't noticed the inside of the truck heating until flop sweat dripped to her chin. She wiped her forehead.

Jon keyed his radio. "Rego, do you copy?"

"Yeah. Where are you? Can't spot your headlights."

"We're still back here."

"Getting worse, the farther north we go. Flames on both sides of the road up here. We'd better gun it to get through this gauntlet of hell. Getting hot in here."

"Same here. Keep us posted."

"Copy that. Clear," replied Rego.

"You heard the man. Give her some gas." Jon peered out the windshield.

Scarlet flame replaced the smoke on their left. While visibility of the dark asphalt highway had improved, the trade-off sucked. Tall spruce burned next to the highway as far as Liz could see, like massive tiki torches lining a corridor. In some spots, the flame centers burned white. They were surrounded by a blast furnace.

Jon scanned left to right. "Fire on both sides. Eighty feet tall."

"We're on the yellow brick road to hell." Her insides inverted, and her hands became sweaty, clutching the steering wheel. She was so hot, it felt like the fire tattooed her. She let go with one hand and wiped her clammy palm on her thigh.

Jon reached in the glove box and pulled out a spare bandana. "Wipe your hands and grip the wheel with that. Gun it!"

Liz slammed her foot down, and the truck lurched while the engine whirred upward like a NASCAR leaving the start line. Her shirt stuck to her back. Beads of sweat dripped down her neck.

The radio squawked with Tupa's voice. "Boss, you copy?"

Jon lifted the radio and keyed it. "Copy. How is it up there?"

"Visibility is bad. I'm hauling ass best I can. Suggest you do the same."

"Copy that, thanks." Jon rested the radio on his leg.

Liz pressed the accelerator. "Those mother effing flames are a hundred feet now." A dark cloud of roiling smoke rolled in front of the truck, blinding her. "Dammit!"

"Steady as she goes. Don't slow down. And they're not mother effing."

How could he be so damn glib? "They're mother effing if I say they are," she hissed, fisting the steering wheel so hard she could break it.

"Say the *real* thing. You know you want to."

She gave him an exasperated look. "All right! Mother *fucking* flames!"

"Love it when you talk civilian. Now doesn't that feel better? I distracted you, and you sailed through the zero visibility." He winced and pressed a hand to his side.

"If we crash, we'll become crispy marshmallows—"

He cut in. "We *won't*. You're doing good. Keep going."

When the smoke cleared, a barrage of sparks struck the windshield. Large chunks of fire debris flew at them. One glowing piece smacked the windshield, and Jon raised his hands in defense. "Holy shitballs! That one cracked the glass."

"Look, visibility! I'll take it." She loosened her grip and swallowed. "Switch the radio to Ryan's air attack frequency. I want to hear what's going on."

When Jon switched the channel, concerned voices streamed in-between Incident Command, retardant ships, and rotor wing aircraft. High winds had powered the fire across all containment lines, and it burned wildly out of control. The state troopers had evacuated Sockeye Landing and Silverleaf. Ryan O'Connor's voice ordered retardant and water drops along the Sterling Highway.

"Hopefully, they won't drop mud on our windshield." Jon leaned forward to peer up. "Impossible to see anything." He switched back to the frequency they'd agreed to use.

Tupa spoke on the radio. "Silva, me and Rego got through, but the highway is closed and Sockeye Landing is deserted. Where should we take your ex?"

Jon keyed the radio. "Can you get to Seward?"

"Yeah, there's no fire in that direction."

"Good. Take Roxanne to the Seward Police Department. Tell them to contact Trooper O'Donnell in Rockfish to make sure she's arrested for arson."

"ADOT knows you guys are still in there. They aren't happy about it."

"I bet not. Thanks, Tupa." Jon rested the radio in his lap. "Doesn't sound good up—" He stopped, gaping out the windshield.

Liz fixated on it at the same time.

"Ass pucker at eleven o'clock!" shouted Jon as a black spruce leaned out and dropped in flames across the highway.

Liz slammed the brakes and swerved to the right, hoping the truck would miss it.

Sparks and flame covered the windshield as her side of the truck scraped past the burning treetop. Somehow, the truck kept going. They hadn't hit the tree dead-on, thank God. It would have mangled the truck. She shivered to think what could have happened and blew out a sigh of relief.

Too soon. Another tree toppled into a graceful, burning descent all the way across the highway. This time, Liz slowed to a stop.

"We're blocked. We can't get around this tree with this guardrail on our right. Turn around," ordered Jon.

"We can't—there's nowhere to go." Her breath came fast. Pulsing veins thumped her temples.

The orange and red flames sprang up in tall, eerie spires, as if sucked by a hole in the sky.

Jon craned his neck in both directions. "We don't have a choice. Turn around, Harrington."

"This truck better not freaking melt," she muttered, grasping the gear shift lever. "I'm a gambler, Silva, so hold on."

Liz took a shaky breath, stopped the truck, and threw it in reverse. She backed up, then pitched forward toward the flame towers—braked hard and backed up fast, grinding the gears. She flipped the gear into drive, just as another fiery spruce hurtled toward them.

"Oh no, you don't!" she screamed at the helpless, burning tree, as if it were the tree's fault. She slammed her foot damn near through the floorboard, punching the gas. She prayed for warp speed.

Fire chunks pummeled the truck while it bounced from the impact of the flaming spruce. Luckily, it hit the truck bed, and not the cab. A loud ripping noise followed as the doomed tree snapped in half. The lower half fell to the highway, while the top half burned like a lit rocket inside the truck bed as they sped down the highway.

Jon hooted like a wild man. "Look at my badass woman— turned us into fucking *Ghost Rider!*" He had a death grip on the wimp handle above his window. His crazed expression was a cross between stark terror and the thrill of surviving another hellacious gauntlet of masochistic horror.

His chortling became contagious, and it felt good to laugh. "High five, Johnny Blaze." She took her hand off the wheel and held it up.

"You're the one named Blaze." He high-fived her, and they hooted as flaming debris blew out the back like afterburners.

"Only in Vegas. Not in Alaska." Liz let out a wobbly breath and reached for the bandana she'd tossed on the dash. She wiped her eyes and lobbed it at him. "Should have seen your wild-assed look when that spruce hit us."

Jon snatched the bandana and wiped his forehead. "Good driving, Tex, but we aren't out of Fuckville yet. Still must get around that first killer tree." He pointed. "There. Ease left."

She slowed and inched the truck past the burning treetop.

The tip of the smoking trunk scraped Jon's door, and he squeezed his eyes shut. "This truck is beat to shit. Keaton will crap a brick."

"Blame it on the fire. Hope you have good insurance." Once Liz left the killer tree behind, she stayed left as far as possible from the searing white flames on her right. The inside of the truck felt like a sauna. Flop sweat dripped down her face like a sling load of water.

Jon swiped his forehead. "Get past this before we charbroil."

She increased their speed until the flames lessened to a low broil instead of high. "Now what?"

"I'm thinking." Jon tapped his empty plastic bottle on the door. "Head back to the clearing on the spur road. At the rate of spread this puppy traveled, the clearing will be in the black by now. We can wait there until the highway opens."

She eyed fresh blood that had saturated his bandages.

"That could be a while. I have to get you to an ER. Call Ryan, maybe he can free up a chopper." She continued through heavy smoke, on the lookout for killer trees.

"Anything's worth a shot at this point." Jon keyed his radio. "Air attack, this is Silva, do you copy?" His voice sounded weak, and it alarmed her.

Ryan O'Connor's voice. "Copy, Silva. Tara relayed your situation. You guys need help?"

"Affirmative. Can you free up a helo to pick us up? There's a clearing in the burned black next to a spur road about a half-mile past the turnoff."

"I'll see if Mel can fly in with Juliet. If anyone can navigate smoke, he can. What are you driving and what are the GPS coordinates for the clearing?"

"Red and black pickup—uh, it *used to be* red. It got stir-fried with some spruce," he said, chuckling. "We're coming up to the clearing. Stand by for the GPS location."

Liz had found Jon's GPS tracker, powered it up, and zeroed in on the clearing. She held it out to Jon, who relayed the coordinates to Ryan.

"Copy that. Stay in radio contact," responded Ryan.

Jon set down the radio and pointed out the windshield. "There's the road. Turn left."

Liz turned and hit the brakes, lurching them forward, then back against their seats.

A tangle of smoldering black spruce had collapsed, blocking the narrow, rutted road, like black spears guarding a castle under siege.

"Oh no!" erupted Liz, beating her fists on the steering wheel.

Trapped. Again.

CHAPTER 41

*J*on let out a long, exhausted sigh. "Cut the engine. We have to get to the clearing." He glanced at her bloodied side. "I need to check that wound. Take off your shirt."

Liz switched off the ignition. "Nice try, Horn Dog. Not in the mood for a strip tease at the moment." She lifted her shirt high enough for him to see her cuts.

"Aw, you're no fun." He gave them a close inspection. "Bleeding stopped."

She leaned over to peer at his side. "Can't tell if yours has. We're out of water. You need hydration."

He tilted his head back on the headrest, holding his side. The nighttime pain meds had kicked in, and he was drowsy as hell. He'd hid his queasiness and dizziness the best he could after Roxanne shot him. Didn't want to alarm Liz. Now it was difficult. "We need flares so Mel can spot us."

"I used your flares, remember?"

"Oh, forgot. Feels like we battled scorch beasts in a video game." He talked slow and winced, his brow furrowing.

She peered at him. "Your nighttime meds have kicked in. Stay here while I go to the clearing and watch for Mel."

"How will you signal him?" Jon peered at the tendrils of

smoke rising from the blackened landscape. Smoke still hung in the air, though not as thick.

She stared at him. "I'll make a fire."

"Yeah, we could use more fire." He gave her an exasperated grin. "Why not? We're on the precipice of hell."

The irony twitched his mouth, but it hurt too much to laugh. At least it sidetracked his mind from his pain for a millisecond or two. He wanted to lift Liz's spirits before the next crocodile popped its head out of a hole.

"Let's review the insanity. You spent the day fighting fire only to escape another fire when my ex tried to kill you. Then she tried to kill you again but shot *me* instead. After that, dragon-fire monsters and predacious trees attacked us and tried to eat our truck." He put a palm on his forehead let out a long sigh, and grimaced.

"We survived the whole bloody ordeal, only to find we couldn't get to Mount Doom to toss in the ring, because the flying monkeys blocked us with Maleficent's black forest." He gestured at the FUBAR spruce trees pitched in every direction except straight up.

Liz gave him an insane look, then burst out laughing, clutching her side. "You sure you only took acetaminophen, and not a hallucinogen?"

That grand spiel wore him out. He heaved out a painful sigh. "Tell me this was all a video game." Her laughter energized his drained battery. He wanted to gather her up and carry her off somewhere safe. Make passionate love to her. But he could hardly move.

"You always make me laugh." She unbuckled her seat belt, leaned across the consul, and kissed him full on the lips.

This took him by surprise, but not enough to prevent his tongue from easing into her mouth, even though his side felt like gremlins were in there chewing on it. Her mouth was an elixir for his pain. She tasted good. He shifted closer, but searing pain pierced him. He broke the kiss and winced.

She winced along with him, holding her own side.

"Helping you when you're injured is getting to be routine. I'm having déjà vu all over the place."

It was time he told her. Let her know in case something bad happened. At the rate they were going, Mother Nature could toss anything in the mix, including flying monkeys.

He clasped her hand in a solid grip. "Ever notice we've been inside each other's heads from day one, like a Spockian mind meld?"

"Ha," she chuckled. "I like that about us."

He took a breath. "I love that about us—because I love *you*." He studied her watery chocolate eyes.

A deafening silence knocked around, like a black hole had sucked up all sound inside the truck. Their breaths were all that broke the quiet.

She spoke haltingly. "So, we've graduated from Main Squeeze status?"

"I'd say our Main Squeeze status has definitely inched up a notch or two."

"You've complicated my life," she whispered, a catch in her voice.

He caressed her thigh. "I figured as much. Just as you've complicated mine."

"How have I complicated yours?"

His face twisted into a smirk. "Seriously?"

"Oh, that's right. Darth Roxanne." She glanced at his once-yellow sleeve, now wearing the remnants of the Crane Lake Fire. She rested her hand over his. "I'm—I'm still trying to process things."

"I get it. That was a heavy thing to lay on you. I wanted you to know in case a herd of brown bears stampedes us or the fire-breathing dragons swoop down again."

She stared at him. "Lots going on right now. How about we get out of here first?" She opened her door.

"Leave the headlights on high beam. Mel might spot them by some divine miracle." Jon opened his door to a lungful of smoke. "Mmm, love the smell of a burned forest in the evening."

He knew his "I Love You" timing sucked, but he'd felt compelled to tell her in case more shit happened.

His only regret was not telling her a long time ago.

🔥

*L*iz came apart upon hearing those three words.

He'd sprung it on her without warning, and it left her reeling.

Should I have said it back to him?

Something had stopped her. *Fear.*

She couldn't say it out loud. Saying it would cost her independence and freedom. Saying it meant her protective, comfortable castle would crumble at her feet.

Love meant solid commitment. How could they move forward when each lived worlds apart...tundra vs. desert? And what about Jon's son? Always complications.

Her mind spun as she turned on the high beam truck headlights, grabbed her day pack, and hopped out of the truck. She hurried to him, leaning on the side mirror, his face bunched in pain. She had to get him to a doctor.

She wanted to throw her arms around him for what he'd just said, but every second counted right now. "Jon, get back in the truck, and I'll come get you."

"No. Will take too long. Check the toolbox for flares." He leaned against the door of the truck, his head tilted back. "So Mel can see us."

"Okay." She hurried back to find the tailgate missing, along with the rear bumper—collateral damage from their foray through the hurricane of fire. The once red truck now sported a demolition-derby mottled black, its side panels and bed tortured by flame. No sign of the toolbox. Another casualty of their great escape.

She moved to Jon and placed his arm around her shoulders. "Everything's gone."

"Okay. Let's go." His words slurred as he leaned on her, his frame towering over hers, as they gimped along the rutted dirt road.

She examined the smoking, charred forest, and skinny black spruce, stripped of needles and branches. Nothing to use for a walking stick. She'd have to bear his weight, like last year. Only this time they weren't scaling a vertical ascent. Just breathing shitloads of smoke, and their sides felt gutted.

Jon erupted into a coughing fit.

Oh God, no, his asthma! Coughing will make him bleed.

He stopped to rest, and Liz noticed his bleeding had indeed started again. Her scariest moment of the day hit her hard—what if Jon collapsed? How would she get him to the clearing?

"Come on, Silva. Slow and easy. Keep going."

He faltered, and she sensed him weakening. They were out of water, and she couldn't offset his blood loss.

"Uh—" He grunted and sunk to the ground.

Liz could no longer hold him up. Her muscles ached, and her arms shook from the strain. "Lie here and rest, and I'll be right back. I need to flag down Mel. I have to get out in the open with the radio and guide him in." She eased him down to rest on his back, then kissed his forehead.

"Don't forget to come back...Blaze." He squinted at her.

"Flying monkeys won't keep me away—and don't call me that," she gently admonished him, smoothing his hair back from his forehead. She wanted to say she loved him, but the words wouldn't form. *Why can't I say it?*

A metallic rotor chop sounded, faint but distinctive. The *whup-whup* of Juliet's rotors were music to her ears. Pressing her hand to her side, she broke into a painful run to cover the quarter-mile to the clearing.

Won't do any good to scream. No way could Mel hear her. She hoped he would find the clearing. She looked back toward the truck, hoping Mel would see the headlights, dimmed by the yellow haze.

"Come on, Mel, spot the darn lights," she muttered as he circled overhead. She couldn't glimpse Juliet with all the smoke. She lifted Jon's radio. "Juliet, this is Harrington. Do you copy?"

Rotor noise on the radio. "Copy. Do you have a flare to show your position? It's clearer toward the river. I'll get a bearing and swing back over."

"We don't have flares but left the headlights on at the truck. It's parked at the turnoff from the Sterling. We're due east about half a mile from the highway."

"Copy. I'll watch for that."

Liz didn't like leaving Jon alone back there in the festering, putrid black. She hoped no crazed bear or moose would happen upon him.

The rotors faded for a few minutes, then became loud again as Mel flew a grid to find the highway. "I see the headlights."

"Thank God." Liz keyed the radio. "We're about a thousand yards east of the headlights. Fly low, and you'll see a big clearing. I'm in the middle of it."

"My spotlight's on," reported Mel. "I should be able to find you."

Liz waited several more tense moments until catching a potent beam of light cutting through thin smoke. She waved and jumped frenetically, like an orangutan.

"Clear the area," Mel instructed on the radio.

Rotor wash whipped up a stinging black spray of debris. She scooted back, trying not to trip over downed, burned trees and vegetation. She turned her back to protect herself from whirling ash as Mel lowered Juliet to the ground. He slowed the rotors, and she turned around.

Liz keyed the radio. "Mel, would you mind helping me get Silva? He's a quarter of a mile down the spur road. He has a side injury."

"Sure. I'll shut her down." Mel cut the engine, and the rotors slowed to a stop. He jogged out, adjusted his baseball cap, and put on clear goggles.

She hugged him. "I'm beyond relieved that you're here."

He drew back. "Are you okay?"

"Yes. Now that you're here."

"I kind of wish you meant that in another way." He gave her a lopsided smile.

His unexpected comment threw her, heating her cheeks. "Well, I..." She trailed off.

He must have sensed her unease. "Let's get Jon."

"Okay, this way." She led off, back down the road.

"How did you and Silva get caught in this mess?" Mel's voice wiggled as he jogged to keep up.

"Silva's ex-wife is the arsonist. We intended to turn her over to the Alaska State Troopers, but the highway closed after she tried to kill me. Jon made a grab for the gun, and she shot him through his side."

"A gun?" Mel sputtered. "Whoa—she shot Jon? Wait, which ex? They're all out of state."

"His first ex, Roxanne. She came up here to help her brother run a lodge on the Kenai River. And get this—she's the one who's been setting the fires."

"You're shitting me." Mel's eyes grew enormous.

"Tell me about it." She squinted as Jon's form came into view on the dark char of the road. "There's Jon."

Liz hurried to him, with Mel on her heels.

She dropped down and squatted next to Jon, cupping his scruffy cheek. "Hey, Big Boy. Mel's here. We're getting you on board Juliet."

"About damn time, Faraday," Jon croaked out, his eyelids drooping.

"Don't give me any crap, Silva, or I'll kick your ass," teased Mel.

Jon tried lifting a brow and failed miserably. "So you've said."

"Liz, I told him if he ever hurt you, I'd beat the shit out of him," confessed Mel.

"You're a good friend." She patted Mel's shoulder, delighted with the off-handed compliment.

"Faraday, stop sucking up to my woman and get us the fuck out of here," mumbled Jon.

"All out of airspeed and altitude, aren't you, bro? Hang on, we'll get you flying again." Mel's voice had a husky twinge that made Liz nervous.

Jon's skin paled under the soot, and Liz wavered. "Silva, stay awake so we can get you to the chopper. It's not far," she said firmly, tapping his cheek.

She turned to Mel and lowered her voice. "He's lost a fair amount of blood. And he took four nighttime pain meds."

"I see that. He's a sleepy boy." Mel reached down to pull one of Jon's long arms across his shoulders, while Liz took her place on the other side. They muscled Jon to his feet and half-dragged, half-limped him to Juliet.

Mel slid the helicopter's rear door open and climbed inside. "I'll hoist him up, you get his legs."

They loaded Jon on board, his tall frame sucking up most of the floor space. Liz hopped inside, and Mel nodded at a small compartment. "Blankets are in there."

He hopped out and opened the pilot's side door. A bottle of water appeared in his hand, and he unscrewed the lid and offered it to her. "Make him drink this. I'll take you to Peninsula Hospital in Rockfish. There's a flight restriction, but I broke it to get here. Only me and Ryan know about it."

"I hope we don't get you into trouble." Liz hadn't stopped to consider the risk Mel had taken to help them out. "I'm so grateful. I don't care where we go as long as Jon gets treatment."

"Aviation regs are just guidelines when it comes to saving my good friends." Mel gave her a lopsided grin.

Upon hearing his name, Jon roused himself. "Got to help Tupa—" His head rolled to the side, and he let out a long breath.

"You aren't helping anyone. Here, drink this." She sat next to him on the floor and dribbled water into his mouth. "If anyone can handle your ex, Tupa can."

He licked his lips, and his eyelids cracked open. "Thanks, Harrington. My hero." He closed his eyes.

"You'll be fixed up in no time." She didn't like how Jon was weakening, and her own side stung like a bee swarm had moved in. "What a pair we are," she muttered, lifting strands of hair stuck to his forehead.

Mel stuck his head in. "I'll radio ahead to Peninsula Hospital ER with an ETA in twenty minutes. Don't worry, we'll fly out of the smoke, then above it." He winked at her.

She gave him a relieved smile. "Thanks, Mel."

He slid the door shut, climbed into the pilot seat, and ramped up the motor.

Liz appreciated the *whup-whup* of the rotors as they whirred up to speed. Thank God Mel had found them in this hot mess.

She pulled blankets from the helo's compartment and folded them under Jon's legs, then tugged her fleece from her day pack and covered his shoulders and chest. Her blood turned to ice as she watched Jon weaken. She'd experienced gut-splitting terror today, but nothing compared to the fear that seized her now.

The next thirty minutes were the longest minutes of her life. Jon worsened by the second as she cradled his head in her lap.

He said he loved me. Liz couldn't remember the last time she'd heard those words. She locked onto them, a lifeline as the helicopter rose and lifted high over the billowing smoke and flew south toward Rockfish. She bent to kiss Jon's cheek.

His lids lifted halfway. "You came back."

"Of course I did—" She choked up.

He reached for her, but his arm flopped to his side, and his eyes closed.

She brushed his hair away from his forehead.

"You better be okay, Silva. There's so much I want to say…"

The knocking of Juliet's blades absorbed her words as they broke free of smoke and flew toward the most glorious sunset Liz had ever seen.

Colors of hope.

CHAPTER 42

hree Weeks Later

Jon felt better with each passing day. The flight to the ER in Rockfish had been a foggy blur. He'd lost blood, and despite Liz's best efforts at dressing the gunshot wound in the aftermath, dirt and bacteria had caused an infection. The medical staff repeatedly told him how lucky he was—that it was nothing short of miraculous the bullet had passed through the tissue below his ribs, narrowly missing his liver. If the bullet had lodged inside, or been a scant millimeter off, Jon's thoracic surgeon told him he'd either be dead or in chronic pain for the rest of his life. But he should fully recover, given his toned fitness level.

"It'll hurt for a while because there's a tunnel through your muscle," said his doctor. "But the pain will lessen with time."

After treatment of her side injury, Liz spent every evening after work with Jon in his hospital room until it was time to return to camp to prepare for work the next day.

Two weeks later, Liz drove Jon back to the Alpenglow Hotel in Rockfish, to finish his recovery. She was a godsend, waiting on him hand and foot every evening after work. She had him moved to a room with clear, clean water so he could bathe without leaving his room. Before leaving each night, she made sure his devices were charged, so he could keep in touch with his investigation team as he continued to mend. She'd even done his laundry. He could get used to this.

Jon Zoomed online each day with the fire investigation meetings at the mayor's office in Rockfish, providing verbal accounts of what had transpired. He'd been careful not to let the cat out of the bag about beating the troopers to Coho Lodge and doing his own search and investigation. He gladly let Trooper O'Donnell take care of those details.

Liz had provided her phone recording of Roxanne's confession to the state troopers. Her phone had captured most of it, except for a few muffled, indistinct sections. She had no desire to listen to it, and Jon didn't blame her for not wanting to relive that horrible afternoon.

Jon asked Trooper O'Donnell to help Liz file an attempted murder charge against Roxanne. It wouldn't be pleasant for her, but Jon felt responsible since Liz had been targeted by his ex. She filed a murder charge in the first degree.

The Alaska State Troopers had collected the arson evidence for processing and obtained the forensic lab results from Anchorage. Jon prepared his final investigation report for the BLM Alaska Fire Service and the state prosecution, with Keaton's help. He still had a shitload of paperwork to do for each of the fires he'd investigated.

Keaton moved his files and laptop to Jon's hotel room during the day, so they could wrap up their investigation. Simone sometimes joined them. Keaton teased Jon it was because Jon had his shirt off in the hot afternoons, with only the white wrap binding his side.

Tupa had done what Jon asked and deposited Roxanne to the police department in Seward. She'd slept most of the way after trying to wriggle loose. Liz had taped her so tight to her seat, an army of samurai couldn't have freed her. When the Sterling Highway opened, Tupa and Rego drove back to Rockfish.

Roxanne was remanded to the Anchorage jail until a court date could be set. The forensic lab had confirmed a positive DNA match on the cigarette butts found at three of the fires.

After sifting through the case, the troopers and the State Fire Marshal's office charged her with two counts of second-degree arson, and one count of third-degree arson. Tyler agreed to cooperate as Jon advised, since he was suspected as an accessory to his sister's fire setting activities.

Jon thought about her son, now that the boy would be without his mother permanently. She'd mostly abandoned him anyway, and Tyler said he and Roxanne's parents would see to the boy's care. The private investigator had called to report the paternity test results were negative, after Jon sent him his DNA in a saliva tube. Roxanne's son wasn't his. Jon couldn't help feeling relieved, though he felt bad for the boy.

The media loved dishing dirt upon learning the arsonist was an ex-wife of the federal fire investigator. Jon's name was all over local and national news. Keaton and Dave Doss helped run interference, while he'd recovered. The agency public affairs staff provided Jon with the standard soundbite: *"The Alaska State Troopers and the State Fire Marshal's Office are continuing the investigation. Details won't be available until after the trial."*

Liz and the Aurora Crew mopped-up after containment of the Crane Lake Fire. Mother Nature had saturated the Kenai Peninsula with endless days of rain, allowing crews to get the fire out. Wind gusts now and then kicked up hotspots, but the Aurora Crew and other firefighters quickly contained them.

Each evening after work, Liz filled him in on what she did that day. Jon had never required constant contact with any woman. Now, he couldn't let a day pass without seeing Liz or hearing her voice.

Trooper O'Donnell spent an afternoon with Jon in his hotel room, accompanied by Dave Doss, who wanted to know why the hell an arsonist shot a U.S. Bureau of Land Management fire investigator. Everyone from the BLM Washington Office and the National Interagency Fire Center wanted to know too. Not to mention the governor of Alaska. The agency had opened its own investigation. Jon had sworn testimonies to make when the time came. In the meantime, he'd provided his own statements in written reports, along with

Liz's witness statement to the shooting and the attempt on her life.

Jon liked that it gave them something to work on together while they healed from their physical and mental trauma. It also provided a sense of closure to the whole fiasco.

He rested at ease on his bed, propped up by pillows. The steady diet of antibiotics had aided his recovery from the severe infection. He sure didn't miss the heplock, that had been inserted in the top of his hand during his hospital stay.

He *tap-tapped* on his laptop on yet another report, when a knock on his door caused him to stop and look up. Keaton always left his door open a crack during the day, so people could come and go without Jon getting up.

"Hey, look who's here." Jon smiled as Keaton and Simone entered the room.

Simone laid a small bouquet of flowers on his bed. "We've wrapped things up and we're driving back to Anchorage. Thought we'd stop to say goodbye."

Jon pushed up to sit straighter. "Keaton said you were heading home this week. Are you driving back together?"

Keaton stood behind Simone and wiggled his eyebrows. "Yep, thought we'd save the State some money." He had a playful smirk that Jon had come to appreciate. Maybe Keaton would score with Simone.

Simone stood next to Jon's bed. "How's your side?"

Jon flicked his eyes up at her. "Good as new. Had a bit of infection, but she's under control now."

Simone lifted her chin. "Excellent work sniffing out the arsonist. I must admit, it's rather odd it turned out to be your ex-wife. Too bad she shot you."

Jon shook his head. "Imagine my shock at finding that out. I should have seen the signs. The acetone. Her nail salon. Her mental instability. She even set fires in northern California."

"Can't make this shit up." Keaton's bluntness was always on point. "Once she had a taste for it, she couldn't stop."

"Smart of your little firefighter to record the confession. How did she manage that?" Simone gave him a pointed look.

He raised his brows and nodded. "Liz is solid under pressure. I'm proud to know this firsthand." *I plan to show her how proud the first chance I get.*

Keaton offered Jon a file folder. "Here's a list of evidence collected and compiled by Trooper O'Donnell. He wants you to make sure it's comprehensive. Don't have to tell you it's confidential, of course. The computer files from Coho Lodge are also listed. The place has crime scene tape around it. AST questioned the brother—"

"Tyler Kettleman."

"Yeah. Turns out he'd been oblivious to most of his sister's arson activities, save for one or two. When he noticed her acting funny, he chalked it up to her mental condition."

"Tyler's always been a good kid. Not like his sister."

"Nice of his sister to keep him employed fighting fire." Simone shoved her hands in the pockets of her raincoat.

Jon looked up at her. "It was a pleasure working with you, Simone. Truly. I mean that."

"Too bad other things couldn't have worked out," she murmured, adding a sultry wink.

Keaton raised his brows at her remark.

Jon gave them both a close-mouthed smile. "Have a nice drive back to Anchorage."

Simone leaned over and gave him a peck on the cheek. "I still envy her," she whispered in his ear. "I'll wait for you in the car," she said to Keaton, then headed out the door.

Keaton extended his palm. "Good working with you, Silva. I suppose you'll be going back to Fairbanks now that the rainy season has set in."

"Yep. Good working with you." Jon shook his hand. "Uh, about the state truck I trashed…"

"Yeah, about that. How the hell did you mangle a perfectly good truck, anyway? All things considered, I'm sure the State will write it off as a loss, given the fact that you caught the fire setter. She sure didn't fit the FBI arsonist profile."

"Not when male fire setters outnumber females nine-to-one." Jon smiled wryly. "She's always had issues."

"And revenge, to spite her fire investigator ex-husband. Lucky you. Did she ever torch anything during your marriage?"

"Nothing besides burning meals. She must have turned pyro after we split."

"She won't be doing any cooking where she's going." Keaton smirked. "No one'll let her near a heat source in prison."

"So, do you and Simone plan to meet up in Anchorage?"

Keaton gave him a look. "Like on a date?"

"Well, yeah." Jon gave him a knowing smile.

"She's slightly out of my league." Keaton winked. "However, stranger things have happened. Keep in touch, Silva." Keaton dipped his chin at him and left.

Jon's phone sounded. He fixed on the Caller ID photo of his woman, draped in fur, framing beautiful breasts, surrounded by snow.

He answered. "Miss Harrington. When will you be here to rescue me again? I should draw up a contract and hire you on a retainer."

"You sure sound chipper. Still taking your meds?"

Jon fingered a prescription bottle on his bed table. "Yep. All signs of infection are gone. Did Tara approve your leave?"

"She gave me three days off before I report to work in Fairbanks." She paused for a moment. "I'm inviting you on a vacay with me. Want to return the favor."

His ears perked up. "Where?"

"Alyeska Resort. Figured we could finish what we started the night of the wedding. Plus, it has sentimental value. And I promise to stay sober this time."

"I like the sound of that. What's the sentimental value?" He smiled into his phone.

Her voice turned soft. "It's where I first heard you sing."

He liked that. A lot. "And Steller's Jay Lodge is where I first saw you dance."

She did that provocative giggle thing he liked. "We're a crack team, Fire Boy. I'll pick you up at noon tomorrow."

"I'll be waiting, Tiny Dancer."

She chuckled. "Tara found an AFS truck for me to return to Fairbanks. One that's not beat to shit."

He laughed. "Hopefully, we won't trash this one."

"Knock on wood. See you later." Her sultry tone waved through him.

He ended the call, then settled back to talk himself down from his erection.

He couldn't wait for tomorrow.

CHAPTER 43

*L*iz had mixed feelings at leaving her crew camp behind. Aurora Crew had packed up their gear and loaded all of it onto the transport van for the drive up to Fairbanks. Rego would follow with the crew equipment truck.

Tupa had bestowed his abalone fishhook necklace to Liz and told her she was family. What an honor for him to say that. He'd confided that he asked Kenzie out on an official date once they were back in Fairbanks. Liz was happy for them.

Before she left town, Liz had gone to see Cohen. As his squad boss she felt partially responsible for what had happened. Tara had arranged for him to move into the Alpenglow Hotel after his stay in the hospital. His injuries hadn't been life-threatening, but he'd cracked two ribs and crushed the tissue on the left side of his back. He'd mended enough to join Aurora Crew for the drive back to Fairbanks. She wished Jon and Cohen could find a way to get along now that she was officially Jon's girlfriend.

I like the sound of that.

She pulled into the parking lot of the Alpenglow Hotel. Just as she raised her phone to call Jon, he strolled out the front door, smiling, as if he were filming a TV ad. A hotel baggage attendant followed, rolling a luggage carrier with all of Jon's gear. She was glad he didn't try to carry it all himself. He was still healing.

A breeze lifted his hair and Liz's heart somersaulted as he came toward her, flowers in hand. He wore jeans and a navy-blue Henley she'd laundered for him. He could waltz out in a tattered burlap sack full of holes, and she'd still salivate. Something about the way Jon swaggered toward her sizzled her algorithms in dozens of obscene directions.

Liz opened the passenger door and beamed. "Hey, Fire Inspector." She helped the hotel attendant heft the gear into the back seat of the crew-cab pickup.

Jon tipped the attendant, then turned and planted a kiss on Liz so tender and sensuous, she'd let him do her right there in the parking lot. She recalled the first time he'd kissed her in another parking lot and how hot they'd been for each other.

When Jon lifted from her lips, the air fluttered and unicorns flew.

"You taste delicious." He accorded her a predatory look. "Can't wait to taste more of you."

"Behave yourself," she purred as he folded himself in the passenger side. She closed his door and climbed into the driver's seat, grinning at the windshield.

"Déjà vu with you driving a truck and me sitting here," Jon commented as Liz pulled onto the Seward Highway and headed north. "Gee, when have we done *this* before?"

"Except this time, we have rain instead of fire." Liz cranked up the windshield wipers.

As they headed north along the Sterling Highway toward the intersection with the Seward Highway, Liz's heart hollowed at the blackened devastation. She gazed out the rain-pocked windshield, mile after ravaged mile. Nothing but sullied, denuded mountainsides. Green spruce had morphed into skeletons…branchless sentinels, sharp as spears standing silent…ghastly witnesses to the ruin. Others had succumbed to the charred confusion on the forest floor.

They observed it in silence for a while, and then Jon spoke. "Never underestimate the power of fire. Like the ocean, it's impossible to tame."

Liz glanced at him. "You said that last fire season after our foray up the mountain from Deadman's Ravine."

"I remember." He gazed out the window, shaking his head at the devastation.

Fire vehicles still lined the side of the road as crews worked along the highway, mopping up to make sure hotspots were out.

"What can't be contained are the areas where fire burns underground. They'll smolder all winter and flare up next spring. Alaska has its fair share of subsurface holdover fires that keep firefighters working every spring." Jon glanced at her.

She nodded, thanking God, she and Jon had emerged from their situation alive and mostly in one piece. Night terrors had stalked her sleep—the sensation of steel pressed against her neck, while burning alive. She'd wakened in cold sweats, struggling to calm herself back to sleep. She had longed for Jon to put his arms around her and say it would be all right.

Now it would be, but something had bugged her these past few weeks. She'd waited until Jon had mended before bringing it up. If they were to move forward together, Liz needed to know certain things.

"Roxanne told me you and she have a son."

He stiffened and quieted for a moment. "I planned on telling you but haven't had the chance. She sprang it on me that day she entered my hotel room with my stolen key card. The last few months of our marriage, she gave her cat away to anyone who would look at her. Any number of guys could be the father." He stared out the windshield. "I had a P.I. in California handle the paternity test. Results were negative. Roxanne's son isn't mine."

"Oh." That bit of news made her breathe easier.

"Would it have made a difference—with us?" asked Jon.

"Not really." She studied the low-hanging clouds hiding the

jagged mountaintops. "I want to be with you, no matter what. Nothing would have interfered with that."

"Not even your Vegas plans?"

She let out a sigh. "Ravish and Jasper, my so-called biz partners, screwed me over. They drained my savings account. All my fault. I trusted Ravish—kept my username and password on a sticky note on my laptop, and she helped herself to my accounts. As if that wasn't bad enough, she threatened to send my nude photos to the Alaska Fire Service if I didn't pony up more money."

"Chrissakes, when did you find out?"

"That night after I left your hotel room. I called Dad's cop buddies on the Las Vegas police force. Sent them texts and voice messages Ravish left on my phone. They helped me file charges. Ravish and Jasper have a court date after their arraignment on charges of felony theft and extortion. I'll have to fly down to testify, but it won't be for a while."

"What about the money they stole?"

"Vegas PD gained some of it back. It was my firefighting savings from last year, along with the dance money left over after Dad's expenses. I called Amethyst Corporation and told them the deal was off. And called the bank to cancel the business loan."

"Why didn't you tell me? I'd have helped you with all that, had I known."

"I didn't tell you before now because you needed to heal. You had enough cats to juggle, wrapping up your investigation and dealing with everything. Besides, I wanted to handle things myself. I got myself into the mess and I had to get myself out." She chuckled. "Kenzie and Tara started a *Go Fund Me* page, and Kenzie's Aussie fireys have already donated to make up for my stolen funds. I'm blown back by their generosity."

"From now on you won't have to shoulder those things alone." He glanced at her. "You can count on all of us to help."

"Not sure what I'd do without my Alaska fire family." She forced back the hitch in her voice.

"And that includes me." He reached over and squeezed her shoulder. "Hey, let's stop at the Wildlife Conservation Center on the way to Girdwood. The Bird Treatment Center in Rock-fish called to say they transported Birdzilla up there. Want to pay a quick visit?"

"I would love that." Liz laughed. "Tara asked me how Birdzilla was doing."

"I'll text her and tell her to stop at the Wildlife Center on their way up to Fairbanks. Are they on the road yet?" Jon plucked his phone from the cupholder on the dash and tapped the text.

"They're right behind me." She glanced his way. "Cohen told me you and he got into a fight. Saw the shiner you gave him."

"Did he tell you why?"

"He said you came to see me the morning after I left the hotel that night. I called him to come get me——"

Jon cleared his throat. "Saw that. He had his arms around you like a gorilla in heat. He's in love with you, like every other guy in Alaska."

"Present company included?" She smiled out the wind-shield, at a green "Summit Lake" sign, admiring the peaceful lake to her right. "We have less than an hour to go, but enough for a catnap. I'll wake you when we get there."

"Sounds good." He reclined his seat and didn't take long before he settled into slumber.

Liz embraced the down time. She turned up the radio and tuned it to the KBAY station she and Jon had listened to at Steller's Jay Lodge, where they played a mix of classic rock and golden oldies. The radio personality cheerfully announced, "Great listening for the Greatland."

She'd had time to think while Aurora Crew worked to mop up the Crane Lake Fire and Jon spent time recovering. She'd reflected on his declaration of love, and she'd arrived at a decision.

Early this morning, she called her boss at the Wild Iris to

give notice she wouldn't be returning. *Ever.* Exotic dancing was officially part of her past.

And she had something to say to Jon. She'd rehearsed it all morning before picking him up.

She didn't want to blow it.

CHAPTER 44

*J*on woke from his dream of a naked Liz, but he couldn't remember why she was naked, and he didn't care. He'd wakened with a smile, and it felt good.

The truck was stopped at a small shack with a pay window at the entrance to the Wildlife Conservation Center, just twelve miles south of Alyeska Resort, on the Seward Highway. Jon rubbed his eyes, while Liz paid the admissions guy and drove inside the compound.

Jon pointed. "There's the eagle enclosure."

They climbed out, and Jon flagged down a woman standing next to the birds of prey enclosure. He introduced himself and explained how Liz found the eagle on a fire.

"Come this way." She motioned for Jon and Liz to follow, and led them to a long, rectangular building behind the outdoor enclosure with smaller birds of prey. She opened a small door into the building leading to the indoor eagle habitat.

Liz checked out the eagles perched on raised logs and branches and the tops of tall poles. "Are these all birds you've rehabilitated?"

"Yes, we hold the birds of prey here until there're openings at the Alaska Raptor Center in Sitka, where they get good care from avian specialists."

Liz pointed to the opposite end at an eagle perched alone on a log, resting on the floor. "There's Birdzilla. I'd know that zany hairdo anywhere."

"I'm impressed, Harrington. You know your eagle." Jon laughed.

The woman motioned them to follow and stopped a short distance from the bird. The eagle turned her head with a wary eye as they approached, a white bandage and splint attached to her right leg. She tilted with her weight on her good leg.

Liz turned to Jon. "The three of us are healing in one way or another, aren't we?"

"You're right." He chuckled and asked the woman, "Will Birdzilla travel to the Alaska Raptor Center down in Sitka?"

"She's scheduled on an Alaska Airlines flight next week. They'll finish rehabilitating her there."

"Good to hear." Jon made a squeaky bird sound, and Birdzilla turned her head to give him a stern stare. "She still has bedhead feathers fluffed out, same as when we dropped her off in Rockfish."

"Gives her a wild and crazy vibe, doesn't it?" The woman laughed.

Liz guffawed. "She's a zany bird. And boy, what a temper. You should have seen us try to catch her."

"She arrived here with the Birdzilla name tag. Appropriately named, as she's a feisty one," the woman said with a laugh. "Good that you rescued her. You'd be surprised how many predators eat eagles when they're injured and stranded on the ground or in the water. Sea lions get them in the water, and bears and wolves get them on land."

"Glad she's doing so well." Liz waved at the eagle. "Bye-bye, Birdzilla. Have a pleasant flight on the airplane. At least you don't have to fly yourself."

The eagle turned her head toward Liz and opened her beak as if to say something.

Jon nudged her. "She remembers you."

"Really?"

"Sure. Eagles have excellent memories." He winked at the

woman and put his finger to his lip in a shush. He didn't want to pop Liz's bubble.

Jon set his hand on the small of her back as they exited the building. "You and Birdzilla have much in common."

When she opened her mouth to ask why, she noticed the Aurora Crew climbing out of their transport van.

"Tara," hollered Liz. "We visited Birdzilla. She's in this building."

Tupa and Rego strode up to Jon and took turns giving him a guy slap and a palm press. "Hey, Silva. How's your side doing?"

Jon tapped it. "Better than a few weeks ago."

"We'll meet for a brew at Snowcastle, and you can fill us in." Rego pointed at him.

"Sounds like a plan." Jon smiled.

"That's some cool stuff you did, catching the arsonist, Boss." Tupa stood with folded arms.

Kenzie stood next to him. "Jonno, did Liz tell you about the GoFundMe we started?"

Jon nodded. "That's a wonderful gesture you did."

"Liz is a bloody good firey. Good on ya for taking up with her."

Cohen slowly straggled over, supporting himself with a walking stick. He stopped in front of Jon and leaned on his stick.

Jon slipped an arm around Liz, still feeling edgy and territorial whenever this dickhead was around.

"Silva. You're out of the hospital."

Jon reined in his sarcasm. "You are, too. Sorry about what happened. You're lucky, Tremblay."

The crew stared at Jon, then Cohen. Word had obviously spread about their altercation. Jon extended his hand.

Cohen stared at it, then gripped it, his eyes darting to Liz, then Jon. "You're the lucky one."

Jon knew what he meant, and he wasn't referring to trees. Hands clasped, they locked stares like two bull moose in a standoff.

They finally released each other. Despite Tremblay's incredible talent at being a dickhead, Jon couldn't help liking the guy. He had excellent taste crushing on Liz, though it had irritated Jon to no end.

Liz broke the tension. "That amiable woman over there will take you to Birdzilla. They wrapped her leg, and she still has that crazy feather-do on her head. Jon said she recognized me."

Rego and Tupa lifted their brows in a *Yeah, right.*

Of course, Rego had to be the one to ruin it. "Eagles don't remember shit. They don't even recognize their own offspring."

"Is that true?" Liz gave Jon a disappointed look.

"Not always." He figured a fast escape was best in this case. "I'll be in the truck. Have to make a phone call." He waved at Tupa and Rego. "See you in Fairbanks. Beers are on me."

"It's a date, Boss." Tupa gave him a hang loose sign with his thumb and pinky raised.

"Later, Boss." Rego gave him a two-fingered salute.

No one on the crew had called him "Boss" since last season. He sensed Tupa and Rego knew he appreciated it. Their show of respect for finding the arsonist.

Jon had risen like a phoenix from the ashes. Born again with renewed hope and a renewed sense of self because of his work as a fire inspector, but mostly because of Liz. She'd helped him understand the meaning of self-forgiveness and that life went on, no matter what. He admired her brave, generous nature and had noticed a change in her—a relaxed, calm manner that hadn't been there before.

Jon sat in the truck, delighting in watching Liz. Tara and Kenzie hugged her, then Tara whispered in her ear, and they laughed. Maybe Tara was dispensing more tips about icebreakers.

Liz's financial situation concerned him since she told him what had happened. He had an idea how to help her out and what he had to do.

He smiled to himself as he pulled out his phone to call Risa.

CHAPTER 45

*L*iz and Jon hauled their gear inside the Hotel Alyeska lobby. She felt welcomed by the rich cherrywood and the northern lights display, with snowy mountain vistas on the walls. A polar bear and cub stood sentinel in a diorama over the grand entrance. Carved totem poles with red and black accents graced either side of the double doors.

Liz loved the simple elegance of this place, and she loved the pond out back of the property with fountains and lush grass and spruce. And of course, the cerulean glaciers, like old friends, welcoming them back.

She'd requested a room with a view of the snow-capped blue mountains and the glaciers, underscored by lush greenery. Alaska's summer dress-up colors of blue, white, and green.

After Liz checked them in, they entered the same elevator as the last time they stayed here. This was her second chance at a redux without an alcohol haze to mess things up.

"Feels like coming home, doesn't it?" Jon stood close as the elevator opened on the seventh floor. *Damn.* He looked wonderful standing there, all casual and relaxed.

"You're right. It does." Lightheaded anticipation tingled her as she led him along the carpeted corridor. She waved her key card, swung the door open, and moved to the vast picture windows to take in the spectacular view.

"Isn't this incredible?" She gazed at the lush stands of Sitka spruce and hemlock, thankful the trees hadn't succumbed to the invasive spruce bark beetle.

He came up behind her and rested his hands on her shoulders. "You have no idea how long I've waited for this—and I can't wait any longer."

She turned into him, placing her palms on his chest. "I don't want you to wait any longer."

He gathered her up and kissed her, then slid his lips along the side of her neck. "I plan to drown myself in you," he breathed.

Sirens went off in every girl part she owned, and she eyed the king bed and led him over to it. What a luxury having a bed with so much real estate after months of sleeping on a single cot. She sat on the edge and tugged him to sit. "I want this to be the same, if not better than our weekend on Kachemak Bay. And that night in your hotel after you doctored my eagle scratches."

"Speaking of which, let's see them."

Liz showed him the underside of her forearm. "Birdzilla left two scars."

"She didn't want you to forget her. Let's see how your other wound is healing."

Liz lifted the side of her Aurora Crew T-shirt.

"I need a better view." Jon tugged her shirt up over her head so fast, her mind whirled. "There. Now I can see." Tossing her shirt aside, he bent to kiss the mostly healed lacerations on the side of her rib cage.

"That tickles," she purred, goose bumping as his lips kissed her healed stitches.

He straightened. "Now, doesn't it feel good to give your girls fresh air? Hello ladies, I've missed you," he murmured to her breasts, brushing his lips across the tops. His head lifted. "FYI, I intend to make love to you until neither of us can walk."

"Oh, I'll always be able to walk," she assured him.

"Not this time, you won't." He slipped his tongue into her mouth.

She tasted the cinnamon and coffee in his luscious mouth, with a scent of brawn that made her ache even more for him. Their unfettered access to one another drove her insane with want. As much as she wanted him right now, she wanted—no, needed to bare her soul to him first.

It was important to her.

She broke the kiss. "Before we—um, do this, I have something to say. I would have before, but I'm a dancer, not a wordsmith. And certainly not a gifted songwriter like you."

"I'd have to write a gazillion songs to describe my feelings for you."

"You're such a charmer," she teased. "But seriously."

"Okay, but understand how difficult this is, when all I want to do is tear off the rest of your clothes." He kissed her neck, driving her wild.

"It won't take long, I promise," she whispered, gently pushing him away. "I really appreciate the sacrifice you're making."

"The struggle is real." He gestured at his swollen crotch and gave her an urgent look. "All right, I'm listening."

"Sorry about the buzzkill." She stared at her lap. "My mom left Dad and me when I was a freshman in high school. As an only child, I had no female influence other than teachers and dance instructors. I bonded with one who encouraged me to study dance. I won a scholarship, and Dad paid the rest. I graduated from UNLV with a bachelor's degree in dance. I promised myself I would desert no one the way my mother deserted me…and I owed my dad big time."

She glanced up at him. "I'm telling you this because you need to know, I will never desert you. I'll never be the one who leaves."

He nodded, solemn-faced.

She took a deep breath and continued. "After my mother left us, Dad and I buried our hearts in the sand. Now he doesn't even remember he had a wife *or* a daughter." She swallowed hard. "It hurt so bad. I buried my heart deeper and distanced myself. I didn't visit him as often. He has no clue who I am." The tremor in her voice took over. "I'm a terrible daughter…" A sob shook loose.

He brushed her tears with his thumb. "You're the best daughter a father could ever have. You gave up your dream to help him. There's no greater love." He offered her his bandana.

She took it and blew her nose. "I created a mental fortress to safeguard myself against the world. Added a moat for extra protection to make myself impenetrable. That way, no one could hurt me. I became cynical, hard, and calloused. I hated myself."

She swiped at her cheeks. "I'd been closed off for so long, that what I felt for you last year frightened me. I stayed casual working with you when all I wanted was to tell you how much…" She shook her head. "I spent the winter talking myself out of you."

"I guess both our heads were in messed up places." He reached for her hand and threaded his fingers with hers. "What about now?"

"I'm not that person now. You crashed through my fortress by trusting my ability and making me a squad boss last year. That meant the world to me. You've always treated me as your equal. I can be real with you. I like who I am when I'm with you."

He stroked her hand and kissed it.

"The Iris laid me off in the summer when business slowed. I still needed money for Dad, so I took a job with a Bureau of Land Management fire crew in Vegas. Then I found out about the Alaska Fire Service. I applied, and you know the rest."

"I'm glad you did." He pushed strands of hair from her face. "Even if you hadn't, I would have found my way to you."

She gazed into his eyes and found honesty. *God, I love him so much.* "I quit my dance job at The Iris. Gave my notice this morning."

"What? Why did you do that?" His astonished tone delighted her.

"That night after the fire, in the truck. You said you loved me." She looked him in the eye. "I didn't say it back."

"I wanted you to know in case we didn't make it out of there. Truth is, you restored my soul. I fell in love with you when we fought fire together last year. Should have told you back then." He smirked at her. "Never could resist a woman with a Pulaski in her hand."

Liz chuckled. "Your words terrified me. And now, for the first time in my life I know exactly what I want and what I don't want. I don't want to dance in strip clubs. I never did. I only did it to repay Dad for helping me get my college degree. He never knew I worked at the Iris. And he never will."

"My lips are certainly sealed." He waited patiently, looking at her like she was the only woman on the planet.

"I tore down my castle and blew up my moat because I wanted you, badly. Not just sexually." She smiled through her tears. "Although that's a big plus. I want all of you. Mind, heart, and our weird, psychic thing that feels like we share a computer chip."

He reached around her and pulled her in tight. "You have all of me—mind, body, and soul. I was a jackass. Mired myself down with self-centered pity and guilt after last year. I talked myself out of you, too, but for a different reason—didn't think I deserved you."

She sighed. "We were both messed up."

He looked relieved. "Geez, Harrington. For a minute there I thought you were going to launch into that 'you complete me' thing."

She made a face. "Give me more credit than that."

"I've done some thinking, too, and I have a proposal," he intoned, studying her.

She drew a quick breath. "Uh-huh?"

He held up a hand. "Relax. Not that kind of proposal. What would you say to my helping you get the dream you've always wanted?"

She raised her brows, curious. "How so?"

"Remember when Risa told us she had a friend with a dance studio in Fairbanks? The reason is, the friend is still looking for a partner to open a dance studio in Vegas, which I didn't know until I spoke with Risa. I immediately thought of you."

Her jaw dropped. "Are you serious?"

"Risa gave me her contact info, and her friend wants you to call her ASAP. What do you say after fire season ends in Alaska, we drive down in my truck, and you can check into it? I won't mind going with you. That is, if you'd want me to."

"You would do that?"

He cradled her face. "I didn't expect you to want to live in Fairbanks. In the winter anyway."

"Nothing personal, but I'm a bona fide desert rat. Ravish and Jasper moved out of my apartment, so we could stay there for a while."

Jon's eyes sparkled. "I wouldn't mind spending winters in Vegas. I could finish my bird doctorate at UNLV and do wildland fire investigation down there. Maybe do training for firefighters. We could drive to Sonoma and visit my brother at our winery. And more importantly, you could be near your dad. We'd be back next spring for Alaska's fire season." He paused for a moment. "And here's the good part. I'll help you finance your half of the studio."

His generous offer took her breath away. "Wow, that's—I don't know what to say. You have this all planned out?"

"What do you think I thought about all that time I was recuperating?" He studied her intently.

Her hands flew to her cheeks, and she thought a minute. "Okay, but on two conditions."

He gave her an eye roll. "Here we go with the conditions again."

"First, I pay you back every penny. And it's non-negotiable." She glanced at him. "Second, we'll still take it one step at a time. I don't want pressure to be Wife Number Four. This commitment thing is a whole new gig for me."

"I get that. No pressure." Jon laughed. "Sound like a plan?"

She slid her palms up his arms and rested them on his shoulders. "Hmm, so I get year-round unfettered access to you? I suppose that's an okay trade-off," she teased.

He brushed her lips, then devoured them. He broke the long kiss and brushed back hair from her face. "And I have a condition. Help me teach firefighters how to preserve points of origin on fires. I'm putting a training contract together for AFS when I get back to Fairbanks."

"I would love that." She threw her arms around his neck and hugged him. "And you can teach me about birds." She drew back, gazing up at him. "That reminds me, what do Birdzilla and me have in common?"

He snorted. "That's easy. You're both batshit crazy, strong, and independent. Not to mention fearless and stubborn. You both have a sharp vision of what you want, and you're focused, despite obstacles. Your feathers ruffle when people force you to do things you don't want to do. And you both resist people who try to help you."

Liz put her hand on her heart. "Birdzilla is my spirit animal."

He took her hands in his. "We can go down to the Alaska Raptor Center in Sitka when they release her into the wild. They have release days where the public is invited. It's a big deal. I volunteered there as an avian specialist."

"Gosh, I would love that." She gave him a slow smile. "Birdzilla brought us together, you know. Ever since then, whenever I see an eagle soar overhead, I think of you."

"Well, I am a bird man." His gaze dropped to her necklace. "I see Tupa bestowed you with his family emblem. He considers you family now. Looks good on you."

Liz fingered the necklace. "Yes, I'm honored. He deemed me worthy after everything that happened." She warmed inside, knowing Tupa respected her, and that meant the world to her.

Unable to control herself any longer, she stood and gave him a seductive grin. "Tear my clothes off, Silva."

"No." He pushed off the bed, grabbed a chair, and set it in the middle of the room. "It's my turn to make *you* wait."

"Oh, hey, you're not—you aren't going to—oh my God, you *are*..." Liz's mouth fell open as Jon steered her to the chair and pushed her to sit.

He fished his phone from his jeans and slid a finger across the screen. His impressive biceps brushed both sides of her when he bent to grip the back of her chair, causing her nipples to stand and salute.

He moved close and nipped her bottom lip with his teeth. "No touching. Only watching. I can touch, but you can't. Copy that, Squad Boss?"

"You're seriously going to lap dance me?" She laughed.

He displayed his resting man face. "Answer the question. Do you copy?"

"Copy. Are you sure you can do this with that hole in your side?"

"Let me worry about that." He tapped his phone. *I'm Too Sexy*, by Right Said Fred, began its lively beat.

Jon bestowed a bad boy look on her and moved to the beat, undulating from his chest on down. Not bad moves. Not bad at all.

She gulped, entranced and slack-jawed, as he matched the beat perfectly. *Did he frigging practice this?*

When the singer sang that he was too sexy for his shirt, off came Jon's Henley. He twirled it over his head, reminding her more of a goofy orangutan than a male stripper. The small, square bandage over his healed wound gave him a bad boy vibe.

Suddenly, his shirt smacked her face and fell to her lap. She squealed with laughter as he pointed his fabulous ass at her and wiggled it.

Liz put her fingers in her mouth and whistled, then hooted as Jon did whatever the song directed him to do. He disco-danced, pointing up and down, a la John Travolta from

Saturday Night Fever. Next, he pretended to be a runway model, strutting, then stopping to pose in front of her.

She reached out to pinch his nipple, and he tapped her hand away with a no-no gesture. She laughed even harder.

Rut-roh, there go the pants.

She covered her face, giggling like a high schooler, as he stuck his thumbs in the waist of his jeans and slowly pushed them down. She suppressed a laugh when he had trouble getting them off.

She reached out and tugged them down, on that long jaunt down his legs. They puddled around his ankles.

"Hey, no touching, lady," he growled, undulating like a *Chippendale's* dancer. He had to have watched YouTube videos to nail down those moves.

Jon went to kick off his shoes, forgetting about the pants holding his feet prisoner. He lost his balance and wobbled forward. "Whoa-a-a…"

Laughing, she caught him, along with a heavy whiff of male. He righted himself and kicked away his jeans. He continued dancing in his tight-fitting gray boxers and white crew socks, his long, hairy legs making her laugh even more.

Now a sexy car joined the mix and Jon pantomimed driving. He moved close, sliding his palms up and down her arms.

Ooh, she liked that.

The song ended. He stopped in front of her, clasped his hands together, and flexed his biceps over his head. An impressive pose for someone still ripped, despite lounging around for the past few weeks.

"Encore, encore!" She came off her chair in a standing ovation and whistled and cheered as he backed up to give her a slight bow.

"You liked that?" He straightened, brushing his hair back. "That's the most I've worked out in weeks."

"You'd give the Thunder Down Under guys a run for the money down in Vegas." Liz laughed and clapped at the panty-smoldering, semi-naked hunk standing in front of her, the splendid chest heaving from his workout.

She took him by the hand and led him to the bed. "Make love to me."

He stood before her with parted lips. "I want you to undress for me first. Here's something to get you in the mood." He tugged her in for an undie-vaporizing kiss that plunged her into full-on strip mode when he lifted off from her lips.

Her professional skills came in handy. She could see this as the requisite prelude to their lovemaking from now on. They each enjoyed lap dancing and entertaining the other, so why not?

Eyes locked on his, she slanted him her *come-do-me* look, unsnapping her jeans. Ever so slowly, she lowered her zipper. She prided herself on her expertise at building anticipation.

He watched her every move and softly hummed an evocative melody to underscore her movements. His impish grin thrust her lust lever to its highest setting.

She fixated on his chest movements and how they were choreographed with his humming. Something only a dancer would appreciate. The tip of her tongue glided across her lower lip as she deposited her jeans to her ankles. An artful toss with pointed toes, and she was rid of them.

He loved that maneuver, judging by his spellbinding expression and increased rise and fall of those glorious pecs. Exotic dance taught her that next to touch, sight aroused guys the most. Jon was putty in her hands when he watched her dance.

"Shall I continue?" she drawled, sliding her palm up her abdomen to caress her breast. She looked down at it, then feasted her gaze on him.

She saw the raw need in his eyes as he let out a passionate exhale. "Oh, yeah."

Enticing him this way turned her on. Settling into her relaxed seduction, she eased one strap at a time from her shoulder and moved to him. He reached around her to unclasp her bra and tugged it off, dipping his head to kiss each breast.

Her breath came fast when he trailed his fingers down

her sides and tracked around her thong. He lifted his head to kiss her while slipping a hand underneath, lightly massaging her.

"You know right where to touch. How do you do that?" she whispered, welcoming the tenderness and affection he offered.

Her thoughts deserted her as he tugged her thong down and backed her up to the bed. They both sank down on it, the glacial twilight streaming in, casting an aqua glow. Water played nature's song in a stream below the open window.

She opened herself to him, and he moved inside her with a sweet tenderness, fragile and new. They relished their sensations, making them last. Slow, gentle glides of kindred, mended souls, each grateful for and appreciating the other.

Making love had new meaning now. For the first time ever, Liz understood the enormity of a physical, emotional connection with another human being, and how powerful it could be...magical enough she shouted Jon's name repeatedly while exploding like a Roman candle.

"Liz-z-z..." He dragged her name out, sounding like a buzzing beehive.

This wasn't sex—it was rapture. A blissful contentment she'd never known. She didn't care how much time passed after losing herself in him. Afterward, there was something so personal, so intimate, about sleeping close to him. A trust like no other. They remained entangled until falling into a deep, relaxed sleep.

During the night, she woke and rolled her head to the side to find Jon awake in the all-night twilight, studying her.

"Why aren't you sleeping? What are you thinking?"

"Seafret's *Wildfire* song keeps playing in my head. It's about us. Our love *is* like a wildfire." He brought her hand to his lips and gave it a tender kiss. "I was also thinking that yours is the last face I want to see when I leave this planet."

"Oh, Jon." She leaned in for a deep, passionate kiss, then traced his lips with her fingertips. "Hopefully, that won't be for a long, long time." She nuzzled his neck. "And yours is the one I want to see when you make love to me under the aurora, since we met on the Aurora Crew. Can we do that before we drive south?"

"I can arrange that. I've a perfect view out my bedroom window. We'll lie in bed as the northern lights dance with the Big Dipper on their green and purple piano. So close and bright, you'll want to reach up and touch them. When we're back in Fairbanks, how about you move in with me for the rest of the fire season?"

"I would love nothing more." She kissed him, delighted with his generous invitation. She was truly and sincerely happy for the first time in her life.

"Remember when you blew out the candles on your puffin cake across the bay?"

"Yeah?"

"What did you wish for?"

He stroked her cheek. "I wished for you to love me."

She gazed at him, loving him so much it hurt. "Well, then. It seems your wish has come true."

EPILOGUE

FIVE MONTHS LATER IN LAS VEGAS

*L*iz and Jon had driven from Fairbanks to Haines, Alaska to catch the marine ferry down to Seattle. They'd loaded his truck and camper onto the ferry and enjoyed the stops along the way at Juneau, Sitka, and Ketchikan.

They'd timed it so Jon could take Liz to the raptor release day at the Sitka Raptor Center, on Baranof Island, on the outer coast of Alaska's Inside Passage. They only had the afternoon to spend, to stick with the strict sailing schedule.

Liz's breath had caught at seeing Birdzilla, good as new with her healed broken leg. When Liz called out goodbye, Birdzilla turned her head and cocked it at her, opening her beak as if to say goodbye in return. Then she lifted off from the arm of the avian specialist, circled overhead, and disappeared into the mist of the overcast morning, to soar the skies over southeast Alaska.

Liz's chest had swelled at seeing the healed eagle take flight. Another mended soul, eager to take on the world once again. "She remembered me!" Liz exclaimed to Jon.

He'd slid his arm around her and drew her close. "She appreciates the one who rescued her. Just as I treasure the one who rescued me."

Liz had tucked herself into him, thankful he'd returned to his old, charming self. They'd been through a lot together and she was grateful for Jon's comforting reassurance of safety and strength.

And now, here she was—standing in the wings of the Mojave Performing Arts Center stage, in the Vegas suburb of Henderson, applauding her ballet students, after a rigorous rehearsal schedule before she'd turned them loose to rehearse with the professional ballet company. She couldn't believe it.

Five months ago, none of this seemed remotely possible, she thought, watching the closing scene where Clara flies off in the sleigh with the Nutcracker Prince. Her eyes flicked up to the stagehands working the pulleys, to make sure the dancers landed safely on the raised platform at the end of the show. The stagehands helped usher them down the stairs, to join the rest of the dancers for the company bow.

The audience applauded Liz's students as they took their final bow after the ballet. She'd worked hard to get her students up to snuff, to win the teen and children's roles in the auditions for the Desert City Ballet Company. She'd hit the ground running as the new partner of "Blazing Danceworks," and she'd initiated an aggressive marketing campaign to enlist registration for classes. Now they had a healthy waiting list.

Jon had talked her into performing a solo at the end of their program as a bonus for the audience. She'd protested until his reasoning won out, that if the parents and public at large saw her perform, she'd have patrons and sponsorships of their fledging studio pouring in like crazy.

"I'll do it on one condition," she'd said, winking at him. "That you play and sing while I dance."

Jon's eyes had bugged out in protest, but she firmly stated, "You don't play. I don't dance."

And now, from the opposite wing Liz watched Jon lift the guitar strap over his shoulder and they locked gazes across the stage. He gave her a thumbs up and they moved out to center stage.

She didn't know what to expect. Jon had squirreled himself

away for weeks to compose and practice the song to be at performance level for tonight. He'd wanted it to be a surprise. She'd choreographed a routine that she could adapt to whatever he composed.

Liz stepped onstage after the *Nutcracker* company bow and the curtains closed. A stool and microphone had been placed on stage left. She removed the mic from the stand to address the audience.

"Thank you for supporting our new Danceworks Studio by attending tonight's performance. As a special thank you, I've prepared a dance piece I hope you enjoy. It has a little bit of everything in it that my good friend, Jon Silva and myself experienced this past year." She paused and caught Jon's eye as he took the stool, poised and ready.

Liz returned the large microphone to its stand, positioned in front of Jon's twelve-string acoustic guitar. She checked to make sure he'd clipped the wireless black mic to his collar.

The lights dimmed. A soft spot lit Jon, while a spray of light focused on Liz as she assumed her pre-dance pose. Her heart fluttered with anticipation of performing on stage with the love of her life. Never in a million years could she have envisioned this. Life was like that.

Jon plucked several notes of his intro, then spoke into his mic. "This is a song I wrote, called *Lizzy's Song*."

Liz resisted snapping her head up in surprise at the sound of her name in the title. She was so moved by the ethereal quality of the melody, that a tear pushed itself out and fell to her breast, creating a spot on her lavender leotard.

She listened intently as she moved, letting Jon's voice carry her as she sailed around the stage, spinning, twirling, and leaping. She let go of her choreography and improvised, soaring like a mended eagle on the wing.

The love inside her flowed through every movement. She'd announced this dance piece as a thank you to the audience. When, in reality, it was her thank you to Jon, for believing in her. For treating her as his equal. And for crumbling the fortress that had fiercely guarded her heart—to heal her guilt about her dad.

But mostly, for loving her.

Jon ended the song and plucked the last, haunting notes. Liz timed her finish along with his, assuming her final pose. There was a moment of silence, followed by thunderous applause that brought tears to her eyes.

The applause was intense and heartfelt, taking Liz by surprise and judging by the look on Jon's face, he was astonished as well. Jon stood and moved to center stage and she joined him and grasped his hand. They took a bow together, then stepped back as the curtain closed and the applause died down.

"That was beautiful. I love you, Slick." She couldn't hold back the catch in her voice.

Jon wordlessly lifted his guitar strap from over his shoulder and held it out for a passing prop guy to grab. He wrapped his arms around her and kissed her so soundly he left her mouth burning with fire. He eased off her lips and stepped back as the stage lights dimmed and they stood in shadow.

"I got my birthday wish and your dream came true. I'd say we're two lucky people." Jon smiled down at her.

"You're my dream come true." She gestured around her. "My dance studio is just frosting on the cake."

"Happy Birthday, Fire Woman. Say, when is your birthday, anyway? You haven't gotten around to telling me."

She gave him a coy smile. "Today."

A horrified look crossed his face followed by an incredulous grin. "No way. I just said that randomly. When were you planning to tell me?"

"This is payback for you not telling me when it was your birthday at Steller's Jay Lodge. Remember?"

"In that case, I have the perfect birthday gift for you when we get home." His eyes twinkled with amusement.

"Another lap dance?" she purred, loving how the subdued backstage light bathed him in a sexy glow.

The mischievous Silva smile formed, and his eyes twinkled. "You'll have to wait and see."

She ignited into an inferno of desire and anticipation. "I seriously can't wait."

He kissed her again. Deep. Hot. Then lifted away. "I know, Fire Woman. I know."

LIZZY'S SONG

We have a second chance to get it right
Two lives born
Out of smoke and fire
Let's set our pasts ablaze
Leave these old sins and walk away
My wish is for you to love me
From this moment until we die
Your face is the only one I want to see
Every morning as I arise

And I say dance Lizzy
We're going to get this right
And I'm singing to you this birthday song
As my candles I blow out tonight

Saved an eagle, set him free
Two llamas down the Kenai
Kayaking with birds and whales
Confirmed my thoughts for you were real
My wish is for you to love me
From this moment until we die
Your face is the only one I want to see
Every morning as I arise
And I say dance Lizzy
We're going to get this right
And I'm singing you this birthday song
As my candles I blow out tonight.

~~ Jon Silva

THANKS FOR READING!

I hope you enjoyed reading ALASKA INFERNO!
It only takes a moment to post a review of this book on Amazon and
Goodreads and makes a huge difference for my author career and success as
a writer. I would very much appreciate it. Thank you! ~ LoLo Paige

Post a review on Amazon here
amzn.to/2QFQpCO
My Bookbub Page at
www.bookbub.com/profile/lolo-paige
And Goodreads at
bit.ly/3yv2ITG

Join LoLo Paige's spam-free mailing list to find out about new
releases and giveaways at lolopaige.com

Visit LoLo on Facebook
facebook.com/LoLoPaigewildlandfire

Listen to Alaska Inferno Playlist on Spotify at
https://spoti.fi/33NKPBi

Let me know what you think of this series. I'd love to hear from you!
Email me at lolo@lolopaige.com
Thank you! ~~ LoLo Paige

ACKNOWLEDGMENTS

First of all, a super huge thank you to Cherry Adair and Bobbi Scopa for their wonderful endorsements!

Another mega thank you to my fantastic editor at The Word Slayers, Karen Boston, and the coordination and promotional work of Amber Thomas. You guys are priceless!

I'm so grateful for my fellow writer and talented poet who writes poems for each of my books. Thank you, S. R. Cyres, for your insightful, beautiful words. I'm also grateful to a super talented songwriter and my hometown classmate, Craig Kuchler, for being so generous in sharing his talents to write a song for Liz. Thank you so much!

Many thanks to the subject matter experts who helped me with arson, fire investigation, law enforcement protocols, and birds of prey: John Maclean, Marc Cameron, Patrick O'Donnell with Cops & Writers, Keenan Powell, Jerri Williams, Cris Hartman, Gordon Snyder, and Caryl Christy. Any errors or inaccuracies are my sole responsibility.

Thanks to my state and federal agency subject matter experts in wildland fire investigation: Carrie Balboa, National Interagency Fire Center (NIFC) Boise, Idaho; Beth Ipsen, Public Affairs Specialist, U.S. Bureau of Land Management, Alaska Fire Service; and the lead fire investigators with the BLM Alaska Fire Service, and the Alaska Department of

Natural Resources, Division of Forestry. Any errors or inaccuracies are my sole responsibility.

And a great BIG mondo thank you to Uncle Steve Stripling for the promotional support on *The Big Alaska Show* on KFQD Radio in Anchorage, and on the KFQD book review website!

Thanks to fellow writers and authors for helping me with plot and story: Lynn Lovegreen, Bee Murray, Liz Harris, Laura Culp Elliott, and Claire O'Sullivan; thanks to Sian Musgrave and Sophia Aves for all things Australian, and Giselle Roeder and Gwen Knight for all things Canadian. And special thanks to Steven Moore for proofreading my final manuscript.

I'm grateful for the promotional support of April Maye, Erin Ember, Diane Wigg, C.J. Ivy Lopez with the Authors Porch, the Ripped Bodice Bookstore in Culver City, CA, and my local Alaska bookstores. And thanks to Chris Story, of Top of the World Radio, Homer Alaska; and James Blatch of Hello Books and Mark Dawson's Self-Publishing Show.

Last but not least, I'm grateful to my esteemed critique group in our Romance Writers of America, Alaska Chapter, who suffered through my early drafts and kept me accurate on all things Alaskan: Lynn Lovegreen, Deb Maynard, Gwen Knight, and Christa Looney.

ABOUT THE AUTHOR

Who knows where real-life adventures will lead? Living in The Land of the Midnight Sun is the place for such adventure. In 2015, *The Anchorage Press* published a short, nonfiction story about the author's narrow escape while wild- land firefighting. The following year, *Embers of Memories* won an Alaska Press Club award for best historical piece in all media. One of the judges suggested  turning it into a novel. Four years later, the suggestion became reality.

 In 2019, ALASKA SPARK won the honor of being a finalist in the Romance Writers of America, Wisconsin Chapter, Fab Five novel contest, competing with writers from around the country. It went on to win three awards for Independent Publishing in 2020 and 2021. While these books are works of fiction, they're loosely based on true life events and the author's experience as a wildland firefighter. She has lived in Alaska most of her life. Early in her federal career, she worked as a wildland firefighter for the U.S. Forest Service and the U.S. Bureau of Land Management, having fought fires in Montana, California, and Alaska.

Want more hot romantic reads? Try my other books!

ALASKA SPARK

Book One of the Blazing Hearts Wildfire Series

Winner of an Indie B.R.A.G. Medallion Award, and finalist in the Eric Hoffer, and Next Generation Indie Book Awards!

Tara Waters loves being a wildland firefighter and the adrenaline rush of fighting wildfires is her calling. She must be on her game to join an elite hotshot crew in Montana. But when Tara is sent to fight fires in Alaska, her dream falls out of reach.

Sexy Alaskan smokejumper, Ryan O'Connor takes Tara under his wing and counsels her when she fails to save someone on a wildfire. She owes him one, but not her heart just because of his irresistible charm and good looks. Ryan has his own story with plenty of demons in his past. And Tara may be the spark his life needs.

But when a mysterious adversary sabotages Tara on the fire line, she discovers a threat far more dangerous than fire—a threat that can destroy everything she's worked for, including a second chance for love that could be extinguished before it ignites.

Listen to Alaska Spark Playlist on Spotify at https://spoti.fi/3tR2vqm

ALASKA BLAZE

Book Three of the Blazing Hearts Wildfire Series

The epic firefighting adventures continue in Book Three of *the Blazing Hearts Wildfire Series, ALASKA BLAZE.* Cohen Tremblay and the

Aurora Crew are sent to battle flames at the base of the mighty Alaska Range, in the shadow of Denali Mountain, to protect sled dog kennels of celebrated Iditarod mushers. When Cohen meets the fearless and feisty Iditarod musher, Riley Atwood, barks and sparks fly! And there's a heck of a lot more heat going on than just the wildfire!

Be the first to know about upcoming book updates and sneak peeks and watch for the release of ALASKA BLAZE by signing up for the author's newsletter at www.lolopaige.com/

CPSIA information can be obtained
at www.ICGtesting.com
Printed in the USA
JSHW020958280521
15278JS00001B/4

9 781736 095102